GENA SHOWALTER

THE
DARKEST
PASSION

D1449684

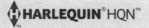
HARLEQUIN® HQN™

Recycling programs
for this product may
not exist in your area.

ISBN-13: 978-0-373-77991-8

The Darkest Passion

Copyright © 2010 by Gena Showalter

Printed in U.S.A.

Dear Reader,

Book ideas come to me in many different ways. Something I see or hear. Dreams. Even sitting in a quiet corner and thinking...thinking...banging my head against my desk... thinking some more. *The Darkest Passion* was first released in 2010, which means I wrote it the year before, but I've never forgotten how this particular idea came to me. There I was, cutting my split ends one by one because it's a habit I've never broken, when all of a sudden an image downloaded straight into my brain—which just happened to become the idea for a story I wrote later. But I digress. I saw Olivia, the heroine, clawing her way out of the ground. Blood soaked her usually pristine robe. Dirt clumped in hair that had been intertwined with sweet-smelling flowers only hours before and streaked once flawless skin. Terror filled her eyes. The moment she reached the surface, only one word screamed from the depths of her soul. A name.

"Aeron!"

I heard her desperation. Felt it. Everything you read in the book sprang from that single scene.

But of course, *The Darkest Passion* is book number five in my Lords of the Underworld series, so some background for the Aeron and Olivia romance had already been laid and I couldn't veer from it. (Shall we call them Aerivia? Olivon?) The two had never spoken, but Olivia had secretly watched him. Here's where the new scene came into play— she watched him and *craved* him...despite the fact that she had been commanded to kill him.

As an angel, all commands had to be heeded...or else. (Little bit of trivia: when the angels received their own spin-off series, the Angels of the Dark, I got to delve deeper into their history. That's when they became known as the Sent Ones.)

So why was Olivia underground? Why was she so frantic to reach the man she was supposed to harm? What would happen when she got to him?

Finding out…so much fun! It's one of the reasons I enjoy my job as much as I do. There's something so satisfying about taking a thousand puzzle pieces and fitting them together to create a beautiful picture. (Oddly enough, it's not the fifteen-hour workdays, the intensity of multiple looming deadlines or the lack of vacations.)

During the course of the story, I cried with Aeron and Olivia, ached for them, cheered for them…wanted only the best for them. And, okay, I might have just slumped down in my chair a little. "Best? Best! You put us through hell," they shout.

Guilty as charged. But I knew they had to hit rock bottom before they'd ever see the light waiting for them up top. "You're welcome," I shout back.

What can I say? I'm a giver.

I hope you enjoy reading their story as much as I enjoyed writing it.

Warm wishes,

Gena Showalter

This one is for Max, my demon—
which makes me his angel. Of course.
And now that it's been printed, it can't be denied.
Max = demon. Gena = angel.

This one is also for Jill Monroe, but don't tell her I said so.

Acknowledgments:

I want to thank all the wonderful people at Harlequin
for the continued support and encouragement.
I am very blessed to work with you!

CHAPTER ONE

"THEY DON'T SEEM to care that they're dying."

Aeron, an immortal warrior possessed by the demon of Wrath, was perched atop the roof of the Bübájos Apartments in central Budapest, peering down at the humans so blithely going about their evening. Some were shopping, some talking and laughing, and some snacking while they walked. But none of them were dropping to their knees and begging the gods for more time in those feeble bodies. Nor were they sobbing because they wouldn't get it.

He shifted his focus from the people to their surroundings. Muted moonlight spilled from the sky, blending with the amber glow of the street lamps and casting shadows on the paved pathways. Buildings stretched on every side, some of the higher points wrapped in light green awnings, the perfect contrast to the emerald trees rising from their bases.

Pretty, as far as coffins went.

Humans knew they were fading. Hell, they grew up knowing they'd have to abandon everything and everyone they loved, and yet, as he'd already observed, they didn't demand or even request more time. And that...fascinated him. Were Aeron to learn he'd soon be separated from his friends, the other demon-possessed warriors he'd spent the last few thousand years protecting, he would have done anything—yes, even beg—to change his fate.

So why didn't the mortals? What did they know that he did not?

"They aren't dying," his friend Paris said from beside him. "They're living while they have the chance."

Aeron snorted. That wasn't the answer he sought. For how could they *live while they had the chance* when their "chance" was a mere blink of time? "They're frail. Easily destroyed. As you well know." Cruel of him to say because Paris's...girlfriend? Lover? Chosen female? Whatever she was, she'd recently been shot to death in front of Paris. Still, Aeron couldn't regret his words.

Paris was the keeper of Promiscuity, forced to bed a different human every day or he would weaken and die himself. He couldn't afford to mourn the loss of one specific lover. Especially an *enemy* lover, which was what his little Sienna had been.

Aeron hated to admit it, but on some level, he was glad the woman was dead. She would have used Paris's needs against him and ultimately ruined him.

I, however, will ensure his safety always. It was a vow. The king of the gods had given Paris a choice: the return of his female's soul or Aeron's freedom from a horrific blood-craze that constantly danced thoughts of maiming and killing through his mind. Thoughts, he was ashamed to admit, he had acted upon. Over and over again.

Because of that curse, Reyes, the keeper of the demon of Pain, had almost lost his beloved Danika. In fact, Aeron had been poised to strike that final blow, blade sharpened, raised...falling toward her pretty neck.

But just before contact, Paris had chosen Aeron and the craze had instantly left him, sparing Danika's life.

Part of Aeron still felt guilty about what had almost happened—and about the consequences of Paris's choice. A guilt that was like acid in his bones, eating away at him. Paris now suffered while *he* reveled in his freedom. That didn't mean he would show Paris mercy in this matter, however. He loved his friend too much for that. More than that, Aeron owed him. And Aeron always repaid his debts.

Hence the reason they were on this roof.

Taking care of Paris, though, was not an easy task. For the past six nights Aeron had carted his friend here amid ceaseless protests. Paris had only to pick a woman, then Aeron would procure her and ensure the two were safe while they had sex. But each night the choice was made later. And later.

Aeron had a feeling he and Paris would sit here and talk until sunrise this time.

Had the now-depressed warrior eschewed these weak mortals as Aeron did, he would not currently be wishing for something he couldn't have. He would not be desperate for it—and denied it for all eternity.

Aeron sighed. "Paris," he began. Then stopped. How should he proceed? "Your mourning must end." Good. To the point, just as he preferred. "It's weakening you."

Paris ran his tongue over his teeth. "As if you're one to talk about weakness. How many times have you been Wrath's bitch? Countless. And in how many of those countless instances can you blame the gods? Only once. When that demon overtakes you, you lose all control of your actions. So don't add hypocrisy to your list of sins, okay?"

He didn't take offense. Sadly, Paris's claim was irrefutable. Sometimes Wrath would seize control of Aeron's body and fly him through town, striking at everyone within reach, hurting them and gorging on their terror. During those instances, Aeron was aware of what was happening, but unable to halt the carnage.

Not that he always wanted the carnage to halt. Some people deserved what they got.

But he did loathe losing control of his body, as if he were merely a puppet with strings. Or a monkey who danced on command. When he was reduced to such a state, he despised his demon—but not as much as he despised himself. Because with the hatred, he also experienced pride. In Wrath. Wresting the reins of control from him required power, and power of any kind was to be prized.

Still. The love-hate tug-of-war disturbed him.

"You might not have meant to, but you've just proven my point," he said, jumping back into conversation. "Weakness births destruction. No exceptions." In Paris's case, *mourning* was simply another word for *distracted*. And such distraction could prove fatal.

"What does that have to do with me? What does that have to do with the humans down there?" Paris pointed.

Big picture time. "Those people. They age and deteriorate in a heartbeat of time."

"And?"

"And let me finish. If you fall in love with one of them, you might have her for the better part of a century. Maybe, if disease or an accident do not befall her. But it will be a century spent watching her wither and die. And during it all, you'll know an eternity without her awaits you."

"Such pessimism." Paris *tsked*—hardly the reaction Aeron had expected. "You see it as a century spent losing that which you are unable to protect. I see it as a century spent enjoying a great blessing. A blessing that will *aid* you the rest of eternity."

Aid? Absurd. When you lost something precious, the memories of it became a tormenting reminder of what you could never have again. Those memories added to your troubles, distracting you—unlike Paris, he wouldn't wrap the word in a pretty bow—rather than strengthening you.

Proof: that's how he felt about Baden, keeper of Distrust and once his best friend. Long ago, he'd lost the man he'd loved more than he would have loved even a blood brother, and now, every time he was alone, he pictured Baden and wondered about what could have been.

He didn't want that for Paris.

Forget big picture. Time for a little more mercilessness. "If you're so capable of accepting loss, why do you still mourn Sienna?"

A beam of moonlight hit Paris's face, and Aeron saw that his eyes were slightly glazed. Obviously, he'd been drinking. Again. "I didn't have my century with her. I had but a few days." Flat tone.

Don't stop now. "And if you had been given a hundred years with her before she died, you would now be at peace with her death?"

There was a pause.

He hadn't thought so.

"Enough!" Paris slammed a fist into the roof and the entire building shook. "I don't want to talk about this anymore."

Too bad. "Loss is loss. Weakness is weakness. If

we don't allow ourselves to grow attached to the humans, we won't care when they leave us. If we harden our hearts, we won't desire that which we cannot have. Our demons taught us that very well."

Each of their demons had once lived in hell and desired freedom, and so together they fought their way out. Only, they ended up exchanging one prison for another, and the second had been far worse than the first.

Rather than enduring sulfur and flames as they had before, they spent a thousand years trapped inside Pandora's box. A thousand years of darkness and desolation and pain. They'd had no independence, no hope for something better.

Had those demons been stronger, had they not craved that which was forbidden to them, they would not have been captured.

Had *Aeron* been stronger of will, he would not later have helped open that box. Would not then have been cursed to house the very evil he had released inside his own body. Would not have been kicked from the heavens, the only home he'd ever known, to spend the rest of eternity in this chaotic land where *nothing* stayed the same.

He would not have lost Baden while warring with Hunters—despicable mortals who abhorred the Lords, blaming them for the world's evil. A friend just died of cancer? Of course the Lords were responsible. A teenage girl just discovered she was pregnant? The Lords had clearly struck again.

Had he been stronger, he would not be caught up in that war once again, fighting, killing. Always killing.

"Have you ever yearned for a mortal?" Paris asked, drawing him from his dark thoughts. "Sexually?"

A quiet laugh escaped him. "Welcome a female into my life one day, only to lose her the next? No." He was smarter than that.

"Who says you have to lose her?" Paris withdrew a flask from the inside of his leather jacket and took a long swig.

More alcohol already? Clearly his little pep talk hadn't done his friend a bit of good.

After swallowing, Paris added, "Maddox has Ashlyn, Lucien has Anya, Reyes has Danika and now Sabin has Gwen. Even Gwen's sister, Bianka the Terrible, has a lover. An angel I had to oil-wrestle, but whatever. We won't talk about that part."

Oil-wrestling? Yes. Best to avoid. "Those couples have each other, but each of those women has an ability that sets her apart from the others of her kind. They're more than human." That didn't mean they would live forever, though. Even immortals could be slain. *He'd* been the one to pick up Baden's head—without the warrior's body. He'd been the one to first glimpse that eternally frozen expression of shock.

"Well, hello, solution. Find a female with an ability that sets her apart," Paris said dryly.

As if it were that easy. Besides… "I have Legion, and she's all I can handle at the moment." He pictured the little demon so like a daughter to him and grinned. When standing, she only reached his waist. She had green scales, two tiny horns that had just sprouted atop her head and sharp teeth that produced poisonous saliva. Tiaras were her favorite accessory and living flesh her favorite meal.

The first he enjoyed indulging, the second they were working on.

Aeron had met her in hell. Well, as close to the blistering pit as a man could get without actually melting inside its flames. He'd been chained next door, so to speak, drunk with that cursed bloodlust, determined to slay even his friends, when Legion had dug her way to him, her presence somehow clearing his mind, giving him the strength he so prized. She'd helped him escape, and they'd been together ever since.

Except for now. His precious baby girl had returned to hell, a place she despised, all because an honest-to-the-gods angel had been watching Aeron, skulking in the shadows, invisible, waiting for…something. What, he didn't know. He only knew that intense gaze wasn't on him right now, but it would return. It always did. And Legion couldn't stand it.

He leaned back and peered up at the night sky. The stars were vivid tonight, like diamonds scattered across black satin. Sometimes, when he craved even the illusion of solitude, he would soar as high as his wings would take him and then fall, fast and sure, only slowing seconds before impact.

As Paris downed another mouthful of his liquor, the scent of ambrosia wafted on the breeze, as gentle and sweet as baby's breath. Aeron shook his head. Ambrosia was his friend's drug of choice, the only thing capable of numbing mind and body for men such as them, but its use was getting out of hand, making the once fierce soldier sloppy.

With Galen, leader of the Hunters and a demon-possessed warrior like them, roaming the streets, he needed his friend lucid at the very least. Factor in the angel, and well, he needed his friend in top fighting form. Angels, as he'd recently learned, were demon-assassins.

Did this angel want to kill him? He wasn't sure, and Bianka's consort, Lysander, wouldn't tell him. But then, the answer really didn't matter. He planned to gut the coward, male or female, the moment it grew some balls and appeared in front of him.

No one separated him from Legion. Not without suffering for it. Legion could even now be hurting, mentally and physically. At the thought, Aeron's hands clenched so tightly the bones nearly fractured. The little darling's brethren enjoyed taunting her for her kindness and compassion. They also enjoyed chasing her, and gods knew what they'd do to her if they actually caught her.

"Much as you love Legion," Paris began, once again dragging Aeron from the sharply tangled mire of his thoughts. He tossed a stone at the building across from them before draining the rest of the flask. "She can't meet all your needs."

Meaning sex. Could they not abandon this topic once and for all? Aeron sighed. He hadn't bedded a woman in years, perhaps centuries. They simply weren't worth the effort. Because of Wrath, his desire to hurt them soon outweighed his desire to please them. More, as tattooed and battle-hardened as Aeron was, he had to work for every scrap of affection he received. Females were scared of him—and rightly so. Softening them required time and patience he didn't have. After all, there were a thousand other, more important things he could be doing. Things like training, guarding his home, guarding his friends. Indulging Legion's every whim.

"I have no such needs." And for the most part, that was true. Disciplined as he was, he rarely indulged in pleasures of the flesh. Only time he did so was while alone. "I have everything I desire. Now, did we come here to share our feelings or find you a lover?"

With a growl, Paris tossed the empty flask as he'd tossed the stone. It slammed into the building's wall, plumes of dust and rock filling the air. "One day, someone's going to fascinate you, draw and ensnare you, and you'll crave her with every cell in your body. I hope she drives you insane. I hope, for a little while at least, she denies you, leading you on a merry chase. Perhaps then you'll understand a glimmer of my pain."

"If that's what's necessary to repay the favor you did me, then I'll gladly endure such a fate. I'll even beseech the gods for it." Aeron couldn't imagine ever wanting a female, immortal or human, so much that it disrupted his life. He wasn't like the other warriors, who constantly sought companionship. He truly was happiest when he was alone. Or rather, alone with Legion. Besides, he was too proud to chase after someone who didn't return his ardor.

But he'd meant what he said. For Paris, he'd endure anything. "Did you hear that, Cronus?" he shouted to the heavens. "Send me a female. One who will torment me. One who will deny me."

"Cocky bastard." Paris chuckled. "What if he actually sends you this unattainable female?"

Gods, that amusement pleased him. It was so like the old Paris. "Doubtful." Cronus wanted the warriors focused on defeating Galen. Which had been his obsession ever since Danika had predicted the god king would die by Galen's hand.

As the All-Seeing Eye, Danika's predictions were always accurate. Even the bad ones. But there was a silver lining: those visions could be used to elicit change. At least in theory.

"But what if?" Paris prompted when his silence dragged on too long.

"If Cronus answers my plea, I'll enjoy the ride," Aeron lied with a grin. "Now, enough about me. Let's do what we came here to do." He sat up and peered down at the street, scanning the thinning crowd.

To preserve the roads, cars weren't allowed in this part of town, so everyone had to hoof it. That's why he'd picked this location. Pulling a female out of a moving vehicle wasn't something he enjoyed. This way, Paris had only to make his selection and Aeron would spread his wings and fly the warrior down. One glance at the gorgeous blue-eyed devil, and the chosen female would stop and gasp. Sometimes a smile was all that was needed to convince her to strip, right there in public, where anyone lurking in the alleyways could watch.

"You won't find anyone," Paris said. "I've already looked."

"What about…her?" He pointed to a plump, scantily dressed blonde.

"No." No hesitation. "Too…obvious."

Here we go again, he thought with dread, but gestured to another woman. "And her?" This one was tall and perfectly curved with a short cap of red hair. And she was dressed conservatively.

"No. Too mannish."

"What the hell does that mean?"

"That I don't want her. Next."

For the ensuing hour, Aeron pointed out potential bedmates and Paris shot them down for various—ridiculous—reasons. Too pristine, too rumpled, too tan, too pale. The only rejection that mattered was "I've had her before" and as many as Paris had had, Aeron heard that one a lot.

"You're going to have to settle on one eventually. Why not save us both the hassle, close your eyes and point. Whoever you're pointing at will be our winner."

"I've played that game once before. Ended up—" Paris shuddered. "Never mind. It's not good to wander down that particular memory trail. So no. Just no."

"What about—" His words halted abruptly as the woman he'd been eyeballing disappeared in the shadows. She hadn't faded from view, as was natural. Normal. She had simply ceased to exist, there one moment, gone the next, the shadows somehow tugged to her as if they'd been jerked on a leash.

Aeron jumped to his feet, wings automatically pushing from the slits in his bare back and expanding. "We have a problem."

"What's wrong?" Paris, too, sprang to his feet. Even though he wavered slightly from the ambrosia, he was still a soldier and palmed a dagger.

"The dark-haired female. Did you see her?"

"Which one?"

That answered Aeron's question. No, Paris hadn't seen her. If he had, the warrior wouldn't have needed to ask of whom Aeron spoke.

"Come on." Aeron snaked his arms around his friend's waist and leapt from the building. Wind blasted through Paris's multicolored locks, whipping several strands against his face as the ground loomed closer... closer still... "Be on the lookout for a woman with shoulder-length black hair, straight as a pin, roughly five-ten, early twenties, black clothing. Most likely she's more than human."

"Kill?"

"Capture. I have questions for her." Like how she'd disappeared like that. Like why she was here. Like who she worked for.

Immortals always had an agenda.

Just before they hit concrete and stone, Aeron flapped his wings. He slowed just enough to land upright with only a mild jarring. He released his charge, and they instantly branched in separate directions. After thousands of years of fighting together, they knew how to proceed without first outlining every move.

As Aeron sprinted down the alleyway to his left, the direction the woman had been heading, he folded his wings back under their slits. He spotted several people—a couple holding hands, a homeless male draining a bottle of whiskey, a man walking his dog—but no dark-haired female. He reached a brick wall and spun. Damn this. Was she like Lucien? Able to whisk herself to any location with only a thought?

Scowling, he kicked back into motion. He'd search every alley in the area if need be. Only, halfway down, the shadows around him thickened, consuming him, choking out the golden glow of the street lamps. Thousands of muted screams seemed to seep from the gloom. Tortured screams. Agonized screams.

He stopped, lest he slam into something—or someone—and palmed two blades. What the hell was—

A woman—*the* woman—stepped from the shadows, only a few feet away from him. She was the only light in that sudden, vast expanse of dark. Her eyes were as black as the gloom around her, her lips as red and moist as blood. She was pretty, in a feral kind of way.

Wrath hissed inside his head.

For a moment, Aeron feared Cronus had actually listened to him after all and sent a female to torment him. But as he stared over at her, there was no heat in his veins, no flutter in his heartbeat, as he'd heard the other Lords expound on whenever one found a female he just "had to have." She was like any other to him: easily forgettable.

"Well, well, well. Aren't I a lucky girl. You're one of them, a Lord of the Underworld, and you came to me," she said, her voice as raspy as smoke. "I didn't even have to ask."

"I am a Lord, yes." There was no reason to deny it. The townspeople recognized him and the others on sight. Some even thought they were angels. Hunters recognized them on sight, as well, but were all too quick to renounce them as demons. Either way, the information could hardly be used against him. "And I did come looking for you."

At his easy confirmation, her features revealed a hint of surprise. "A great honor, to be sure. Why were you looking?"

"I want to know who are you." Better question— what was she?

"Maybe I'm not as lucky as I thought." Those lush red lips dipped into a pout and she pretended to wipe away a tear. "If my own brother doesn't recognize me."

Well, he now had part of his answer: she was a liar. "I don't have a sister."

She arched a black brow. "You sure about that?"

"Yes." He hadn't been born to a mother and father;

Zeus, King of the Greek gods, had simply spoken him into existence. Same with all the Lords.

"Stubborn." She *tsk*ed, reminding him of Paris. "I should've known we'd be just alike. Anyway, it's so nice to finally catch one of you alone. Who'd I get? Fury? Narcissism? I'm right, aren't I? Admit it, you're Narcissism. That's why you plastered your body with tattoos of your own face. *Nice.* Can I call you Narci?"

Fury? Narcissism? None of his brothers carried those demons. Doubt, Disease, Misery and many others, yes, but not those. He shook his head—only to remember that other demon-possessed immortals *were* out there. Immortals he'd never met. Immortals he was supposed to find.

As he and his friends had been the ones to open Pandora's box, they'd always assumed they were the only ones cursed to house its evil. But Cronus had recently corrected that false assumption, gifting the Lords with scrolls bearing the names of others like them. Apparently, there had been more demons than warriors, and with the box nowhere to be found, the Greeks—the gods in power at the time—had placed the remaining demons inside the immortal prisoners of Tartarus.

A discovery that did not bode well for the Lords. As Zeus's former elite sentries, they'd locked many of those prisoners away—and criminals often lived only for vengeance. Something Wrath had taught him well.

"Hello," the woman prompted. "Anyone home?"

He blinked down at her, cursing himself. He'd allowed himself to be distracted in the presence of a possible enemy. *Fool.* "Who I am is none of your concern." That *was* information that could be used against him. Especially since lately, Wrath was so easily provoked the most innocent of statements could send it—and therefore Aeron—into that murderous craze, placing this town and all of its citizens in danger.

He blamed the angel stalking him.

Except he couldn't blame the angel when Wrath began snarling inside his mind, clawing at his skull, desperate to act. To hurt. The demon's keenest ability was, and had always been, sensing the sins of anyone nearby. And this woman's, he suddenly realized, were vast.

"I'll take your sudden black expression as a no. You're not Narci, and no one's home."

"Stop…talking…" He gripped his temples, cool blades pressed against his skin, trying to stop the mental bombardment he knew was coming, another distraction he could ill afford. Useless. Her multitude of sins played through his head at once, like movies on split screens. She had recently tortured a man, had chained him to a chair and set him on fire. Before that, she had gutted a female. She had tricked, and she had stolen. Had abducted a child from his home. Had lured a male to her bed and sliced his throat. Violence…so much violence…so much terror and pain and darkness. He could hear the screams of her victims, could smell burnt flesh and taste blood.

Perhaps she'd had good reason for doing those things. Perhaps not. Either way, Wrath wanted to punish her, using her own crimes against her. First it would chain her, then gut her, then slice her throat and set her on fire.

That was the way of Aeron's demon. It beat beaters, murdered murderers, as well as everything in between. So yes, at Wrath's urging, *Aeron* had done those things. Many times. Now, he clenched every muscle in his body, locking his bones in place. *Steady. Can't lose control. Have to stay sane.* But gods, the need to castigate…so strong…a need he liked more than he should have. As usual.

"Why are you here in Budapest, woman?" Good. That was good. Slowly he lowered his arms.

"Wow," she said, ignoring his question. "That was quite a display of restraint."

She'd known his demon wanted to hurt her?

"So let me guess." She tapped a nail against her chin. "You're not Narci, so you have to be…Chauvinist. Right again, aren't I? You think a pretty little thing like me can't handle the truth. *Mistake.* But no matter. Keep your secrets. You'll learn, though. Oh, yes, you'll learn."

"Are you threatening me, female?"

Again she ignored him. "Word on the street is Cronus gave you the scrolls and you plan to use them to hunt us down. To use *us*. Perhaps even slay us."

Aeron's stomach bottomed out. One, she knew about the scrolls when he and his friends had only just learned of them. Two, she knew she was on that list. Which meant this woman was indeed an immortal—and a criminal—and if she was to be believed, she was also demon-possessed.

Aeron didn't recognize her, which meant he and his friends hadn't been the ones to imprison her. That meant she'd come *before* their time in the heavens. And *that* meant she was a Titan and a greater threat, for the Titans were far more savage than their Greek counterparts.

Worse, the now-freed Titans were currently in charge. She might have godly help.

"Which demon do you carry?" he demanded, not above using its weaknesses against her.

She offered a wicked grin, his hard tone clearly amusing her. "You didn't share that information with me. Why should I share anything with you?"

Infuriating woman. "You said *us*." He looked over her shoulder, half expecting someone to leap forward and attack him. All he saw was darkness…and all he heard were more of those muted screams. "Where are these others?"

"Hell if I know." She splayed her arms, her hands out and empty, as if she didn't think he warranted the use of a weapon. "I'm on my own, just like always, and that's the way I like it."

Probably another lie. What woman would approach a fearsome Lord of the Underworld without backup? He didn't relax his guard as he met her gaze. "If you're here to war with us, know that—"

"War?" She laughed. "When I could kill you all while you sleep? No, I'm just here to deliver a warning. Call off the dogs or I'll wipe your presence from this world. And if anyone can do so, it's me."

After the things he'd seen in his mind, he believed her. She attacked in gloom, a phantom who delivered no warning. Without a doubt, there was no crime she found too vile. That didn't mean he was going to heed her demands. "You might think yourself powerful, but you can't defeat us all. War is what you'll get if you continue to issue such *warnings*."

"Whatever, warrior. I said what I wanted to say. You just better pray this is the last time you see me." The shadows thickened again, enveloping her and leaving absolutely no sign of her presence. Until, right next to his ear, he heard, "Oh, and one last thing. This was my courtesy call. Next time, I won't play nice."

Then the world around him crashed back into focus: the buildings at his sides, the trash bags littering the concrete, the inebriated male now passed out cold. Finally, Wrath calmed.

Aeron remained on alert, eyes scanning, body ready. He listened, heard only the deliberate drags of his own breath, the patter of human footsteps beyond the alley and the song of night birds.

Once more his wings expanded and he shot into the air, determined to find Paris and return to their fortress. The other Lords had to be notified. Whoever the bloodthirsty female was, whatever else she could do, she needed to be dealt with. Soon.

CHAPTER TWO

"Aeron! Aeron!"

At the fortress, Aeron's booted feet hit the balcony that led into his bedroom. Jolted by the unfamiliar female voice, he released Paris.

"Aeron!"

At that third ear-piercing feminine cry of terror and desperation, both he and Paris spun to face the hill below them. Thick trees knifed toward the sky, obscuring visibility, but there, amid the dappled greens and browns, he could just make out a figure draped in white.

A figure rushing toward their home.

"Shadow Girl?" Paris asked. "How the hell did she make it past our gate so quickly? And on foot, no less?"

Aeron had explained what happened with the woman from the alley along the way. "That's not her." This voice was higher, richer and far less confident. "The gate… I don't know."

Weeks ago, after he and Paris had recovered from battle wounds inflicted by Hunters, they had erected an iron gate around the fortress. That gate stretched fifteen feet tall, was wrapped with barbed wire and had tips sharp enough to cut glass. It also vibrated with enough electricity to send a human into cardiac arrest. Anyone who attempted to climb it wouldn't live long enough to reach the other side.

"Think she's Bait?" Paris tilted his head, his study of her intensifying. "She could have been dropped from a heli, I guess."

Hunters had been known to use beautiful human females to lure the Lords out into the open, distract them and capture them for torture. This one certainly seemed to meet the criteria, possessing long wavy hair the color of chocolate, skin as pale as a cloud and a curved, ethereal body. Aeron couldn't make out her facial features just yet, but he would bet they were exquisite.

His wings unfolded from their slits as he answered, "Maybe." Damn Hunters and their *perfect* timing. Half his friends were gone. They'd traveled to Rome to search the Temple of the Unspoken Ones, ruins that had recently risen from the sea. They hoped to find *anything* that would lead them to missing godly artifacts. Four artifacts that, when used together, would then lead to the location of Pandora's box.

Hunters hoped to use that box to lock the demons back inside, destroying the Lords since man could no longer live without demon. The Lords simply hoped to demolish it.

"There are trip wires out there." The more Paris spoke, the more Aeron noticed a tremor in his tone. Because of Shadow Girl, as Paris had called her, there hadn't been time for him to bed anyone in town, so his strength must be draining. "If she's not careful… Even if she *is* Bait, she doesn't deserve to die like that."

"Aeron!"

Paris fisted the balcony railing and leaned down for a better look. "Why's she calling for you?"

And why was she using his name with such familiarity? "If she's Bait, Hunters are probably out there right now, lying in wait for me. I'll try and help her and they'll attack."

Paris straightened, face suddenly bathed in moonlight. Bruises had formed under his eyes. "I'll get the others, and we'll take care of her. Of them." He was off before Aeron could reply, striding out of the bedroom, boots thumping against the stone floor.

Aeron kept his focus on the girl. As she continued to race upward, closer and closer to him, he realized the white cloth draping her was actually a robe. And the back of it, which he hadn't been able to see before, was bright red.

She wasn't wearing shoes, and when her bare toe slammed into a rock, she fell, that mass of chocolate hair cascading around her face. There were flowers woven through the curls, some of the petals missing. There were also twigs, but he didn't think she'd placed those there intentionally. Her hands were shaking as she reached up and pushed the strands away.

Finally, her features came into view and every muscle in his body jumped, tensed. She was exquisite, just as he'd supposed. Even splotchy and swollen from tears as she was. She had huge sky-blue eyes, a perfectly sloped nose, perfectly sculpted cheeks and jaw, both just a little rounded, and perfect lips that formed a lush heart.

He'd never met her before, he would have remembered, but suddenly there was something almost…familiar about her.

She lumbered to a stand, grimacing and groaning, then started forward. Once again, she fell. A pained sob escaped her, but still she persisted, rising, edging toward the fortress. Bait or not, such determination was admirable.

Somehow she managed to dodge all the traps, weaving around them as if she knew where they were, but when she hit another rock and tumbled to the ground for a third time, she stayed down, shuddering, crying.

His eyes widened as he studied her back. The red... Was that...blood? Fresh, still wet? The metallic tang of it drifted on the breeze and reached Aeron's nostrils, confirming his suspicions. Oh, yes. It was.

Hers? Or someone else's?

"Aeron." No longer a scream, but a pathetic wail. "Help me."

His wings expanded before he could think things through. Yes, Hunters would purposely injure Bait before sending her into the lions' den, hoping to gain sympathy from the target. Yes, he'd probably end up with arrows and bullets in his back—again—but he wasn't going to leave her out there, injured and vulnerable. Wasn't going to allow his friends to risk their lives to save—or destroy—his little visitor.

Why me? he wondered as he shot from the balcony. Up, up he soared before falling toward her. He zigzagged to make himself less of a mark, but no arrows whizzed by and no gunshots sounded. Still, rather than land beside her, he increased his speed, reached out his arms and scooped her up without ever slowing his pace.

Perhaps she was afraid of heights and that was the reason for her sudden stiffening. Perhaps she'd expected him to be killed before ever reaching her and, when he'd actually managed to latch onto her, had stiffened from terror. Either way, he didn't care. He'd done what he'd set out to do. He had her.

She began flailing weakly against his hold, grunting in shock and pain. "Don't touch me! Let me go! Let me go, or I swear to—"

"Be still, or by the gods, I *will* drop you." He had her by the stomach, her face aimed toward the ground. That way, she could see just how far she would fall.

"Aeron?" She craned her neck to see him. The moment their gazes connected, she relaxed. Even smiled slowly. "Aeron," she repeated on a sigh of pleasure. "I was afraid you wouldn't come."

That pleasure, undiluted and untouched by malice, surprised—and confused—him. Women never looked at him like that. "Your fear was misplaced. You should have feared I *would* come."

Her smile faded.

Better. The only thing that disturbed him now was the radio silence from his demon. As with Shadow Girl, images and urges should have bombarded him by now. *Worry about it later.*

Continuing to zigzag, he flew into his bedroom, not stopping on the balcony as usual. He needed cover as quickly as possible. Just in case. Except, just as he was retracting his wings, they slammed into both sides of the doorway and fire rushed from the tips to the arches.

Aeron ignored the pain as he skidded to his feet. When he righted himself, he strode to the bed and gently laid his charge atop the mattress, facedown. He ran a fingertip along the ridge of her spine and her heart-shaped lips parted on an agonized groan. He'd hoped she'd been doused with someone else's blood, but no. Her injuries were real.

The knowledge wouldn't soften him. She'd probably inflicted the damage herself—or allowed the Hunters to do it—just for the sympathy it would evoke. *No sympathy from me. Only irritation.* As he stomped to his closet, he drew his wings into his back, but broken as they now were, they wouldn't fit under their flaps. That only increased his irritation with her.

He didn't have rope and didn't want to leave the room to find some, so he grabbed two of the neckties Ashlyn had given him in case he ever wanted to "dress up." He returned to the bed.

Her cheek pressed into the mattress, her gaze tracking his every move, as if she couldn't help but peer at him—and not in revulsion as most females did. She watched him with something akin to desire.

An act, surely.

And yet, that desire...there was something familiar about it. Something unsettling. *That's* what he'd noticed earlier, he thought. When she'd called his name, that same desire had been evident and deep down, he'd known he'd encountered it before. When? Where?

From her?

He continued to stare down at her, and Wrath—was still silent, he realized. This was (supposedly) the first time he'd ever been in her presence, yet his demon still wasn't flashing her sins through his mind. That was odd. Had happened only once before. With Legion. Why, he'd never figured out. Gods knew his baby girl had sinned.

So why was it happening again? With possible Bait, no less?

This woman, had she never sinned? Had she never said an unkind word to another? Never purposely tripped someone or stolen something as simple as a piece of candy? Those pure, sky eyes said no. Or, like

Legion, had she sinned but for whatever reason, flew under Wrath's radar?

"Who are you?" His fingers wrapped around one of her fragile wrists—mmm, warm, smooth skin—and anchored it to a bedpost with the tie. He repeated the action with her other wrist.

Not once did she protest. It was as if she'd expected— and already accepted—that she would receive such treatment. "My name is Olivia."

Olivia. A pretty name. Fitting. Delicate. Actually, the only thing that *wasn't* delicate about her was her voice. Layer after layer of…what was that? The only word he could think to describe it was *honesty,* and so much drifted from her, he was knocked backward.

That voice had never told a lie, he would bet. It couldn't have.

"What are you doing here, Olivia?"

"I'm here…I'm here for you."

Again, that truth…it was a force that flowed into his ears, through his body, and sent him staggering. There wasn't room for doubts. Not a single one. He was simply *compelled* to believe her.

Sabin, keeper of Doubt, would have loved her. Nothing pleased the warrior's demon more than tearing down another's confidence.

"Are you Bait?"

"No."

Again, he believed her; he had no choice. "Are you here to kill me?" He straightened and crossed his arms over his chest, glaring down at her, waiting.

He knew how fierce he looked, but again, she didn't react as females usually did: trembling, cowering, crying. She fluttered her long, black lashes at him, seemingly hurt that he'd maligned her character.

"No, of course not." She paused. "Well, not anymore."

Not anymore? "So. At one time, you meant to slay me?"

"I was once sent to do so, yes."

Such honesty... "By whom?"

"At first, I was sent by the One True Deity to merely watch you. I didn't mean to scare your little friend away. I was only trying to do my job." Fresh tears filled her eyes, turning those beautiful blue irises into pools of remorse.

No softening. "Who is the One True Deity?"

Pure love lit her expression, momentarily chasing away that sheen of pain. "Deity of you, Deity of me. Far more powerful than your gods, though mostly content to remain in the shadows, and so rarely acknowledged. Father to humans. Father to...angels. Like me."

Angels. Like me. As the words echoed in his head, Aeron's eyes widened. No wonder his demon couldn't sense any wickedness in her. No wonder her gaze felt familiar to him. She was an angel. *The* angel, actually. The one sent to kill him, by her own admission. Though she didn't plan to end him "anymore." Why?

And did it matter? This delicate creature had been, at one point, his appointed executioner.

Suddenly he wanted to laugh. As if she could have overpowered *him.*

You couldn't see her. Would you truly have been able to stop her, had she gone for your head?

The thought hit him and he lost his amusement. *She* was the one who had been watching him these many weeks. *She* was the one who had followed him, unseen, driving a pained Legion away.

Which begged the question of why Wrath wasn't reacting as Legion always did. With fear and even physical agony. Perhaps the angel controlled which demons sensed her, he considered. That would certainly be a handy ability to possess, keeping her intended victims ignorant of her presence—and intentions.

He waited for brutal rage to fill him. Rage he'd promised to unleash on this creature time and time again should she ever reveal herself. When the rage failed to appear, he waited for resolve. He must protect his friends at any cost.

But that, too, remained hopelessly out of reach. What he got instead? Confusion.

"You are…"

"The angel who has been watching you, yes," she said, confirming his suspicions. "Or rather, I *was* an angel." Her eyelids sealed shut, tears catching in her lashes. Her chin trembled. "Now I'm nothing."

Though he believed her—how could he not? That voice… Seriously, he wanted to doubt her about something, *anything,* but couldn't manage it—Aeron extended a shaky hand. *What are you, a child? Man up.*

Scowling at his display of weakness, he steadied his hand and flipped away her hair, careful not to touch her injured skin. He pinched the scooped neck of her robe and gently tugged. The soft material ripped easily, revealing the expanse of her back.

Once again, his eyes widened. Between her shoulder blades, where wings should have protruded, were two long grooves of broken skin, tendons torn to the spine, ripped muscle and even a peek at bone. They were savage wounds, violent and unmerciful, blood still seeping from them. He'd had his own wings forcibly removed once, and it had been the most painful injury of his very long life.

"What happened?" The hoarseness of his voice threw him.

"I've fallen," she rasped, shame dripping from her tone. She buried her face in the pillow. "I'm angel no more."

"Why?" Never having encountered an angel before—well, besides Lysander, but that bastard didn't count because he refused to speak to the Lords about anything of importance—Aeron didn't know much about them. He only knew what Legion had told him, and of course, there was a very good chance her recounting had been colored by her hatred of them. Nothing she'd described fit with the female on his bed.

Angels, Legion had said, were emotionless, soulless creatures with only one purpose: the destruction of their darker counterpart, the demons. She'd also claimed that, every so often, an angel would succumb to the lures of the flesh, intrigued by the very beings he—or she—was supposed to loathe. That angel would then be kicked straight into hell, where the demons she had once defeated were finally allowed a little vengeance.

Was that what had happened to this one? Aeron wondered. A trip to hell, where demons had tormented her? Possible.

Should he untie her? Her eyes...so guileless, so innocent. Now they said *help me*. And *save me*.

But most of all, they said *hold me and never let go*. He'd been tricked by such innocence before, he thought, stopping himself before he could act. Baden had been tricked, as well, and had died for it.

A smart man would learn a little more about this woman first, he decided.

"Who took your wings?" The question emerged as a gruff bark, and he nodded in satisfaction.

She gulped, shuddered. "Once I was cast—"

"Aeron, you stupid shit," a male voice said, hushing her. "Tell me you didn't—" Paris stalked into his bedroom, but ground to a halt when he spotted Olivia. His eyes narrowed, and he ran his tongue over his teeth. "So. It's true. You really flew out there and grabbed her."

Olivia stiffened, keeping her face hidden from view. Her shoulders began shaking as if she were sobbing. Was she finally scared? Now?

Why? Women adored Paris.

Concentrate. Aeron didn't have to ask how Paris knew what he'd done. Torin, keeper of the demon of Disease, monitored the fortress and the hill it sat upon twenty-eight hours a day, nine days a week (or so it seemed). "I thought you were gathering the others."

"Torin texted me, and I went to him first."

"And what did he tell you about her?"

"Hallway," his friend said, motioning to the door with a tilt of his chin.

Aeron shook his head. "We can discuss her here. She's not Bait."

Another swipe of his tongue over his straight, white teeth. "And I thought *I* was stupid when it came to females. How do you know what she is? Did she tell you and you couldn't help but believe her?" His tone was sneering.

"She's an angel, despot. The one who's been watching me."

That wiped the scorn from Paris's expression. "An actual angel? From heaven?"

"Yes."

"Like Lysander?"

"Yes."

Very slowly, Paris looked her over. Female connoisseur that he was—or used to be—he probably knew everything about her body by the time he was done. The size of her breasts, the flare of her hips, the exact length of her legs. That did *not* annoy Aeron. She meant nothing to him. Nothing but trouble.

"Whatever she is," Paris said, far less angry than he'd been, "it doesn't mean she's not working with our enemy. Need I remind you that Galen, the world's biggest blowhard, says *he's* an angel?"

"Yeah, but he's lying."

"And she can't be?"

Aeron scrubbed a hand down his suddenly tired face. "Olivia. Are you working with Galen to harm us?"

"No," she mumbled, and Paris stumbled backward, just as Aeron had done, clutching his chest.

"My gods," his friend gasped. "That voice…"

"I know."

"She's not Bait, and she's not helping Galen." A statement of fact from Paris now.

"I know," Aeron repeated.

Paris shook his head as if to clear his thoughts. "Still. Lucien will want to search the hill for Hunters. Just in case."

One of the many reasons Aeron had always followed Lucien. The warrior was smart and cautious. "When he finishes, call a meeting with whoever's here and tell them about the other woman. The one from the alley."

Paris nodded and suddenly there was a sparkle in his blue eyes. "Quite an evening you've had so far, huh? I wonder who else you'll meet tonight."

"Gods help me if there's another," he muttered.

"You shouldn't have challenged Cronus, my friend."

Aeron's stomach clenched as his gaze swung back to the angel. Had the god king actually answered his dare? Was Olivia to be the one who led him for a merry chase? His heart *was* pounding, he realized, and his blood *was* heating.

He ground his teeth. Didn't matter whether she was or not. She could try to tempt him, but even she, with her fall of chocolate hair, baby blues and heart-shaped lips, would fail to do so.

"I don't regret my words." Truth or lie, he didn't know. He hadn't thought Cronus had any power over the angels. So how then would the god king have sent her here? Or was he not responsible? Perhaps Aeron was mistaken and Cronus had nothing to do with this.

Again, it didn't matter. Not only would the angel fail to tempt him, he would ensure she left before she had time to cause a single moment of concern.

"Just so you know," Paris said, "Torin saw this one on the hill with his hidden cameras. Said she dug her way out of the ground."

Out of the ground. Did that mean she *had* been tossed into hell, and had then been forced to claw her way free? He couldn't picture the fragile-looking female doing such a thing—and surviving, that is. But then he recalled the determination she'd displayed while running toward the fortress. Maybe.

"Is that true?" He looked her over with new eyes. Sure enough, there was dirt under her fingernails and smeared on her arms. Besides the blood, however, her robe was perfectly clean.

In fact, as he watched, the tear he'd made wove itself back together, much like his body did when wounded. A piece of cloth with healing properties. Would wonders never cease?

"Olivia. You will answer."

She nodded without glancing up. He heard a sniff, sniff. Yes, she was sobbing.

An ache bloomed in his chest, but he ignored it. *Doesn't matter what she is or what she's endured. You will* not *soften, damn it. She frightens and hurts Legion and has to go.*

"A real, live angel," Paris said, clearly awed. "I'll take her to my room, if you'd like, and—"

"She's too injured for bedsport," Aeron snapped.

Paris eyed him strangely for a moment, then grinned and shook his head. "I wasn't sizing her up or anything, so let go of your jealousy."

That didn't even deserve a response. He'd never experienced jealousy, and wasn't about to start now. "So why were you offering to take her to your room?"

"So I can bandage her wounds. Who's the despot now?"

"I'll take care of her." Maybe. Could angels tolerate human medicine? Or would it hurt them? He knew well the dangers of giving one race something meant for another. Ashlyn had almost died when she'd drunk wine meant only for immortals.

He would have called for Lysander, but the elite warrior angel was currently living in the heavens with Bianka and if there was a way to reach him, Aeron hadn't been told what it was. Besides, Lysander didn't like him and wasn't the type to willingly offer information about his race.

"You want to be the responsible one, fine. But admit it." Paris tossed him another grin. "You're staking a claim on her."

"No. I'm not." He didn't have even the smallest desire to do so. It was just that she was injured and couldn't take care of herself, and was therefore in no position to be anyone's bedmate. And that's all Paris would want her for. Sex. No matter what the warrior claimed.

Besides, she'd called for *Aeron*. Screamed *Aeron's* name.

Undeterred, Paris continued, "An angel isn't technically human, you know. An angel is something more."

Aeron popped his jaw. Of all the things for the man to remember from their earlier conversation. "I said I'm not staking a claim."

Paris laughed. "Whatever you say, compadre. Enjoy your female."

Aeron's hands curled into fists, his friend's laughter not so welcome now. "Go and tell Lucien everything we've discussed, but under no circumstances are you to inform the women that there's a wounded angel here. They'll raid my room wanting to meet her and now is not the time for that."

"Why? Do you plan to make out with her?"

His teeth ground with so much force he feared they would soon be nothing but a fond memory. "I plan to question her."

"Ah. So that's what the kids are calling it these days.

Well, have fun." With that, a still-grinning Paris strolled from the room.

Alone once more with his charge, Aeron gazed down at her. Her silent sobbing ended, at least, and she faced him again.

"What are you doing here, Olivia?" Saying her name shouldn't have affected him—he'd said it before, after all—but it did. His blood heated another degree. It must be those eyes of hers...piercing him...

A shuddering breath escaped her. "I knew the consequences, knew I was giving up my wings, my abilities, my immortality, but I did it anyway. It's just...my job changed. Joy was no longer mine to give. Only death. And I hated what they wanted me to do. I couldn't do it, Aeron. I just couldn't."

His name on her lips, uttered with such familiarity, affected him, too, and he sucked in a breath. What was wrong with him? *Toughen up. Be the cold, hard warrior I know you can be.*

"I watched you," she continued, "as well as those around you, and I...ached. I wanted you, and I wanted what they had—freedom and love and fun. I wanted to play. I wanted to kiss and to touch. I wanted joy of my own." Her gaze met his, bleak, broken. "In the end, I had a choice. Fall...or kill you. I decided to fall. So here I am. Yours."

CHAPTER THREE

YOURS. SHE SHOULDN'T have said that.

Olivia froze in horror, one thought blasting through her mind louder than any other: she'd just ruined everything.

She should have eased Aeron into the truth. After all, every time she'd approached him these past few weeks, he'd threatened her with agony and death. That she'd been invisible hadn't mattered. He'd known she was nearby. How, she still hadn't figured out. She should have been imperceptible, as insubstantial as a phantom of the night. And now that she was here, in the flesh and spilling her secrets, he probably viewed her as even more of a threat. He probably viewed her as an enemy.

Probably? She laughed without humor. He did. His questions had lashed at her, cutting deep. Yep. She'd ruined. He'd want nothing to do with her now. Well, except to bestow that agony and death upon her.

You didn't fight your way from the depths of hell to be slaughtered in this fortress. She'd fought her way out of hell for a chance with Aeron. *Despite* the chance of failure.

You can do this. Having surreptitiously watched him time and time again, she felt she knew him pretty well. He was disciplined, distanced and brutally honest. He trusted no one but his friends. Weakness was not a trait he tolerated. And yet, to those he loved, he was kind, nurturing and solicitous. He placed their well-being above his own. *I want to be loved like that.*

If only he could have seen her before she'd been kicked out of the only home she'd ever known. If only he'd seen her before her ability to fly had been taken away. Before her newfound skill of creating weapons from air had been obliterated. Before her capacity to shield herself from this world's evil had been removed.

Now…

She was *weaker* than a human. Having relied on her wings rather than her legs for the whole of her centuries-long existence, she didn't even know how to walk properly. What if she *couldn't* do this?

A sob escaped her. She'd given up her home and friends for pain, humiliation and helplessness. If Aeron kicked her out, too, she'd have nowhere to go.

"Don't cry," Aeron ground out.

"I can't…help…it," she replied between shuddering whimpers. Only once before had she shed tears—and those had sprung because of Aeron, as well, when she'd realized her feelings for him were completely overshadowing her sense of self-preservation.

The magnitude of what she'd done was now a screaming force inside her head. She was alone, trapped in a frail body she didn't understand, and dependent on the mercy of a man who sometimes wreaked deathly havoc on an unsuspecting public. A public she, as a bringer of joy, had once been responsible for making happy.

"Try, damn you."

"Can you…maybe…I don't know…hold me?" she said between gasps of air.

"No." He sounded horrified by the thought. "You will simply desist immediately."

She cried all the harder. Had she been home her mentor, Lysander, would have gathered her close and cooed until she quieted. At least, she thought he would have done so, since the theory had never been tested.

Poor, sweet Lysander. Did he know she was gone? Did he know she could never return? He'd known she was fascinated with Aeron, spending every free moment in this plane to watch him in secret, unable to complete the terrible task she'd been given, but Lysander had never expected her to give up everything for the man.

To be honest, she hadn't, either. Not really.

Perhaps she should have since her troubles had begun even before she'd first laid eyes on Aeron.

A few months ago, golden down appeared in her wings. But gold was the color of the warriors, and a warrior she had never longed to be. Even though it would have elevated her station.

Remembering her unhappiness, she sighed. There were three angelic castes. The Elite Seven, like Lysander, worked directly with the One True Deity. They had been selected at the beginning of time and never wavered in their duties to train other angels and monitor evil happenings. Next were the warriors. They destroyed the demons who managed to escape their fiery prisons. Last were the joy-bringers, as Olivia had once been.

Many of her brethren had experienced instant wing envy at the arrival of the golden down—nothing malicious, of course—but for the first time in her existence, she'd been uncertain of her path. Why had *she* been chosen for such a duty?

She'd loved the job she had. She'd loved whispering beautiful affirmations in human ears, bringing them confidence and pleasure. The thought of hurting another living being, even a deserving one... She shuddered.

That's when she encountered those first thoughts about falling, about starting a new life. They'd been innocent thoughts, really. What if and maybe... And when she spied Aeron, those thoughts had intensified. What if they could be together? Maybe they could live happily ever after.

What would it be like to be human?

So by the time the Heavenly High Council, a daunting body composed of angels from each of the three factions, had called her into their tribunal chamber, she had expected to be chastised for her failure to destroy Aeron. Instead, she'd received an ultimatum.

She'd stood in the center of a spacious, white room, the ceiling domed, the walls forming a perfect circle. Columns had stretched all around, even the ivy climbing them a stark, pristine white. A throne sat between each of those columns, a regal form perched in every one.

Do you know why you are here, Olivia? a resonant voice had asked.

Yes. Though she trembled, her wings never ceased their graceful glide. They were long and majestic, the feathers a glorious white threaded with moonlit gold. *To discuss Aeron of the Underworld.*

We've been patient for weeks, Olivia. The emotionless voice had echoed like a war drum inside her head. *We've given you countless opportunities to prove yourself. You failed each time.*

I'm not meant to do this, she'd replied shakily.

You were. You are. There is no better way to spread joy than to save humans from evil. And that is what you will be doing with the completion of this task. This is your last chance. You will end Aeron's life or we will end yours.

The councilor's threat hadn't been meant as a cruelty, she knew. That was simply the way of the heavens. A single drop of poison could ruin an ocean, and so every corrosive drop had to be wiped out before hitting the waves. Yet she'd protested anyway.

You cannot kill me without the True Deity's blessing. And He would not give it. He was all that was tender and kind. He cared for his people, *all* of his people. Even wayward angels. Quite simply, He was love.

But we can *send you away, ending life as you know it.* The speaker had been female, but her voice was no less flat.

For a moment Olivia had had trouble catching her breath, and bright sparks of light had danced around her eyes. Lose her place? She'd just purchased a newer, bigger cloud. She'd promised to take over one of her friend's joy-bringing shifts so that he could go on vacation—and she'd never before broken a promise. Still she'd persisted. *Aeron isn't evil. He doesn't deserve to die.*

That is not for you to decide. He ignored an ancient law and must be punished for it before others think that they can do the same without consequence.

I doubt he even knows what he's done. She'd spread her arms, beseeching. *If you would just allow him to see me and hear my voice, I could talk to him and explain—*

Then we *would be ignoring an ancient law.*

True. Faith was built on the principle that you believed in what you could not see. Only the Elite Seven were allowed to reveal themselves in the mortal plane, as they were sometimes tasked with rewarding people for that faith.

I'm sorry, she'd said, head bowed. *I should not have asked such a thing of you.*

You are forgiven, child, they'd replied in unison.

Forgiveness was always granted so easily here. Well, except when commandments were ignored. Poor Aeron, she'd thought, even as she'd said, *Thank you.*

It was just...Aeron drew her. He looked every inch the demon with his tattooed flesh, yet seeing him for the first time had roused desires inside her that had been too strong to ignore. What would it be like to touch him? What would it be like to be touched *by* him? Would *she* finally know the joy she brought to others?

At first, those thoughts had shamed her. And the better she'd come to know Aeron, the stronger the desires had become—until falling and being with him had been all she could think about.

Finally, she'd told herself it was acceptable to feel so strongly about him because, despite his appearance, despite what the Council said, he was honest and good. And if he was honest and good, she could do the things that he did, and be honest and good, as well. More than that, it would be okay because he, protector that he was, would keep her safe. From others, from herself.

If he were killed, however, she would live the rest of eternity never knowing how...exquisite experiencing him in every way could have been. She would regret. She would mourn.

But to save him, from her own hand, at least, meant giving up everything she knew, as the Council had proclaimed. More than losing her home and her wings, however, she would also be stuck in a world where forgiveness was not always granted, patience was rarely rewarded and rudeness was a way of life.

He is your first assassination, so we do understand your reluctance, Olivia. But you cannot allow that reluctance to ruin you. You must rise above it or you will pay the price forevermore. Which will you choose?

That had been the Council's last-ditch effort to save her. Yet she had raised her head and uttered the words that had been churning inside her for all those weeks—the words that led her here. Before fear could change her mind.

I choose Aeron.

"Woman?"

The hard voice shook Olivia from the past; it was deeper, richer than anyone else's and…necessary. She blinked, her surroundings slowly coming into focus. A bedroom she knew by heart. Spacious, with silver stone walls plastered with portraits of flowers and stars. The floor was composed of dark, polished wood, and draped by a soft pink rug. There was a dresser, a vanity and a young girl's lounge.

Many would have scoffed at the fact that this strong, proud warrior possessed such a feminine room, but not Olivia. The furnishings merely proved the depths of Aeron's love for his Legion.

Did he have room in his heart for one more?

Her gaze landed on him. Still he stood beside the bed she was sprawled upon, gazing down at her with… no emotion, she realized, disappointed. And who could blame him? What a sight she must be. The tears had dried on her cheeks, making her skin feel tight and hot. Her hair hung in tangles, and dirt streaked her exposed skin.

Meanwhile, *he* looked gorgeous. He was tall and mouthwateringly muscled, with the most amazing violet eyes fringed by long black lashes. His dark hair was cropped nearly to his scalp, and she wondered if the choppy strands would prickle her palm when she caressed them.

Not that he would allow her to caress him.

He was heavily tattooed, even on the perfectly sculpted planes of his face. Each of those tattoos depicted something gruesome. Stabbings, stranglings, burnings, blood—so much blood—each skeletal face etched in torment. Yet amid all the violence were two sapphire butterflies, one riding his ribs and one outlining the wings on his back.

The other Lords, she had noticed, only had one butterfly tattoo, each a mark of their demon-possession, and she'd often wondered why Aeron had the extra. Wasn't as if his body contained two demons or anything.

More than that, he despised weakness. Didn't the butterflies remind him of his folly? For that matter, didn't the other tattoos, the violent ones, remind him of the terrible things his demon had forced him to do?

As for Olivia, why didn't this man repulse her as he would have repulsed any other angel? Why did he continue to fascinate her?

"Woman," he repeated, impatient now.

"Yes?" she managed to croak.

"You weren't listening to me."

"I'm sorry."

"Who wanted me dead? And why?"

Rather than answer, she begged, "Sit down, please. Looking up at you like this is straining my neck."

At first, she didn't think he would comply. Then he surprised her by easing to his haunches, his expression gentling. Finally, their gazes were level and she could see that his pupils were dilating. Odd. That usually happened when humans were happy. Or angry. He was neither.

"Better?" he asked.

"Yes. Thank you."

"Good. Now answer me."

Such a commander. She didn't mind, though. The reward was too great. Now she could drink in the wonderfully wicked sight of him without effort, while talking to him as she'd dreamed of doing all these weeks. "The Heavenly High Council wants you dead because you helped a demon escape from hell."

He frowned. "My Legion?"

His Legion? Olivia nodded, winced. Pain wasn't something she'd ever experienced before—mentally or physically—and she wasn't sure how she was withstanding it. Lucidly, at least.

Or maybe she did know. Humans produced adrenaline and other hormones, which numbed them somewhat. Maybe she was producing those things, too, human that she now was. More and more, she began to feel pleasantly distanced from her new body and its unfamiliar aches and emotions.

"I don't understand. Legion had already crawled free by the time we met. I did nothing to earn anyone's... wrath." His mouth tightened on that last word.

"Actually, you did. Without you, she wouldn't have

been able to reach the surface because she was bound to the underground."

"I still don't understand."

Olivia's eyelids, suddenly heavy and seemingly laced with sandpaper, closed—*oh, to discuss something else*—but she forced them to reopen. "For the most part, demons are able to leave hell only when they're summoned to earth. It's a little loophole we didn't catch until too late. Anyway, when they're summoned, their bond with hell breaks and in its place they become bound to the summoner."

"But again, I didn't summon Legion. She came to me."

"Maybe you didn't consciously summon her, but the moment you accepted her as yours, it was as if you'd done so."

He flexed and unflexed his hands, a gesture she knew he made while trying to get himself under control. Perhaps he *was* angry. "She has every right to walk this earth. I am demon, and I have done so for thousands of years without punishment."

True. "But your demon is trapped inside you. Therefore *you* are its hell. Legion is now unfettered, able to come and go as she pleases. Which means she has no hell, and that defies all heavenly rules."

She could see he was preparing to argue. Perhaps it would help to explain the origins of hell.

"The more powerful demons were once angels. Only, they fell. They were the first to fall, actually, and their hearts were blackened, all goodness wiped from them. So, rather than lose their wings and powers, they were punished to suffer forevermore. A tradition that has continued with their offspring. There can be no exceptions.

Demons must be bound to some sort of hell. Those who break that bond are killed."

Red seeped into his irises, glowing brightly. "You're saying Legion has no hell, and because of this, she must die?"

"Yes."

"You're also saying she was once an angel?"

"No. Once in hell, the demons learned how to procreate. Legion is one of those creations."

"And you think to punish her, even though she has caused no harm?"

"Not me, but yes. Even though."

"Understand me now. I will allow no harm to befall her." Calmly stated, but no less violent.

Olivia remained silent. She wouldn't lie to him and tell him what he wanted to hear. That he and Legion were safe now, their crimes forgotten by those in the heavens. Eventually, someone would come to do what Olivia had been unable to.

"She didn't deserve to be there," he growled.

"That wasn't for you to decide." The rebuke emerged softly, as gently as she was able. That the words were an echo of what the Council had said to her left a bad taste in her mouth.

Aeron drew in a rough breath, his nostrils flaring. "You fell. Why aren't you being thrown into hell?"

"The first angels to fall turned their backs on the One True Deity, hence their blackened hearts. I did not turn my back. I merely chose a different path."

"But why were you sent to me *now?* Not as one of the fallen, but as an executioner? Thousands of years ago, I did far more terrible things than break a little demon's bond to hell. All of us here did."

"The Council agreed with the gods that you and your brethren were the only ones capable of housing, and perhaps one day controlling, the escaped demons. As I said, you are their hell, and you have been punished for those early crimes sufficiently."

Victory claimed his features, as if he'd caught her in an untruth. "Wrath will be freed the moment of my death, escaping his so-called hell. What of that? You still think to kill me?"

If only that loophole had not been closed... "Once, we were forbidden to kill demon High Lords, and that is what your Wrath is. Then they escaped the depths, forcing us to change our rules accordingly. So...I was to kill Wrath, as well."

The admission caused his victorious expression to fade. "You fell. That means you didn't agree with the edict. With killing me, my demon and Legion."

"Not true," she said. "I think you should be spared, yes. And Wrath, too, since the demon is a part of you. Do I think Legion should be permitted to live in this world? No. She is a menace in ways you haven't yet learned, and she'll most likely cause untold harm. I fell because—"

"You wanted freedom and love and fun," he said, parroting her earlier words. Only, his were sneered. "Why were you chosen for this task? Have you killed before?"

She gulped, not wanting to admit how things had unfolded but knowing she owed him an explanation. "The dark one, Reyes...he has visited the heavens many times because of his woman, Danika. I saw him once and followed him here, curious about the life a demon-possessed warrior could have built for himself."

"Wait." Aeron scowled over at her. "You followed Reyes."

"Yes." Hadn't she just said that?

"But you followed *Reyes*." Anger radiated from him, body and tone.

"Yes," she whispered, understanding. Suddenly she wished she'd kept that part of the story to herself. She knew how protective Aeron was of his friends, and his dislike of her had to be growing by the minute. "I didn't hurt him, though. I...I spent every day afterward traipsing these grounds." *Following you. Wanting you.* "I was chosen because I, better than anyone, knew your routine."

Or had the elders sensed her mounting desire for him, and thought that if she were the one to eliminate Aeron, she would eliminate that appalling desire, as well? She'd often wondered.

"Just so you know, Reyes has a woman." Aeron arched a brow, disrupting the etching of ghostly souls on his forehead. Screaming souls rising toward damnation. "But that hardly matters. I want to know how you would have killed me."

She would have formed a sword of fire, just as Lysander had taught her, and taken his head. That was the quickest death an angel could deliver, she was told. The quickest and the most merciful, over and done with before a single thread of pain could be felt.

"There are ways," was all she said.

"But you fell and are now unable to complete your mission," Aeron replied, and now his voice was tight with dread. "Someone else will be sent in your place, won't they?"

Finally he was beginning to understand. She nodded.

His frown gave way to another scowl. "Like I said, I will allow no harm to befall Legion. She's mine, and I protect what's mine."

Oh, to be his, she thought, the longing inside her fiercer than her lingering pain. That's why she was here, after all. Better to experience a moment with him than a lifetime with anyone else.

She would have liked more than a moment, yes, but a moment was all they had. When her replacement came, and he would, Aeron would die. Though her heart sank at the thought, the circumstances were as simple as that. Aeron would be defenseless against an opponent he could not see, hear or touch. An opponent who would be able to see, hear and touch him.

And, knowing heavenly justice as she did, that replacement would be Lysander. Olivia had failed, and so her mentor would be held responsible for her shortcoming.

Lysander wouldn't hesitate to deliver the final blow. He never did. Yes, he was different now that he'd mated with Bianka, a Harpy and descendant of Lucifer himself. But to walk away from Aeron meant that Lysander, too, would have to fall. He would have to give up his forever with Bianka, and that was not something the elite warrior would do. Bianka had become his everything.

"I thank you for the warning." Aeron pushed to his feet. If he'd said something before that, she'd missed it, distracted as she'd been. What was wrong with her? She'd come here for him, but since her arrival, she'd mostly retreated into her mind.

"You're welcome. But there's something I'd like in return. I—I would like to stay here," she rushed out. "With you. I can even help with your maid duties, if you'd like." So many times she'd watched Aeron clean this fortress, grumbling about his hatred for the assigned chore.

He bent down to untie her wrists, his motions so tender he elicited only the barest twinges of pain. "I'm afraid that isn't possible."

"But...why? I won't be any trouble. Honest."

"You have already caused trouble."

Her chin started trembling again, the emotional numbness she'd experienced fading quickly. *He still plans to get rid of me.* Fear, confusion, despair all bombarded her. She buried her face in the pillow, not wanting Aeron to see. She was already at enough of a disadvantage with him.

"Woman," he growled. "I told you not to cry."

"Then don't hurt my feelings." The words were muffled from the cotton pressed against her lips—and yes, from her tears.

There was a rustle of clothing, as if he were shifting from one foot to the other. "Hurt your feelings? You should be grateful I haven't killed you. You caused me untold grief this past month. I had no idea who followed me or why. My loyal companion couldn't remain with me and had to return to a place she loathes."

A place she deserved to be, despite Aeron's earlier assertion, but whatever, as some of the Lords were fond of saying. "I'm sorry." Despite everything, she really was. Soon, he would lose all he valued and there would be nothing either of them could do to stop it from happening.

Don't think like that or you'll start crying again.

He sighed. "I accept your apology, but that doesn't change anything. You aren't welcome here."

He forgave her? Finally, a step in the right direction. "But—"

"You are fallen, but you're still immortal. Yes?" He didn't give her time to reply. Her clothing had healed itself, so in his mind it probably stood to reason that she would, too. "You'll be fine by morning. And then I'll want you out of this fortress."

CHAPTER FOUR

AERON PACED THE LENGTH of the hallway. He'd been at it for hours, but saw no reprieve in his immediate future. Someone had to guard the angel. Not from intruders but from *her* intrusion, just in case she was here to sneak about and listen to things she shouldn't.

A rationalization that didn't make a lot of sense, but one he would stick with. Yes, she could have listened to things she shouldn't have as an angel, invisible and protected, but she was vulnerable now, and she could one day be captured by the Hunters and used to hurt his friends.

His hands fisted, and he forced his mind to retreat from thoughts of her torture and their deaths before he punched a wall. Or a friend.

Besides, when Olivia was well enough, which should be any time now, part of him expected her to try and escape his room to hunt for Legion. Even though Legion was absent, that wasn't something Aeron would allow. Not that Olivia, fallen as she now was, could do much damage during her search.

Still. She could reveal her findings to another angel, the one she predicted would come, and that angel could attempt to see the deed done.

Not on my watch, he thought.

His friends had already had their meeting—he'd

heard their mutterings, then their laughter, then their footsteps as they parted—but he had no idea what had been decided. No one had visited him. Were they going to pursue the odd female he'd met in that alley? Had Lucien found any sign of Hunters on the hill?

Aeron hadn't changed his mind; he didn't believe Olivia was involved with them. But they could have followed her here. Sneak attacks were their specialty, after all.

And really, an invasion would be the perfect end to this terrible night.

Half an hour ago, he'd called for Legion to warn her about what was happening. Usually, no matter the distance between them, she heard his cry and came to him. Not this time. Like Lucien, she could flash from one location to another with only a thought, but she hadn't appeared.

Was she hurt? Bound? He was tempted to formally summon her, just as she'd taught him—though until Olivia's explanation, he hadn't understood what she meant—for that wasn't something she could ignore. The more he'd considered the possibility, the more he'd thought it likely that the angel—fallen or not—had to be out of the fortress before Legion would feel comfortable enough to return. He remembered her fear, the way she'd trembled even uttering the word *angel*.

He could have asked Olivia to stop doing whatever she was doing that pained the little demon and not him. Or his friends, for that matter. They'd never sensed Olivia, not in any way. But he hadn't asked. She was healing, and he didn't want to disturb her.

Especially when she'd done so much for him already. *No softening.*

So he'd left Legion alone, as well. For now.

Not that he could imagine the fragile Olivia hurting anyone. Even at full strength—whatever that was. Should it come to a fight, Legion would have the angel pinned, those poisoned fangs deep inside Olivia's vein, in seconds.

That's my girl, he thought, grinning. Only, his grin didn't last. The thought of Olivia dying didn't sit well. She hadn't killed him as she'd been ordered. Not that she could have, but she hadn't even tried to do so. Nor had she harmed Legion, as she'd probably wished to. She wanted only to experience the joys of life she'd clearly been denied.

She didn't deserve to die.

For a moment, only a moment, he thought about keeping her. As calm as Wrath was around her, not demanding he punish her for some crime she'd committed twenty years ago, a day ago, a minute ago, she would be the perfect companion for him. She could see to his needs, as Paris had said.

Needs he'd claimed not to have. But he couldn't deny that while he'd been crouched beside her, *something* had stirred inside him. Something hot and dangerous. She'd smelled of sunshine and earth, and her eyes, as blue and clear as the morning sky, had regarded him with trust and hope. As if he were a savior rather than a destroyer. And he'd liked it.

Idiot! A demon, keeping an angel? Hardly. Besides, she's here to have fun and you, my friend, are as far from fun as a man can be.

"Aeron."

Finally. News. Relieved to push Olivia from his thoughts, Aeron whipped around and saw Torin leaning one shoulder against the wall, gloved arms crossed over his chest and an irreverent smile curling his mouth.

As keeper of Disease, Torin couldn't touch another being skin to skin without beginning a plague. The gloves protected them all.

"Once again, a Lord of the Underworld has a woman locked in his chambers while he tries to figure out what to do with her." Torin chuckled.

Before Aeron could reply, images began flashing through his head. Images of Torin lifting a blade, expression intent, determined. That blade descended... nailed its target in the heart...and emerged wet and red.

The man who'd been stabbed, a human, collapsed into a heap on the ground. Dead. There was a figure eight tattooed on his wrist, the symbol of infinity and the mark of a Hunter. He hadn't hurt Torin, hadn't even threatened to do so. The two had simply passed each other on the street, some four hundred years ago, when the warrior had left the fortress to finally be with the woman he'd fallen for, but had first spied the brand and attacked.

To Wrath, the act was malicious and without provocation. To Wrath, the act deserved punishment.

Aeron had seen this particular event many times already, and each time he'd had to suppress the urge to act. Now was no different. He actually felt his fingers curling around the hilt of his dagger, the need to stab Torin as Torin had stabbed the Hunter strong.

I would have done the same thing, he mentally shouted at the demon. *I would have killed that Hunter, maliciously and without provocation. Torin doesn't deserve castigation.*

Wrath growled.

Calm. Aeron's arm fell to his side, his hand empty.

"Demon wanting a go at me?" Torin asked matter-of-factly.

His friends knew him very well. "Yes, but no worries. I've got the bastard under control."

He thought he heard the demon snort.

The more he denied Wrath, the more its desire to penalize would grow—until the need overtook Aeron so completely, he would snap. That was when he'd fly into town, no one safe, the slightest sins met with absolute cruelty and ruthlessness.

Those vengeance sprees were the reason Aeron had tattooed himself as he had. As he was immortal and prone to heal quickly, he'd had to mix dried ambrosia into the ink to be permanently marked and it had been like injecting fire straight into his veins. Had he minded, though? Hell, no. Every time he looked into the mirror, he was reminded of the things he'd done—and what he would do again if he wasn't careful.

But more than that, the tattoos assured him that the people he'd killed, the ones who hadn't deserved to die, would never truly be forgotten. Sometimes that helped ease his guilt. And sometimes it helped dim his irrational pride in the demon's strength.

"—sure you have control?"

"What?" he asked, pulling himself from his thoughts.

Torin grinned again. "I asked if you were sure you had control of your demon. You're winking in and out, and your eyes are glowing red."

"I'm fine." Unlike Olivia, there wasn't utter truth in his voice. The lie was there for all to hear.

"I believe you. Really. So…back to our conversation?" Torin asked.

Where had he gotten sidetracked? Oh, yes. "I'm sure you didn't come here to compare me to our mated friends. I'm hardly the love-struck fool all of them were when they brought their women here."

"And just like that, you've ruined my next three jokes. You're no fun."

Exactly what Aeron had thought when Olivia had mentioned her three desires. Having the knowledge confirmed, though, scraped him up inside for reasons he couldn't explain. "Torin. Your purpose, please."

"Fine. Your angel's already causing problems. Some of us want to get rid of her, and some want to keep her. I'm on Team Keep. I think we need to charm her to our side before you make her hate us all and she decides to help the enemy."

"Stay away from her." Aeron didn't want the warrior anywhere near Olivia. And it had nothing to do with the man's white hair, black brows and green eyes that never seemed to take anything seriously, ensuring Torin didn't need to touch a woman to win her.

Torin rolled those eyes. "Moron. You should be thanking me, not threatening me. I came to tell you to hide her. William's on my team and he wants to be the one to do the charming."

William, an immortal with a sex addiction. An immortal with black hair and blue eyes even more wicked than Torin's. A warrior who was tall, muscled and untamed. A warrior whose only tattoos were hidden under his clothes. If Aeron was remembering correctly, there was an X over his heart and a treasure map on his back. A treasure map that crossed his ribs and dipped around his waist, finally ending over his "fun zone."

He was a "real beefcake"—if human females could be believed—and was the *epitome* of fun.

Olivia would probably like him.

Why did Aeron suddenly want to bash the man's face into the wall, ruining those pretty looks? Something he'd never wanted to do before, despite Wrath's intense need to punish the man, breaking his heart into hundreds of pieces the way he'd done to hundreds of women. Only, Wrath wanted Aeron to use a blade.

Aeron had always resisted because he liked William, who may not be a true Lord, but who could be counted on during battle. The man had no limitations when it came to killing.

Without Legion, you're looking for a fight. That's all. Yes. Clearly he was on edge.

"Thank you, Torin, for the warning about William," he said, hoping he sounded properly wry. "Though Olivia won't be here long enough to be charmed by anyone."

"I'm sure William would tell you he only needs a few seconds."

Do not react. Although, if William showed up, Aeron could "accidentally" lose control of Wrath, allowing the demon to finally have a go at the immortal.

Wrath purred his approval.

"Oh, hey," Torin said, claiming his attention. "Switching the topic from one sex addict to another, Paris wanted me to tell you that Lucien flashed him into town to find a woman. Lucien planned on leaving him there, so he won't be back until morning."

"Good." His relief had nothing to do with Paris being far away from Olivia. "Did Lucien see any sign of Hunters while he was out there?"

"Nope. Not on the hill and not in Buda."

"Good," Aeron repeated, kicking back into motion. From one corner to the other he paced. "Was there any sign of the dark-haired woman?"

"No, but Paris promised to continue looking for her. Once he regained his strength, of course. And speaking of lost strength, Paris mentioned that the angel is injured. Do you want me to have someone fetch a doctor?"

"Fetch" meant "abduct" in this household. "No. She'll heal on her own." They'd been on the lookout for a doctor to permanently employ for some time, but they'd had no luck. Now time was of the essence, since Ashlyn was pregnant. But no one knew if the baby would be mortal or demon, so they had to be careful whom they chose.

Hunters, as they'd recently learned, had been breeding immortals with mortals for years, spawning half-ling children in the hopes of creating an unstoppable army. The demon of Violence's baby would be a prize among prizes, someone every Hunter would love to use. And in the hands of the wrong doctor, the Lords' secrets would be anything but safe.

Torin shook his head in sympathy, as if Aeron were too dim-witted to think things through properly. "You sure she'll heal? She was kicked out of the heavens."

"*We* were kicked out of the heavens, yet we heal as fast as ever. We even regenerate limbs." Which Gideon, keeper of the demon of Lies, was now in the process of doing. The warrior had been captured during their last battle with Hunters and tortured for information— information he had not given. In retaliation, the Hunters had removed both of his hands.

Gideon was still bedbound and a major pain in everyone's ass.

"Good point," Torin said.

A woman's scream suddenly burst from Aeron's bedroom.

He stopped pacing, and Torin straightened. By the time the second scream sounded, both were running for the room, though Torin kept a good distance between them. Aeron threw open the door, the first inside.

Olivia was on the bed, still lying on her stomach but now thrashing. Her eyes were closed, and despite the shadows her lashes cast, he could see that bruises now branched under them. That dark hair was in tangles around her trembling shoulders.

Her robe had obviously cleaned itself, most of the blood gone. Yet there were two new stains where her wings should have already begun to grow back, both bright crimson and wet.

THE DEMONS WERE tugging on her.

Olivia could feel their claws digging into her skin, cutting, stinging. She could feel the sticky slime on their scales and the burn of their putrid breath. She could hear the glee in their laughter and wanted to vomit.

"Lookie what I found," one of them cackled.

"A pretty angel, fallen right into our arms," another chortled.

Plumes of sulfur and rot thickened the air, and the stench was sucked into her nostrils as she tried to catch her breath. She'd just fallen, the clouds opening up under her feet, sending her tumbling from the heavens, down…down, no end in sight, flailing for something, anything to catch and stop herself…and when the end had finally appeared, the ground had opened up, too, the flames of hell swallowing her whole.

"A warrior angel, at that. She has wings with gold."

"Not anymore."

The tugging became harder, more violent. She kicked and hit and bit, trying to fight her way free to run and hide, but there were too many demons around her, the jagged, rocky landscape behind them unfamiliar to her, so her efforts elicited no results. The tendons anchoring her wings in place began to tear; the scalding pain spread, consuming her until every thought in her head revolved around the easiest way to stop it: dying.

Please. Let me die.

Stars winked over her eyes, suddenly the only thing she could see. Everything else had gone black. But black was good, black was welcome. Still, on and on the laughter and tugging continued. Dizziness soon flooded her, and nausea began churning in her stomach.

Why wasn't she dead? Then one of her wings ripped free completely and she screamed, that scalding pain morphing into what she now knew was true agony. Not even death could end this kind of suffering. No, this would follow her into the afterlife.

The other wing quickly followed, and she screamed again and again and again. Claws continued to scrape at her clothing, damaging more of her skin and sinking inside the fresh wounds on her back. Finally, she did vomit, emptying her stomach of the heavenly fruits she'd consumed just that morning.

"Not so pretty now, are you, warrior?"

Hands squeezed at her, touching her in places no one had ever touched her before. Tears streamed down her cheeks, and she lay there, helpless. This was it. The end.

Finally. Except, one thought glimmered in that sea of black: she'd given up her beautiful life, only to die in hell without ever knowing joy, without spending time with Aeron. No. *No!*

You are stronger than this. Fight! Yes, yes. She was stronger than this. She would fight. She would—

"Olivia."

The hard, familiar voice swept through her mind, momentarily blocking the hated images, the pain and the sorrow. The determination.

"Olivia. Wake up."

A nightmare, she thought, with a small hint of relief. Only a nightmare. Humans often had them. But she knew the assault had been much more to her. A memory, a replay of her time in hell.

She still thrashed atop the bed, she realized, her back even now aflame, the rest of her bruised and knotted. Forcing herself to cease, she pried her eyelids apart. She was panting, chest swiftly lifting and falling against the mattress, air burning her nose and throat as if she were inhaling acid. Sweat dripped from her, soaking her robe to her skin. That blessed numbness she'd experienced earlier was completely obliterated; she felt *everything.*

Death might have been preferable, after all.

Once more Aeron was crouched beside the bed and peering over at her. A male—the one named Torin, she recalled—stood beside him and watched her through haunted green eyes.

Demon, Olivia thought. Torin was a demon. Just like the others. The ones who had ripped out her wings. The ones who had touched her and taunted her.

A piercing scream coiled from her raw throat. She wanted Aeron, only Aeron; she didn't trust anyone else.

Didn't want anyone else even looking at her right now. Especially a demon. That Aeron himself was possessed by Wrath had no bearing on the situation. To her, Aeron was simply Aeron. But all she could think about when she looked at Torin was how scaled hands had pinched her nipples and sunk between her legs. How those hands would have done far more if she hadn't begun fighting.

Fight. Yes. She kicked out her leg, but the foolish limb flopped uselessly, the muscles too tense to work properly. *Helpless.* Again. A sob joined her scream, both choking from her as she then tried to scramble from the bed and throw herself into Aeron's arms. But once more, her feeble body refused to cooperate.

"Make him leave, make him leave, make him leave," she shouted, burying her face in the pillow. Even looking at the newcomer was painful to her. She might know Torin on sight, but she didn't know him the way she knew Aeron. Didn't crave him the way she craved Aeron.

Aeron, who could make everything better, as he did for his friend Paris every night. Aeron, who could protect her as he did his little Legion. Aeron, who was so fierce he had scared her nightmares away.

Strong hands settled on her shoulders and held her down to stop her renewed thrashing. "Shh. Shh now. You have to calm down before you injure yourself further."

"What's going on?" Torin asked. "What can I do to help?"

No. No, no, no. The demon was still here. "Make him leave! You have to make him leave. Now. Right now."

"I'm not going to hurt you, angel," Torin said gently. "I'm here to—"

Hysteria was bubbling up inside her, about to consume her and sweep her under. "Make him leave. Please, Aeron, make him leave. Please."

Aeron growled low in his throat. "Torin, damn it. Get the hell out of here. She's not going to calm down until you do."

There was a heavy sigh, sadness in the undertones, then blessedly, footsteps sounded.

"Wait," Aeron called, and Olivia wanted to scream. "Did Lucien flash to the States as planned the other day and purchase Tylenol for the women?"

"As far as I know, yes," Torin replied.

They were conversing? Now? "Make him leave!" Olivia shouted.

"Bring me some," Aeron said, talking over her.

The door creaked open. *Finally,* the demon was leaving—but he would return with human medicine. Olivia whimpered. She couldn't go through this again. Would probably die from fear alone.

"Just throw it inside the room," Aeron added, as though sensing her thoughts.

Thank you, sweet merciful Deity in heaven. As Olivia slumped onto the mattress, the door clicked shut.

"He's gone," Aeron said softly. "It's just you and me now."

She was trembling so violently, the entire bed shook. "Don't leave me. Please, don't leave me." The plea proved just how weak she currently was, but she didn't care. She needed him.

Aeron smoothed the sweat-damp hair from her temples, his touch as soft as his voice. This couldn't be her Aeron, speaking to her so sweetly, caressing her so tenderly. The change in him was almost too vast to be believed. *Why* had he changed? Why was he treating her, a virtual stranger, as he usually only treated his friends?

"You wanted me to hold you earlier," he said. "Do you still wish it?"

"Yes." Oh, yes. Whatever the reason for the change, it didn't matter. He was here, and he was giving her what she'd desired for so long.

Very slowly, he eased beside her, careful not to jostle her. When he was stretched out, she inched forward until her head was resting in the groove of his strong, hot shoulder. The action lanced more of that debilitating pain through her, but being this close to him, finally touching him, was worth it. *This* was why she'd come here.

He wrapped one arm around her lower back, still so careful of her wounds, and his warm breath trekked down her forehead. "Why aren't you healing, Olivia?"

She loved when he uttered her name. Like a prayer and a plea, wrapped in the same pretty package. "I told you. I fell. I'm fully human now."

"Fully human," he said, stiffening. "No, you didn't tell me that. I could have brought you medicine sooner."

There was guilt in his tone. Guilt and dread. The dread she didn't understand, but was too wrung out to question. And then she forgot all about it. In the center of the room, an amber light sparked. That light grew... and grew...brightening so much she had to squint.

A body took shape. A big, muscled body draped in a white robe very similar to hers. Pale hair appeared next, waving to thick shoulders. She saw eyes like liquid onyx and pale skin with the slightest dusting of gilt. Last to fill her gaze were wings of pure, shimmering gold.

She wanted to wave but could only manage a faint

grin. Sweet Lysander, here to comfort her at last, even as a figment of her imagination. "I'm dreaming again. Only, I like this one."

"Shh, shh," Aeron whispered to her. "I'm here."

"As am I." Lysander's gaze swept his surroundings and his lips curled with distaste. "Unfortunately, this is no dream." As always, he spoke true, his voice as filled with certainty as hers.

This was truly happening? "But I'm human now. I shouldn't be able to see you." Actually, seeing him was now against the rules. Unless her Deity thought to reward her? Given that she'd just turned her back on her heritage, that hardly seemed likely.

Now he peered straight into her eyes—straight, it seemed, into her soul. "I petitioned the Council on your behalf. They've agreed to give you one more chance. And so, right now, a part of you is still angelic and will remain so for the next fourteen days. Fourteen days in which you may change your mind and reclaim your rightful place."

Like a bolt of lightning, shock lanced through her, burning and sizzling. "I don't understand." No fallen angel had ever been given a second chance before.

"Nothing to understand," Aeron said, still trying to soothe her. "I've got you."

"I am of the Seven, Olivia. I wanted fourteen days for you, and so you were given fourteen days. To live here, to…enjoy. And then, to return." Lysander's affronted tone proclaimed his status should explain everything.

It did not, but still the hope in his voice saddened her. The only thing she regretted about her choice was hurting this amazing warrior. He loved her, desired only the best for her.

"I'm sorry, but I won't change my mind."

He appeared thunderstruck. "Even when the immortal is taken from you?"

She barely managed to stop her horrified cry. *I'm not ready to lose him.* But weak as she was, there was nothing she could do to save him, and she knew it. "Is that why you're—"

"No, no. Calm yourself. I'm not here to kill him." The word *yet* was unsaid, but present all the same. "If you decide to stay, his new executioner will not be decided until your fourteen days have passed."

So. She was guaranteed two weeks with Aeron. No more, no less. That would have to be enough. She would make so many memories, they would last a lifetime. If she could convince Aeron to let her stay here, that is. As stubborn as he was...

She sighed. "Thank you," she told Lysander. "For everything. You didn't have to do this for me." And had probably had to fight the Council mercilessly for such a concession, one of the Seven or not. Yet he'd done so, without hesitation, just so she might experience the joy and passion she craved before reclaiming her place in heaven. She wouldn't tell him that she could not go back. No matter what happened.

In fourteen days, if she did return, she would be expected to kill Aeron, she knew—and still she would not be able to do so. "I love you. I hope you know that. No matter what happens."

"Olivia," Aeron said, clearly confused.

"He cannot see, hear or even sense me," Lysander explained. "He now realizes you are not talking to him and thinks you are hallucinating from the pain." Her mentor stepped toward the bed. "I must remind you that the man is a demon, Liv. He is everything we fight against."

"As is your female."

He squared his wide shoulders, and his chin lifted. Ever the stubborn warrior, her Lysander. Just like Aeron. "Bianka broke none of our laws."

"But even if she had, you would have wanted to be with her. You would have found a way."

"Olivia?" Aeron repeated.

Lysander paid him no heed. "Why would you choose to live with him as a human, Olivia? Just for a few minutes in his arms? That can bring you nothing but heartache and disappointment."

Once again, there was undiluted truth in his tone. Lies were not permitted in their—no, *his,* she thought sadly—world. Still, she refused to believe him. Here, she would do things she desperately wanted to do. Not only would she live as a human, but she would feel as one, too.

The bedroom door swung open, saving her from replying. A small plastic bottle was tossed inside. It landed on the floor a few inches from Lysander's sandaled feet.

"Here are the meds," Torin called. The door shut before Olivia could work up another scream.

Aeron made to rise, but Olivia settled her weight more firmly atop him. "No," she said, grimacing as another of those burning bolts struck her. "Stay."

He could have pushed her aside, but didn't. "I need to get the pills. They'll help ease your pain."

"Later," she said. Now that they were touching, now that she felt the warmth of his body, wrapping around her, soothing her, she didn't want to lose it. Even for a moment.

At first, she thought he would disregard her plea, but then he relaxed and tightened his hold on her. Olivia sighed with contentment and met Lysander's hard gaze once more. He was scowling.

"This is why," she told him. Cuddling wasn't something angels did. They could have, if they'd so wanted, she supposed, but none ever had. Why would they? They were like brothers and sisters to each other, physical desire not part of their makeup.

"Why what?" Aeron asked, confused all over again.

"Why I like you," she answered honestly.

He stiffened, but didn't reply.

Eyes narrowed, Lysander spread his wings in one smooth jerk, the gold glistening in the moonlight. A single feather drifted to the floor. "I'll leave you to your recovery, pet, but I *will* return. You don't belong here. As the days pass, I have a feeling you, too, will realize that."

CHAPTER FIVE

THAT FIRST NIGHT, after Olivia finished her strange conversation with herself, she finally fell back asleep, once again moaning and groaning with her pain, thrashing and hurting herself further. The second night, the mutterings about demons began. *Don't touch me, you filthy wretch.* Whimper, gag. *Please, don't touch me.* The third night, a deathly stillness claimed her.

Aeron almost preferred the begging.

Through it all, he mopped her brow, kept her company—even reading one of Paris's romance novels to her, though she remained unaware—and forced liquids and crushed pills down her throat. He would not have her death on his conscience.

More than that, he wanted her out of his life—no matter how strongly his body reacted when he neared her. Or thought of her. He hadn't lied. Once she was healed, she was gone. *Because* of how his body reacted.

Worse, the way his demon reacted. Not to her, but *for* her.

Punish, the demon said for the...what? Hundredth time? *Punish the ones who hurt her.* During Aeron's blood-curse, the demon had spoken to him—in one-word commands—in addition to flashing violent images through his mind. For the past three days, though, extended speech was Wrath's preferred method of communicating, and Aeron wasn't quite used to it. Where was the peace Olivia elicited?

Also, he wasn't sure what Olivia had been through when she'd been kicked from her home, and he couldn't allow himself to find out. He might not be able to stop his demon from acting. Could barely stop the demon now. And if he knew the truth, he might not *want* to stop his demon. If ever there was a time to enjoy what Wrath could do...

Don't think like that. Aeron didn't want to soften toward Olivia any more than he already had, and he didn't want her sinking deeper into his thoughts and decisions. His life had enough complications. And already she'd added more.

She wanted to have fun. As he'd assured her, *fun* wasn't a word he was acquainted with, nor did he have time to learn. And he wasn't disappointed about that. Truly.

She wanted to love. In no way was he right for that task. Romantic love wasn't something he would ever bring to the table. Especially with someone as fragile as Olivia. And he wasn't disappointed about that, either. *Truly.*

She wanted freedom. *That* he could give her. In town. If she would just get better, damn her!

She *would* get better, or by the gods he would finally unleash his demon, willingly and without restraint.

Punish. Punish the ones who hurt her.

Why did the demon like her? And Wrath had to like her. Nothing else explained the urge to strike at beings they hadn't personally encountered. He'd had time to think about this, way too much time, yet no answers had materialized.

Aeron scrubbed a hand down his face. Because he refused to leave Olivia's side, Lucien had had to continue seeing to Paris's care and ensuring the warrior fed his own demon properly. Torin, in turn, had had to see to Aeron's meals, bringing him trays of food throughout the day, but never staying to talk with him. If Olivia were to awaken and see the male… He didn't relish a repeat of her earlier terror.

Unfortunately, the women of the house had learned of the angel's presence and had descended en masse to welcome her. Not that he'd let them past the door. No telling how Olivia would react to them. Besides, none of them had known how to help the angel. He'd asked. Fine. He'd snarled.

Although he might have endured fits of terror from Olivia if it meant seeing her conscious again. Why the hell would she not awaken? And now, as still as she was… He rolled to his side, careful not to jostle her, and stared down at her. For the first time, she didn't curl into him but remained as she was. Her skin was ghostly pale, her veins visible and garish. Her hair was a matted nest around her head. Her cheeks were hollowed out and her lips scabbed from where she'd chewed them.

Yet she was still beyond beautiful. Exquisite, even, in a protect-me-forever kind of way. So much so, his chest constricted at the sight of her. Not in guilt, but in a possessive need to be the one doing the protecting. A need that ran bone-deep.

She had to heal, and he had to get rid of her. *Soon.*

"At this rate, she's going to die," he snarled to the ceiling. Whether he was speaking to her One Deity or to the gods he knew, he wasn't sure. "Is that what you want? One of your own to suffer unimaginably before perishing? You can save her."

Look at you, he thought, disgusted with himself. *Pleading for a life as the humans never do.*

That didn't stop him. "Why won't you?"

The barest hint of a...growl? hit his ears. Aeron tensed. As he palmed one of the daggers he'd placed on his nightstand, his gaze zoomed through his bedroom. He and Olivia were alone. No godly being had appeared to chastise him for his impudent tone.

Slowly he relaxed. Lack of sleep was finally catching up with him, he supposed.

Night had long since fallen, moonlight shimmering through the windowed doors leading to his balcony. So peaceful was the sight, so fatigued was his body, he should have finally drifted into slumber. He didn't. Couldn't.

What would he do if Olivia died? Would he mourn her as Paris mourned his Sienna? Surely not. He didn't know her. Most likely, he would feel guilt. Lots and lots of guilt. She had saved him, yet he wouldn't have done the same for her.

You don't deserve her.

The thought whispered through his head, and he blinked. It hadn't belonged to Wrath, the timbre too low, too gravelly—and yet, somehow familiar. Had Sabin, keeper of Doubt, returned from Rome, attacking his self-confidence as was the warrior's unintentional habit?

"Sabin," he spat, just in case.

No response.

She's too good for you.

This time, Wrath rumbled inside his head, prowling through his skull, suddenly agitated.

Not Sabin, then. One, Aeron hadn't heard Sabin return and, two, he knew the warrior wasn't due to arrive for another few weeks. Plus, there was no gleeful undertone to these doubts, and Sabin's demon found great joy in the spreading of its poison.

So, who did that leave? Who possessed the power to speak in his mind?

"Who's there?" he demanded.

That does not matter. I am here to heal her.

Heal her? Aeron relaxed just a little. There was a ring of truth in the voice, just as there was in Olivia's. Was this an angel? "Thank you."

Save your thanks, demon.

Such anger from an angel? Probably not. Or was this a god, perhaps, answering his prayers? No, couldn't be, Aeron decided. The gods enjoyed their fanfare and would have relished the opportunity to reveal themselves and demand gratitude. And if this were Olivia's Deity, surely there would have been a hum of power in the air, at the very least. Instead, there was…nothing. Aeron sensed, smelled and felt nothing.

I have every faith that, when she awakens, she will begin to see you for what you really are.

Because of the being's certainty that she would awaken, Aeron didn't mind the implied insult. He was too relieved. "And what am I?" Not that he cared. But in the answer, he might learn who this speaker was.

Inferior, wicked, malicious, foolish, single-minded, rotten, unworthy and doomed.

"Tell me how you really feel," he replied dryly, hoping his sarcasm hid his actions as he slowly edged over Olivia, using his body to shield hers. Wicked and malicious—the beliefs of the Hunters. Yet a Hunter would have attacked Aeron before offering anyone aid. Even their Bait.

Again he wondered if this newcomer was an angel. Despite that anger. And clearly, hatred.

Another growl echoed. *Your insolence only proves my point. Which is why I will allow her to get to know you as she desires, for I have a feeling she will not like what she learns. Just...do not soil her. If you do, I will bury you and all those you love.*

"I would never soil a—"

Silence. She awakens now.

To prove the words, Olivia moaned. In that moment, the amount of relief that flooded him was irrational. Too much for someone he didn't know and wouldn't mourn. One thing he did know: whoever the speaker was, he was indeed powerful, to draw Olivia from that deathly slumber so quickly.

"Thank you," he said again. "She suffered unjustly and—"

I told you to be silent! If you dare disturb her healing process, demon...actually, I've had all of you I can stand for one evening. Sleep.

Though he fought against it, his body seemed unable to refuse the command and sagged against the mattress, a few inches from Olivia. His eyelids closed and lethargy beat through him, dragging him kicking and screaming into the darkness he would have previously welcomed. Still, that darkness couldn't stop him from reaching for Olivia and drawing her into his side.

Where she belonged.

EYES STILL TOO HEAVY to open, Olivia stretched her arms over her head and arched her back, the knots unwinding from her muscles. *Sooo* good. Grinning, she drew in a deep breath that brought with it the scent of exotic spice and forbidden fantasies. Her cloud had never smelled this...*sexy* before. Nor had it ever been this warm, almost decadently so.

She wanted to stay just like this forever, but laziness wasn't the way of the angels. Today she would visit Lysander, she decided. *If* he wasn't away on a secret mission as he often was, and if he hadn't locked himself away with his Bianka. Afterward, she would head to the fortress in Budapest. What would Aeron be doing today? Would his contradictions fascinate her once again? Would he sense her again, as he shouldn't have been able to do, then demand she reveal herself so that he could kill her?

Those demands always hurt her feelings, though she couldn't blame him for his anger. He didn't know who she was or what her intentions were. *I want him to know me,* she thought. She was likeable; she really was. Well, to other angels, she was. She wasn't sure what a demon-possessed immortal warrior would think of the real her, his supposed opposite.

Only, Aeron didn't seem like a demon to her. Not in any way. He called Legion his "precious baby," bought her tiaras and decorated his room to fit her tastes. He'd even had his friend and fellow Lord Maddox construct a lounge chair for her. A lounge chair that rested beside his bed and was draped with pink lace.

Olivia wanted her own lacy lounge chair in that bedroom.

Envy is not a good look for you, she reminded her-

self. *You might not have a lacy lounge, but you have
helped countless people laugh and rejoice and learn to
love their lives.* Yes, she took a great amount of satisfaction from that. But...now she wanted more. Maybe
she'd always wanted more, but just hadn't realized it
until her "promotion."

So greedy, she thought with a sigh.

The rock-hard yet smooth mattress underneath her
shifted and moaned.

Wait. Rock-hard? Shifted? Moaned? Jarred into lu-
cidity, Olivia now had no trouble prying her eyelids
apart. She jerked upright at the sight she beheld—or
didn't behold. The indigo haze of a rising sun and fat,
puffy clouds were nowhere to be seen. Instead, she saw
a bedroom with jagged stone walls, a wood floor and
polished cherrywood furniture.

She also saw a lacy pink lounge chair.

Realization slammed into her. *Fallen. I've fallen.*
She'd descended into hell, and the demons—*do not
think about them.* Already, with only that small memory, her body had begun trembling. *I'm with Aeron now.
I'm safe.* But if she truly was mortal, why did her body
feel so...fit?

Another realization: because she wasn't truly human.

Fourteen days, she recalled Lysander saying, before
she lost all of her angelic traits. Did that mean... Could
her wings have...

Biting her lower lip, afraid to hope, she reached behind and felt her back. What she encountered caused her
shoulders to slump with both relief and sadness. No injuries remained, but her wings had not regrown, either.

Your choice. Your consequences. Yes. She accepted
that. It was strange, though. This wingless body be-

longed to her. A body that would not live forever. A body that felt both the good and the bad.

And that was okay, she rushed to assure herself. She was in the Lords' fortress, and she was with Aeron. Aeron, who was underneath her. How fun. So far this body had only experienced the bad, and she was more than ready for the good.

Olivia scooted off him and twisted to study him. He was still sleeping, his features relaxed, one arm tossed over his head, the other at his side, where she had been. He'd been holding her close. The corners of her lips lifted in a dreamy smile, and her heart fluttered wildly.

He wasn't wearing a T-shirt, and the knowledge caused her heart's fluttering to pick up speed. She had sprawled across the colorful expanse of his chest, had lain on those tiny brown nipples, those ropes of muscle and that intriguing navel.

Unfortunately, he was wearing jeans. His feet were bare, though, and she saw that even his toes were tattooed. Adorable.

Adorable? Really? Who are you? People were being murdered on those toes. Still, she wanted to trace her fingertips over them. She did trace a fingertip over the butterfly on his ribs. The wings curled into sharp points, destroying any illusion of delicacy.

At her touch, breath pushed from his lips, and she jolted backward. No way did she want to be caught molesting him. Well, without his permission. The action proved more forceful than she'd meant, and she propelled off the bed completely, plummeting to the floor with a painful *thwack*. Hair danced over her face, and when she brushed the strands aside, she realized she'd awoken Aeron.

He was sitting up, glaring down at her.

Olivia gulped and waved up at him shyly. "Uh, good morning."

His gaze roved over her, narrowed. "You look better. Much better." His voice was rough. Probably from sleep, and not desire as every cell in her body hoped. "Are you healed?"

"Yes, thank you." At least she thought she was healed. Her heart had yet to calm, its continued erratic beat foreign to her. And there was an ache in her chest. Nothing terrible, as the pain in her back had been, but odd. Her stomach was even quivering.

"You suffered for three days. Any complications? Any lingering twinges?"

"Three days?" She hadn't realized so much time had passed. And yet, three days hardly seemed long enough for her to have healed so thoroughly. "How am I all better?"

He glowered. "We had a visitor last night. He didn't give me a name, but he said he would heal you, and I guess he was true to his word. He didn't like me, by the way."

"My mentor." Of course. Healing her would have meant bending the rules, but Lysander had helped *make* those rules. If anyone would know ways around them, it was him. And an angel who didn't like Aeron? Lysander for sure.

Once more Aeron's gaze raked her, as if searching for injuries despite the truth in her claim. His pupils dilated, gobbling up every bit of that lovely violet. Not with happiness, but with...anger? Again? She had done nothing to quash his earlier tenderness. Had Lysander said something to upset him, then?

"Your robe..." he croaked, and quickly turned away from her, giving her his back. His second butterfly tattoo greeted her, and her mouth watered. What would those jagged wings taste like? "Fix it."

Frowning, she looked down at herself. Her knees were drawn up and her robe was bunched at her waist, revealing the small, white panties she wore. He couldn't be angry about that. Anya, Lucien's wife and the minor goddess of Anarchy, wore much less on a daily basis. Still, Olivia smoothed the soft, flowing material to her ankles. She could have stood and rejoined him on the bed but decided not to risk either falling or a rejection.

"I'm covered now," she said.

When he faced her, those pupils still blown, he tilted his head to the side, as if he were replaying their conversation through his mind. "Why do you have a mentor?"

Easy enough to answer. "Like humans, angels must learn how to survive. How to help those in need. How to fight demons. My mentor was—is—the greatest of his kind, and I was blessed to work with him."

"His name." The two words lashed like a whip, hard and sure, cutting.

Why such a negative reaction? "I believe he's an acquaintance of yours, actually. You know Lysander, yes?"

Aeron's pupils finally retracted, the violet irises once more visible—and drowning her in their irresistible depths. "Bianka's Lysander?"

She smiled at the description. "Yes. He visited me, too."

"The night I thought you were talking to yourself," he said, nodding.

"Yes." And he planned to return. That, she didn't

mention. Lysander loved her and wouldn't hurt Aeron—yet—because that would, in turn, hurt her. At least, that was the hope she clung to.

Aeron scowled. "The angelic visits have to stop, Olivia. Between Hunters and our demons, we have enough to deal with already. Even though Lysander helped you, even though I'm grateful, I cannot allow the continued interference."

She laughed. She just couldn't help herself. "Good luck with that." Stopping an angel was like stopping the wind: in a word, impossible.

His scowl intensified. "Are you hungry?"

The subject change didn't bother her; it actually delighted her. He'd often done the same thing with his friends, moving from one topic to another without warning. "Oh, yes. I'm starved."

"Then I'll feed you before taking you into town," he said, throwing his legs over the side of the bed and standing.

Still Olivia remained in place, but this time the immobility was because her limbs felt as if they were anchored to rocks. First, he was *gorgeous*. All muscle and danger and mouthwateringly colorful skin. Second— "You still mean to cast me out?"

"Of course."

Don't you dare cry. "Why?" Had Lysander said something, as she'd suspected?

"Better question. When did I ever imply otherwise?" He strode to his bathroom and she lost sight of him. There was a rustle of clothing, and then a burst of water upon porcelain.

"But you held me in your arms all night," she called. "You cared for me for three days." That had to mean something. Right? Men didn't do such things unless they were besotted. Right? In all her time with Aeron, she'd never seen him with a female. Well, besides Legion, but the little demon didn't count. He'd never held her in his arms all night. So his attention to Olivia was special. *Right?*

There was no reply. Soon, steam and the scent of sandalwood soap were drifting through the room. He was showering, she realized, and her heart once more picked up speed, even skipping a beat altogether. He'd never showered when she'd been here before. He'd always waited until she had left.

Seeing his naked body had become an obsession.

Was he tattooed *there,* between his legs? If so, what design had he chosen?

And why do I want to lick that design the same way I want to lick the butterflies? Imagining doing so, Olivia traced her tongue over her lips before freezing in astonishment. *Bad, naughty girl.* Such a desire…

Well, I'm not fully an angel anymore, she reminded herself, and she wanted to see—and taste—him. So see him—and hopefully taste him—she would. After everything she'd endured, she deserved a little treat. Or maybe a big treat? Either way, she wasn't leaving this fortress until she'd gotten a peek.

Determined, Olivia finally pushed to her feet. Without her wings to center her, she had no sense of balance, and quickly toppled over, sharp pains exploding from her knees and making her wince. This pain, however, was bearable. After the wing extraction, *everything* was probably bearable.

Again, she stood. Again she fell. Argh! All too soon,

the water shut off. There was a slap of wet flesh against marble, and then a glide of cotton from metal.

Hurry! Before it was too late.

For balance, she placed one foot in front and one in back and spread her arms wide. Slowly she inched to her full height. She wobbled left, then right, but managed to stay upright this time. *Go, me!*

Then Aeron emerged from the bathroom, and disappointment filled her. There was a towel wrapped around his waist and another winding around his neck. Too late. Double argh!

"You showered so swiftly. Surely you missed a spot," she said.

He didn't flick her a glance, but kept his attention on the dresser in front of him. "No. I didn't."

Oh.

"Now it's your turn," he said after placing a T-shirt on top of the wood. He used the second towel to dry what little hair he had.

Had she called him gorgeous before? She should have said *magnificent.* "My robe cleans me." Did she sound as breathless to him as she did to herself?

He frowned, still not facing her. "Even your hair?"

"Yes." Her hands were shaking as she pulled the hood over her head, gave it time to work its magic, and then cast it back. As the material fell, she smoothed a hand through her now silky, smooth locks. "See? All of me."

Finally, he looked her over, gaze sliding down her body, lingering in certain places, heating her blood, making her skin tingle. When their eyes met, his pupils were once again dilated, black overshadowing violet.

Seriously, what was she doing to cause such anger?

"That it does," he growled. He turned on his heel and strode forward, entering his closet and disappearing from view. The towel soared out and landed in a heap on the floor.

He was naked again, she thought, forgetting his anger. *Now's your chance.* Grinning, Olivia propelled into motion. She managed two steps before toppling and landing on her knees—then launching the rest of the way to her stomach, air whooshing from her lungs.

"What are you doing?"

Up, up she looked. There was Aeron, in the closet doorway, dressed in that black T-shirt, now paired with jeans. He'd also pulled on a pair of boots and weapons were probably strapped all over his muscled body. His eyes were narrowed, his lips drawn tight in a frown.

Foiled again. She sighed in dejection.

"Doesn't matter, really," he said, clearly done waiting for her reply. "It's time for us to go."

Now? "You can't take me into town," she rushed out. "You need me."

He sputtered for a moment. "Hardly. I need no one."

Oh, really? "Someone else will be sent to do the job I couldn't do, remember? As you couldn't sense Lysander when he visited me, you won't be able to sense another angel."

Aeron crossed his arms over his massive chest, the very picture of male stubbornness. "I sensed you, didn't I?"

Yes, he had, and she still hadn't figured out how he'd done so. "Well, like I said, you didn't sense Lysander. I, however, can see the angels. I can warn you when another approaches." Not that they would come for him until her fourteen-day reprieve ended—wait, they had an eleven-day reprieve now, since three had already passed—but he didn't need to know that.

He popped his jaw left and right, disrupting the flow of the images etched there. "You told me you were hungry. Let's find you something to eat."

Again with the subject change. This time, she hated it, but still let it slide, sensing further argument was futile. Besides, she *was* hungry. She crawled to her knees, then eased to her feet. One step, two…three… Soon she was in front of Aeron, smiling at her success.

"What was that?" he asked.

"Walking."

"Took you so long, I'm officially fifty years older."

She raised her chin, pride undiminished. "Well, I didn't fall."

He shook his head—in exasperation?—and took her hand in his. "Come on, angel."

"Fallen," she automatically corrected. The feel of his fingers curled around hers, warm and strong, made her shiver. A sensation she wasn't allowed to relish.

When he tugged her forward, she tripped over her own feet. Thankfully, before she could kiss the ground again, he jerked her up and into his side, anchoring her there.

"Thank you," she muttered.

Now *this* was the life. She snuggled as close to him as she could get. Throughout the centuries, she'd watched many humans succumb to their baser desires, but until that golden down had appeared in her wings, she hadn't truly wondered why they did so. Now she knew: every touch was as delicious as Eve's apple had probably been.

She wanted more.

"You are a menace," Aeron mumbled.

"A *helpful* menace." Maybe, if she reminded him enough, he would begin to realize that he did, in fact, need her.

He didn't offer a response, but led her down a hallway, keeping her upright the entire time. Even better, he had to carry her down the flight of stairs. Something she would have enjoyed far more if she hadn't been so distracted. The walls were lined with portraits of the heavens—angels she recognized flying through the clouds—as well as hell. The latter she avoided studying, not wanting any reminders of her time there.

Also lining the walls were pictures of naked men, most lounging on beds of silk. Those she stared at, a fact that didn't embarrass her. Really. Even when she had to mop up her drool. All that skin...that brawn...that sinew... Too bad they weren't tattooed from head to toe.

"Anya's been doing some decorating. You should cover your eyes," Aeron said, his deep voice cutting into her ogling.

"Why?" Covering her eyes would be a crime. One that would surely insult her Deity, for wasn't it her duty to admire his creations?

"You're an angel, for gods' sake. You aren't supposed to look at such things."

"I'm fallen," she reminded him. Again. "And how do you know what I'm supposed to do?"

"Just...close your eyes." He dropped her legs, forcing her to stand, and ushered her around a corner.

A bevy of voices suddenly assaulted her ears, and she stiffened, stumbled, unprepared to deal with anyone but Aeron.

"Careful," he said.

She slowed her steps. People were unpredictable, and

his immortal friends more than most. Worse, her body was now susceptible to all forms of injury. They could torture her, physically, mentally and emotionally, and she wouldn't be able to fly away.

In the heavens, everyone loved everyone else. There was no hate, no cruelty. Here, kindness was often an afterthought. Humans often called each other terrible names, tore down each other's self-esteem and purposely broke one another's pride.

Olivia would have been happiest spending every minute of her humanity alone with Aeron.

You weighed the good versus the bad, remember? You thought the possibility of pleasure worth any price. You can deal. You have to.

"You okay?" he asked.

"Yes." She was determined.

They rounded another corner, entering the dining room, and Aeron stopped. Immediately, the voices tapered to quiet. Olivia did a quick scan and saw that four individuals sat at a table piled high with food. Four potential torturers.

Fear sparked inside her chest, and she had trouble catching her breath. Before she realized what she was doing, she had pulled from Aeron's clasp and inched behind him, hiding from view. To remain upright, she had to flatten her palms against his back.

"Finally. Fresh angel meat," a woman said with a husky laugh. "We were beginning to think Aeron planned to keep you hidden forever. Not that I would've allowed such a thing, you understand. I'd already dug out my trusty lock pick and had a rendezvous scheduled for midnight."

A nice-to-meet-you rendezvous or a how-does-the-tip-of-my-blade-feel rendezvous? Probably the latter. Olivia recognized the raspy voice as that of Kaia Sky-hawk, Bianka's twin and Gwen's big sister. She was a stealing, lying Harpy, and the spawn of Lucifer. She was also aiding the Lords in their quest to find Pandora's box, and would destroy anything she viewed as a threat. Like an angel.

Gwen, the youngest Skyhawk, lived here with Sabin, though the pair was currently in Rome, last Olivia had heard, along with several others, searching one of the Titans' newly risen temples for artifacts that had once belonged to Cronus.

Silly Cronus, whom the Lords assumed was all-powerful. If they only knew...

"I'd keep my mouth shut if I were you," the one called Paris warned the Harpy.

Olivia peeked around Aeron's shoulder.

"Why?" Kaia asked, unconcerned. "You think Aeron will attack me? You should know by now that I like to wrestle. In oil."

Paris's lips pursed at the unpleasant reminder of his own oil-wrestling experience. With Lysander. Something Olivia would have loved to watch. "No, I don't think you should be quiet because of Aeron. I think you should be quiet because you're prettier that way."

There was a feminine snort, and Olivia smiled in response. No longer drunk with pain and memories, she found, to her surprise, that her fear of the demons was fading. Maybe she really could do this.

"So, Olivia," Paris said. "How are you? Feeling better?"

Though she didn't move from behind Aeron, she replied, "Yes, thank you."

"Mmm. I'd love to give you something to be *really* thankful for." This speaker was William, she realized. He was handsome, wickedly so, with black hair and blue eyes. He was also an untamable rogue with an odd sense of humor Olivia didn't always understand.

"Someone needs to remove your *something* for the good of womankind." That pronouncement came from Cameo, the only female Lord. Well, the only one the Lords knew about. She was possessed by Misery, and all the world's sorrows rested in her voice.

Just then, Olivia wanted to give the woman a hug. No one here knew it, but Cameo always fell asleep crying. It was heartbreaking. Maybe…maybe they could become friends now, she thought, again surprised by her still-fading fear.

"Now that that's out of the way," Aeron said, once again taking Olivia's hand and dragging her with him as he marched forward. When he reached the table, he pulled out a chair for her.

She kept her eyes downcast as she shook her head. "No, thank you."

"Why?"

"I don't want to sit alone." Not after she'd experienced the bliss of having him as her mattress and then her cane.

Sighing, he plopped into the chair himself. Fighting a triumphant grin, Olivia perched herself on his lap. Well, she fell into his lap. No longer able to use him as a cane, she'd had no anchor to steady her. He stiffened, but didn't rebuke her.

She had no idea what everyone thought of her display because she kept her gaze downcast. For the moment, she was calm and she wanted to stay that way.

"Where's everyone else?" Aeron asked, picking up the conversation as if it had never tapered off.

"Lucien and Anya are in town, still looking for your Shadow Girl," Paris replied. "Torin's in his bedroom, of course, watching the world and keeping us safe. Danika—" Aeron flinched at the girl's name, and Olivia patted his hand in comfort. Clearly, he still felt guilty for almost killing her. "Danika is painting something, but she won't tell us what yet, and Ashlyn is looking over the scrolls Cronus gave us, trying to remember if she ever heard a conversation about any of the people listed."

The scrolls in question documented nearly everyone who had been possessed by one of the demons released from Pandora's box, Olivia knew. Angels had kept watch over them throughout the centuries, so she knew where a few lived. Would she be marked for death by her own kind if she told? Would that break an ancient law?

"Gods, Sex. We should rename you Boring. Let's get to the good stuff. Introductions are in order, yes?" William prompted. "It's only polite, really."

"Since when do you care about politeness?" Aeron barked.

"Since now."

Behind her, she heard her warrior's teeth grind. "This is Olivia. She's an angel," he said to no one in particular. His harsh tone didn't invite further conversation.

"Fallen angel," she corrected anyway. She spied a bowl of grapes and couldn't stop her squeal of delight. Three days of neglect caught up with her.

Sharing and moderation, creeds she had lived by all her life, abandoned her as she grabbed the bowl and pressed it into her chest. One by one (handful), she popped the delicious fruit into her mouth, savoring, moaning her satisfaction. But all too soon, the bowl was empty and she frowned—until she spied a plate of apple slices.

"Yummy." Olivia leaned forward. She would have tipped to the side, but Aeron's big hands settled on her hips, securing her in place and making her shiver. "Thank you."

"Welcome," he rasped.

Grinning, she swiped up the plate and settled back in his lap. He tensed as she did so, and poked her in the lower back, but she barely noticed. The slices, too, were consumed amid happy moans. Food tasted even better as a human. Sweeter. Necessary rather than an afterthought.

Finally full, she glanced up to offer someone the last remaining slice. Everyone was staring at her, and the food settled like lead inside her stomach. "I'm sorry," she said automatically. What had she done wrong?

"Why are you apologizing?" Kaia asked. There was nothing malicious in her tone, only genuine curiosity.

"Everyone is watching me, so I thought..." More than that, Aeron was tenser than before.

"I'm with the Harpy," William added, wiggling his eyebrows. "I love a woman who molests her breakfast."

She had *not* done that. Had she?

Kaia slapped the back of his head. "Shut it, playboy. No one cares about your opinions." To Olivia, she said, "In case you had trouble grasping my meaning, I'm staring at you because I'm curious about you."

Just as Olivia was curious about her, she realized. The Harpies could only eat what they stole, lied unabashedly and killed with abandon. In short, they were the antithesis of the angels, yet they enjoyed life to its fullest, which was why Lysander had chosen to be with one.

Soon, I will enjoy life to the fullest, as well.

"Do you know Lysander, my twin sister's man?" Kaia asked.

"Yes. Very well."

The Harpy propped her elbows on the table, rattling dishes. "Is he as ironfisted as I think?" Disgust layered her voice.

"Probably more so."

"I knew it! Poor B." Sympathy darkened her features, but she quickly brightened. "I know. You and I can put our heads together, because two gorgeous heads are always better than one, and plan ways to loosen him up a bit. We can even get to know each other better. The girls of the house have to stick together."

"Not possible. I'm taking Olivia into town." Aeron's hold, which had never fallen away, tightened further. "There'll be no planning. No loosening up. Definitely no getting to know each other."

Olivia's shoulders slumped. Had Aeron always been so harsh and she just hadn't noticed? Or was this attitude for her benefit? "Are you sure you want to get rid of me?" she asked him. "I'm good for you. I promise!"

"Because you can help me?" A question when it should have been a statement.

She wanted to shake him, the stubborn man. "Yes."

"Well, we've got enough helpers here, so, yes, I'm sure."

"I can also make you smile. That was my job, you

know." Her old job, anyway, and one she missed. "Would you like to smile?"

He offered no hesitation. "No."

"I would." William clapped. "I like to smile when I'm in bed and naked, so I say we keep her."

Aeron's nails dug past her robe and into skin, but she didn't protest. If she did, he would remove his hands, and she liked them where they were. "Like Kaia said, your opinion doesn't matter."

"Besides," Kaia added. "I doubt the big guy even knows how to smile."

"I do, too," Aeron snapped, causing everyone to laugh.

"Sure you do, Grumpy." Kaia tossed her bright red hair over her shoulder. "Listen, there's no need for you to take her into town. News flash—I'm taking myself up on my offer and getting to know her. I'm totally impressed by the fact that she got herself booted from the heavens, and I need all the juicy details."

"As will I." Cameo nodded to emphasize her determination. "Be getting to know her, that is."

"You can include me, too." William blew Olivia a kiss, and her cheeks heated with a blush. "No need to say anything. I already know what words are perched on your tongue. Stop me if I'm wrong, but my getting to know you will be your pleasure."

Aeron growled low in his throat. "She's not staying, and there will be no pleasure. As I said, I am taking her into town and leaving her there. Today."

"But why?" Olivia asked. She might have hated her duties as a warrior angel and might not have ever made a kill, but that didn't mean she was a complete pushover. "You said you didn't want any more helpers, but

I promise you, those you have can't help you with the next angel sent to kill you."

She expected someone to speak up and agree with her, but no one seemed to care that a heavenly assassin would be coming to snuff out their friend. Everyone at the table, including Aeron, probably assumed the Lord was invincible.

So of course, he remained stubborn. "I don't care."

She slapped the apple plate back where she'd found it, rattling the dishes far more than Kaia had. "I can also help you defeat the Hunters." Truth.

"Olivia," he said, and she didn't have to see him to know he was gazing up at the ceiling and praying for patience. Except, if she wasn't mistaken, the prayer she actually heard him mutter was for strength. "We are demons, and demons and angels do not mix. Besides, Legion can't return until you're gone."

The one argument she couldn't refute absolutely. "But...but...I'm willing to try to get along with her." If he heard her panic, he gave no indication. "And I'll be nice to all your other friends, too. How could I not? I gave up everything to save you."

"I know." The words were snarled.

"The least you can do is—"

"I didn't ask you to give up anything," he snapped. "So, no. There is no *least I can do.* You're healed. We're even. I owe you nothing."

Cameo ignored him, propped her elbows on the table and leaned forward, closer to Olivia. "Forget about him. He just hasn't had enough caffeine yet. Let's backtrack a bit. How can you help us with the Hunters?"

Finally. Interest, even if Cameo's tone was more morose than encouraging. Olivia raised her chin another notch. "For one thing, I know where other demon-possessed immortals are located." Thankfully, lightning didn't strike her at the confession, and angels didn't appear with fiery swords raised. "You said you were looking for them, I believe."

A moment passed in shocked silence, all eyes hitting—and staying on—her.

"Aeron," Cameo said.

"No. It doesn't matter," his hard voice proclaimed. "We have the scrolls for that."

"Yes, but they give names, not locations." The female Lord's stare became penetrating. "Sabin will want to talk with her when he returns."

"Too bad."

"If that dickwad Sabin wants to talk to her, that means Gwennie will want to, as well." Kaia drummed her nails against the tabletop. "And as you know, puppy, I ensure that my sister gets what she wants. Besides, I'm about to die of boredom since no one has attacked the fortress as promised."

"Harpy," Aeron snapped. "Don't try my patience. You will obey me in this and let the angel go."

"Warriors are so adorable when they think they're all tough and commanding." Kaia's arm shot out, again rattling dishes, and she snatched up a handful of eggs. A handful she then launched at Aeron.

Olivia quickly dodged, and the eggs slapped Aeron in the face. His lips curled in a grimace as he wiped away the yellow mess. Rather than touch her again, however, he flattened his palms on the arms of the chair.

Kaia giggled like a schoolgirl. "Don't act surprised by our insistence that she remain here. Paris told me what you said to Cronus the other night on that rooftop. 'Send me a woman who will deny me,'" she mocked.

"Oh, really? When did you and Paris have time for a heart-to-heart?" William asked as he buttered a blueberry muffin.

Kaia shrugged, her focus remaining on Aeron. "A couple nights ago, I was looking for a little fun, and he was looking a little weak." Another shrug. "He was feeling chatty afterward."

Paris merely nodded in confirmation. Every time Olivia had seen the keeper of Promiscuity, he'd appeared sad. Just then, he looked almost…happy, if a little tired. That must have been some chat.

"But I offered you a place in *my* bed," William whined to the Harpy.

Bed? Oh. *Oh.* Kaia and Paris had apparently accomplished more than talking during that heart-to-heart.

"You suck at 'Guitar Hero,' so I figure you're bad with your hands. Besides, someone else we all know and love has staked prior claim on you."

"Who?" Olivia asked before she could stop herself.

Kaia ignored her, continuing on. "Therefore, I picked Paris to keep me warm the other night. And I can't wait to give Bianka the down-and-dirty details."

"Oh, no. No, no, no. You can't kiss and tell," Paris sputtered.

The Harpy smiled lazily, evilly. "Just watch me. Anyhoodles. You want your little demon to return, Aeron-bo-barren, you'll have to go into town and play with her there. The angel stays."

The heat of Aeron's breath was like fire on the back of Olivia's neck. "This. Is. *My.* Home."

"Not anymore."

Kaia and William had spoken in unison. They shared a smile, though William still looked sulky over Kaia's choice of bedmates.

"Yeah," Olivia said, chin lifting yet another notch. "Not anymore." She wanted Aeron here with her, yes, but he apparently needed time away to reflect on how lucky he actually was to have her.

That wasn't egotistical of her, she told herself. Truth was never egotistical. Besides, it shouldn't take him more than a few hours to realize just how much he needed her and wanted to be with her. He was smart. For the most part.

Please, let him want to be with me.

Once more Aeron's hands settled on her waist. This time, he squeezed hard enough to make her gasp. "Do you know where Pandora's box is, Olivia?"

Of course he'd ask the one question she didn't have an answer for. "Well...uh...no."

"Do you know where the Cloak of Invisibility and the Paring Rod are being held?"

Okay. Two questions. "No," she admitted softly. What she did know was that the Lords had found two of Cronus's artifacts: the Cage of Compulsion and the All-Seeing Eye. What they lacked, as Aeron had mentioned, was the Cloak of Invisibility and the Paring Rod. As the One True Deity had no use for such relics, her kind had never searched for them.

Aeron lifted her to her feet and released her. Olivia had to grip the table to keep from toppling over. She also had to press her lips together to keep from moaning in disappointment. *Touch me.*

"Still want her here?" he asked the others, emotionless. "Her, rather than me?"

One by one, they nodded. Unrepentant.

"Fine." He ran his tongue over his teeth. "She's yours. Get what information you can from her. As suggested, I'll be in town. Someone text me when she's gone. Only then will I return."

CHAPTER SIX

THERE WAS A CONSPIRACY to drive him mad, Aeron thought darkly.

First, his friends had kicked him out. Second, his demon had screamed at him to stay. *To stay.* With Olivia. A being Wrath should despise. A being *Aeron* should despise. Instead, he understood his demon's dilemma.

She was enchanting.

This morning, when he'd woken up and realized she was fully healed, the desire he'd denied only a few days ago had sparked to life. Ever since, it had refused to fade. She'd fallen to the floor, robe bunched at her waist, and her panties—shit, her panties. Too white, too pure. Made a man want to rip them apart with his teeth and dirty the wearer up a bit. He'd wanted to tear her robe away, too, and devour her.

Somehow, some way, he'd managed to stop himself.

Maybe because he'd realized—and reminded himself, over and over again—that Lysander had been the voice he'd heard the day before. That Lysander had been the one to heal Olivia, the one who wanted her happy and whole.

"Unsoiled," he muttered.

And Lysander would be a terrible enemy to have.

The Lords could fight Hunters, yes. But Hunters *and* an angelic army? Hardly.

So Aeron had finally gotten himself under enough control to leave the bed without falling on top of Olivia in a desperate rush to touch and taste her. He'd finally convinced himself to get rid of her. He'd finally, blessedly forgotten there was a throbbing erection between his legs while she wiggled on his lap and made love to her food.

Only to have Wrath insist on "more."

"I liked you better when you were merely a presence. An urge," he told the demon now.

A snort was the only reply. At least there was no more of the demon's pleading. Wrath had only quieted a few minutes ago, when realizing what Aeron planned.

Aeron scrubbed his face so hard his calluses scratched his cheeks. He was in Gilly's apartment in town. A spacious three-bedroom on the wealthier side. Gilly was a young friend of Danika's who now lived in Budapest. Torin, their first line of defense at the fortress, had loaded her apartment with state-of-the-art security, just in case Hunters ever discovered her connection to the Lords. Even though she was fully human and as innocent as a person could be—a miracle in and of itself, given what Danika had told the Lords about Gilly's troubled childhood—those bastards wouldn't hesitate to hurt her.

She was currently at school—high school, that is—and undoubtedly happy for the distance between them. She still wasn't comfortable around him. Understandable. Though Gilly was only seventeen, she'd seen the dark side of man and had been on her own for years. They'd offered her a room at the fortress, but she'd desired a place of her own. Good thing, too. Now Aeron wouldn't have to roam aimlessly until dark; he could summon Legion at last.

He stood in the center of the living room, the couches and chairs pushed back to make space for the circle of salt and sugar he'd sprinkled just in front of him. He was going to summon her in a way she couldn't ignore.

He splayed his arms and said, "Legion, Quinientos Dieciséis of the Croisé Sombres of Neid and Notpe·hocil," just as Legion had taught him. It was her name, number, and title in a mix of different languages. Legion, Number Five Hundred and Sixteen of the Dark Crusaders of Envy and Need. If he didn't say it all, he could accidentally summon someone else. "I command you to appear before me. Now."

There was no flashing light as Cronus liked to employ when materializing, nor did time stop. One minute Aeron was alone, the next Legion was inside the circle. Simple, easy.

She collapsed to the floor, panting, sweat glistening on her scales.

"Legion." He bent down and scooped her up, careful not to let a single grain of salt or sugar touch her. It would burn, she'd told him.

Wrath purred, happy again.

Immediately Legion snuggled into his arms. "Aeron. My Aeron."

The action reminded him of Olivia. Sweet, beautiful Olivia, who was now with Kaia, a demented Harpy with a warped sense of humor, and Cameo, a ruthless killer with a tragic voice. He'd leave William and Paris, two unabashed sex addicts, out of the equation. Because if he didn't, he would destroy Gilly's apartment in a fit of rage. Rage, not jealousy, just to be clear. If they messed with the angel, they'd be inviting Lysander's wrath—and it was that prospect, not the thought of Olivia being attracted to one of his friends, that infuriated him. Of course.

Gilly's wall would look better with a few holes, he thought then. He'd be doing the girl a favor, helping her decorate.

Plus, as leery as Olivia was with others—anyone but himself, that was, not that he was proud about that— she might not be faring well. Even now she could be hiding, crying, praying for his return.

Surely Gilly's couch would be more comfortable if it were sawed in two.

Harden your heart, as you so unflinchingly told Paris you could do. Olivia's state of mind didn't matter. Her tears didn't matter. They couldn't. Actually, they would help. She would leave the fortress that much faster.

Legion was the most important thing to him. The child he'd secretly wanted but had never been able to have. Not just because he'd never committed to a woman, but because he knew how weak babies could be. Becoming a father, something he'd never had himself, hadn't been worth the agony of watching his own child wither and die.

With Legion, he didn't have to worry. She would live forever.

"What's wrong, precious girl?" he asked, carrying her to the couch and falling into its cushions. The scent of sulfur clung to her, and Wrath sighed, clearly homesick. Once his demon had hated that aroma. But now that the fiend knew the horrors of Pandora's box, hell seemed like Paradise.

"They chassse me." She rubbed her cheek against his pectoral, abrading skin, and purred. "Almost got me thisss time."

Her forked tongue always caught on and prolonged her *S*'s, something he found endearing. When he'd first met her, she'd even spoken like a baby, using the wrong tenses and pronouns. At her request, they'd been working on her grammar, and he was very proud of her progress.

"You're here now. You're safe." He rubbed the two little horns atop her head, knowing how sensitive they were and how much she liked it. "You don't have to go back."

"Angel dead?"

"Not exactly," he said, sidestepping the question for the moment.

They sat like that, silent, for several minutes, while she fought for control of her breathing. Finally, she calmed and the burning heat of her scales cooled. She sat up and that red gaze looked around.

"Thisss isssn't home," she said, confused.

Aeron scanned their surroundings, trying to see the place as she must. Furniture in a rainbow of colors: red, blue, green, purple and pink. A wood floor draped with a floral-print rug. Walls dripping with different-sized portraits of the heavens, gifts from Danika.

"We're in Gilly's apartment."

"Pretty," she said, the awe in her voice unmistakable.

Her sense of femininity had ceased surprising him. When he moved back to the fortress, he would give her a room of her own. A room she could decorate as she wished. He wasn't sure how much more pink he could stand in his own.

"I'm glad you like it. We might be here awhile."

"What?" Her awe was replaced by fury as she faced him. "You're living with Gilly now? Isss ssshe... Doesss ssshe love you?"

"No."

Slowly she relaxed. "Okay, then, but I wanna go home now. I misssss it."

Me, too. "We can't. The angel is there."

Legion stiffened, fury returning. "Why isss ssshe there and not usss?"

Excellent question. "She's going to help the others with the Hunters."

"No. *No. I* help with Huntersss."

"I know, I know." She might be little, but she was fierce. And killing was a game to her. But she'd endured so much strife in her life that Aeron desired only peace for her now. He didn't want to drag her into yet another battle. He wouldn't.

She meant too much to him.

"We can be alone here," he said.

"Fine." Again, she relaxed against him. "We'll stay, but I *will* help more than her."

Or Olivia would lose her head. Warning received. Time to distract his little darling. "Want to play a game?"

Jumping up, grinning, she wound herself around his neck, slithering like a snake. "Yesss, yesss, yesss."

Always ready to play, his Legion. Despite her improved speech, she hadn't lost her childlike needs. "Pick something. Whatever you want." He reached up to pet her, and his gaze fell to his arm. There was a single patch of bare skin on his wrist. He should have a snake tattooed there, to remind him of Legion. A tattoo to remind him of the good in his life, rather than the bad.

Yes, he liked that idea.

"I want to play...Clothes Optional."

Also known as Shred Everything Aeron Wore. "Maybe pick something else. What about Beauty Shop, like we played a week ago? You can paint my nails."

"Yeah!" Legion clapped, her excitement palpable. "I'll go get Gilly'ssss polisssh." Off she raced, disappearing around the corner.

"Gilly's room is the last one on the right," he called. He would spend an hour or two indulging her and then he would patrol the city for any sign of Hunters, as well as Shadow Girl. After what Legion had endured in hell, he owed her a little recreation, damn his duties.

Owed. The single word blasted through his head, and he cursed. He also owed Paris.

Even though he'd claimed he wouldn't return to the fortress until Olivia was gone, he had to take care of Paris. That wasn't a duty he would relinquish for any reason, yet he'd already allowed Lucien to see to Paris's needs for the last three days. He sighed, disappointed in himself. Just because Lucien had taken the warrior into town didn't mean Paris had picked anyone.

And while Paris might have slept with Kaia the other night, the strength he'd derived from it wouldn't last long. Despite his smiles, he'd looked fatigued at breakfast. As Aeron had learned, fatigue was the first sign of trouble.

Aeron was willing to bet the warrior hadn't been with anyone since Kaia. And that just wouldn't do.

Legion skipped back into the living room, holding

a plastic purple case and grinning widely. "Your nails will look like rainbowsss when I'm done."

Rainbow. He supposed that was better than the bright pink flares she'd made them last time. "I'm sorry, baby, but our game will have to wait. I need to go back to the fortress and take care of something, which means I need you to stay here."

The case fell to the floor with a crash. "No!"

"I won't be gone long."

"No! You ssssumoned me. You sssaid you'd play."

"But if Gilly returns before I do," he continued, as if she hadn't spoken, "please, please, please don't try and play with her. All right?" The human wouldn't survive. "I just have to grab something." Or rather, someone. "Be a good girl and wait for me."

Legion stalked to him. She flattened her hands on his chest, her claws slicing past his skin, drawing beads of blood. "I'll go, too."

"You can't, baby. Remember?" He reached up and scratched her behind the ears. "The angel is there. She's lost her wings and is now visible, but that doesn't make her any less dangerous to you. She—"

The little demon jumped up and perched in his lap, staring up at him. Already big eyes widened. "Ssshe doesssn't have wingsss no more?"

"No. She doesn't."

"Ssshe'sss fallen, then?"

"Yes."

Once again, Legion clapped happily. "I heard an angel had fallen, but I didn't know it wasss her. I could have helped them hurt her! But I can fix that. I can snatch my home from her now. I can kill her."

"No," he said, more fiercely than he'd intended.

Even Wrath reacted fiercely, growling inside his head, snapping at Legion for the first time.

Because his demon wanted to be the one to destroy the angel? No. Aeron shook his head. That made no sense, considering Wrath's earlier desire for "more." Perhaps the demon didn't want her destroyed by *anyone*. A suspicion that still made no sense, but was a better fit.

Why did the demon like her?

Later. Aeron cupped Legion's chin and forced her to keep her attention on him so that he would know she was not already daydreaming about the killing. "Focus on me, baby. Good. Now. You can't hurt the angel."

Legion blinked up at him. "I can! I'm ssstrong enough, I promissse."

"I know you can, but I don't want you to. She was supposed to hurt me but didn't." Instead, she'd given up everything for him.

Why? he wondered for the thousandth time. What kind of person did that? He'd scoffed at her earlier when she'd reminded him of her sacrifice, but truly, he was fascinated and confused. And humbled.

She didn't know him. Or maybe she did, since she'd followed him for weeks—but that made her decision all the more bizarre. More than that, he wasn't *worth* saving. Not to an angel, all that was good and right and perfect. And certainly not to a woman whom he would never allow himself to have.

"Ssso?" Legion persisted.

"So. In return, we're going to be nice to her."

"What? No! No, no, no." If she'd been standing, she would have been stomping her feet. "I can hurt her if I want."

"Legion," he said, using his most authoritative tone.

"This isn't a negotiation. You will leave her alone. Promise me."

Scowling, she sprang from his lap and paced the length of carpet in front of him. "You only want me to be nice to your friendsss. Ssso ssshe hasss to be your friend. But you can't be friendsss with a disssgusssting angel."

The words didn't seem to be directed at him, so he didn't reply. He let her continue to rant, hopefully getting it out of her system.

"Isss ssshe pretty? I bet ssshe'sss pretty."

Again, Aeron remained silent. Legion, he knew, was protective of him and liked to be the center of his world. As was not uncommon among children of single fathers, she didn't like him turning his attentions elsewhere.

"You like her," she accused.

Finally he spoke up. "No. I don't." But even he could detect the uncertainty in his voice. He'd liked holding Olivia in his arms the last few nights. Liked it way too much. He'd liked her sitting in his lap at breakfast. He'd liked having her wild-sky scent in his nose. He'd liked the softness of her skin and the purity of her eyes. He'd liked her gentleness and her determination.

He'd liked the way she'd looked at him, as if he were part savior, part temptation.

"You like her," Legion repeated, and this time there was so much fury in her words, they nearly scorched his skin.

"Legion," he said. "Even if I like another woman, that doesn't mean I'll love you any less. You are my baby, and that will never change."

Poison dripped from her too-sharp teeth—teeth she bared in a snarl. "I'm not a baby! And you *can't* like her. You jussst can't. I'll kill her. I'll kill her right now!" With that, Legion disappeared.

"WHAT DO YOU THINK?"

Olivia twirled clumsily in front of the full-length mirror, taking in the knee-high black boots, the so-short-it-barely-covered-her-bottom skirt and the cerulean-blue tank top she wore. The matching blue thong she had shimmied into even came up over the waist of the skirt. Talk about naughty. She'd never revealed this much skin before. Not even to herself. There'd never been a need.

She'd asked for this, however. "Make me beautiful," she'd said to Kaia the moment Aeron had stomped from the fortress.

"Oh, goodie! A slut-it-up makeover," the Harpy had responded.

The other two warriors, William and Paris, had groaned. Paris had even sung, *"Boor-ring,"* under his breath before leaving. William had tried to stick around to "help," but Kaia had threatened to use his balls as earrings.

After that the Harpy had eyed Olivia with amusement. "You want Aeron to realize his mistake, huh?"

"Yes, please." More than that, she'd wanted to shed her angelic image completely. Once and for all. She'd thought, by removing her robe, she could remove her fear and uncertainty, too. She'd thought, by donning the "slut-gear," she could also cloak herself in confidence and aggression.

And as she spun a second time for a look at her backside, she realized she'd been right. Well, she realized she was right after her dizziness faded. Thankfully she was getting used to her legs—kind of—and managed to remain upright.

"I love it," she said, grinning. She looked like a new person. She even looked human. But most of all, she looked radiant, and seeing that radiance was like swimming in a pool of power.

I'm strong. I'm beautiful.

What would Aeron think? In all the time she'd watched him, she'd never seen him pay any specific female attention—besides herself, the past few nights and this morning. So she wasn't sure what kind of woman attracted him.

And it was better that way, she supposed. She couldn't pretend to be something she wasn't. Otherwise she'd still be in the heavens. So he would have to like her for herself. Which was what she wanted most. If he couldn't do so, well, he wasn't worth her time anyway.

He'll like you. How could he not?

Confidence was nice.

"Those are make-a-man-beg clothes for sure," Kaia replied. The redhead had spent the last hour rifling through her closet to dress Olivia exactly right. "I stole them from a little place in town."

Wait. "These garments haven't been paid for?"

"That's right."

"Really?" Why did she suddenly feel sexier? Olivia wondered. Was she becoming as bad as the demons? Maybe she'd send the shop a little money. *You don't have any money.* Maybe she'd send the shop some of Aeron's money.

"Now sit," Kaia commanded, motioning to the chair in front of the vanity mirror with a tilt of her chin.

Cameo moaned. "You're not done yet?" She sat upon

the bed, waiting (im)patiently for the slut-it-up session to end. "I have so many questions."

Kaia shrugged. "Ask her while I do her makeup."

Olivia perched on the plush cushion as commanded and Kaia crouched in front of her. The Harpy had already palmed an eye-shadow brush and a case of azure powder. Never having worn makeup before, she wasn't sure how she felt about that much color, but she didn't complain. This was one of the reasons she was here, after all. To experience everything the world had to offer.

"Close your eyes," Kaia said. When she complied, the brush began to dance gently over her lids. "You're up, Cameo."

No other prompting was needed. "You said you know where some of the demon-possessed immortals are staying," Cameo said, getting down to business.

"Yes." Again, no lightning struck and no angelic army swooped in.

"Aeron met a girl the night he saved you. She was surrounded by screaming shadows, whatever that means. Do you know her?"

Olivia was nodding before she could stop herself.

"Be still," Kaia told her. "Now I have to fix your eye. It looks like I hit you. While *I* like that look, I don't think Aeron will."

"Sorry." She straightened her spine, keeping her chin immobile. "That was Scarlet, daughter of Rhea. Oh, and if you don't know, Rhea is the self-proclaimed mother to all the earth and embittered wife of Cronus."

"What?" Cameo gasped out. "Shadow Girl's a daughter of the gods? And not just any gods, but the king and queen of the Titans?"

"Well, one god. Cronus isn't her father. Rhea spent forbidden time with a Myrmidon warrior when she and Cronus first began warring with each other."

"Why were they warring?" Kaia asked. "I feel like I should know the answer, but I never kept up with heavenly politics."

Easy enough to explain. "Cronus planned to lock their children, the Greeks, in Tartarus because his old All-Seeing Eye had predicted they would usurp his power. Rhea merely wanted them banished to earth. But he locked them away, anyway."

Cameo muttered a quick "hmm" before saying, "So this Scarlet was conceived…when?"

Such a sad voice…Olivia's heart actually bled, hurting more intently with every word the female spoke. "Rhea had her affair as she deliberated ways to help the Greeks escape Tartarus and overthrow Cronus. Her lover even helped her enact that plan, and died for his efforts. However, the Greeks were ultimately freed. Rhea expected to continue ruling, but Zeus feared she would later aid Cronus and locked her away right alongside his father. Scarlet was born and raised inside the prison."

As she'd spoken, brush, sponge and stick had been used on her face, one after the other. Nervousness bloomed, burning her stomach. She prayed she wouldn't resemble a clown when Kaia finished.

"So this Scarlet is possessed by…Shadows?" Cameo asked. "Darkness? If so, I'm not sure how either one can be considered evil. They seem like gifts rather than curses. To always be able to hide…to strike your enemy without being seen…"

"You're thinking in terms of absolutes," Olivia explained. "Your demon, Misery, isn't necessarily a curse, either, for without pain there couldn't be pleasure. Think about it. Everyone must experience the dark emotions on some level to appreciate what they have. Your demon is simply the extreme of the emotion. As is the case with the other Lords. And with Scarlet. But the demon she carries is neither darkness nor shadows. What she has inside her is Nightmares."

"Okay, wow," Kaia said. "And I thought the guys here were lucky. That has to be, like, the coolest demon ever."

Nightmares? Cool? Hardly. "The darkness Scarlet summons is a complete absence of light. It's an abyss within her, a never-ending pit of gloom. And inside that gloom lie the very things humans fear most."

There was a rustle of clothing and she pictured Cameo shifting on the bed, leaning closer to her. "How do you know so much about this?"

"I've encountered many demons over the centuries. As a former bringer of joy, I saw how and why demonic influence ruined human lives."

"Ohhh, cool. So what did you do with those demons?" Kaia asked. "Start with how you kicked ass and end with mopping up the blood."

Adorable Harpy, to view her as so strong. "I didn't fight them myself. If my presence alone failed to send them fleeing, I would have to summon a warrior angel to dispatch them."

"Let's backtrack a minute," Cameo said. "That kind of experience wouldn't tell you where Scarlet was and what she could do."

Busted. Olivia's cheeks heated. "I've been watching Aeron for a while and knew he wished to meet the others of his kind. I made sure to study those nearby—the closest of whom just happened to be Scarlet. There are a few others also scattered about, but most are hiding around the world."

"Interesting. Are they—"

"Nope. My turn to ask a question," Kaia interjected. "So is this Scarlet a good guy or a bad guy?"

Olivia pondered her answer. "I suppose that depends on your definition of *good* and *bad*. She was raised in a prison, surrounded by criminals. That's all she knew before being paired with her demon and later cast to Earth. Everything she's done, she's done to survive."

"As have we," Cameo muttered.

Which wasn't true for Olivia. Everything she'd recently done, she'd done to suit her own needs. She should feel guilty about that, she thought, but... she didn't. In discovering the path to her happiness, she just might discover Aeron's, as well.

No "just might" about it, her newfound confidence piped up.

Finally Kaia finished applying the makeup, the brush strokes ceasing. The Harpy clapped her hands and whistled. "All done, and damn, I'm good."

Slowly, Olivia cracked open her eyelids. The moment she found the mirror, she gasped. And she'd thought herself radiant before... The blue shadow complemented the color of her eyes, making them appear electric. The black mascara added so much length to her lashes, they nearly reached her brows, offering the perfect frame. The rosy blush on her cheeks gave her a just-roused-from-bed glow, and the bloodred lipstick gave her lips a kiss-me glaze.

"No need to offer your firstborn in thanks," Kaia said. "I only accept cash. Now, if you'd like, we can go into town, find Anya, 'cause I think she's still there, grab a beer and a man and continue your miseducation."

Still entranced, Olivia reached up and grazed a fingertip over the half ring of black under her eyes. They were smoky, sultry. Perfect.

Try to resist me now, Aeron, she thought. *I dare you.*

Confidence was more than nice. Confidence was soul-changing.

"You can't leave," Cameo protested. "I'm not done with my questions."

Kaia rolled her eyes. "So ask them in town while we're drinking ourselves into a stupor. I'm thirsty, and Anya will decapitate us if we fail to include her."

"You have an answer for everything," the female Lord grumbled.

"I know, right? Isn't it wonderful?"

"Hardly."

As the two bantered back and forth, Olivia next traced her lips. Soon she would know the feel of Aeron's. Again, no "might" about it. He wouldn't be able to resist her. She could barely resist herself. Would his lips be hard or soft? Would they plunder or be gentle? Didn't matter, really. She would finally taste him, and that's what she craved most.

"Isss thisss her? Isss thisss the one? Well, guesss what? You will die, angel," a new voice suddenly proclaimed, and there was enough hate in that voice to slay an army.

Olivia jolted up and spun, barely managing to remain upright. A tiny demon stood across the bedroom, its eyes bright red with malice. Its claws were elongated and ready for attack, its teeth sharp and bared. Even its green scales seemed sharpened, standing on end like pieces of broken glass—ready to cut.

This time, she hadn't fallen into hell. Hell had come to her.

No! A scream formed in her throat, but just before it could unfurl, it lodged in the knot growing there, so all that emerged was a choking sound.

Calm, steady. She'd caught a glimpse of this creature a few times while following Aeron and knew who it was. Legion. *You don't have to be afraid.*

Squaring her shoulders, she tried to unfold her wings for balance—only to be reminded that she no longer had them. She gulped. "Hello, Legion. My name is Olivia. I—I mean you no harm."

"Sssorry, but I can't sssay the sssame."

"Now, now." Cameo jumped in front of Olivia, acting as a shield. "There'll be none of that. We're all friends here."

"I'll kill you, too, if you get in my way," Legion snarled. "Move! That angel isss *mine.*"

Kaia pressed into Cameo's side, the two more than a shield. They were a wall. "Well, I guess you'll have to kill me, too, then."

They were...protecting her? Guarding her? Despite her fear, Olivia's chest swelled with pleasure. They didn't know her, yet they were treating her as one of their own. As if she already belonged.

"So?" Kaia demanded. "What's it gonna be, demon girl?"

"I accept your offer. I'll kill you, too." Then Legion...disappeared.

O-kay. After her words, that disappearance was a relief. But why would—

She reappeared between the two warrior women. Before either had time to deflect or prepare, she'd bitten them both on the neck. Both women collapsed on the ground, writhing and moaning in pain.

Olivia barely had time to process what she'd witnessed. "How could you do such a thing! I thought they were your friends. They hadn't hurt you, only wanted to save me."

Those red eyes locked on her, the hate intensifying. "Aeron isss mine. You don't get to have him."

"Well, I'm afraid I can't agree with you." Though Olivia trembled—she was alone, weaponless, defenseless and unstable—she stood her ground. "Aeron will be mine." One way or another. She wouldn't lie about that, even to save herself.

A forked tongue swiped over those pointed teeth. "You gonna pay for that, angel. With your life."

Legion leapt at her.

CHAPTER SEVEN

SEVEN DAYS. SEVEN damn days, and not a single result. Strider, keeper of Defeat, wiped his sweaty face with a towel. He propped himself against the boulder at his back and surveyed his surroundings. The sun was shining brightly, hotter here than it had ever been in Buda. Pristine water gently washed toward this island near Rome, the soft hum of it a balm for his ears.

All that remained of the Temple of the Unspoken Ones were battered pillars identical to the one at his back—some fallen, some standing—and an altar still stained and splattered with crimson. There was a vibration of energy in the air. Energy that caused his hair to stand on end. And yet, despite the altar and the energy, Strider felt an odd sort of kinship with the place. After all, a lot of people considered him an unspoken one. Evil and unnecessary.

Not that he agreed. He was paired with Defeat and couldn't lose a single challenge without suffering for it. Where was the evil in that? Wasn't like he killed indiscriminately just to win an Xbox game or anything.

Anyway. Last time he'd been here, archaeologists had been studying every nook and cranny. Hunters had been among their numbers, hoping to find one of Cronus's powerful artifacts or even Pandora's box itself. They weren't here anymore. Why?

Though the temple had risen from the sea only a few months ago, trees had already grown, tall and lush and green. They circled the area where the temple had once stood proud, but they didn't quite touch that temple. They actually arched *away* from it, as if afraid of getting too close.

What was here that hadn't been the last time he'd visited was bones. Human bones. The archaeologists', most likely. What had killed them, he could only guess. There was no trace of flesh or blood. Yeah, an animal could have devoured so many people in the handful of months since he'd last been here, but wouldn't there have been some trace of the feasting? Well, besides the bones. A bloodstain here, a piece of rotten meat there. Claw marks where the humans had fought for freedom. Footprints where they had tried to run away.

There weren't.

So. What could consume so cleanly? A godly creature, that's what.

Anya, (minor) goddess of Anarchy and Lucien's girl-friend-slash-soon-to-be-wife—horror of horrors, the naughty little vixen had decided to plan a wedding for herself—didn't know much about these Unspoken Ones, so wouldn't verify his idea that they had turned the humans into meals-on-heels. The gods had never, well, spoken of them, she'd said, so she wasn't sure what they could do. The gods *had* feared them, however.

Still, Strider wasn't leaving. He had to find those artifacts. He had to find Pandora's box. He had to destroy the Hunters. Finally. His life depended on it. Hell, his peace of mind depended on it. Every day Defeat spoke a little louder inside his head, so every day he was reminded more and more of the first days of his possession. Days he wanted to forget.

His demon had been a roar, a constant scream, the consuming need to challenge everyone he encountered driving him. No matter the consequences. Kill a friend? So be it. As long as he won.

He'd hated himself back then. His friends had probably hated him, too. Well, not true. They'd been as wild from their demons as he'd been from his. It had taken centuries to learn how to control themselves. But while they now had control of their darker halves, he was edging closer to its loss.

"Looks like someone decided to take his break before the rest of us," a raspy voice teased from behind him.

Strider turned. Gwen, a redheaded beauty who was stronger and more vicious than any of the Lords, approached him, a glistening bottle of water in her hand. She tossed it at him, and he easily caught it. Within seconds, he had the entire thing drained. Gods, the cold felt good as the liquid moistened his dry throat.

"Thanks."

"You're welcome." Slowly she grinned, and he knew exactly why Sabin had fallen in love with her. Naughty women ruled. "I stole it from Sabin."

"I heard that, wife," Sabin said, striding around the boulder across from them. He increased his speed until he reached Gwen's side, then draped an arm around her shoulders.

Immediately she reached up and twined her fingers with his. She even leaned her head against his side, trusting the man to hold her up and keep her safe. They might enjoy one-upping each other, but they were unified. That much was clear.

Their pairing had initially shocked Strider, truth be told. After all, Gwen was Galen's daughter and Galen was leader of their greatest enemy. More than that, Sabin was the keeper of Doubt and Gwen had been a timid little mouse the first time the two had met. The demon had practically eaten her alive.

Now, there wasn't a more confident woman alive. How the two had reached this point and made things work, Strider wasn't sure. He was just glad he wasn't the one in a committed relationship. He liked women—even the un-naughty ones. Oh, did he like women. But relationships? Not so much.

He'd had a few girlfriends over the years, and at first, he'd loved it. Loved the commitment, the exclusivity. When they'd discovered his penchant for winning, however, most of them had tried to work it to their advantage.

"Bet you can't make me fall in love with you."

"I doubt you can convince me that we're meant to be together forever."

He'd played that game too many times before, winning hearts he'd no longer had any interest in winning. Now, he enjoyed them once—maybe twice—fine, maybe three times—and then it was goodbye old, hello new.

"What's this about breaking early?" Sabin ushered Gwen to the altar and leaned his hip against the stone. He guided her in front of him, again wrapped her in his arms and held her tight against his chest, her head resting under his chin.

Strider shrugged. "I was thinking." Rather than examining the stones for symbols or messages as he'd been ordered.

Sabin had been Strider's leader his entire life. Yeah, Lucien had been commander of the elite army while they'd lived in the heavens, but it had been Sabin that Strider had looked to for advice and guidance. Still did. The man would have beheaded his own mother if it meant winning a battle. Not that any of them had a mother. They'd been born fully formed. But Strider valued that kind of commitment.

"Did I hear someone say it was break time?" Kane, keeper of Disaster, asked with a grin of his own as he rounded a corner. His hair, which was a mix of brown, black and gold, as well as his eyes, which were a mix of brown and green, gleamed in the amber sunlight.

Had he always been that colorful? Strider wondered. They'd been together forever, but Strider didn't think he'd ever seen the man so…happy. Almost glowing. Maybe the temple agreed with him.

A gust of wind suddenly rose among the trees. A branch snapped off and flew toward the men. Of course, it smacked Kane in the back of the head. Used to such catastrophes, his stride didn't even slow. Maybe the temple *didn't* agree with him.

Strider chuckled. That wouldn't be the last of Kane's woes, he was sure. Rocks tended to fall and ground tended to crack whenever the warrior arrived at the scene.

Behind him, gravel crunched under boots and Strider turned again. Amun, Reyes and Maddox, the last of their group, were closing the distance.

"Break?" Amun said, his deep voice almost raw from disuse. He was dark from head to toe and as the keeper of Secrets, he rarely spoke, too afraid he would reveal devastating truths the warriors wouldn't be able to recover from. But as he'd recently spilled many of those secrets, anyway, to calm Gideon from a rage, he'd been a bit more talkative.

The change did Strider's heart good.

"Guess so," he replied.

Sabin rolled his eyes. "Look what you've started."

"What's wrong with a break? I'm tired. And gods know we're not making any progress." Maddox was, perhaps, their most dangerous member. Or rather, had been. Before he'd met his Ashlyn. Now, there was a gentleness to his violet eyes that none of the other Lords possessed.

Too bad that gentleness only extended to the delicate Ashlyn. Maddox was paired with the demon of Violence and when that boy erupted… Ouch. Strider had been on the receiving end of the man's need to hurt and maim a time or two. And yes, Strider had won, even then, dishing more punches and slices than he'd received. He just couldn't help himself.

"We've searched the grounds, x-rayed the stones hoping to find something inside them, and spilled our own blood hoping to draw the Unspoken Ones out with a sacrifice." Reyes, as dark as Amun but far more tense, splayed his arms, still cut and bleeding from his latest offering. Or from self-torture. One never knew with Reyes. "What's left for us to do?"

Everyone looked to Sabin.

"They were the ones who told us Danika was the All-Seeing Eye. I don't understand why they won't help us out again," the warrior said, his own frustration clear.

The All-Seeing Eye could see into heaven and hell. She knew what the gods were planning, what the demons were planning, as well as the outcome of all those plans—but not necessarily at the right time. Details came to her in spurts, out of sequence.

Sabin spun in a circle, calling, "All we want to know is where the other two artifacts are. Is that too much to ask?"

"Just help us, damn it," Kane shouted, getting into the spirit.

"Otherwise, I'll rip each stone from this island and toss them into the sea," Maddox added.

"And I'll help him," Strider vowed. "Only I'll piss on them first."

As his voice echoed from the rocks, the air seemed to thicken with challenge. The insects in the trees even quieted.

"Whoa—maybe you shouldn't have threatened to violate their property," Reyes muttered.

Oopsie.

Next, the world around them faded, leaving only the pillars and the altar. Only, every one of the pillars was suddenly upright and the altar was now gleaming white marble scrubbed clean of debris.

Unsure what was happening, each of the warriors stiffened, straightened and grabbed for a weapon.

Strider was proficient with both guns and knives, but usually preferred to slice and dice. Today, however, he'd make use of his Sig Sauer. He kept the muzzle down, but that didn't mean it was any less dangerous. He could aim and fire in less time than it took to blink.

"What's happening?" Gwen whispered.

"Don't know, but be ready for anything," Sabin warned.

Any other warrior would have shoved the woman behind his back to protect her. Not so with Sabin. Men and women had always been equals to him, and even though he loved Gwen more than life itself and wanted her protected more than he wanted victory, everyone here knew that Gwen was the strongest among them. She'd saved more than one Lord already.

Strider, though, did inch to the front—of her, of everyone. That sense of challenge... He had to be the one to win this thing.

His demon was already chanting. *Win...win...must win...can't lose.*

I know, he growled. *I will.*

He pivoted, gaze roving, searching. Finally, he spotted his prey. A huge man—no, that thing couldn't be called a man. A huge beast had materialized between two of the pillars.

Even as Strider's stomach tightened, he took his quarry's measure. The beast wasn't dressed, but then, he didn't need clothing. His skin was furred like that of a horse. Snakes danced and hissed from his head, their thin bodies acting as his hair. Two long fangs protruded over his bottom lip. He had human hands, but his feet were hooves.

Muscle was stacked upon muscle on his torso, and his nipples were pierced by two large silver rings. Metal chains circled his neck, wrists and ankles, and those chains kept him tethered to the pillars.

"Who are you?" Strider demanded. No need to ask *what* the thing was. Ugly as shit covered it.

He hadn't expected an answer, but damn if the ensuing silence didn't irritate him.

Then, beside the beast, between two other pillars, another monster appeared, and Strider blinked at the sudden addition. This one was male, as well, but only the lower half of his body was covered by carmine fur. His chest was a mass of scars. He, too, was anchored in place by chains.

Still. Those chains didn't detract from the menace radiating from either of them.

"My gods. Look," Kane breathed, pointing.

A third beast appeared, and this one was female. Like the men, her torso was bare. Her breasts were large, her nipples also pierced, though with diamonds rather than silver hoops. A leather skirt wrapped around her waist and thighs. She stood in profile, and Strider could see the small horns protruding from her spine. The horns he actually liked—they'd give a man something to hold on to when things got rough. Her face, however, was beaked like a bird's. So bed her? No. She, too, was furred and chained.

In quick succession, a fourth and fifth appeared, both so tall and wide they were like living mountains. They didn't have snakes for hair, though. What they had was worse. One was bald, yet shadows seemed to be seeping from his skull. Thick and black and putrid. The other had blades. Small but sharp, they spiked from his scalp, each glistening with something clear and wet.

The Unspoken Ones.

Without a doubt. Strider let out a breath. They should have remained the Unseen Ones, as well. 'Cause damn. *Win.*

No challenge has been issued yet, moron. Thank the gods, he added, just for himself. Would he be able to defeat these things?

The female stepped forward, her chains rattling. The Lords held their ground, and this seemed to please her. She grinned, her too-white teeth sharp as razors.

Thankfully, she couldn't get far, couldn't reach them, bound to the pillars as she was.

"Once more, you have darkened our doorstep." Her voice rang with the cries of a thousand souls trapped in hell, desperately trying to escape. They screamed from her, echoing through the temple, their tears practically soaking him. "And once more, we grant you the honor of our presence. But do not think, even for a moment, that your threats moved us. Desecrate our temple, will you? Go ahead. However, I suggest you say goodbye to your cock before you do so."

Win!

Not a challenge, not a challenge, not a fucking challenge. Please don't let that be a challenge. He had a feeling the woman meant what she'd said. If he whipped out Stridy Monster to relieve himself, he'd lose Stridy Monster. And there was no greater tragedy than that. Ask anyone who'd been with him.

"Uh, our apologies," Sabin said in an effort to smooth things over.

"Accepted," she replied easily.

That ease seemed out of place. Wrong.

Damn. Where was Gideon when you needed him? As the keeper of Lies, that boy knew when someone spoke true—or not. Strider had been apprehensive since the beasts had appeared, but now he wondered, what was their angle? The question churned his apprehension into straight-up fear.

"Now, the reason for our appearance," she continued. "Your determination to defeat your enemy is admirable, and we have chosen to reward you for it."

A reward? From these creatures? His formerly tight

stomach now did a little dance: twist, twist, knot, twist, twist, knot. Wrong, he thought again.

"So you'll help us?" Reyes asked. Gullible fool. "Help us defeat the Hunters at long last?"

A laugh. "As you said yourself, we have already helped you. And we did so without seeking anything in return." Her gaze, so much like a black hole he already felt as if he were falling, shifted, landed on him and pinned him in place. "Did we not?"

Just like that, understanding dawned. Anytime you wanted to hook someone on your drug, you gave them the first taste for free. Their aid had been the drug, and the Lords were now the addicts.

They would have to pay for any further assistance, Strider realized. And pay dearly. Ding, ding, ding. Finally, *right*.

"Perhaps we can help each other," Kane suggested, the ground cracking under his feet. He hopped to the side to avoid falling into a black hole of his own.

Her chin lifted in haughty disdain. "We need nothing from you."

"We'll see," Sabin said, tone unconcerned. But Strider could see the wheels turning in the back of his friend's mind. "Do you know where the Cloak of Invisibility is? And the Paring Rod?"

"Yes." She offered them another grin, this one loaded like a gun and ready to fire. "We do."

Yep, I'm hooked.

Win! Defeat repeated.

Strider licked his lips in anticipation, bones already humming at the thought of victory against the Hunters. Finally, the Super Bowl of wins, here for the taking. Once they had those artifacts, they could find and destroy Pandora's box. That wouldn't destroy the Hunters, of course, but it *would* ruin their plans to use the box to draw the demons out of the Lords, killing the warriors.

Man couldn't live without demon, not anymore. They were two halves of a whole, bonded forever. Defeat was as much a part of him as Stridy Monster.

The demons were equally bound, though they wouldn't die if man and spirit were parted. However, they would be crazed, forever hungry to feed their depraved needs but unable to quench themselves.

After the Hunters had killed Baden, the demon of Distrust had sprung from his body, tortured, screaming, destroying everyone it encountered. Strider had watched, helpless.

Worse, that demon was still out there, still causing havoc.

That was the reason the Hunters no longer sought to kill him and his friends. They didn't want the demons free and unable to be captured. But with the box, they could do both.

Yet thanks to Danika, they now knew the Hunters had a new plan of action. Somehow, they *had* found the demon of Distrust. They had managed to capture it and were trying to force it to possess another body. If they succeeded... Strider shuddered. They wouldn't have to wait for the box. They could kill the Lords, place their demons inside bodies of their choosing and do whatever they wished.

They claimed they wanted a world without evil, but would they say the same thing if they were in control of all that evil? Hell, no. Power wasn't easy to give up. As he well knew. No way he'd be able to give up his. He liked winning—and not just because of his demon.

"So what do you want from us?" Sabin asked, cautious now. "In exchange for those artifacts?"

Strider almost grinned. Sabin didn't like miscommunication. He wanted the facts laid out so everyone knew what they were getting into.

The Unspoken One laughed, and it was a far crueler sound than before. Maybe because this time, she mocked with that laughter. "Think you it is that simple? That you give us a token and in return we give you that which you desire most? How wrong you are, demon. You are not the only ones who seek what we have to offer. Behold."

Above the altar, the air thickened, coagulated, and colors sparked to life before bleeding together and forming what seemed to be a movie of some kind. Strider strained to decipher the images—then tensed as Galen came into view. His blond hair, his handsome features, his white feathered wings. As usual, he wore a white robe, as if he truly were an angel rather than a demon-possessed warrior like the rest of them.

Beside him was a tall, slender female. She was pretty in a sturdy sort of way, with sharp features, dark hair and pale skin. He'd seen her before, he thought, flipping through mental files of ancient Greece, ancient Rome and everywhere else he'd been throughout his very long life, but coming up blank. He pored through more recent times, but again—oh, shit, there. Danika, he realized. Danika had painted her. An enemy.

Shit, he thought again. Danika had painted this woman in a scene set twentysomething years in the past, yet nothing about her had changed. There wasn't an age line on her.

She wasn't human, then.

Today she was dressed in black leather and strapped to a table, but she wasn't struggling against her bonds. There was determination in her expression, her gaze following— No. Surely not. That couldn't be... It wasn't possible... But as Strider watched, he saw a ghostlike creature bouncing from one corner of the room to another. Its eyes were red, its face skeletal, its teeth long and sharp.

No question; it was a demon. A High Lord, like the very being that possessed Strider.

Strider stopped breathing, every muscle in his body clenching his bones.

"Baden," Amun rasped in that unused voice of his, so much longing in his tone that it actually hurt to hear. There'd been something about Baden, something they'd all gravitated to. Something they'd all needed. They'd loved Baden more than they'd loved themselves. More than they loved each other.

Still did, despite his death.

"No damn way." Kane shook his head almost violently.

Strider agreed. No damn way. That demon did *not* carry the essence of their friend. Couldn't possibly. But there *was* something familiar about that ghostly being... something gut-wrenching.

"Enter her," Galen commanded. "Enter her and your torment will end. You'll finally have a host. You'll finally be able to feel, to smell, to taste. Don't you remember how wonderful that is? Finally you'll be able to destroy, to shred human trust as you were meant to do."

Shred human trust. As Distrust was meant to do. No, he thought again.

The spirit groaned, and its speed increased. Clearly,

it was agitated. Did it know what was happening? Did it want another host? Or was it simply too crazed to understand?

"Please," the woman begged. "I need you. I need you so badly."

So. She was willing. That didn't mean she knew what would happen to her if she got her wish. For the first century—at least—there would be no remnants of the person she was. She would be fully demon and many, many humans would suffer because of that.

"Do it," Galen continued. "It's what you want. What you need. All you have to do is touch her and relief is yours. What could be easier?"

Could the demon understand? he wondered again. As keeper of Hope, Galen could make anyone or thing crave a future they never would have wanted without his influence. Even a demon. That's how he'd formed his Hunters, by convincing them the world would be a better place without the Lords. A utopia of peace and prosperity.

As Galen crooned persuasively, even Strider was affected. *He* wanted to touch the female. There would be relief…his future would be assured…better…

The demon darted toward the woman, changed its mind, then darted in the other direction. Oh, yes. It understood.

Don't do it, Strider projected. He wanted his friend back, yes. More than anything in the world. And in some ways, the demon of Distrust was his friend. Essence of Baden or not. But he didn't want his friend to be housed in the body of his enemy.

"Do it!" Galen snarled. "Do it! Now."

On and on the spirit circled the room's ceiling.

Impatient, Galen threw up his hands. "Fine. Forget it. You can spend the rest of eternity the way you've spent the last few thousand years. Miserable. Hungry. Unfulfilled. We're leaving." He reached out to release the woman's bonds.

There was another groan, then a growl, and then the spirit was again darting from one corner to another, gaining speed, nothing but a blur. It fell...fell...and finally slammed into the female's stomach.

Had she not been tied down, she would have hurt herself, so intense was her sudden thrashing. Thrashing that increased with every second that passed. She grunted and groaned, her muscles spasming, her features contorting. Then the screams began.

No. Godsdamn it, no. Strider nearly fell to his knees.

Galen smiled an evil smile of satisfaction. "It's done. At last. Now all we have to do is wait and see if she survives."

The door to the room swung open and a group of his followers marched inside. Such perfect timing. They must have been watching nearby on monitors.

"Do we return to the temple, Great One?" the one in front asked.

Galen's answer was lost as the vision wavered, then disappeared altogether.

Time suddenly seemed suspended, caught in threads of horror and shock.

Sabin was the first to shake himself loose. "What the hell just happened?"

What happened? Hell's gates had just opened, the repercussions he'd already contemplated suddenly *real*. If the woman survived, Hunters would now be out for blood, as Strider had feared. They would no longer con-

142 THE DARKEST PASSION

would crave death. And if their demons were freed,
those demons would be caught, paired with someone
new, and Galen could build an army of demonic immortals all under his command.

"Bring the images back," Maddox commanded.
"Show us what followed the possession."

"Such a tone will earn you nothing but discontent,
Violence, for your enemy wants what you want. The
Paring Rod." The Unspoken One splayed her arms, her
nails so long they curled back into her fingers. "*We* will
choose whom to bestow such a blessing upon."

Maddox popped his jaw before bowing his head.
"My apologies."

"What do you want from us? Name it, and it's yours."
Strider didn't care what they desired. He would give it
to them.

She smiled, as if she'd expected nothing less. "If you
wish to acquire the Rod, you will bring us the head of
your king."

There was another beat of horrified silence.

"Wait. You want...Cronus's head?" Gwen swept her
gaze over the Lords. "The *god* king?"

"Yes." No hesitation.

Could Strider give that to them? The god king had
helped him win several battles. The god king was on
his side and would do anything to destroy Galen and the
Hunters. So...kill him? Kill the most powerful immortal
ever to live? And if he failed, make an enemy of him?

"Just how are we supposed to do that?" Kane demanded.

"I told you it wouldn't be simple. But though he is a
god, and destroying him will prove the most difficult

task of your existence, he is very much like you," the Unspoken One replied. "More so than you have realized. Use the knowledge to your advantage."

Kane shook his head, and a lock of hair slapped his eye. "But he's on our team."

"Is he?" Another cruel laugh. "Do you not think he will slay you the moment he no longer has need of you? Besides, if you do not bring us his head, your enemy will. And they will receive our prize."

Strider's eyes widened, another answer finally sliding into place. *This* was why Galen would try for Cronus's head. This was why Danika had predicted what she had.

They couldn't allow Galen to curry favor with these beings. The consequences could be too great—far greater than pissing off Cronus. Shit. Damn it! Fuck. No curse word seemed strong enough.

"Why do you want him dead?" Strider asked. As Sabin always said, knowledge was power. Perhaps in the answer, they could find redemption.

The creature's teeth gnashed together. "He has made us slaves and we will not tolerate such a fate. Surely *you* understand."

Understand, yes. For too long, he'd been a slave to his demon. But there was no redemption in her answer. These beings were determined. They would not be swayed.

What would happen if they were freed? Roaming unfettered? Nothing good, that much he could guess.

"You need time to think," she continued. "Time we will grant you. And to prove our magnanimous intentions, we will even give you another gift. Enjoy. I know we will."

Her eerie, smiling face was the last thing Strider saw before he and the others found themselves transported to another location, a jungle—Hunters suddenly surrounding them.

CHAPTER EIGHT

OLIVIA AND LEGION circled each other. When the little demon had lunged, Olivia had jumped out of the way, and Legion had slammed into the wall. Now, Olivia studied her foe. She'd seen this type of being—a minion, also known as a demon servant—defeated before. All angels had, even those whose sole purpose was to bring peace and joy to the world. But of course, she'd never fought one herself.

Destroying them had never seemed like much of a battle for the warrior angels, though. Not really. They had merely stretched out their arms, their swords of fire appearing. Once those flames—which hadn't been created in hell, but had instead sprung from her Deity's mouth, his breath far hotter than the blazes all demons so loved—made contact with scales, the demons disintegrated. This, well, this would not be anything like that.

Kaia and Cameo were still on the ground, still writhing, their skin now a light shade of green. As an angel, Olivia would have been able to soothe them, taking their pain into herself and dispatching it. But trapped as she was in this feeble body, she could do nothing.

Nothing but watch. And fight.

If she hoped to survive, she needed that which she'd never experienced or embraced before: fury. That was what strengthened humans, after all. Wasn't it? They seemed to expand, destroy, *defeat* when they hosted the emotion.

So...what made her angry? Her time in hell, definitely.

Though she would rather have plucked out her eyes, Olivia allowed the memory of her time in hell to play through her mind. The flames...the stink...those oozing, roving hands... Sickness churned in her stomach, fear and disgust blending with that first spark of fury. After that, instinct took over and her shock at Kaia's and Cameo's mistreatment joined the fray, numbing the fear. Only, thankfully, the fear.

"You die thisss day, angel."

Her hands curled into fists. *I'm strong.* "You can never be with Aeron the way you desire, demon," she said, knowing the truth in her voice had to be distasteful to a creature raised among liars. "I tell you this not to be cruel, but to—"

"Ssshut up. Ssshut up!" Legion swung out her arm, claws bared.

Olivia bowed her back, leaning out of reach. Without her wings to balance her, she stumbled and nearly fell to the floor.

"Aeron lovesss me. He told me ssso."

Most of her fury drained, and there was nothing she could do about it. Compassion was hardwired inside her, as was the need to give happiness rather than heartbreak. They desired the same thing, she and Legion. "And it's true. He loves you, but he doesn't love you as a man loves a woman. He loves you as a father loves his daughter."

"No." A stomp of a foot. A hiss. "I'll marry him one day."

"If that were the case, I probably wouldn't have given up my entire way of life to come here and save him. I wouldn't have wanted to be with him." She spoke as gently as she was able. Emotionally wounding the demon wasn't her goal. For whatever reason, Aeron did like the...thing. But Olivia knew how demons operated and knew Legion would berate and undermine her unless she was made to understand. "Already I've slept in his bed, curled into his side."

Legion didn't accuse her of lying. How could she? Angels never had the need, and the little fiend knew it. Rather, she stopped and gaped at Olivia, her breathing choppy, shallow. More poison dripped down her fangs.

"You want what you cannot have. You envy, you crave. That's your nature," Olivia said, "and I understand that nature better than I ever did before because that is the very reason I am here. I envy, I crave. But what you don't realize is that your leaving hell to be with Aeron has sentenced him to death. *You* are the reason I was sent to him. You are the reason I was ordered to kill him. You are the reason another assassin will be sent in my place." She drew in a breath. "You are the reason he will die."

"No. No! I'll kill the next dirty angel just like I plan to kill you now."

That was the only warning Olivia had. One moment Legion was in front of her, the next she was on top of her, and they were falling...down, down. Olivia took the brunt of the impact, her skull cracking on the ledge of the hearth and oxygen shoving from her lungs like a heat-seeking missile. Bright lights winked over her vision, but not enough to obscure the teeth descending toward her neck.

Lysander had begun training her for her new warrior duties the very day that golden down appeared in her wings, so Olivia knew to jam her palm into Legion's chin and shove, grinding the demon's teeth together painfully.

She'd never relished the thought of battling demons. Especially when Lysander told her that warriors had to distance themselves from their task completely, leaving only a hardened determination to take down their prey. Could she?

A shock of cold bloomed in her fingers and spread up her arms...into her chest...and that cold numbed more than fear this time, destroying what little remained of her fury, right along with the compassion and disgust.

Yes. She could, she realized. *Shocking.*

Do what you must, a voice whispered through her head. *You are angel. She is demon. Let your instincts guide you. Let your faith flow through you.*

For a moment, she thought Lysander was beside her. But then Legion growled, snapping her from her sense of relief, and it didn't matter. Olivia was ready. Rather than using emotions she had no experience with, she allowed that which was natural to her, faith and love, to consume her, as the voice had instructed. *This* was true strength.

With a flick of her arm, she tossed Legion across the room. The demon slammed into the wall and slid to the floor. All the while, those red eyes remained narrowed on her.

Up. Now.

Olivia jumped up and pressed her back into the

hearth. The new position limited her range of motion, but she needed something to balance her when—

Legion sprang at her.

Olivia ducked and once again the demon hit the wall. As she ricocheted backward, plaster dusted the air, filling Olivia's nose and making her cough. Still, she didn't hesitate to kick out her leg and propel Legion to her bottom. Faith—she could win this. Love—good against evil. The heel of Olivia's foot must have somehow cut past those scales because crimson seeped from the demon's breastbone.

"I will not allow you to hurt me, demon."

"You won't be able to ssstop me."

Again Legion leapt up. Again she threw herself onto Olivia, clinging like a vine. Teeth snapped and nails clawed. Olivia punched left, right and forward, working one knee between them to preserve some distance, but barely managing to keep herself upright. Legion shifted her head from side to side to avoid impact, but she wasn't always successful. A cheekbone cracked. Her nose broke.

Across the room, glass shattered. Then a dark winged figure was there, wild gaze searching…landing on the still-struggling women. Aeron. Their eyes met, and time suddenly seemed suspended. His lips were pulled back in a tight scowl, and his tattoos were so black they were like shadows on his skin.

A bubble of excitement burst through her and Olivia lost her focus. Her hand collided with the demon's mouth, an area she'd been avoiding; Legion took full advantage and bit, those razor-sharp fangs cutting deep, thick poison dripping straight into her veins.

Olivia screamed. The burn, like acid and salt and

fire…oh, Deity. Her hand was turning to ash, surely. But when she looked down, she saw the flesh was merely cut and bleeding, a little swollen.

"Olivia," Aeron shouted, rushing to her.

Her knees gave out and she slid to the floor, no longer able to hold her own weight. She clutched her hand to her chest, breathing suddenly too difficult. The pain was just too intense, like having her wings ripped out all over again.

Before, during the fight, stars had winked over her eyes. Now she saw black spots and they were a thousand times worse. They grew and intertwined, ruining her sight and leaving her in a dark void of solitude and pain.

"What did you do to her?" Aeron snarled, cutting through the illusion of aloneness. And even though he was angry, she welcomed the intrusion.

"Pro-protecting myself," Olivia managed to work past trembling lips.

"Not you," he said, and this time his tone was gentle. Callused fingers smoothed over her brow, just as gentle, brushing her hair out of the way.

Despite the agony still blistering and sizzling in her hand, she offered him a weak smile. Aeron might not have wanted her to stay in the fortress, might even have run from her, but on some level he cared about her well-being. He'd bypassed Kaia and Cameo and come straight for Olivia.

Her newfound confidence had not been misplaced.

There was a shuffle of footsteps. Then, "Aeron, my Aeron. Ssshe'sss nothing. Leave her and—"

"The only one leaving her will be you. I told you to stay away from her, Legion. I told you not to hurt her."

Aeron's hands fell away from Olivia and she moaned, bereft. "You disobeyed me."

"But...but..."

"Go to my room. Now. We'll talk about this later."

Silence. Then a sob. "Aeron, pleassse."

"Don't argue with me. Go." Clothing rustled. He must have turned away from her. "What did she do to you, Olivia?"

"H-hand," she managed to work past chattering teeth. She still felt as if she was on fire, and yet, now she was as cold as ice. "Bite."

Those strong, callused fingers returned to her, only this time, they circled her wrist and lifted her hand. Probably to inspect the injury, but that didn't matter. The action increased the velocity of her blood-flow, which increased the intensity of the pain, and she whimpered.

"I'll make it better," he promised.

"Others were bitten first. Help them, then me."

He didn't reply. Instead, he fit his warm lips around her wound and began sucking. In this, he was not gentle. Her back arched and another scream ripped from her. She tried to jerk from his clasp but he held tight, sucking, sucking, and then spitting. Sucking, sucking, spitting.

Gradually, the pain ebbed. The burn cooled and the ice melted, and she slumped against the floor like a doll. Only then did Aeron stop.

"*Now* I'll take care of the others," he said, voice hoarse.

The black faded from her vision, and she watched fuzzily as he strode to Cameo and gave her the same treatment, sucking the poison from the wound in her neck and spitting it out. When the warrior woman finally stilled, sighing in relief, he turned his attentions to the Harpy.

As he was spitting out the last mouthful, the bedroom door burst open and two warriors rushed inside. Paris and William. The two searched the room, weapons drawn. Paris wielded some type of gun. William, two blades.

"What's going on?" Paris demanded. "Torin texted us that you busted through Kaia's window."

"Great timing," Aeron replied dryly.

"What?" William said, all innocence. "We did you a favor, taking our time. We thought you were playing kinky sex games."

"I will…kill that…fucking bitch!" A scowling Kaia lumbered to her feet. "She bit me. She fucking bit me!"

"I'll deal with her." Aeron rose, as well. His expression was bleak but no less determined. "Not you."

Kaia pointed a finger into his chest and lifted to her tiptoes, but that still didn't place them nose to nose. "No, you'll baby her like you always do."

"I'll deal with her," he repeated firmly.

"Hold everything. I missed a four-way chick fight. *Then* I find out someone's been nibbling." William's attention shifted to Olivia, who was still lying on the floor. "Please tell me our sweet little angel is the biter. It'll make me want her ever so much more."

Aeron growled low in his throat, closed the distance and crouched beside Olivia. "Get out of here, *Willy*. You're not wanted or needed."

"I beg to differ," William huffed.

"Rather than allow Aeron to kill you, I'll explain

what happened on the way out." Cameo scrubbed a hand down her face before holding out her arm expectantly.

William just arched a brow. A frowning Paris strode forward, clasped her hand and tugged her upright.

"Thanks," she muttered with an irritated look to William.

He shrugged. "You're not my type, so I don't feel the need to help you."

She rolled her eyes. "Every woman's your type."

That should have made everyone in the room laugh, but tragic as Cameo's voice was, everyone cringed.

Aeron scooped Olivia up. Good thing. All energy had abandoned her. Her muscles were still trembling, reminding her of the aftershocks of an earthquake. Without a word to the others, who hadn't left as planned, he carted her into the hall.

"Every time I stumble upon you, you're injured," Aeron said.

True, but she wasn't going to ask him to stay away. "I suppose I should thank you for saving me."

"You suppose, angel?" He snorted.

Fine. No supposing about it, but no way would she admit it. He'd called her angel. Again. Which meant he still saw her as she'd once been, not as she now was. He needed to realize she'd left her sweetness behind with her robe.

"With that attitude," she said, "you'll get no thanks from me. Ever."

No response.

She fought a wave of disappointment. "So?" she prompted.

"So what?"

Impossible man. "Do you now assume I'm weak and easily breakable?"

Again, he gave no reply. Which meant that, yes, he did. She frowned. As much as he hated weakness, she would never be able to work her way into his bed—with him in it and naked, that is—if this kept up.

She'd have to find a way to prove how strong she really was.

The words *faith* and *love* once more drifted through her mind. She doubted he was ready for either one, however. And besides, she didn't love him. Did she? She just didn't know. What she felt for him was different from what she'd ever felt for anyone else, but she'd never loved anyone in the romantic sense.

All she really knew about that kind of love was that it meant being willing to die for the other person. As Ashlyn had for Maddox. As Anya almost had for Lucien. Was *she* ready to die for Aeron? No. She didn't think so. She hadn't offered such a compromise to the Council when she'd had the chance, something they might have considered. Sacrifice *always* earned a reward.

"Where are you taking me?" she asked, changing the subject. She was still too groggy to reason things out. More than that, Legion was in his bedroom and Olivia was *not* ready for another run-in. If that was where he was headed, then—

"My bedroom," he said, and her stomach clenched. Ugh. He was. "But—"

"Legion isn't there. As always, she disobeyed me. I felt her leave this plane of existence."

Olivia's eyes widened in surprise. She'd known they were linked, but that was...wow. "You're *that* connected to her?"

He nodded.

Maybe Legion was right. Maybe she *was* meant to be with Aeron. The thought was like another injection of acid in Olivia's veins. She herself wanted to be more than Aeron's acquaintance, more than his friend. She wanted to be his lover. That had never been clearer than now, this moment, as his strong arms banded around her and held her close. As his heart hammered against her ear and his warm breath trekked over her skin. But she wouldn't share him with Legion, no matter how much she desired him.

You won't have to. You're a confident, aggressive woman now, and you go after what you want.

True.

"I'm sorry she hurt you," Aeron said gruffly, surprising her. "She's just a child, and I—"

"Wait. I'm going to stop you there." Though she did like hearing him apologize. "Legion isn't a child. She's not much younger than you."

For a moment, he just blinked down at her. "But she's so innocent."

Innocent? Now Olivia was the one to snort. "What kind of life have you led that you consider that little fiend innocent?"

His lips twitched as he pounded up a flight of stairs. Her weight didn't seem to bother him. "It's just…her lisp, I guess. And her joy at dressing up and playing princess."

"She's spent her life in hell, surrounded by evil, souls being tortured in every corner. Of course dressing up is fun to her, but that doesn't mean her mind is childlike. She loves you, Aeron." Or so she said. Would Legion die for him? "She wants you the way a woman wants a man." There was no question of that.

He stopped in the middle of another hallway, one foot raised midair. He tilted his head until their gazes locked together, his violet irises wild. "You're wrong. She loves me like a father."

"No. She plans to marry you."

"No."

"Yes. You hear me and you know I speak true."

A muscle in his jaw ticked. "If what you say is correct—"

"It is. Again, you hear the truth in my voice."

Aeron gulped, shook his head as if to dislodge her claim. At least he didn't try to deny it this time. "I'll talk to her, tell her a romantic relationship isn't possible. She'll understand."

Only a man could delude himself in such a way.

He kicked back into motion, silent now. At his door, he shouldered his way inside. Olivia tensed, but sure enough, Legion was nowhere to be seen. She sighed with relief as Aeron laid her atop the soft mattress.

"Aeron," she said, not ready for him to leave and suspecting he intended to do so.

"Yes." He remained in place, hovering over her, and smoothed a hand through her hair.

She almost purred as she leaned into the touch. "I didn't mean it before. When I said I wouldn't thank you. I truly am grateful for your aid."

What are you doing? He'll never see you as a potential lover if you constantly remind him of your angelic nature.

"Yeah, well." Clearly uncomfortable, he coughed as he straightened. "Are you hurt anywhere else?" He didn't wait for her reply, but cast his gaze over the length of her. Perhaps that was his first full glance at her new clothing, because his jaw suddenly dropped. "You... you're..."

Perhaps her potential lover status wasn't in jeopardy, after all. *Confident.* "Isn't it pretty? Kaia helped me." *Aggressive.* She smoothed her hands down her breasts, stomach and hips, wishing he were touching her instead. Goose bumps broke out over her skin. Oh, now that was a surprise. It felt good. Really, really good. She'd have to remember to touch herself like this again.

"Pretty," he said thickly, hotly. "Yes."

"What do you think of my makeup?" When his gaze lifted to her face, she traced a fingertip over her lips. "I hope Legion didn't smear it."

"It's...nice." Again, his voice was thick and hot.

Was that good or bad?

Did it matter? She wanted him; she'd decided to go after him. She would have him.

Licking her lips—and tasting coconut, hmm—she sat up, propping her weight on one elbow and reaching for Aeron with the other. She flattened her palm over his pounding heart. Part of her blushed at such boldness, screaming to pull back. The other part preened, shouting to rush onward.

To achieve great joy, she reminded herself, you often had to step out of your comfort zone.

So step out already. "You can kiss me if you want." *Please, please, let that be what he wants.*

For a moment, he stopped breathing. At least, his chest stopped moving. A blaze erupted in his eyes, expanding his pupils, and his muscles twitched under her grip. "I shouldn't. You shouldn't. You're an angel."

"Fallen," she reminded him. Again. "I could have died the other day. I could have died today. In both cases I would have died without knowing the taste of you. What a shame that would be, since it's all I've ever really wanted."

"I shouldn't," he repeated, leaning...leaning... Regrettably, he stopped himself just before contact.

She tried not to scream in frustration. How close had she come to finally getting her wish? "Tell me why." So that she could obliterate each of the reasons.

"I don't need the distraction." At least he didn't move away. "I don't need a woman. I don't need *anything*."

There was no way to refute that. Never had a man been more unwavering about remaining alone. So, rather than argue, she simply said, "Well, I *do* need a distraction," and slid her hand up to his neck. She wouldn't step out of the zone this time; she would sprint.

Determined, she jerked him down.

He could have resisted. He could have stopped her. He didn't. He allowed himself to fall on top of her. They remained like that for a long while, simply looking at each other, his body pinning her down, neither of them able to catch their breath.

"Aeron," she finally rasped.

"Yes?"

"I don't know what to do," she admitted, all the longing she felt wafting from the words.

"I may be a fool, but I've got it from here," he replied, and claimed her mouth with his own.

CHAPTER NINE

SHE'S WEAK, PRACTICALLY HUMAN. Worse *than human,* Aeron reminded himself as their tongues twined, but he couldn't make himself care. Later he would. Later he would regret, but for now, all he wanted was...her. Olivia. A woman his little Legion despised, a woman who had just gotten her ass handed to her—although, if he were honest, he would admit that she'd been holding her own until he'd distracted her—and a woman he *would* kick out of the fortress very soon.

The way she calmed and charmed Wrath made him uneasy, throwing him off his game. Even now, the demon purred, enjoying what was happening. Eager for what was to come.

Foolish. Olivia was a distraction he couldn't afford. He hadn't lied about that. He couldn't waste time worrying about her, saving her when she got herself into trouble—and she would. She wouldn't be able to help herself. The woman was determined to have "fun," for the love of the gods.

Any other man would have been willing to help her with that, he thought next, hands falling beside her temples and fisting the sheet. Look at William. Sex-happy William. Bastard.

Mine. The angel is mine.

Wrath? Staking a claim? Laughable.

Not yours, and certainly not mine. But oh, how he wished otherwise.

In her new clothing, she'd exposed luscious skin and dangerous curves. Both of which were sins in their own right, pure temptation no man could hope to resist. Not even him. She'd wanted a kiss and there'd been something inside him that had demanded he give it to her. For once, he hadn't had the strength to pull away. Had only been able to press their lips together, open her teeth with his tongue, and take. Take her sweetness, take her innocence. Take everything he could from the kiss.

And holy hell, the taste of her... She tasted of grapes, sweet with just a little tart, as her tongue tentatively sought his. Her nipples were hard and every few seconds she arched upward to brush her core against his erection. In contrast, her hands slid through his cropped hair and remained soft, her kiss gentle.

She would be a tender lover, just as he'd always preferred.

He'd never understood why some of the other warriors gravitated to women who scratched and bit and even hit during this most intimate of acts. Had never wanted to do so himself before. Why bring the violence of the battlefield into the bedroom? There was no reason good enough. Not to him.

Aeron's past lovers, the few he'd allowed himself, had expected more intensity from him than he'd been willing to give. Probably because he looked like a biker, was a confessed warrior and killer, and backed down from nothing. But he hadn't allowed them to push him into going faster or harder.

One, he was too strong and they too weak. He could too easily break them. Two, harder and faster might have roused his demon and Aeron refused to participate in a three-way with a creature he sometimes couldn't control. Again, he could break his partners, morphing from lover to punisher.

Except...if he were completely honest with himself, there was a desire, small though it was, to push Olivia past all boundaries, to hurtle her over the edge of her own sense of control, so much so that she would attack and plead and do anything necessary to reach her climax.

Wrath's purring increased in volume.

What was wrong with him? What was wrong with his *demon?* With this much interaction, Aeron should have feared hurting Olivia more than he'd ever feared hurting another. He didn't. He deepened the kiss, taking more than she was probably willing to give.

Yes. More.

Wrath's voice was a whisper, but still it jarred him back into reality; he raised his head from Olivia. *I'm not edging into bloodlust. You should be quiet.*

More!

Even though the demon had always been silent around Legion, his baby calming it much the same way Olivia did, Wrath had never wanted to kiss her.

Why was it responding this way to Olivia, then? An angel?

We need to slow down, he replied, not knowing what else to say.

Like a petulant child denied his favorite treat, the demon whined, *More heaven. Please.*

More...heaven? Aeron's eyes widened. Of course. To Wrath, Olivia must represent a place the demon would never have been welcome, making the unattainable seemingly within reach. Though, to be honest, Aeron had never before suspected that the demon wished to visit the home of the angels. Angels and demons were enemies, after all.

And maybe he was wrong, but nothing else explained the demon's…affection for her.

"Aeron?" Her eyelids cracked open, her lashes thick and black, the perfect frame for those magnificent baby blues. Her lips were wet and red, and she licked them slowly. "Your eyes…your pupils…but you're not angry."

What about his pupils? "No, I'm not angry." Why would she think so?

"You're…aroused, yes?" Those lips curved into a wanton grin, saving him from having to reply. "So why'd you stop? Am I doing it wrong? Give me another chance, please, and I promise I'll learn the way of it."

He pulled back a bit more and blinked down at her. "This is your first kiss?" He'd known that. *I don't know what to do,* she'd said earlier. But the truth hadn't really hit him until now. Angels remained utterly innocent, even in this? No wonder Bianka had chosen to linger in the sky with Lysander. This was…intoxicating.

Olivia nodded. Then, surprisingly, she offered him another grin. "You couldn't tell? You thought I was experienced?"

Not entirely, but he didn't want to spoil her excitement. Plus, he liked her inexperience a little too much. He liked being her first, her only. Liked the possessiveness now flooding and consuming him.

A possessiveness that was wrong on so many levels. "Perhaps we should—"

"Do it again," she rushed out. "I agree."

Innocence and eagerness, wrapped in such a pretty

package. Oh, yes. Intoxicating. "Not what I was going to say. Perhaps we should stop." Before he introduced her to far more than a kiss.

Before he introduced himself—and Wrath—to heaven. A heaven they might never want to leave.

"Only this time," she added, as if he hadn't spoken, "I'll be on top. I've always wanted to try that. Well, since I met you."

She was stronger than she appeared and managed to shove him to his back, cool cotton pressing into his bare skin. Without awaiting permission, she straddled his waist. Her skirt was so short it rode up her thighs and gave him a forbidden peek at her panties. They were blue this time, like her shirt, and tiny. So very tiny.

His mouth watered and he found his hands on her knees, pushing them farther apart and rubbing her against his erection before he could stop himself. Sweet heaven. Damn, damn, damn. Heaven. He shouldn't be doing this.

More.

Moaning, she tilted her head back, and the silky length of her hair tickled his stomach. Her breasts arched forward, her nipples still hard and visible through her shirt. Clearly, she wasn't wearing a bra.

That did not delight him.

Her gaze met his, burning him to his soul. "I wasn't kidding when I told you I needed a distraction. Legion's attack reminded me of what the other demons did to me. And I want to forget, Aeron. I *need* to forget."

"What did they do to you?" he found himself asking, even though he'd once told himself he didn't care to know.

Some of the passion-haze left her, dulling those

pretty irises, and she shook her head. "I don't want to talk about it. I want to kiss."

She leaned down, but he turned his head away. "Tell me." Finding out was suddenly more important than finding pleasure.

"No." Her lips dipped into a pout.

"Talk." He would learn the truth and he would avenge her. Simple as that.

Wrath snarled in agreement.

A growl escaped the angel, surprising them both. "Who would have thought a man would rather converse than do...other things."

His teeth ground together. Stubborn woman. "Even if we kiss, I will not fu—sleep with you," he said. Lysander's warning chose that moment to echo in his head. *Do not soil her. I will bury you and all those you love.*

He stiffened. How could he have forgotten such a threat?

"I didn't ask you to sleep with me, now did I?" How prim and proper she sounded. "Like I said, I just wanted another kiss."

Maybe that was true. Maybe it wasn't. Yes, her voice claimed it was, but he refused to believe it. Didn't *want* to believe it. Not that he would ever admit such a thing aloud. If he were to sleep with her as *she* so clearly craved, she would expect more. Women always expected more, whether he pleased them or not. And more he couldn't give her. Not just because of her powerful mentor. Complications, he reminded himself. He didn't need them.

More!

"If I kiss you again," he said, thinking, *shut up, shut the hell up,* "I won't hold you afterward." A kiss was not "more," he told himself. A kiss was not something that soiled. A kiss was just a kiss, and she was on top of him, for gods' sake. "It won't change anything between us." Best she understood that now. "Also, I'll expect you to tell me what was done to you."

Bargaining? Really? *Way to resist.*

"I'm a confident, aggressive woman, so I'm okay with the not changing anything between us thing," she said with a casual—forced?—shrug. "Cuddling isn't a top priority, anyway. But talking about what happened? I can't promise."

Did this "confident" and "aggressive" woman truly not care to burrow into his side and hold him tight once their lips parted? Did she truly want him for a kiss and nothing else? That delighted him. Truly. That did *not* disappoint him. Not even a little.

"Right now, I just want to use your mouth and your body," she added with a blush. Not as confident as she seemed, perchance? "But don't worry. I'll only rub against you a little bit. So if we're done with this conversation, I'd like to get to it."

Despite his disappoint—uh, utter delight—that she was willing to kiss him without expecting anything else, fire sparked in his blood, caught and spread. Soon his veins were like rivers of lava, every muscle clenched and ready, burning. Use his body? Please, please, please.

I said more!

What an odd mix of innocence and hedonism she was.

What an odd mix of reluctance and enthusiasm *he* was.

He should stop this now, finally, before things spun out of control.

Control. Damn it. He needed to exercise some and act rationally, rather than talking himself into and out of being with her. Actually, he needed to talk himself—and his demon—out of it one final time and then leave.

"As you reminded me, you could have died today," he said darkly. Good. Nothing upset him more than thoughts of death. "You're easily breakable." Except that.

"So?"

"So?" He could only shake his head. Like the humans he always observed, she didn't seem to care. She wasn't on her knees, begging for more time, and obviously had no plans to do so. His jaw clenched painfully. She should be begging.

"Are we done chatting now?" she asked, blush reigniting. "If not, I guess I could touch myself some more. I liked it before. Maybe I'll like it again." Without waiting for his response, she cupped her breasts and moaned. "Oh, yes. I like."

Perhaps she wasn't blushing, after all. Perhaps she was simply flushed with pleasure.

He gulped. "No, we aren't done chatting. Why aren't you afraid of dying?"

"Everything and everyone has an end," she said, carnal ministrations never ceasing. "I mean, you're going to be killed soon, and though I loathe the thought, you don't see me crying about that, either. I know what will happen, and I accept what cannot be changed. I'm trying to live while I can. While *we* can. Dwelling on the bad is what destroys all hint of joy."

He felt a muscle tick beneath his eye. "I will not be killed."

She stilled, some of the sparkle fading from her expression. He tried not to mourn the loss. "How many times do I have to tell you?" she said. "You won't be able to beat the angel sent to slay you."

"Tell me something else, then. You gave up your immortality for fun and immediately ran to me. That means you expect me to supply this fun. Why would you do that, why would you give up so much and rely on me so heavily if I'm to be destroyed?"

She offered him a sad smile. "I would rather be with someone a short time than not at all."

Her claim reminded him of what Paris had said the other night, and he bristled. He wasn't wrong in this. *They* were. "You sound like a friend of mine. A very foolish man."

"Then silly me for not choosing him instead. Better a fool who plays the game than one who remains on the sidelines."

He bared his teeth in a scowl. *Don't even think about being with someone else,* he wanted to roar.

Wrath, too, erupted. Not at Olivia, but at Paris. The demon flashed images of the warrior's head on a platter—minus his body.

Aeron instantly sobered. *Oh, no, you don't. You will leave Paris alone.*

She's mine.

No, mine, he snapped, then realized what he'd done. *I mean, she belongs to neither of us. I've told you that. Now will you please shut up?*

"Are we done chatting *now?*" One of Olivia's fingertips traced down the flatness of her stomach and circled her navel. "Or shall we make this conversation more interesting?" She nibbled her bottom lip, considering. "Oh, I know what we can discuss. Can people really die of pleasure?"

Oh, hell, no. She hadn't just asked that.

Do not soil her. "We'll never know." He sat up, meaning to toss her aside and leave her here. Alone. Aroused, but alone. The desire to murder his friend had done nothing to temper his need, nor had the reminder of Lysander's threat. Retreat was his only other option.

"Well, you might not, but I promise you I'll find out."

He froze. Just how far would this angel go to discover the truth? As the question drifted through his mind, his cock pulsed. The image of her splayed out, her own hand between her legs, fingers sinking deep, consumed him. Dear...gods...

"No. You will behave yourself." The words croaked from him. "Now, I have to go."

Stay! Wrath commanded.

Gods help him, he did. He stayed. As easily as if he'd been chained to the bed, his fight gone before it had time to fortify him.

"Fine. But I really wish— No. No!" she repeated more forcefully. "You can go when we're done. Only then." Olivia's arms wound around his neck, her hands firm against his hair, her nails sinking into his scalp. "I know what to do now." She jerked his mouth to hers and her tongue instantly plunged deep.

Oh, yes. A quick study.

Her lips slanted over his, their teeth scraping. The heat...the wetness. Consuming, destroying his resolve. Everything he needed, everything he ached for. Chasing every thought but one from his head: *finish.*

Yes. Yes! More.

She moaned, and he swallowed the decadent sound.

And when she rubbed against him, he could feel how damp she was, even through his pants. His gentleness— gone. His tentativeness—abolished. He arched up to meet her. When that wasn't enough, he clasped her ass and forced her to move faster, harder. Deeper.

"I want to touch you everywhere," she rasped as she plundered. "I want to taste you everywhere."

"Me first. I—" No. No, no, no. *Do not soil her, do not soil her.*

She nipped her way to his chin, then lower, sucking on his neck to ease the sting.

Yes, please. Soil her all day, all night.

More, Wrath demanded again.

More. Yes. More— No! Damn it. Threaten her, Wrath. That'll send me fleeing the room, surely.

More.

Is that the only word you know?

More, damn you.

Aeron snarled. No one wanted to cooperate today.

"Why me?" He rolled Olivia over, pinning her down again, meaning to stop the madness but licking the hollow between her neck and shoulder instead. That hammering pulse looked too delicious to ignore. Foolish man. Stupid demon. Beautiful female.

Hands seeking of their own accord, he kneaded her breasts. Fucking mistake. They were perfect, her nipples harder than he'd realized. *Keep the conversation going. Pull those hands away.* "I must be everything your kind despises." After all, his evil deeds were etched over his body for the entire world to see.

"You're both the goodness I know and the exhilaration I crave." She wrapped her legs around him, closing any lingering hint of distance. "What's not to like about that?"

Shit, shit, shit. Another perfect fit. "I'm not good." Not compared to her. Not compared to anyone, really. If she knew half the things he'd done or half the things he would do, she would be running from him. "How can I be to someone like you? You're an angel." An angel who tempted him like no other.

Heaven.

"I'm fallen. Remember? And I'm a little tired of hearing you say *my kind* and *someone like me*. It's irritating. And do you know how hard it is to irritate an angel? Even one of the fallen?" Her hands roved over his back, over the slits that hid his wings. She probed inside, found the delicate membranes. "I'm sorry if my chastisement hurts your feelings, but— No. I'm not sorry!" She caressed.

A roar of bliss parted his lips. He had to reach over his head and grab the headboard to keep himself from clawing or punching something, so drunk did the sudden influx of pleasure make him. Damned. He was damned. There would be no resisting now.

Sweat beaded over his skin, and his blood heated yet another degree. No one had ever... That was the first time anyone had... How had she known to do that?

"Again," he commanded.

More, Wrath agreed.

Again Olivia's fingertips grazed his hidden wings. Again he roared at the bliss, unable to catch his breath. With that first touch, his thoughts had splintered. With the second, they had aligned, an echo of his need. *Finish*.

More than a kiss? Hell, yes. He would give it to her.

More, more, more.

Olivia raised her head and flicked her tongue over one of his nipples. "Mmm, I've always wanted to do that." She licked again. And again. But soon that wasn't enough, and she nibbled on the hard little bud with her teeth.

Aeron let her bite him. Something he'd never allowed another woman to do. He was too lost to stop her, and part of him didn't *want* to stop her. Part of him, like his demon, only wanted more. Hell, *all* of him did. Control be damned.

Her attentions turned to his other nipple. There was no licking this time, only the biting. He was surprised to find himself leaning into the sting, anticipating, eager. To his surprise, the action wasn't a reminder of Wrath's vengeance sprees, as he'd always assumed it would be. It wasn't even a reminder of his first time with a woman, as he'd also assumed. A time he'd rather forget. It was a declaration of his partner's intense, *uncontrollable* excitement.

And still he wanted harder. Faster.

More!

He released the headboard and rolled once again, placing Olivia on top. She nipped her way down his stomach, her nails scraping at his skin, her raspy pants echoing in his ears. He gripped the hem of her shirt and jerked the material over her head, freeing those magnificent breasts. He'd only touched them before, the shirt a hated barrier, but now he saw nipples like frosted plums. Hungry, he was hungry. He shifted his gaze before he lifted her, devoured. Her stomach was beautifully soft.

Oh, yes, soft, he thought as he splayed his fingers on

her warm skin. His tattooed hands were almost obscene on so delicate a woman, but he couldn't force himself to pull away. *Where's your prized strength now, huh?*

Gone, like his sense of control.

Her fingers wrapped around his and she stared down at the contrast they made. Innocence and wickedness.

"Beautiful," she gasped.

She thought so?

"I'm going to get it pierced, I think," she said, tracing a fingertip around his hand.

His gaze shot to her passion-glazed face. "Get what pierced?"

"My navel."

"No." *Unsoiled.* A gorgeous jewel would sparkle against her skin and draw his eyes constantly. Make his mouth water. Make him want to tongue her there. Then move lower. Soiling. "You aren't going to do that. You're an angel."

"Fallen." Her grin was slow and wicked. "I thought we were done chatting. Especially since we were doing something I liked very, very much and I want to do it again. *Tasting.*" She scooted backward on his legs and licked at *his* navel, tongue swirling on some of his tattoos.

Groaning, Aeron relaxed on the mattress. That naughty tongue was hot, her teeth still sharp, but damn if he wasn't already addicted to the feel of them. *More.* A plea from him this time. Maybe they all had been.

Until…her fingers worked at the button on his jeans and reality intruded. *You'll finish.* He couldn't allow it, he reminded himself. Too much was at stake.

Hated reality.

Rational. Be rational. He grabbed her wrists to stop

her. "What're you doing?" Did that slurred tone belong to him?

"I want to see your—" she licked her lips, cheeks coloring again "—your penis."

He nearly choked on his tongue. *Unsoiled. Rational.*

"Then I want to suck on it," she added, a slight tremor to the words.

Dear...gods...he thought again. Someone needed to tell Lysander she was halfway soiled already—in the most delicious way—and it wouldn't be Aeron's fault if he completed the job. "You're not doing that to me."

Fool!

Lookie there. His demon knew another word.

She traced one of those naughty fingertips up his stomach and around his nipple, her hand trembling just as her voice had. "But I want to. *So badly.*"

"You're an angel," he reminded them both for the thousandth time, shaking his head for emphasis. And he might be a killer, but he wasn't a debaucher.

You could be. The demon?

Gods, he wanted to be.

"No," he said, again for everyone's benefit. His, Olivia's and Wrath's. *Now go back to your corner,* he shouted to the demon. *You aren't welcome here anymore.* Even though Wrath had been on its best behavior.

"Argh! How many times do I have to tell you? I've fallen."

"Yes, but I won't be responsible for your ruin."

Eyes narrowing, she slammed a fist into his chest. "Fine. As a confident, aggressive woman, I know I can find someone else. I wanted it to be you, but as I've learned the past few days, we don't always get what we want. William flirted with me, I think, and it's clear that he likes to have...you know. *Sex*."

When she lifted from him, as if she truly meant to follow through with her threat—and perhaps she did, the determined little wildcat, despite the fact that she'd faltered on the word *sex,* proving she wasn't quite as confident and aggressive as she wanted him to believe—a snarl of rage erupted from him and he grabbed her by the arm. He tossed her back onto the mattress.

William would not be touching her. Ever.

When she stopped bouncing, he covered her with the full measure of his weight. "Just because I won't let you do things to me doesn't mean I won't do things to you. I'm already ruined." As he spoke, he slid his hand up her thigh. Soft...warm...

Mine.

Another claim from Wrath, but he couldn't protest this time. Automatically her knees parted. Warm? No. Hot. He tunneled past her panties to the heart of her. She was perfect and wet, dripping. His thumb, shaking now, pressed into her sweet spot.

"Yes," she gasped. "Yes. That's so good...just what I'd imagined..." Her eyes closed and she dug her nails into his back.

Away from his wings, but even that was a stimulant to him. He meant to ease one finger inside her, but that gasp...her praise...her caress... His desire was once again spiraling to new heights, and he actually shoved inside her. *Careful.* She didn't seem to mind, though. No, she seemed to enjoy.

"Yes." A moan this time. Her knee rubbed against his hip. "More."

Helpless but to obey—would it always be so with

her?—he sank in a second finger. She writhed and thrashed and he thought she might even have drawn his blood. His cock wasn't free, thank the gods, or in that moment, he would have pounded inside her.

Scratch that. His cock wasn't free, *curse the gods,* or in that moment he would have pounded inside her.

Inside her. He wanted inside her so bad.

After this, after she erupted in his arms, screaming and begging and praising his name, he had to get rid of her. She caused too many problems, fogged up his common sense, distracted him.

Unsoiled, he reminded himself. *Take her into town unsoiled.*

Keep her, Wrath whined.

I told you to be quiet, he snapped. He didn't need to war with his demon as well as with his own needs.

And why was Wrath so vocal? he wondered again. Over a female, no less, rather than someone's punishment. Yes, he'd already figured out the demon liked what Olivia represented. Heaven. Odd though that was. But this insistence…

Was the demon more like him than he'd realized? Both liking and hating what they did, how they killed. He'd always assumed the demon enjoyed the blood-crazes—and the ensuing results. But what if Wrath had always been as helpless as Aeron? As desperate for absolution?

"Aeron?"

"Yes," he gritted out, Olivia's voice drawing him out of his head.

"You stilled," she said through her panting. "I need more. Do continue, please."

Reverting to her sense of propriety. Enchanting.

But he didn't want to hear her ask him for more; it only weakened his resolve. And he didn't want to hear Wrath, either.

He silenced them the only way he could. He pressed his mouth into Olivia's and kissed her.

He meant to gentle things, as he was used to, as he could handle, but she was having none of that and lifted to meet him, her tongue dancing over his, her teeth sliding against his.

Soon she was writhing against him again, moaning. Even reaching between their bodies, tunneling inside his pants and gripping his cock. He hissed in pleasure, in pain. She wasn't gentle about that, either, and though she didn't know the way of it, her motions a little too jerky, her touch was so welcome he found himself moving into her hold. Hard, fast, uncontrollable.

A knock sounded at the door.

He didn't still. He couldn't. She'd thumbed the slit at the head of his cock, spreading moisture, and in the span of a few seconds, he'd catapulted past the point of return. Reality would not intrude this time.

"Don't stop," he told her.

"It's so...just a little...more..." Her grip tightened. "Aeron."

Again he jerked in pleasure. He had to cut back a roar as another knock sounded.

"Don't you dare stop, either!" Olivia screeched, then her tongue was back inside his mouth, her nails all over him, her knees gripping his sides.

In and out he pumped his fingers. Her grip tightened even more, pulling his skin, but gods, the burn was good. So damn good. And when his thumb found her clitoris again, she screamed, loud and long and with so much pleasure a wave of pride flooded him—and with the pride came a release of his own.

A release so complete he didn't care that he was jetting seed all over her stomach. Didn't care that he was shouting profanities and slamming his free hand into the headboard and cracking the wood. Didn't care that what he'd done could damn him in Lysander's eyes.

As a third knock reverberated, Aeron collapsed on top of Olivia, his strength utterly depleted. Panting, sweating, he rolled to his side so that he wouldn't squish her.

"Okay," she said after a moment, sagging into the mattress. "Now I can cross one item off my To Do list. Good job, and thank you. I know other men enjoy cuddling, but I believe you mentioned earlier that you don't want to do that, so..."

Dismissed, he thought, eyes widening. Just like that.

Hell. No. He was just leaning toward her, meaning to jerk her into his arms and force her to cuddle him, when yet another knock reverberated. Scowling now, frustrated, he drew the sheet around her, popped to his feet and stalked to the door. Someone was about to die.

CHAPTER TEN

WHO WAS HERE?

A naked Aeron threw open the door, and Olivia watched him unabashedly. That beautiful butterfly flew at the top of his back and she had touched it. In fact, his skin was welted and bleeding from where she'd scratched him. Perhaps that should have embarrassed her. It didn't. She was proud. She'd marked him. Marked the man she lusted after. And he had responded; he had climaxed. She wanted to do it again. Only, she wanted to do more. Go all the way.

Stupid intruders.

Who was here and what did they want? If it wasn't life-and-death, Olivia hoped they fell down the stairs later.

The violent thought, so unlike her, gave her pause. Or maybe such violence *wasn't* unlike her. She was new and improved, after all.

And the new and improved Olivia might—might—have gotten Aeron to change his mind about that cuddling by subtly mentioning how much others enjoyed it. And, to be honest, cuddling sounded more delightful by the second. Warmth, strength and raw sex appeal, all wrapped around her.

Maybe next time. If there was a next time. He'd seemed so sure this would be a one-time deal.

"What?" Aeron barked. His big body blocked her view, so Olivia couldn't see who it was.

"Heard some shouting." Cameo stepped to the side for a peek inside the room, finally answering Olivia's unspoken question. The female warrior spotted Olivia's disarray, and her mouth dropped open in astonishment.

Olivia just grinned and waved. She wasn't embarrassed by what had happened with Aeron. Well, not much. She was mostly jubilant. She'd given up everything she'd ever known to be here and experience the glories of the flesh, so inhibitions weren't going to be tolerated.

Besides, over the years, she'd seen humans do all manner of things. Sex, drugs. So much good, so much bad. What she'd done had been beautiful. There was no shame in it.

"You look well," Olivia told her.

"You, too." Had Cameo's voice not been so sorrowful, Olivia thought she might have heard laughter in the undertone.

"Eyes on me, Cam," Aeron said, clearly irritated for some reason. "Why are you here?"

Cameo faced him, lips twitching. "Torin watched some footage he recorded last night and caught a glimpse of Nightmares. Far as he could tell, she went into a building and never came out."

"What are you talking about?"

"Your Shadow Girl. Olivia told us she's possessed by the demon of Nightmares. Anyway, we're going into town to, uh—" her gaze flicked pointedly to Olivia "—*chat* with her. You in or out?"

Aeron stiffened, and there was a beat of silence. Then he said, "In," and glanced over his shoulder at Olivia.

"Don't get comfortable. You're coming with us. While we're out there, we'll find someplace for you to stay until you decide where you want to live permanently."

What? He still planned to get rid of her? After everything they'd done? Sure, she'd told him it wouldn't change anything, but that had been before it changed everything. That one little taste of pleasure wouldn't be enough for her.

You were assertive before, in this bed. You can be that way again. "Sorry, but no can do. I'd probably almost die again," she said, and she almost grinned when his eyes widened. The man had a serious problem with thoughts of her death, expecting it at every corner. "I think I'll stay here." *And you'll like it,* she projected to him. Some people didn't know what they needed to achieve happiness. Clearly, Aeron was one of them. She'd just have to instruct him, as she'd already planned.

He massaged the back of his neck. "We talked about this, Olivia. You can't stay here. No matter what happened between us."

"Okay." She threw her legs over the side of the bed and stood, dragging the sheet with her.

"So you're going into town with me?" he asked, obviously suspicious. And angry and relieved. What a weird combination of emotions.

"Of course not." Placing one foot in front of the other while her knees trembled was difficult, but she managed to do it. Without falling. She brushed past Aeron—oh, sweet Deity, his heat, his strength—and smiled as she did the same to Cameo, who winked at her.

She paused in the hallway as a thought occurred to her.

Glancing at Aeron over her shoulder, she said, "I'm

going to explore your fortress. Oh, and, Aeron. When you fail to find Nightmares, whose name is Scarlet, by the way, please don't come home and take your bad mood out on me. Unless you want me to kiss it better. That would be acceptable."

She didn't wait for his response, but meandered around the corner.

"Olivia," he called.

Ignoring him, she continued on. She had a feeling he wanted to argue with her. Her body was still humming with threads of the pleasure he'd given her and arguing would ruin that.

"Olivia! You're practically naked."

Naked? She stilled, glanced down at the sheet draped over her bare breasts and gulped. Partial nudity was fine when she was with Aeron, but not so fine when she would most likely run into others. And that had nothing to do with a lack of confidence, she assured herself.

Being with Aeron had helped defeat the memory of what had happened in hell, yes. But then, nothing about the two experiences had been similar. Aeron had sought pleasure; the demons had sought pain. Still. Seeing lust in someone else's eye might bring those memories roaring back to life.

With a sigh, she rushed back inside the room, bypassing Aeron and his infuriated expression without comment. Cameo had already wandered off. Olivia dropped the sheet, grabbed her shirt and pulled the fabric over her head. Thankfully, she was still wearing her skirt and panties.

"Better," she said with a nod.

"No, it's not. Not for what we're about to do. And yes, I'm saying you're coming with me."

She closed the distance between them, rose to her tiptoes and kissed his cheek. "See you later. And please be careful." Down the hall she meandered again.

"Olivia."

She ignored him, attention riveted by the many doorways ahead of her. She peeked her head into the first, unsure of what she'd find. Of course. A workout room. She should have guessed, but as many times as she'd secretly been here, her focus had been on Aeron.

"Olivia," he called, and this time he sounded resigned. "Fine. Stay. Whatever. I don't care."

Liar. At least she hoped he was lying.

The second room, she saw, was empty. The third, she heard voices floating from before she reached the doorway. Not allowing herself to be dissuaded by fear or uncertainty, she peeked inside.

It was a bedroom, like Aeron's, only there was no pink or lace. Dark walls, metal furniture rather than wood, and of all things, a karaoke station in the corner. A woman was seated at the side of a large bed, reading to a man who rested atop the mattress.

Olivia must have made a noise because that man's gaze lifted and landed on her. He tried to rise, but the woman protested. "Gideon. What are you doing? Lie down!"

Gideon. Olivia racked her brain. Keeper of Lies?

"I'm resting," he croaked out. "We're alone."

Oh, yes. He was indeed the keeper of Lies, unable to tell a single truth without suffering severe pain. He was also very, very cute, with blue hair, electric eyes and a pierced eyebrow. But he was clearly injured. White bandages were wrapped around his wrists where his hands should have been.

Confident. Aggressive. "Sorry to interrupt. I was just…in the neighborhood." Truth. "I'm Olivia," she said, waving. Though this demon raised her hackles as Torin had done, she didn't scream at him to leave or run away herself. Before, she'd been injured and lost to those terrible memories. Now, her body was stronger—or as strong as a human body could be. She could handle this. "I'm with Aeron."

Which wasn't a lie. He was one of the reasons she'd come here. She'd just kissed him while lying in a bed and oh, her heart had yet to settle over that. She'd never seen him do that with another female.

Just like that, her mind immersed itself in what had happened. Wow. Just…wow. While his body was hard as a rock, his mouth was soft as a rose petal. His hands had moved all over her, she'd rubbed herself on his massive erection, and those big fingers had pushed inside her. The pleasure…the heat…the surprising abandon… she'd never experienced anything like it.

Now she knew. You really *could* die from pleasure.

He'd tasted of mint, sweet and spicy; together, they'd been the perfect aphrodisiac, overwhelming her senses. Completion had become her sole source of survival.

"You're the angel," the woman said with a welcoming grin, tugging her from her thoughts.

"Yes. Fallen, but yes."

Gideon relaxed against his pillows. "Wonderful."

"Pay no attention to him. He's grumpy from boredom. I'm Ashlyn, by the way." Ashlyn had golden hair, golden eyes, and looked as delicate as an iris. "Maddox's wife."

"Maddox, keeper of Violence," Olivia said. A giant

of a man with black hair, violet eyes identical to Aeron's and a seemingly untamable temper. "You've married?"

"In our own private ceremony," Ashlyn replied with a blush. She stood. "He's not so bad, though, I promise." Her hands smoothed over her rounded belly. "He's a sweetie once you get to know him."

Olivia couldn't help herself. She strode forward and placed her own hands on that belly. Pregnant females had always drawn her, for she'd always known she would never bear children herself—another secret wish of hers. Angels were created, not born, so even if she'd experienced physical desire with another of her kind, she wouldn't have conceived.

Now that she was human…perhaps there was a possibility.

With Aeron? A girl could hope. For a moment, she pictured what children of theirs would look like. They wouldn't be born with all those tattoos, of course, and that was a shame, but they might have his beautiful violet eyes, and even his wings. Everyone should experience the joys of flight, if only once. Perhaps their children would even have Aeron's grit and determination, driving her mad while at the same time enchanting her.

She sighed, returning her attention to the task at hand.

"They are strong, your twins," she said, knowing mothers welcomed such news. "Fire and ice. You'll have your hands full, keeping them out of trouble, but you'll be happier for it."

Ashlyn's jaw dropped and for a long while, she simply blinked up at the taller Olivia. "T-twins? How do you know I'm having twins?"

Oh, no. She'd ruined the surprise, hadn't she? "Sensing who grows in a woman's womb is a gift all angels possess."

"That...that just can't be." Her skin was paling by the second, even becoming tinted with green. "There's only one being inside me. I mean, I'm progressing normally. Right?"

How much to tell her? Only enough to calm her, perhaps. "No. You're progressing slowly. Your children are immortal and require a much longer gestation. But don't worry. As you promised me, I now promise you. Both your son and your daughter are healthy."

"A son? A daughter?"

Great. She'd ruined another surprise.

With a shaky hand, Ashlyn brushed a lock of honey-colored hair from her face and hooked it behind her ear. "I need to lie down. I need to call Maddox. I—I—" Her wild gaze swung to Gideon. "Would you mind terribly if—"

"Yes," he said, grinning. "I would mind."

She exhaled heavily. "Thank you." As if she were lost in a trance, the pretty Ashlyn padded from the room, not sparing Olivia another glance.

"I'm sorry," Olivia called. For more than one reason. Now she was alone with Lies. A situation in which she had never thought to find herself. Injured as he was, however, she couldn't leave him. "Would you, uh, like me to continue the story?" she asked. Not waiting for a reply, she lifted the book Ashlyn had left behind— ohhh, a romance novel, how decadent!—and claimed the woman's seat.

"I'd love for you to read to me," he said. "Your voice is not...creepy."

Meaning he wouldn't and it was. *Rejected.*

She fanned the book's pages, doing her best to hide her disappointment. "What you're hearing is a layer of truth. There's nothing I can do about it. Well, except lie, but that's not something I want to do. They taste horrible. Plus, they're too complicated. Feelings get hurt, fights erupt."

"Yeah, I'd know nothing about that. Lies are awesome," he said, but she knew he was agreeing with her. There was envy in his tone. "I wish...nothing. I wish nothing."

Poor guy. He must wish for a lot of things. "So. Do you still want me to leave?"

"Yes."

"Excellent." Progress. "Can I read now?"

"Yes," he said again. "I'd rather not talk."

Oh. Still no romance novel for her, then. "About what?"

"About you. I have no desire to know why you're here."

"So you can help me?" she asked hopefully. From fear to need? And so quickly. Perhaps that proved the depths of her desperation to succeed.

"Sure. Why not?"

Choosing to ignore the lie—perhaps he merely *thought* he couldn't help her, but would surprise himself—Olivia told him about her decision to fall, what she hoped to gain and the progress she'd made with Aeron. It was nice, having an unbiased bystander to share with. Someone who wouldn't judge her.

"So you hate him, then?" the warrior asked, and she knew that he meant love.

Love. Did she love Aeron? "No. Yes. Maybe." She

still didn't know. "I think about him all the time. I want to be with him, give myself to him fully. You know, sexually," she added with a blush, in case he didn't understand. *Confident.* "He said he wouldn't have sex with me, though."

"Smart little shit, our Aeron." Gideon's grin was slow to form, but wicked and sultry because of it. "Listen, here's a little unhelpful advice. Don't consider sneaking into his bedroom tonight—and don't make lots of noise so he doesn't kill you, thinking you're the enemy. Oh, and don't be naked."

"Excellent suggestions, thank you," she said, brightening. She kicked her feet onto the bed. She still wore her boots, and the black leather glinted in the light. "Men do like their nakedness, I've noticed. Aeron didn't want anyone else to see my...breasts."

The new and improved her could still be embarrassed, she realized.

"How wrong you are. Oh, and, Olive? In that position, I can't see your panties," he said, clearly amused. *Confident, you are confident.* "Do you like them?"

He blinked in surprise, clearly having expected her to change positions. "I *hate* them."

"Really?" That wasn't embarrassing, she decided; that was empowering. "Would you like them as a souvenir? Since I plan to take your advice and crawl into Aeron's bed naked, I'm not going to need them anymore."

Gideon laughed outright. "Nope. I wouldn't. I would hate to have them as a souvenir. And not just because I'm sure Aeron will be thrilled to know I have his girlfriend's panties."

Aeron's girlfriend. A lie, from Gideon's point of

view, but she could have melted into a puddle. "Then they're yours. I'll give them to you before I take off."

That earned her another laugh. "I don't like you at all, boy. Not at all."

She beamed. "Ditto. So now that I've told you about me, tell me about him. Aeron. I mean, I know who he is, but I know nothing about his past. I want to understand him. Reach him. Help him stop worrying about my eventual death." And accept his own.

"No way." Meaning *sure thing.*

Gideon shifted on the bed. A lock of blue hair had lodged into the headboard, and it pulled with his movement. He grimaced, reached up, but was unable to clasp a single strand with his bandaged wrists. His frustrated growl propelled her into action.

She dropped her legs, leaned forward and gently smoothed the hair free. "Better?"

"No," he muttered gruffly.

"Good. I like the blue, by the way. Maybe I'll dye mine." She pushed the thought to the back of her mind, to be considered later. Along with that navel piercing. Right now, she wanted to learn about Aeron. Who he'd been, what had shaped him.

"Forgetting Aeron…where do you not want me to start?"

"I know you warriors were kicked from the heavens into ancient Greece. I've heard the stories about the torment you caused, slaying innocent humans, torturing, raiding, pillaging, destroying everything you encountered, and so on and so forth."

He shrugged. "You heard wrong. We had total control of our demons and weren't lost to bloodlust. And when we did finally lose control, the guilt of what we'd done, well, it was minimal."

Guilt. A terrible burden to carry. And from what she'd seen of these Lords, they carried far more than any one person should ever have to bear. They deserved peace, she decided. Once and for all.

"Aeron wasn't a warrior," Gideon continued, "and yet his actions, even when unwarranted, didn't torment him—though I was always sure he hated what he did a little too much and loved himself for it. Even still, he did the least amount of work, making the rest of us do all the killing to protect the god king."

Olivia quickly translated Gideon's meaning. Aeron had sometimes loved his job a little too much and had hated himself for it, but he'd also loved his friends, so he'd done their work, too, sparing them some of the burden, which had probably been torturous for him.

Guilt, she thought again. Even then, he had carried massive amounts of it. He had enjoyed hurting those who'd hurt others, and had most likely considered himself just as evil as they were.

Before he died, before she died, she would teach him otherwise. He wasn't evil. He was a protector. No wonder the thought of her death troubled him. In his eyes, he would have failed to protect her. The sweet, darling man.

"Please, go on," she beseeched.

Gideon nodded. "All those deaths never affected him, making him see fatality around every corner. And then, when our hated enemy, Baden, was not decapitated, Aeron saw that immortals could live forever. That didn't freak him out."

Okay, so. The deaths he'd brought about in the line

of duty had given him a healthy appreciation for mortality, especially when his dear friend was decapitated. Now, he expected everyone around him to die, knowing there was nothing he could do to stop it—nothing he could do to protect them, as she'd just figured out.

To a man who valued strength and power, that helplessness had to bother him greatly. That must be why he kept himself so distanced from everyone but Legion. The fewer people he cared about, the fewer people he had to worry about saving.

So how had Legion snuck her way past his defenses?

More than that, how had Legion escaped his demon's need to reprimand? The little fiend had hardly lived a blameless life. Look what the creature had done to innocent Olivia.

"As for Legion," Gideon said, seeming to read her thoughts. "I think Aeron has never secretly craved a family of his own, and Legion doesn't give him that."

So. Aeron had secretly wanted a family—just as she had—and Legion provided that for him. Somewhat. *I could become his family, as well,* Olivia thought. Not that she wanted to be Legion's stepmother, but for the pleasure of staying with Aeron, she could endure even so heinous a title.

"I don't see the eagerness in your eyes, angel, and I'm very glad for it. You should know that, even in the heavens, he preferred wild women, and I can sense that, at heart, you're as wild as can be—no matter that you clearly haven't convinced yourself otherwise. Though Aeron thinks that's what he wants, I assure you, it's not what he needs."

Oh…no, she thought, suddenly dejected. Aeron preferred tame women, but Gideon thought he needed someone wild. Gideon also thought that, no matter what Olivia did or said, she wasn't wild at heart and would never be.

"Why are you warning me away? Only a few minutes ago, you told me how to seduce him."

"My girl Aeron doesn't deserve a little torment now and then."

Oh. A little *entertainment*. That's what Gideon considered her.

He was wrong. Maybe she'd been gentle before—or had pretended to be—but the more time she spent in this fortress, the more she was learning about herself.

Gentleness was what she'd had her entire life. Lysander had been gentle with her. The other angels had been gentle with her. She'd been gentle with them.

In Aeron's arms, she'd come alive with sensation. She'd wanted more, wanted harder and chaotic, control unattainable. She'd wanted *wild*. A few times, he'd tried to slow things down. He'd tried to soften his touch, proving Gideon's claim that he preferred gentle. Or thought he did.

He did beg you to fondle his wings, she reminded herself, and that fondling had been anything but tender.

Still. He hadn't wanted her to pierce her navel. What would he think when she actually did it? When she got a tattoo, as she also planned to do? Maybe of a butterfly. Would he no longer even want to kiss her?

"This conversation has officially depressed me," she said. "Not that I didn't enjoy talking with you. You gave me the details I begged for, and I'm grateful, but I think I'll read to you now, if that's okay. I need a distraction before I head to the kitchen and try out every bottle in the liquor cabinet." That's what many humans did when they were given news they didn't like.

"Not like we can do both," he said, and motioned to an array of bottles atop his dresser.

"Really?" Eager, Olivia pushed to her feet, crossed the room and swiped up as many of the fuller bottles as she could hold. The liquid swished inside, different scents drifting to her nose. Apples, pears, lemons. Dark spice. "Giggle juice is what I've always called it," she said, "and I've always wanted to try it."

"Now's not your chance. Don't you dare pour any down my throat."

"That would be my pleasure." After tipping one bottle over Gideon's lips while he gulped back mouthful after mouthful, then draining the rest of the contents herself and nearly choking—it didn't taste as wonderful as she'd hoped—she reclaimed her seat and flipped open the book, unmindful of the page.

The words blurred slightly.

"'She gripped her breasts and squeezed,'" she read. Interesting. "'Just as he had done earlier. Her nipples throbbed all the more, wanting his hands. A whimper escaped her. Normally she would have hated herself for making such a sound, but now, this moment, she was owned by her passion.'"

I know the feeling, Olivia thought. Sadly, she might not know it again.

She started on another bottle.

AERON PUSHED HIS WAY inside the fortress, his hands drawn into tight fists. He didn't look around or head to the kitchen even though he was starved. He started pounding up the steps.

"Where're you going?" Cameo asked, keeping pace beside him.

"To find Olivia." To question her. He wouldn't kiss her as he'd been craving these past few hours, thinking about her rather than searching for Nightmares. Worrying that he was becoming obsessed with her in the same way he'd once been obsessed with killing Danika.

Only, he didn't want to kill Olivia.

He wanted to finally finish what they'd started in his bed. Yes, they'd both come, but he hadn't sunk inside her. He hadn't taken her all the way.

Still. He'd already soiled her, he'd decided, by spilling his seed on her belly. He'd already earned Lysander's wrath. Not that he cared anymore. Not that the angel had come gunning for him yet. So what other harm could making love to her cause?

Just like that, his focus switched. Rather than question her when he found her, he'd strip her. *There you go again. Thinking about her rather than taking care of business.*

Didn't help that his demon had yet to shut up. If he heard the word *more* one more time, he was going to erupt in a blood-craze all his own.

Concentrate. Question her. Yes. That's what he'd do. No stripping her. Unless her clothes were too tight, then he would be doing her a favor, removing them and helping her breathe.

Concentrate, damn you. Question. Her. She'd predicted that he would be unable to find Shadow Girl. Nightmares. Scarlet. Whatever. And she'd been right. How had she known the girl would seemingly vanish without a trace?

Looked like he needed her, after all, he thought with

a scowl. That didn't mean he'd keep her, though. Definitely not. Strip her, however...

He punched the wall.

"Wow. You like her that much?" Cameo said, incredulous. "I mean, I know you're fooling around with her, but I've never seen you this keyed up over a woman."

"I don't want to talk about her."

"Fine. Don't."

"But if you insist...I don't understand her and it's driving me insane." He rarely shared his problems with his friends. They had enough to deal with. But just then, he didn't know what else to do. He needed help. Before he lost himself completely.

At the landing, he stopped and Cameo did the same. He scrubbed a hand down his face. "She's making me feel things I've never felt before and want things I've never wanted before. Cronus has to be teaching me a lesson. That's the only explanation for her effect on me." No other woman had ever come close to tying him up like this. "I never should have dared the god king to send me a female I would chase. Except I've hardly had to chase her, so she can't be the one Cronus sent to me. Gods, this makes no sense. Something has to be wrong with me."

Cameo patted his shoulder, her expression understanding even through the misery etched there. She opened her mouth to respond, but an echoing feminine sob stopped her.

They shared a confused look before Aeron kicked back into motion. He recognized that rich, sexy timbre, even in its sadness, but the sound hadn't come from his room, or the one next to it.

Masculine laughter abounded next, and he scowled.

Gideon. Laughing. That should thrill him, with as much pain as Gideon had recently endured. Thrilled was not what he felt, however.

Aeron rushed around the corner and into his friend's bedroom. There was Olivia, lying directly beside Gideon, her head buried in his shoulder as her body shook. Gideon, the insensitive prick, was still laughing.

"What's going on?" he demanded, rushing forward. And no, it wasn't jealousy pouring through his veins like fire. It was rage. Rage that Olivia was bothering his injured friend. Yes. Rage. At Olivia. He didn't want to stab Gideon in the heart with one of his daggers. "Someone better explain before I do something we'll all regret."

Mine, his demon growled.

Better than "more," he supposed.

"Aeron?" Olivia met his gaze briefly before turning her watery eyes away from him. She even reached up and wound her arms around Gideon's neck, holding on for dear life. Her tears soaked his shirt, her body again shaking violently. "Oh, great. Now he's angry."

"If you hurt her…" Aeron snarled. Okay, fine. He wanted to stab Gideon.

He'd never purposely hurt one of his friends. Had he fought them? Yes. Bashing each other's heads into walls was merely a healthy way of blowing off steam. But Sabin had once stabbed him in the back—literally— not to blow off steam but in real anger, and he'd vowed never to make his friends feel that kind of betrayal.

Now, though, he didn't think he'd be able to help himself. And he wouldn't be able to blame his demon, either. There were no vile images flashing through his mind, no desire to punish a sinner. There was just more of that blinding rage.

You don't care about this woman. You're getting rid of her at the first opportunity, he reminded himself, even as he scooped her up. Her sobs intensified, and she tried to hold on to Gideon.

Aeron shook her loose. "Gideon! Answer me. What happened? What did you do to her?"

"Everything. She's just a very happy drunk." Gideon gave him an unapologetic grin.

Pure, sweet Olivia drunk? Worse, someone other than Aeron had corrupted her?

Rage, yes. The dark emotion spread. Surprise, as well. And a jealousy he could no longer deny.

"Oh, Aeron," Olivia said between gasping hiccups, finally deciding to seek comfort from him rather than his friend. "It's so terrible. I have no wings and you're determined to kick me into the streets, alone and desperate. Legion was so mean, and for a few minutes, I was angry. I've never been angry before. Not really. I didn't like it. And I know so much and could help you more than you realize, but you don't want my help. Maybe Lysander was right. Maybe I need to go home."

He recalled how bloody she'd been when he'd found her, those wings freshly removed. He recalled how much pain she'd been in when Legion had bitten her. Guilt replaced every other emotion inside him. He should— Wait. Go home?

"You can go back?" he asked her, astonished.

"Mmm-hmm." Sniff, sniff. "In fourteen…no, ten days. I'm losing count. You told me I was sick for three, right? But if I *do* return, I'll be forced to kill you. That's the only way they'll welcome me back into their fold."

So if she returned home, she'd still have to kill him. Or try to. He could live with that. Hopefully literally. She would be out of reach, away from his dark influence and hurtful urges, safe from harm.

"I can take care of myself, Olivia," he said, and she burst into a fresh round of sobs.

"You shouldn't always have to, Aeron. Someone needs to protect you the way you always protect others."

This was how she would kill him, he mused. Through tears and kindness. Already there was a sharp pang in his chest. He'd always been the protector, the one to keep others safe. That someone else wanted to care for him was nearly irresistible. "Get some rest," he told the still-grinning Gideon before striding out of the room.

That's when he heard Wrath moaning in his head, as upset as Olivia was. *Mine. Hurt. Better.*

I'm doing my best. "I may not be able to fix anything you listed, but if you finally tell me what the demons did to you, I can make that better. Remember how?"

Olivia rubbed her forehead against his slightly stubbled jaw. "With a kiss."

"Yes." His grip tightened. Gods, he was a giver. "Tell me."

Sniff, sniff. "No. I don't want to."

"Did you tell Gideon?"

"No."

So. Even drunk, there was no chance she'd spill. He could have pushed, but didn't. No more tears. Please, gods, no more tears.

Inside his bedroom, he eased her onto the mattress. She peered up at him, her eyeballs practically spinning. "Do you wanna have sex now?" she asked, then hiccupped. "I think I gave my panties to Gideon, so I'm good to go."

"You gave your panties to Gideon? And he accepted them?" Incredulous, Aeron fought the urge to check under her skirt, then fought the even stronger urge to return to Gideon's room and finally attack.

"I did, and he did. So are we going to do this or not?"

Sadly, he was tempted. Even with her swollen eyes and splotchy skin, she looked enchanting—and beddable. His body still craved her, and no one had ever needed comforting more. Not that he knew how to comfort anyone. But she deserved better than a drunken first time.

"Go to sleep, Olivia. In the morning—" at which point she—and he?—only had nine days before he ensured she returned home "—we have a lot to discuss."

CHAPTER ELEVEN

LEGION BATTLED TEARS as she raced through the fires and screams of hell. Once her home, now her hated refuge. She was on all fours, galloping like a lowly animal, a position she knew well. It kept her close to the ground, beneath notice, and increased her speed. Plus, it was the only position allowed for someone like her. Were she to stand and walk, every High Lord within reach would feel compelled to punish her for such impudence.

And speaking of High Lords, they were all around her, torturing the human souls that had been sent here to forever rot. They were laughing, loving every bit of the blood and the pain and the vomit.

Aeron didn't care that she was here, a place he knew she despised, either. Not anymore. How could he? He had protected the angel. Her enemy. He had then saved and, worse, comforted that angel.

Why? Why hadn't he tried to protect Legion? Why hadn't he saved and comforted her? The tears began to fall, and laced with poison as they were, they stung her scales.

When she reached a hidden alcove of shadow and stone, she stopped, stood and pressed her back against a jagged, blood-splattered wall. She was having trouble catching her breath, and her heart—which was now broken in half, damn that Aeron—pounded sharply.

The long length of her forked tongue emerged, and she wiped away a few of the tears. While the tart poison would have sent anyone else to their knees, sobbing and begging for mercy, it merely stung anew. So badly she'd wanted the angel to die from that poison, but it hadn't happened. Aeron had been too determined to save her, and what Aeron wanted, Aeron found a way to get. Always.

What was she going to do? The first time she'd seen Aeron, chained and hungry for blood, she'd loved him. He'd been fighting that hunger, had even hated himself for it, and never before had she encountered anyone who preferred to save rather than destroy. She'd thought, *He can save* me.

In a mere heartbeat of time, she'd decided to live with Aeron. To marry him. To sleep in his bed every night and wake up next to him every morning. Instead, he'd had his friend Maddox build her a bed of her own. Still, she'd wanted to be everything to him. Had known all she needed was time.

Yet time was not a luxury she had anymore. She couldn't return to their home because he'd invited the angel to stay. That stupid, ugly angel, with her long curly hair and cloud-pale skin. Legion—and every demon, really—couldn't remain in the presence of such goodness for long. It hurt. Truly hurt. Somehow eroding everything they were, destroying them little by little.

Aeron didn't hurt, though, she thought darkly. How could he? He'd welcomed the bitch. Maybe Wrath had lived among humans for too long to react to the angel as a normal demon should. Maybe Wrath was buried too deeply inside Aeron.

Either way, Aeron should have cared about Legion's

pain. But he hadn't. Just like he no longer cared about *her*. He'd sent her away.

"What's wrong, sweet child?"

Legion gasped at the sudden intrusion, peering wide-eyed at the newcomer. She hadn't heard him approach, yet he was now in front of her, as if he'd simply materialized. Or had been waiting, invisible, all along.

A tremor rolled down her spine. She would have scrambled away, but the rock behind her stopped her. Bad, bad, bad. This was so bad. A visit she couldn't hope to survive.

"Leave me alone!" she managed to work past the sudden lump in her throat. A lump that held a thousand whimpers.

"Do you know me?" he asked smoothly, completely unoffended. Or seemingly so.

Oh, yes. She knew him. Hence the whimpers. He was Lucifer, brother to Hades and the prince of most demons. He was evil. True, undiluted evil.

Sweet child, he'd called her. Ha! He would stab her in the back the moment she turned away from him and laugh while doing so. Just for "funsies," as Anya would say. She swallowed.

"Well?" He snapped his fingers and in the next instant, they both stood in the center of his throne room. Rather than stone and mortar, the walls of Lucifer's palace were composed of crackling flames. "It's a simple question. Do. You. Know. Me?"

"I—I do. Yesss." Legion had been here only twice before, but the first time, during her birth into this realm, had been enough to convince her that she never wanted to return. The second time, she was brought here for punishment. Punishment she'd earned for refusing to torture a human soul.

"Concentrate," Lucifer snapped.

She blinked and forced herself to focus. Plumes of black smoke wafted from the floor, the walls, even the throne atop the dais, curling around her like fingers of the damned. There were screams trapped inside those plumes, and those screams taunted her.

So ugly, they said.

So stupid.

So unnecessary.

Unwanted. Undesired.

"I asked you another question, Legion. You will answer."

Though she wanted to look anywhere but at him, she forced her gaze to meet his. Lucifer was tall, with shiny black hair and orange-gold eyes. He was muscled, like Aeron, and handsome—but not as handsome as Aeron—despite the inferno always banked in his expression.

What had he asked? Oh, yeah. What was wrong with her? "I—" What should she tell him? A lie, definitely, but something he would believe. "I jussst wanted to play a game."

"A game, hmm?" His lips curled slowly, wickedly as he strolled around her, closing in, studying, taking her measure and clearly finding her lacking. "I have a better idea."

The heat of his breath somehow reached the back of her neck, and she shuddered. At least he didn't stab her as she'd feared. "Yesss?"

"We shall bargain, you and I."

Her stomach twisted into cutting knots. His bargains were notorious, for they always ended in his favor. That's how he'd escaped hell for a year to live unfettered on Earth. He'd bargained with the goddess of Oppression, the very one responsible for ensuring the walls surrounding this underground prison were solid, impenetrable. The one who had allowed many demon High Lords to escape. The one who had then died, her bones used to construct Pandora's box.

"No?" she said, and though she'd meant it as a statement, it emerged as a question.

In front of her once again, he *tsked*. "Don't be so hasty. You haven't even heard what I have to offer."

It wouldn't be good for her, that much she could guess. "I—I ssshould go."

"Not yet." He spun on his heel and glided to his throne, where he eased down, relaxed, utterly sure of himself. Smoke reached him, surrounded him, and flames soon followed, dancing around as if happy just to be near him.

Legion tried to shift from one foot to the other—only to realize her feet had been glued in place. There would be no leaving. Not until he was done with her. Still. She didn't panic. She'd been beaten before and had survived. She'd been called terrible names and laughed at; she'd been thrown into seemingly never-ending pits and kicked into ice fields, unable to transport herself somewhere else.

"I can help you get something you want," Lucifer said. "Something you'll do anything to possess."

Ha! There was nothing he could offer that would—

"I can help you win Aeron's heart."

For a moment, she forgot to breathe. Only when her

lungs and throat began burning, scalding, did she force her mouth to open and suck air inside. He could…what?

"As you like to spy on the happenings here for the Lords of the Underworld—" there at the end, bitterness had filled his tone "—I like to spy on the happenings of the surface. I know you're enamored of Aeron, keeper of my darling Wrath."

Hearing his derision, she raised her chin. "He lovesss me, too. He told me ssso."

Lucifer arched a brow. "Are you sure about that? He was so angry that you'd hurt his precious little angel."

The word *precious* used to describe that pig of an angel caused red spots to wink over her vision. *She* was Aeron's precious. Her. No one else.

Lucifer waved his hand regally, and the air in front of Legion thickened, wavered, dust motes sparkling. Colors burst to life. Then Aeron was there, bending down and gently lifting the angel's wrist to his mouth. He sucked at the poison Legion had injected in her, and her lithe body stilled.

Seeing his mouth on that disgusting interloper caused the red to brighten and rage to flood her. Rage and hate and determination.

"How will you help me?" she found herself asking. The scene disappeared and she was once more looking at Lucifer. Perhaps bargaining with him wouldn't be so bad. Perhaps she would be the one to come out ahead. She was smart. Resourceful. Right?

"Let's face it," he said, gaze raking over her scaled body. "You're as ugly as a creature can be."

Her jaw dropped as wave after wave of hurt hit her, and she tried to backpedal, wanting to hide. She wasn't ugly. Was she? She was different from Aeron, yes. She was different from the angel, as well. But that didn't mean she was *ugly*.

"I can practically hear the thoughts in your head. Allow me to address them. Yes, you are indeed ugly. Actually, saying you're ugly is being kind. I can hardly stand to look at you. In fact, to settle my stomach I'm going to have to stare just over your shoulder while we finish this conversation."

She was ugly, then. Hideous. A monster. The devil himself couldn't even bear to look at her. Tears filled her eyes. "How will you help me, then?" she asked again.

He gazed down at his yellowed, curling nails, as if he hadn't a care. "I, powerful being that I am, can make you pretty."

"How?" she insisted.

"To start, I'd give you silky, flowing hair. Any color you desired and far better than the angel's. I'd give you smooth, creamy skin. Again, any color you desired. I'd give you bedroom eyes no man can resist. A tall, slender body with big breasts. Men go crazy for those, you know. And while a forked tongue has its uses in bed, I'd probably get rid of that. Your lisp is annoying."

He could make her pretty? Pretty enough to win Aeron? Hope bloomed in her chest; the mere thought of finally being with the man of her dreams—living as husband and wife—had her shedding one reservation after another. "What do you desire in return?"

"Oh. That," he said, shrugging as if it were of no importance. "All I'd want is to possess your new body."

She frowned. "I don't undersssstand. How could I win Aeron if I'm not…me? How could I win Aeron if *you* are me?"

He pinched the bridge of his nose. "I see you're stupid, too, which means we'll have to fix that, as well. I didn't mean I'd possess your new body right away, my single-minded friend. I would be allowed to do so only if you failed to win him."

Her frown intensified. Being beautiful didn't mean she'd automatically win?

The silence earned her a shake of his head. "Clearly breaking my meaning down as if I were talking to a child didn't work. What else can I do?"

Her cheeks heated, and it had nothing to do with the fire around them. She wasn't stupid *or* a child, damn him! "You're trying to confussse me on purpossse."

"Actually, I'm not. I don't want you crying foul later. So listen closely. I will give you nine days to seduce Aeron. I would say all you have to do is gain his declaration of love, but you already have that. What you don't have is his sexual attraction, and that's what you really want. So get him in your bed, of his own free will, and you win our bargain. You may keep your new body and live happily ever after. Without my interference."

Everything sounded fair and wonderful and perfect. Everything but the timing. "Why only nine days?"

"Does the reason matter? It won't change anything about the bargain."

Resistance. Of course the reason mattered. "Tell me," she insisted.

"Fine. Nine is my favorite number."

A lie, definitely. She could push, but... Was learning the truth more important than gaining a chance at that which she desired most?

No.

"And if I fail?" she asked. He'd told her what he wanted, yes, but she needed every detail.

"Well." His fingertips traced circles on the arms of his throne. "If you fail to seduce him into your bed, for fucking, *not* sleeping, within the allotted time, you must allow *me* to possess your new body, as I said. For however long I wish."

There it was. The final detail. He would be able to control her for "however long" he wished. In other words, *forever.*

But why would he want— The answer slammed into her and she gasped. Lucifer viewed her as his ticket to escaping hell. Because Legion wasn't bound to hell, but to Aeron, she was allowed to leave this place. Lucifer was not. He was trapped here.

If she gave him permission to overtake her, *he* would then be free to leave. What he wanted, they would do. She would be aware, yes, but her wants would cease to matter.

If it were as simple as taking control of her body and using it to escape, Lucifer wouldn't waste time bargaining with her. But demons couldn't possess bodies, human or otherwise, without permission. Even the demons in Pandora's box had needed the gods' blessing to possess the Lords.

"It all comes down to whether or not you think you can succeed," Lucifer said. "Do you? I certainly do, which makes me feel silly for even offering this bargain. Perhaps I shouldn't have." In one fluid movement, he pushed to his feet. "I mean, there are other, weaker demons I can—"

"Hold on," she rushed out. "Jussst hold on."

Slowly he eased back down.

She couldn't let this chance slip away. The angel, who was incapable of speaking a lie, had told her that

Aeron saw her as a child. That Aeron considered himself a father figure to her. That would never change—unless she did something drastic.

"Termsss must be ssspelled out."

"Haven't they already?"

"Not from my end."

He clutched a hand over his chest. "You don't trust me?"

She shook her head. A bargain was binding, even for creatures such as them. Once they both agreed, she would be trapped, the bargain a living entity inside her. There could be no changing her mind. If she failed, she would concede what she'd promised, unable to stop herself.

"I'm wounded. But very well," he said. "State exactly what you expect from me."

If she didn't, she would receive no more than that, but most assuredly less. "I have to be prettier than the angel, with pale hair, golden skin, brown eyes and big breasts." All the opposite of the little bitch. "I want the entire nine days, with no time warpsss." As she spoke, her excitement grew. She was really going to do this. She was really going to try and win Aeron's heart. "And I want to be awake when I'm with him."

"Damn," Lucifer said, an amused twinkle in those fiery eyes. "You caught me on that one. I planned to put you into a coma until your time was up."

And she had stopped him from doing so. She was feeling very proud of herself at the moment. See? She wasn't stupid, after all. "You can't kill him, either. If he diesss before time runsss out, the bargain diesss, too."

"Agreed. Now, are those your only demands?" he asked, ever the indulgent lord.

"I don't want to ssspeak with a lisssp, asss you ss-said. I want to firssst appear before Aeron, not halfway acrosssss the world, jussst asss I am, and then I want to change bodiesss in front of him." That way, he wouldn't think she was Bait or a Hunter and try to get rid of her before she could seduce him.

"Very doable. Is *that* all?"

She gulped, considered, then nodded.

Once more, he stood. He splayed his arms, fire leaping from his fingertips. "Then it's agreed. You shall have everything you named. But if you fail to lure Aeron, Lord of the Underworld and keeper of the demon of Wrath, to your bed and inside your body within those nine days, you will return to this throne room, where you will willingly consent to my possession of your body."

Another nod.

"Say it," he demanded, no longer the kind and benevolent man he'd pretended to be.

"I agree."

The moment the words left her mouth, a sharp pain tore through her. Grunting, she doubled over. She couldn't breathe, was fading, every muscle she possessed spasming. But just as quickly as the pain had sprouted, the bargain birthing to life inside her, it left her and she straightened.

"And so it is done," Lucifer said. Then he gave her the same smile he'd bestowed on her when he'd first brought her here. Wicked, satisfied. "Did I forget to mention that, when you fail, my first order of business will be to murder each of the Lords of the Underworld and set their demons free?"

CHAPTER TWELVE

As THE NIGHT gave way to dawn, the citizens just now awakening and emerging to begin their days, Aeron stalked the streets, Paris at his side, both remaining in the shadows, silent. Perhaps Paris, who hadn't hesitated in his choice of companion this time—did that mean he was finally getting over Sienna?—was as lost in thought as Aeron was as they headed back to the fortress.

Olivia had cried herself to sleep, and he'd held her through those tears. When she'd finally fallen into unconsciousness, he'd flown her to Gilly's apartment, thinking that things would be easier that way. If she couldn't talk to him, she couldn't tempt him to forget his purpose. But he hadn't left right away. Paris had needed time with his chosen, so Aeron had snuggled in next to the angel.

Once again, he'd found that he liked holding her. Which was all the more reason to finally get rid of her. But as he'd walked away from her, meaning to do so permanently, he'd no longer been sure he *wanted* to get rid of her. Not that he'd ever been sure, but damn, his resolve had been shaken.

Seeing her in Gideon's arms had given life to a possessive streak he hadn't known he possessed, the earlier incidents with William and Paris paltry in comparison. The thought of Olivia roaming these roads, determined to have "fun," alone, so easy for the plucking... His teeth ground together, a common occurrence whenever he thought of her.

A man passed, claiming his attention. A human. Mid-twenties. Large. Instantly Wrath began growling, chomping for freedom, conveying images of meaty hands swinging at—and connecting with—a sobbing female face.

Wifebeater, Aeron realized as Wrath flashed more of those images through his mind.

You're worthless, the man liked to yell, spittle spraying from his mouth. *I'm not sure why I married you. You were a fat cow then and you're a fatter cow now.*

For once, Aeron didn't try to stop himself. What if Olivia had been the target of that rage? What if Legion had been? Allowing Wrath to pull his strings without any resistance, loving his demon more than he should, *without* the taint of guilt, he turned on his heel, raced forward and closed the distance between himself and the man. A man who gasped when Aeron grabbed him and spun him around.

"What the hell?"

"Aeron," Paris called, weary.

Aeron ignored him. "You disgust me, you insignificant little shit. Why don't you try beating *me?*"

The man paled, trembled. "I don't know who you are or what you think you're doing, but you better get out of my face, asshole."

Tourist, he thought, or he would have been recognized. "Or what?" Aeron smiled slowly, cruelly. "You'll call me another bad name?"

There was a snarl low in the man's throat. He had a knife in his pocket, Aeron suddenly knew. He wanted to stab Aeron in the stomach, in the neck, and watch him bleed to death.

Without any warning, Aeron struck. His right fist connected with the man's nose. There was a grunt, a howl of pain. Blood sprayed. He didn't pause, but swung his other hand. His left fist connected with the man's mouth, splitting tissue. The howl became a scream.

Aeron wasn't done.

Can't fight fair. Have to hurt. Wrath was in total control.

Still, Aeron didn't mind.

As the man tried to orient himself, tried to struggle free, Aeron kneed him in the groin. His opponent doubled over, air shooting out of his crimson-soaked lips. No mercy. This bastard had never shown any. Aeron kicked him in the shoulder, and he flew backward. After that, he was in too much pain to stand or even defend himself.

He gazed up at Aeron through tear-filled eyes. "Don't hurt me. Please, don't hurt me."

"How many times has your wife said something similar to you?" Aeron dropped to his knees, straddling the man's waist.

Drawing on a reservoir of strength he probably hadn't known he possessed, the white-faced man tried to scoot backward. Aeron merely tightened the grip of his legs, holding the bastard in place.

"Please." The man's voice was shaky, desperate.

Aeron struck again and again, raining one blow after another. The man's head whipped left and right with each new impact. More blood sprayed. Teeth even flew out like pieces of candy. Skin split and bones broke.

Soon, there were no grunts, no gasps.

A hand patted his shoulder. "You've punished him. You can stop now," Paris said from behind him.

Aeron stilled. He was panting, his knuckles throbbing. Too easy. That had been too easy. The man hadn't paid enough for the damage he'd inflicted. *But maybe he learned a lesson,* a voice of reason said inside Aeron's head. For reason to have returned, control must be his once again.

"Let's go home," Paris suggested.

Home, no. He wasn't ready to return to his room—to see the bed where he'd kissed and touched Olivia. Still, Aeron stood. He gave the man a final kick in the stomach before facing his friend. "I need some time. Alone."

A while passed in silence, Paris studying his hard expression. Finally he nodded. "All right. Maybe use it to decompress, 'cause damn."

"Plan to." Even after Paris walked away, Aeron remained in place, trying to pull himself back together. *I'm in control,* he reminded himself, even though he still didn't want to be. *I'm in control.*

Wrath continued to prowl through his mind, worked into a frenzy and ready for the next victim.

He needed Legion.

Or Olivia, he thought then.

His heart began pounding for a different reason, and it took him a minute to realize why. Arousal mixed with regret was beating through him exactly as his fists had beat at the human. Olivia hadn't woken when he'd left her in Gilly's guest room. She hadn't woken when he'd given Gilly instructions to call him the moment she did. No, she'd lain on the bed, splayed adorably, hair tangled around her, snoring delicately. Fighting the urge to curl beside her again had proved nearly impossible. But he'd done it. He'd headed out to round up Paris.

Perhaps he should return to her, he thought, heading in the direction of Gilly's apartment before he could stop himself. He glanced up at the heavens, hoping for guidance. His gaze never made it to the stars. Instead, he caught sight of white, feathered wings and ground to a halt.

Galen. Leader of the Hunters. False angel. Bastard.

Automatically Aeron palmed two blades and slipped deeper in the shadows. He shouldn't have come into town without a gun, but he'd been so preoccupied with Olivia that he hadn't thought to grab anything extra. Galen was perched on top of a building, those wings outstretched as he scanned the streets.

If he knew Aeron was below, watching him, he gave no notice.

All the while Wrath howled inside Aeron's head. The warrior had committed too many sins for the demon to process, the need to kill simply flooding Aeron. *Control. Absolute control.* He couldn't lose it this time.

Galen straightened unexpectedly. Aeron pressed against the wall of the building behind him, sure he'd been spotted but unwilling to walk away. Perhaps tonight they would end this. Finally.

Galen jumped, falling...falling... His wings stretched farther, flapped once, and he landed softly, several yards away from Aeron.

Aeron tensed. He couldn't kill Galen without severe consequences, but he *could* torture the bastard before locking him away. And then torture him again afterward.

A moment ticked by, then another, Galen simply

tucking his wings into his back and waiting. He never approached.

Every fiber of Aeron's being wanted to leap forward and attack. Surprise attacks were his forte, after all, but he held himself steady. Sometimes battle wasn't the best course of action in a war. Sometimes merely watching and learning reaped far greater rewards. What was going on here? What was Galen doing in Budapest?

He'd come here before, of course, but he'd recently left to fight a contingent of Lords who had raided a facility in Chicago where he'd been raising—and educating—halfling children. Half human, half immortal. All of whom had been taught to hate the Lords.

Now that school was in ruins, the Lords having liberated the kids and found them loving homes. Homes the Hunters would hopefully never be able to track down.

Was Galen here for vengeance, then?

Punish, Wrath said.

Not yet.

"Finally," Galen said, his rich voice filling the silence.

Aeron scanned the area, but saw no one approaching. So, to whom was Galen speaking? To himself? Or—

A pair of legs appeared a few feet in front of Galen. Only, those legs weren't attached to a torso. What the hell? The question had barely formed before a waist appeared, then shoulders, arms—and there, on the inside of the…apparition's right wrist, was a symbol of Infinity, the mark of a true, dedicated Hunter—and lastly, a face. Then a male was standing there, fully formed, holding a piece of dark, flowing cloth.

Not a ghost, then, for there was no shimmering outline around him. Just a man, as real as Aeron was. But how had he— *Cloth*. The word echoed through Aeron's mind, followed by another. *Invisible*.

His eyes widened in dread and astonishment. Cloth. Cloak. The...Cloak of Invisibility?

"I'll take that." Galen confiscated the cloak and folded it once, twice. Rather than cause the material to shrink yet thicken, each fold diminished both size and width, and soon it appeared the warrior held a simple square of paper.

Oh, yes. This could be nothing else but the Cloak of Invisibility.

Galen tucked the artifact into his robe, even as Aeron reached out automatically. *Stay. Wait.* His arm fell to his side. Information first, artifact second.

"There are cameras here," the human said. "I haven't found them, but I know the demons keep the city under surveillance."

"Don't worry." Galen laughed, smug. "They've been taken care of."

Oh, really. How? The cameras hadn't been disabled. Torin would have texted him. Had someone hacked into the system perhaps, and was even now replaying feed? That had happened in one of the movies Paris had forced him to watch. Or could more powerful forces be at work?

Cronus sometimes helped the Lords, so it stood to reason that another god could be helping the Hunters.

"You confirmed that they have an angel in their midst?" Galen asked.

"Yes, though she doesn't seem to be as powerful as you."

"Few angels are. And half their troops are missing?"

"Yes."

Another laugh from Galen. "Very good. Now join the others and stay hidden until I return. Some of our troops disappeared yesterday, and even our lovely queen has lost sight of them. Once I find them, we can attack. And this time, we'll show no mercy."

Punish! Wrath chimed in again.

"No mercy? But I thought—"

Galen shook his head. "Tell the others our experiment was a success."

The man's grin was slow but no less satisfied. "No mercy, then."

Those white wings shot out, flapped, then stilled. Galen frowned. "My daughter. I want her left alone and alive." With that, he leapt into the air.

His surprising concern for Gwen would not save him, Aeron mused darkly, darting into the air himself. His wings were completely healed and he would have no problem following—

Galen disappeared, there one moment, gone the next.

PUNISH!

Damn it, Aeron inwardly fumed. *I can't.* The Cloak was gone, out of his reach, and Galen with it. Only thing left to do was dig up more information. Not that getting it would redeem him from this failure.

His gaze narrowed on the human below him. The male wound around buildings and parked cars, always scanning his surroundings. Aeron followed. Finally his prey entered the newly remodeled Club Destiny—now under new management and renamed The Asylum—and didn't emerge.

Was that where the Hunters had set up camp?

Impossible. Some of the Lords were fond of partying there, so Torin had installed security cameras inside.

They would have picked up their enemy's presence. But...

Maybe not impossible. Perhaps the camera feed was being distorted, as it had been in the streets?

Other questions began playing through his mind. What experiment had been a success? Where had Galen's troops gone? Who was their "queen"?

With Wrath still screaming in his head, demanding he act, he withdrew his cell phone and texted Torin. Call a meeting. Two hours. He had a few things to take care of first. Namely, Olivia. If she had answers, he would get them out of her. Meanwhile, she could calm him as he'd originally planned. I found something. Even saw Galen with the godsdamn Cloak of Invisibility.

Torin, who never seemed to sleep, replied instantly. Make it one. If what you know is more important than our enemy having an artifact, I gotta hear it ASAP.

Done. Aeron pocketed the phone and pivoted on his heel to head back to Gilly's apartment, wake Olivia if he had to and demand those answers. But halfway there, a tall, menacing figure stopped him in his tracks.

Cronus, king of the gods, was frowning. As always, he wore a long, white robe and his feet were wrapped in sandals. His toes were visible, his toenails yellowed and curled.

Still, Aeron couldn't help but notice he looked younger than he ever had before. His hair no longer sported strands of gray, but was thick and sandy-colored. His face was almost unlined, his eyes a brighter brown than Aeron was accustomed to. What had caused the change?

"My Lord," he said, careful to keep his irritation to himself. The god rarely appeared when summoned, but never minded visiting at the most inopportune moments.

Wrath, still primed and ready, didn't flash images inside Aeron's mind, but then, it never did with this god. As had occurred when he spotted Galen, with too many sins to process, he merely experienced an overwhelming rush. Not to kill this time, but, curiously, to steal everything the god possessed. An urge he didn't understand, and hadn't been able to decipher.

"You have disappointed me, demon."

Don't I always? "This isn't the place for such a discussion. Hunters—"

"No one can see or hear us. I've made sure of it."

Just like another god had made sure the Hunters were unobservable? he wondered again. "Then please. Tell me why I have disappointed you. I cannot live another moment without knowing."

Those brown eyes narrowed. "Your sarcasm displeases me."

And as he knew all too well, bad things happened when the god king was displeased. Like Aeron's mind and demon becoming crazed with bloodlust and his friends' lives placed in jeopardy. "My apologies." He bowed his head to hide the hate surely shimmering from behind his lashes.

"Need I remind you that Galen's death is as important to you as it is to me? Yet you have allowed the angel to distract you."

"Isn't that what you wanted?" he couldn't help but ask.

Cronus waved a hand through the air. "Think you I paid any heed to your ridiculous begging? I do not want you distracted, so why would I send a woman to ensure that you are?"

He'd wondered the same thing.

"Get rid of her."

"I'm trying," he said, hands fisting.

Keep, Wrath snapped.

"Try harder," Cronus ordered.

"She'll only be here another ten—no, nine days." With morning approaching, he'd lost a little more time with her. Which was a good thing. Yes, good. "And then she'll be back in the heavens." Where she belonged. He would make sure of it.

A pang of sadness hit him, but he ignored it. Just as he ignored Wrath's whimper.

Cronus looked only marginally appeased at the words. "If she isn't, I will—"

"You will what?" Another male suddenly appeared without warning. This one was tall and muscled, with pale hair and dark eyes. Like Galen, he had wings. Only, his were solid gold.

Lysander.

Aeron had only seen the warrior angel a few times, and as with Olivia, there were no flashes of vile deeds inside his head, no urge to punish in any way. That didn't mean Aeron liked the bastard, though.

She's too good for you, Lysander had said. *Do not soil her or I'll bury you and all those you love.*

Aeron hadn't sensed the angel on any level, then or now, and loathed how helpless that suddenly made him feel. Lysander could have sliced his throat and he wouldn't have been able to fight back.

Olivia had been right.

Cronus paled to an unflattering shade of white. "Lysander."

"Hurt her," Lysander said, gaze darting between them, "touch a single hair on her head, and I will ruin you."

"How dare you threaten me!" Cronus bared his teeth in a scowl, color swiftly returning with his fury. "I, who am almighty. I, who am—"

"A god, yes, but you *can* be killed." Lysander laughed without humor. "You know I never make idle threats. You hear the truth in my voice. Harm her, and your ruin will be ensured by my hand."

Silence.

Thick, heavy.

"I will do as I wish," Cronus finally said, "and you will not stop me." Contrary to his words, however, he disappeared.

Aeron struggled to gain his bearings. The god king had never backed down from anything. That he had now, before an angel...that didn't bode well for Aeron, who was far less powerful.

"As for you." Lysander held out his hand and a sword composed solely of fire suddenly appeared. The tip of that sword was pointed at Aeron's throat before he could blink.

His flesh sizzled, even as his eyes narrowed. "Is this about the...soiling?"

"You have no idea how much I long to kill you," the angel said. "Coldly, without mercy."

"But you will not." Otherwise, the angel would have already struck. They were clearly the same in that regard. When it was warranted, warriors acted without hesitation. They didn't pause for conversation.

"No, I will not. Bianka wouldn't like it. Nor would Olivia." The sword lowered, vanished. "I want her back, but she…likes you." Disgust layered his truthful voice. "Therefore, you will live. For now. But I want you to make her miserable, to make her hate this mortal life, and I want you to do it while keeping her safe."

"Agreed."

"So easily?" Those dark eyes widened. "You do not want to keep her?"

Want—yes. In that instant, at the thought of losing her once and for all, he admitted that part of him did indeed want to keep her. At least for a little while. He wanted to help her have fun, wanted to watch her smile and hear her laugh. He wanted to hold her again. Kiss her again. Touch her again. Finally sink inside that sweet little body. But he wouldn't. She would be better off in the heavens, and he could return to the life he'd made for himself. A life without complications. Or worry. Well, except for the coming attempts to end his life.

If she remained on earth, she would be human. Fragile. She would soon wither and die. And he would only be able to watch her. That wasn't something he would ever allow himself to do. Not for anyone. Not even her. *Especially* not her.

Mine, Wrath growled.

"No," he forced himself to say—to Wrath, to Lysander. No more ignoring or accepting the demon's claim. It was far too hazardous. "I don't want to keep her." Unlike the angel, he could lie unflinchingly.

"Yet you do wish to….soil her completely?"

He pressed his lips into a mulish line. They were *not* having that conversation. Already his body reacted at the thought of bedding her, hardening in all the right places.

"I can see that you do. Very well, then." Or maybe they were. "Be with her in...that way, if that's what you both desire. I will not punish you for it, for no one knows better than I that a woman bent on seduction is irresistible. And no one knows Olivia better than I. If she doesn't experience *everything*—" Lysander, the fearsome angel actually blushed "—she won't leave you. So. After the act, make her miserable like I told you. Convince her to leave you without physically harming her, and I'll do my best to convince the Heavenly High Council to spare you *and* your demon friend."

Lysander's best would equal success. No question in Aeron's mind.

Which meant Aeron and Legion would be alive, and Olivia would be forever protected. Olivia, whom Lysander knew better than anyone. That statement roused more emotion than any other—even the one about being spared.

He should be the one to know her best.

"Thank you," he forced himself to say. Funny. The words sounded like they'd been shoved past blades.

Lysander backed away, one step, two. "I'll go now, but not without first imparting information you have long craved, as you cannot protect my ward the way she needs if you do not know what's happening around you." He didn't wait for Aeron's response. But then, Aeron didn't have one. Had he spoken, he might have accidentally sent Lysander on his way rather than urging him to continue. "You've often wondered why Cronus refuses to harm Galen on his own. The reason is simple. Cronus and his wife, Rhea, despise each other. They have taken opposite sides in your war and have vowed not to capture or kill any Lord themselves. Their way of keeping the fight somewhat fair, I suppose. Rhea is, of course, Galen's shield and informant."

So. A god *was* helping the Hunters. And not just any god, but the Titan queen.

Should have known, should have guessed. Aeron had met her once, when the Titans had first defeated the Greeks and overtaken the heavens. They'd summoned him, hoping he would supply information about the Lords. Rhea had looked as old as Cronus once had, with silver hair and wrinkled skin. She had radiated such coldness and hatred, Aeron had been taken aback—though at the time, he'd been more concerned by the news about the changing of the heavenly guard than by one lone goddess's chilly stare.

"One more bit of information I'll leave you with," Lysander said, "for this will aid you more than any other. Cronus and Rhea are like you."

Like him? "What do you mean?"

"They are gods, yes, but they are also Lords. She is possessed by the demon of Strife and he—he is possessed by Greed."

CHAPTER THIRTEEN

OLIVIA GROANED. HER TEMPLES throbbed and her brain felt as if it had been doused in gasoline and set on fire. Still, she blinked open her eyes, determined to find out what was wrong with her; tears instantly formed, burning hotter than her head. And now, as awareness swept through her, she realized her mouth felt as if it had been stuffed with barbed wire and cotton.

She smacked her lips, confused, concerned.

"That's a good girl," Aeron said. Though the words themselves were positive, he sounded harried. Even upset. And loud. Way too loud. "Wake up. Come on, Olivia. You can do it."

"Hush." Through a foggy haze, she managed to focus on him. He crouched beside her, both hands extended. In one, two little pills rested. In the other was a cup of something dark and steamy. "Please."

"I need you to take these and drink this." At least he whispered this time.

As an angel, her senses hadn't been attuned to this plane and she'd never truly smelled what humans cooked or drank or misted all over their bodies. But she could smell now, and that dark liquid was divine. Like bottled power, promising a fresh start, perhaps even a total body healing.

Coffee, she knew humans called it. No wonder they

stood in mile-long lines and were willing to hand over every cent in their pockets for a single shot of it.

"What are those?" she managed to croak out, motioning to the pills with a tilt of her chin. Mistake! The movement sent a wave of dizziness crashing through her.

"Just take them. They'll make you feel better."

That, he hadn't whispered and she covered her ears. "Do you have an inside voice? Could you use it, please?"

He fisted the pills and gently dislodged her hands. "Stop playing. We don't have a lot of time."

"Shh! Livvie's talking, and she's not averse to crushing your vocal cords if you don't keep it down." Why did she like this man again?

"Up. Now."

Gingerly she sat up and rubbed the sleep from her eyes. Her still-burning brain nearly exploded, and she groaned.

Aeron gave her an impatient scowl. No, not impatient. The emotion in that scowl was dark, yes, but whatever he felt was harder. Needier? Had her groan *affected* him?

She wanted to preen. She did fluff her hair—only to realize the curling mass tumbled down her shoulders in countless tangles. Her cheeks flamed as she pulled up the hood of her robe. Or tried to. Frowning, she looked down. Blue tank top, short black skirt.

Why was— Her slut-it-up makeover, she recalled. Oh, yeah. But that didn't explain her headache. Her lashes lifted and she met Aeron's penetrating stare. "Was I injured?"

He snorted. "Hardly. You drank too much, and are now paying the price."

That wasn't the only price she was paying. One terrible memory after another suddenly flooded her. After that first bottle of giggle juice, which clearly hadn't been so giggly for her, she'd experienced a terrible sense of loss. After the second bottle, a crushing sense of depression had come over her, and she had sobbed uncontrollably. Gideon had held her, and she'd cried all over him. About Aeron. *Mortifying.*

Aeron lifted his hand to her mouth. "Take the pills, but don't chew them. Understand? Swallow them whole."

Could she? Just then, they looked as big as oranges. Her arm was shaking as she pinched the pills between her fingers and tossed them into her mouth. Tried to swallow. Failed. Ugh. The taste! Her face scrunched in revulsion.

"Drink. That'll help." He held the steaming cup to her lips and poured.

Olivia gagged. While the liquid smelled wonderful, it tasted like a mix of battery acid and dirt. How ladylike would she appear if she spit everything onto the bed?

"Swallow," he barked as he set the cup aside.

She did. Barely. The pills slid down her throat, rubbing her raw, as did that disgusting coffee. When she stopped shuddering, she glared up at him. "Don't ever do that to me again!"

He rolled his eyes and settled back on his haunches. "You did it to yourself when you allowed Gideon to get you drunk."

How many times was he going to remind her of her folly?

"Now, I need you to get up. *Livvie.* We've got something to do."

Right now she only wanted to go back to bed. In fact, she fell back onto the mattress and gazed up at the ceiling. There was a poster of a woman in a bikini, her skin golden, her cheeks red and her nipples hard. Long blond hair blew in the wind. Olivia frowned, confusion returning. That hadn't been in Aeron's bedroom before.

She scanned the rest of the room, but didn't recognize anything. There was a walnut dresser with a crystal vase that glistened in the light seeping through white curtains, portraits of different-colored flowers on the walls and pretty beige carpet on the floor.

"This doesn't look like your place," she said.

"That's because it isn't."

Her frown intensified. "So...whose is it?"

"Yours. You'll be staying here with Gilly, in this guest room. Do you know Gilly?" He didn't give her a chance to answer. "Both Paris and William have bunked here before, hence the poster. Anyway, you'll be staying until you decide to return to the heavens."

Realization hit. He was so desperate to be done with her, he'd flown her into town while she slept. Oh, that hurt.

"Olivia?"

Fight past your pain. "Yes, I do know Gilly," she said, voice trembling. She knew the girl better than any of the Lords, actually. Gilly was young and sweet and had lived a tragic life until moving here, her parents having hurt her in so many ways.

At one time, Olivia had been responsible for bringing joy into Gilly's life. That's why, when Gilly ran away from home, she'd led the teen to Los Angeles. On a level even Olivia hadn't understood, she'd known Gilly would find salvation there. What she hadn't known then was that that salvation would be Danika and the Lords of the Underworld.

Her Deity worked in mysterious ways.

"But," she continued, "I'm not going back to the heavens."

Determination glinted in Aeron's eyes, but all he said was, "We'll talk about it later. Right now, as I told you, we have a job to do. You've got time for a fast shower, but it'll have to be a multitasking one. I've got questions for you, so we'll talk while you're cleaning up."

He didn't wait for her response, but scooped her up and carted her to the bathroom. There wasn't time to enjoy the ride. He set her down, severing all contact, bent over and worked the knobs in the stall. He had a nice butt, she observed, hugged just right by his jeans. And by "nice" she of course meant "so exquisite her stomach fluttered."

Hot water suddenly burst from the spigot, startling her into averting her eyes. By the time she realized what she'd done—*need more!*—he'd already straightened. How disappointing. Or maybe not. That water promised strength, vitality and...her lids closed to half-mast. Fun, round two? Possibly. Her first shower, and Aeron would be an observer. Hopefully, he wouldn't be able to look without touching.

The morning was suddenly off to a much better start.

Desire trembled through her.

He turned to her and though he was the same height as always, he seemed larger, more menacing. His eyes glowed that bright violet, his tattoos stark, and the pulse in his neck hammered wildly. He wore a black shirt and black pants—both easily removable—and she could see the bulge of weapons at his waist and ankles.

So beautiful, she thought, heart picking up speed. She wanted to stroke him again. Wanted to dance her lips over his entire body. *Especially* between his legs. When she'd gripped him there, she'd felt that bead of moisture.

What would that bead taste like?

He gulped. Had he sensed the direction of her thoughts? "You know how to take a shower, right? You...strip—" his voice caught on the word "—step under the water and lather the soap from head to toe."

"Are you going to join me?" She pulled the tank over her head, letting the material float to the floor. Revealing her body should have made her uncomfortable, she supposed, but she wanted him to see and to yearn, just as she did. Unbearably. Besides, she was confident, aggressive, and now that she knew the kind of pleasure they could give each other, she would do anything, say anything, to receive it. "Or are you just going to watch?"

If that's the case, you can watch me do this. She cupped her breasts the way she suddenly imagined him cupping them, unable to stop herself. Oh, yes. That felt good.

His eyes widened, seemingly glued to her, the air in the bathroom changing. Charging with electricity. "Don't do that." Harsh, choked.

"Why not?"

"Because your Deity should be rewarded for creating those." He shook his head, though his narrowed gaze didn't leave her. "I mean, because I— Damn you. And damn me. I should be punished. The thoughts in my mind..."

Were they like hers? "Aeron," she beseeched.

"I just realized I never kissed them," he uttered in

a rough voice charged with the same electricity that hummed in the air. "And gods, woman, that's a *crime*."

"Kiss them now." *Please.*

"Yes." He leaned toward her, head bowing, pupils expanding—and this time she *knew* it was desire rather than anger.

Her nipples pearled, waiting...expectant...but just before contact, he caught himself, straightened and growled. She released a breath she hadn't known she'd been holding. He'd almost... Sweet Deity. He really had almost kissed her there.

"Aeron." The ache such knowledge evoked... *Do it. Don't stop now.*

"No."

"Why?"

"Because!" He knew what she craved, what she needed, yet denied her still. Just *because*. Bastard! "You do this alone." He passed her and stepped outside the bathroom, tugging the door shut behind him, leaving only a small crack of light.

So close...

She could have screamed, her skin suddenly too tight for her body. Instead, she removed the rest of her clothing and entered the stall. The moment that first cascade hit her, she wished she *had* screamed. Anything to ease some of the pressure building inside her. Pressure the soft caress of water merely provoked.

She tried to blank her mind, but an array of words kept claiming her attention. *Kiss. Breasts. Bodies. Moving. Kneading.* Argh!

"I don't hear you lathering," Aeron snapped.

"Get bent," she snapped back, an expression she'd

heard humans utter to those who irritated them. And oh, did Aeron irritate her.

Kiss. Breasts. Bodies. Moving. Kneading. Sliding. Taking. Her knees almost buckled.

"Olivia." A warning?

"Zip it, demon!" Shaking, she pumped a few squirts of rose-scented soap into her hands and finally began cleaning herself. Even that disturbed her, doubling the pressure. How had he revved her up this quickly and this intensely? *Without* kissing her?

Kiss. Breasts. Bodies. Moving. Kneading. Sliding. Taking. Possessing. Licking. Sucking.

Soon she would break.

Distraction. Yes, that's what she needed. "Did Paris and William use this soap? And yes, you may speak now."

"I don't know and it doesn't matter. You shouldn't be thinking about them. More than that, I'll be asking the questions here. How did you know we'd fail to capture Scarlet yesterday?"

"I told you. I know a lot of things that can help you, but so far you haven't seemed interested in learning them."

"Well, I'm interested now, so start talking. Are there any other demon-possessed immortals in town?"

Confident, she reminded herself. "You think it's that easy?" *Aggressive.* "You make a demand and I deliver?"

A pause. A hesitant, "What do you want?"

Relief! "We'll start with an apology."

"I'm…sorry."

Grudgingly offered, greedily received. "No," she finally answered. "There aren't any other demon-possessed immortals in town."

"All right, then. I'll need you to take me to where this Scarlet is staying."

"Nope, sorry." Olivia twisted and turned under the water's spray, the bubbles running down and off her body. *Kiss. Breasts*— Argh! "I'm not doing anything for you."

"You will."

Another demand, uttered with such determination... determination that should have been annoying rather than sexy. *Pressure mounting...again...* "Why are you so eager for my aid now?"

"I want you to see the kind of life I lead. I want you to see the fights and the blood and the pain. I want you to see that I don't care about anyone other than my friends and Legion, and I will hurt anyone—*anyone*— who threatens them."

Anyone—even Olivia? Even though he'd chosen to help Olivia yesterday and send Legion away? Undoubtedly. Goodbye, pressure. Hello, emptiness. They had been cold, hard words, more vow than threat. He might not want to do so, but he wouldn't stop himself.

"All right," she said. If he wanted to spend the rest of his life showing her those things, she'd let him. And she'd return the favor! She'd show him exactly what he'd be missing if she left. Like the breasts he should be "punished" for ignoring. Like the mouth that wanted so badly to suck on him.

Pressure...worse than before...

Breathe, she needed to breathe. She manipulated the knobs until the water shut off, the air around her instantly cooling her. Only, that failed to temper her needs. Little bumps broke out over her soaked skin, and she groaned. *No more.*

Perhaps she could give *herself* relief, she thought, intrigued. Aeron had used his fingers...and she did have fingers of her own... She licked her lips, heart pounding anew. He wouldn't have to know. She'd turn the water back on, pretend to need more lathering, and—

"Done?" he asked.

She tensed. "I—I just—"

"Olivia, I believe I mentioned that I'm pressed for time."

True. He wouldn't be alive much longer.

The reminder sobered her, chilled her desire as the air hadn't. She'd thought she had accepted his coming death. But nine too-short days? That was hardly enough time to experience everything she wanted to experience with him. Especially as stubborn as he was being.

You'll have to make it enough.

"All right," she said with a sigh, and stepped from the stall. Going with him now would also grant them more time together. And she supposed she wouldn't torture him with what he'd never have, she thought sourly, hating to abandon so sweet a revenge. She *supposed* she'd offer her breasts and her needy mouth—and anything else he wanted—without restraint.

In between the offerings, she could protect Aeron, as she'd vowed to do, should anyone or anything threaten him.

"All right what?" he asked, confused.

There was a toothbrush on the shower ledge, along with a tube of minty paste. Having seen humans perform the task a thousand times, she knew what to do and managed to brush her teeth without incident. "All right, I'll show you where Scarlet lives."

Mouth fresh and clean, she grabbed the brush on the

counter. The bristles caught on several tangles, making her grimace, but she didn't stop until her hair was smooth. Next time, she'd remember to bring her robe with her even if she didn't plan to wear it.

"What changed your mind?" Suspicion dripped from each word.

"Arguing with you is a waste of precious time." True, if somewhat misleading.

"A rational female. Who would have guessed?"

She tossed the brush into the sink. "An insensitive male who won't get a kiss if he keeps that up." Again, true. And shocking. This vengeful side of her...she liked it.

Silence greeted her. Did that mean he craved another kiss? Despite her new affinity for tormenting, she tried not to hope too intently.

"I haven't hurt Legion, you know," she said. "Even when she hurt me."

"Actually, angel, she hurts whenever you're near. Or she used to, when you had wings. But I never did, nor did the other warriors, and we're just as demonic as Legion is. Why was that? Were you doing it on purpose?"

"Of course not. Though it's true demons hate to be around angels, you've managed to humanize yours. At least somewhat." Now. Enough talk about Legion, even though Olivia had been the one to bring her up this time. "Do you want to know how to capture Scarlet or not?"

"Sorry," he muttered. "Yes. I do."

She fought a grin. Another apology. Just as grudging, but just as sweet. "Here's what I know. Because she's possessed by Nightmares, she's weakened during the daylight hours." As she spoke, Olivia studied herself in the foggy mirror. There were bruises under her eyes and her cheeks were a bit hollowed. She only ever wanted Aeron to see her at her best, not like this, but it couldn't be helped. "She's like vampires in that regard. She sleeps during the day, her body too frail even to walk."

Aeron took a moment to absorb what she'd said. "We'll capture her today, then, while she's sleeping."

"Why the urgency? And what do you plan to do with her?"

"Hunters are in town. We've found their hideout, and we now know they're being aided by Rhea, the god queen. We want to ask Scarlet a few questions, prevent her from helping the Hunters."

"I could have told you they were in town, but you refused to listen to me."

"I know, I know, and I'm sorry about that, too. So what do you know about Rhea?"

Yet another apology from him. The man deserved a reward. "I know that she titled herself Mother Earth, and that she's aiding the Hunters," Olivia said, even though all she could think about was giving Aeron that reward. "I know that she was weakened inside Tartarus, all the Titans were, and that's how the Greeks were able to get the demon of Strife to possess her."

"I can't believe I had the information at my fingertips all along," he muttered. "If her demon is taken from her, will she die? Like us?"

"Yes."

"So why is she helping the Hunters?"

"For the same reason Galen is leading them. They plan to kill you, and save themselves, then use your demons for their own gains. In Rhea's case, taking over the heavens and destroying Cronus once and for all."

If he had more questions, and she was sure that he did, he didn't allow himself to ask. Did he plan to go to his other source, whatever—or whoever—it was? And he did have a source. That much was clear. He hadn't been this knowledgeable before. If he did, he wouldn't need Olivia, and she hated the thought of that.

"Thank you for the information," he said gruffly.

"You're welcome." *Push him. Be confident. Aggressive. Show him that he needs you for more than answers.* "I accept payment in the form of kisses. And anyway, I believe I owe you two. You apologized for your insensitivity, after all."

Aeron cleared his throat. "Yes, well, I never said I'd pay you. Or *accept* payment. We, uh, need to leave."

Disappointing man. "Just let me—" Olivia glanced at the towel. If she donned it, she would be giving up, and she wasn't ready to give up.

She bit her lip as Gideon's words drifted through her head. Well, her translation of his words. Men liked naked women. Men had trouble resisting naked women. So no towel, she mused, nearly humming with anticipation.

Pressure...

"Never mind," she said throatily. "I'm ready."

Arching her back to lift her chest—he *did* like her breasts—she gripped the doorknob and flung the door open fully. *Confident.* Aeron was leaning against the wall and had his back to her. His arms were still crossed over his chest. Unfortunately, he was still dressed.

Aggressive. They'd just have to change that.

Naked and wet, she stepped in front of him, her heart drumming harder and faster than when she'd considered touching herself. When he spotted her, his jaw dropped.

His nostrils flared. His pupils practically exploded, the violet irises completely obscured.

Olivia almost moaned. Well, well. Gideon had been right. Aeron did like looking at a naked woman.

Push harder. The ache…she needed him to assuage the ache… "What do you think of my outfit?" she asked, twirling.

Strangling sounds left his mouth.

She might never wear clothes again. "I'm human now and humans always demand payment for their services." Could he hear the excitement and nervousness in her voice? "So, if you want any more information from me—and believe me, I have a lot to offer—you'll have to earn it."

"How?" The word was a snarl—but that snarl wasn't laced with anger. "With those kisses you mentioned?"

"That was the fee five minutes ago, and you refused to pay it. Therefore, my price has now gone up. If you want to know anything else, you'll have to warm me with your body. I'm cold." *I'm so hot, I'm on fire.*

He gulped. Straightened. His gaze traveled the length of her, lingering on her breasts, between her thighs. His breathing became choppy, shallow. "Holy hell. Dying. I'm dying."

So am I. "Aeron." *Give me. Take me.*

"There…there isn't time."

"Make time," she said, and closed the remaining distance between them. *Must…touch…*

He could have scooted her out of the way, and she wouldn't have been able to stop him, but he didn't. His big hands settled on her waist, his fingers digging deep. Finally!

"I shouldn't," he said. "Told myself I wouldn't, even though he won't—"

"He?" *More.* "Who won't what?"

At first, he gave no response, made no reply. "My... demon," he finally said in a hard tone, his fingers spreading to cover more ground. From lower back to buttocks, he touched her. Burned her. "He won't...hurt you. For once, I don't have to worry."

"He," not "it"? What had changed between the two beings?

Who cared? *Progress!* "So why shouldn't you be with me?" If he'd hoped to dissuade her from this path, he never should have introduced her to passion. His mistake, and one she would take total advantage of. "There aren't any obstacles."

"Obstacles..." He floundered on the word, his gaze glued to her lips. "We are..."

She flattened her palms on his chest, unwilling to listen to him rattle off an entire list of problems. As he'd probably planned. His heart was drumming harder and faster than hers. A good sign. Still. Wanting it even harder, even faster, she arched her lower body into his and moaned. *Oh, yes.*

"You like getting answers, don't you, Aeron? That's important to you? For the good of you and your loved ones. Just *pay me.*"

He licked his lips, leaving a glistening sheen of moisture. One taste, that's all she needed.... "Who would have thought an angel would be such a manipulator?" he asked huskily.

"I'm fallen," she reminded him. Yet again. "Now, enough talking. More paying."

"Yes..."

He leaned down just as she rose on her tiptoes. Their lips smashed together, and at first, he didn't respond. She had to force her tongue past his clenched teeth, but the moment it touched his, he groaned and took over.

Oh, did he take over. His arms banded around her waist and hefted her up. She had to wind her legs around him and lock her ankles, otherwise she would have simply dangled there. The new position was delicious, exactly what she'd needed, placing her aching core at the tip of his hard, thick erection. An erection peeking past the waist of his pants.

Stupid pants.

His hair, cut so close to his scalp, tickled her palms as she rubbed them up and down. One of his hands cupped the base of her neck and angled her head for deeper contact. Contact she felt through every inch of skin, every cell rushing through her veins, every bone screaming for more.

"You have on too many clothes," she told him between deep breaths.

"Not enough," he shot back. His lips settled on her collarbone and sucked. Lower still. He licked a nipple, finally making good on his promise to kiss her there, and she moaned. His other hand moved to her neglected breast and massaged. "I don't think a shield of armor would protect me from your appeal."

Such a sweet admission.

"We should slow down."

What? No! "Speed up." She twisted his ear, earning a growl.

Again he sucked on her other nipple, and the sting made her gasp—then she moaned as he licked where he'd nibbled. She arched into him, rubbing just the way she liked.

"I'm going to get you all wet."

"And that's a bad thing?" he asked.

Bad thing, bad thing. The words were an echo in her brain, and she remembered how she'd tried to lick his penis the last time they'd kissed like this, but he hadn't let her. Had thought her too pure.

She dropped her legs, feet hitting soft carpet.

He frowned. "What are you—"

She sank to her knees, tugging at his pants until his shaft broke free. Thick, long, so magnificently hard.

"Olivia…" A moan, as if she tortured him. "You shouldn't."

Her mouth watered as she pressed her cheek into the satin-smooth flesh. Hot, imprinting. His fingers tangled in her hair. She pulled back only slightly, opened wide, then sucked him in. His girth stretched her jaw, an uncomfortable fit, but the salty-sweet taste of him thrilled her.

"I was wrong. You should," he croaked out. "You really should."

Up and down she rode him with her mouth, hands playing with his heavy sac. She enjoyed him, enjoyed doing this, destroying his reluctance, spurring him into enthusiastic abandon. But he didn't let her take him all the way. All too soon, he gripped her shoulders and yanked her up.

"No more." Sweat glistened on his face as he swung her around and crowded her against the wall. Without a word, he next dropped to *his* knees. His strong hands parted her legs, and then he was there, licking at her, sucking on her, *devouring* her.

She needed an anchor, but couldn't find one as her hands clawed up and down the wall behind her. As her head thrashed from side to side. As her hair tickled her back. *Everything* was a stimulant. And she was close... so close...just needed...

He stormed to his feet, panting, lapping at the moisture she'd left on his face, eyes at half-mast, liquid. "Want to take you...can't take you...taste so good... need more...can't have more..."

More. Yes. "Aeron."

He shook his head, all hint of his resistance fading— only to be replaced by determination. He reached between their bodies and stroked his erection. The other hand gripped her waist. "Can't...can't...have to remember..."

"What? Remember what? Are you going to...are we going to..." *Please, please, please.*

"Can't." He stilled. Their raspy pants were the only sound in the room, tangling together wildly, just as she wanted to be with him. "Can't. We're going to—" Another growl. He tore his hand away from her to scrub down his face. As that hand descended, revealing his features, she saw the change in them. From determined to enraged. "Most humans have to walk around unfulfilled. If you want to be a human, you should know how that feels."

Unfulfilled? She'd rather die. "Teach me next time. Please, Aeron." Too badly did she need him now. *"Please."* She arched her hips, back and forth, this time fitting her moist core against the hot steel of his freed shaft, a shaft she'd tasted. Down she slid, up, down again. Oh, Deity. The pleasure...incomparable. Searing, thrilling...forbidden.

Must have been the same for him because once more he shot into action. He cupped her bottom and slammed her into that shaft. Over and over, again and again. Not once did he penetrate her, but that didn't matter to her weeping body. What he was doing was too good, electrifying, and soon they were both groaning, panting more heavily, trembling.

Even their kiss spun out of control, their tongues dueling, rolling together, their teeth banging, scraping. Her nails clawed at him, at his hidden wings—*too wild?* Gideon had said that Aeron needed a wild woman, but this might be too much, too fast for her warrior and she didn't want him pulling away.

Though it nearly cost her the last remnants of her sanity, Olivia tempered her touch, easing her nails out of his back, away from those sensitive slits.

"What are you doing?" he snapped.

"Enjoying you," she replied. "Or I was, until you opened your mouth."

He frowned, pulled his face away from hers so that he could peer into her eyes. "Well, start enjoying again."

"I'd love to." She bit her bottom lip and arched into him. "But I want your penis inside me first."

A strangling sound left him.

Again she arched. The tip of his shaft rubbed her clitoris, and she gasped. He hissed. So good. *Soooo* good. Her head fell back, and her wet hair swung, once more tickling her skin. So close, she thought. So close to that pinnacle of pleasure he'd propelled her to the last time they'd kissed like this. The pinnacle that would ease the pressure still building inside her, still torturing her.

"Aeron, Aeron. Just a little more," she rasped, "and I can—"

"No. No!" He released her, suddenly and without warning, and she fell off him. She hit the ground and lost her breath. That didn't dull her passion. Or ease her aches. "Can't."

He wiped his shaky hand over his mouth, as if washing away the taste of her, briefly hiding the lines of tension banked there. Then he was refastening his pants with trembling fingers.

"No climaxing," he said in that harsh tone she so despised. Angry, rather than desire-filled.

"I—I don't understand."

His narrowing gaze settled on her, his expression like granite. "I told you. Humans often experience unrequited yearnings. You want to be a human so badly, you can endure them, as well. Now get dressed. Like I also told you, we have somewhere to be."

CHAPTER FOURTEEN

STRIDER HIT THE GROUND as a bullet whizzed past his shoulder.

"Sorry," Gwen muttered with a grimace. Her red hair was pulled back in a ponytail and her silver-gold eyes were gleaming. "I'm having trouble channeling my dark side—" her Harpy "—so I thought I'd better carry a gun."

A gun that she'd never worked with before. A Dead Hunter special he'd augmented himself.

Damn, that'd been close. Nearly taken out by friendly fire. And then things really would have gotten bad. Even though she wouldn't have meant to hit him, his demon would have seen it as a challenge. Gwen would have won, and he would've been writhing on the ground for days, lost to the agony.

As he'd lost a challenge a few weeks ago to Hunters—because Gwen and Sabin had let her father escape, something he was still trying to forgive them for—the consequences of failure were vivid in his mind, and he wasn't eager to repeat the experience.

"Just take your finger off the trigger," he told her. "We don't know where the Hunters ran off to and hid, and they don't know where we are. Gunshots could give away our location."

"Done."

Shaking his head, Strider straightened. Glanced around. Lush, thick trees surrounded him and most of the others who'd been at the temple with him—and who, like him, had been whisked to…wherever the hell they were. Close to water, like before, that much he knew. He could hear the lull of the sea a few yards away, and golden sand sparkled at his feet and clung to his skin.

Amun and Maddox were currently scouting for signs of the enemy.

Evidently the Unspoken Ones' idea of a "gift" had been to whisk them and sixteen armed Hunters to a mysterious location. They'd all been here twenty-four hours, had endured one full-on shoot-out, one scramble to safety to figure things out, and now this. Waiting. Searching. It was like the boxing matches Strider liked to watch on TV: the Lords in one corner, the Hunters in the other. So when was the freaking starting bell going to ring?

Soon, if he had his way.

His phone beeped, drawing his attention and signaling success. In one area at least.

"Yes!" he said, punching a tree trunk in excitement. "My text finally went through to Lucien." He'd been trying to contact his friends in Buda for most of the twenty-four hours with no luck. Either the powerful creatures had refused to let him make contact or cell towers were few and far between out here. His money was on the creatures. He needed Lucien to flash them more weapons and ammo. No way they'd leave this place until every Hunter was captured. Or dead. He wasn't picky.

Now that the text had gone through, communication

lines open, did that mean the Unspoken Ones were taking their hands out of the battle?

Only a few seconds later, his phone beeped again. He raised the screen to read Lucien's reply. Tried to flash to you. Something's blocking me.

Damn. Hands still in, just not as restricting.

He relayed the bad news to the others, scattered around him, and they groaned.

"We'll be fine," Sabin said. "If nothing else, Gwen can rip through them like a knife through silk."

Strider knew the statement wasn't a besotted husband's exaggerated boast, but the truth. When her dark side overtook her, Gwen could immobilize an immortal army on her own. Humans would be child's play.

"Only if my Harpy decides to show," she grumbled. "Wait. No *only* about it. She will. I'll make her." When it came to Sabin, she'd do anything to protect him. A fact everyone in this little camp knew intimately, having been shredded by her Harpy's claws a time or two during training.

Don't worry, he typed, returning his attention to the phone. We've got this.

Good news is, Galen's here in Buda and not among the group.

Surprising, since he'd seen Galen in that vision. You guys good to go?

We'll be fine. But I should warn you, that bastard somehow got his hands on the Cloak. He could be in the fortress, and we'd never know it.

Shit! This just got worse and worse. Galen had an artifact, and a powerful one at that. Soon as this was over, Strider would do whatever was necessary to steal it. Meanwhile, it was his turn to drop a bombshell. Looks like Hope's been a busy boy. I should warn you that Galen managed to merge the demon of Distrust with one of his soldiers. A female. We think he'll be out for blood now.

At first, Lucien didn't reply. Was probably battling shock as Strider and the others had. Distrust, the only thing left of Baden, was now in enemy hands.

Did Galen even need Pandora's box anymore? he wondered now. With the box, he could gather all the demons at once, without having to search for them later. So yeah, probably.

Finally, a new text came in. This is bad. Really bad. And I think it's only going to get worse. Aeron's called a meeting. Found something out. More from me when I know what that something is. Meanwhile, be careful.

You, too.

A twig snapped. Everyone stiffened, half immediately pointing their weapons in the direction of the noise and half aiming in the opposite direction, just in case. Amun and Maddox strode through the bush, and everyone relaxed. Amun was dragging a man, a human, behind him. Expression grim, he tossed the motionless body in the center of the camp.

As Maddox tied the man up, Amun signed what they'd learned.

Strider had always admired Amun's ability to absorb memories. Sure, it left him with a new voice in his head each time he did so, but that seemed like a small price to pay for knowing the thoughts of everyone around you. As he'd just taken a new crop of memories, though, Strider knew it would be a long time before he heard his friend speak again.

"Hunters set up camp about a mile north of us, and

this guy was on guard duty. Their plan is to wait for us to attack them on their turf, where they can more easily injure us while remaining barricaded themselves," Sabin said, interpreting. Then he laughed without humor. "We all saw Distrust merge with that female. They won't just try to injure us. They'll be out for our heads."

"Gets better," Strider said, pocketing his phone. "Galen's back in Buda, and he has the Cloak of Invisibility."

For several prolonged seconds, silence dominated their circle. Then he felt the vibrations of their anger as they considered the consequences. *Then* he heard their muttered curses.

"Obviously we can't stay here much longer, but just as obviously, we can't let these men go. Maddox can lead us to their camp, and we'll fight them on their turf just like they wanted." Sabin stood, hands clenched into fists. "Only, they won't like the results. We show no mercy. Take no prisoners."

Amid murmurs of agreement, Strider and the others pushed to their feet. Knives were palmed by Kane and Reyes. Guns were clutched by Gwen and himself. No, no, no. He crossed the small distance to stand in front of her and plucked the modified Sig Sauer from her fingers.

"I'll take that," he said.

"Fine." She smiled sheepishly, then waved her clawed fingertips. "I'll do better without it, anyway."

"We all will."

Sabin hugged her tight. "I'll help you summon your Harpy after Maddox gives us some direction. Maddox?"

Maddox walked to the center of the group and knelt in the sand. He drew a misshapen circle. "We're on an-

other island. We're here, and they're here." His finger-
tip danced through the golden grains. "The Unspoken
Ones must have given them extra fortifications, because
I found steel traps here, here and here."

Amun signed.

Again, Sabin translated for Maddox and Reyes, who
hadn't spent the last few thousand years with the silent
warrior. "Sleepy there," he said, pointing to the motionless Hunter, "was patrolling the perimeter of their
camp with three others."

"If we split up, we can surround them and close
in, a different warrior taking out each of the remaining guards while giving the others no room to run and
hide." Strider would love nothing more than to pick
them off himself, one by one, but there wasn't time.

"Excellent," Sabin said with a nod. He outlined who
was to go where. "I don't care if you have to scoot on
your stomach. Don't let them see you. They're expecting
us, as Sabin said, so the greater a surprise we manage to
be, the better our chances of success. And once you spy
their camp, don't move until you hear my signal. I want
to let my demon at them before we attack." Doubt could
turn even the bravest of warriors into thumb-sucking
babies. "Move as swiftly as you can. Let's reach them
before they realize we've already eliminated one of their
own. If they haven't already."

Grinning, Strider saluted and was off. For the most
part, he loved this part of his life. Loved the challenge
of battle, loved the rush of victory. Adrenaline always
pumped through his veins, driving him faster, making him stronger. Like now. He dodged tree limbs and
jumped over stones, all the while merging with the
shadows.

Need a triumph, his demon whined.

Some Lords could hear their demons clearly; some simply felt their other half's desires. Strider only heard his before and after a battle. Perhaps that was because that was when Defeat was the strongest—and the most worried.

I'll get you one. Promise.

Sure?

What are you, Doubt? Yeah, I'm sure.

Every so often, the sun would peek through the canopy of treetops and spill onto the ground like a spotlight. Out of habit, he spun until he once again met with shadows. Sadly, he wasn't one of the ones to run into a guard. Finally, though, he reached his destination and slowed. He was careful to avoid anything that might crunch beneath his boots. Then, hearing the murmur of unfamiliar voices, he lay down as ordered and inched his way to a bush bordering the Hunter camp.

All he saw was a wall of rocks, but there were gaps between several of those rocks, gun barrels peeking from them. Then he heard the whispers.

"Rick hasn't returned yet."

"He's only five minutes late."

"Maybe he got lost."

"Please. The Lords of the Underworld are out there. Rick's already dead."

"Yeah, you're right. I know you are. They have no morals, no conscience, so killing an innocent man wouldn't faze them. But damn, I really liked him."

Innocent? Please.

"We shouldn't wait for them to come to us. *We* should attack *them.* Obviously we've got a god or two on our side. Our hideout appeared out of nowhere. Our guns and traps, too. Why else would we have been brought here with the Lords if not to finally destroy them?"

Good question. These Hunters were supposed to be a gift, yet they'd been armed and sheltered. Or maybe the battle was the gift. Not to the Lords, but to the Unspoken Ones. Maybe they enjoyed watching bloodshed.

One man must have stood, because suddenly Strider could see the top of his head. "Shut your fucking mouths, all of you. We're dealing with demons, the plague of our lives. We have to stay on alert."

Fanatics, Strider thought with disgust. They wanted someone to blame for their troubles. Understandable, he supposed, but wrong. Humans had free will. More often than not, that free will was the source of their troubles. They decided what they would eat, how much they would drink and who they would sleep with. They decided whether or not to do drugs or get in a car destined to crash.

"What if—what if they're too strong and we die out here?"

"They want revenge for what we did to Lies, I know it. They're going to cut off our hands like we cut off his."

Strider fought a grin. Doubt was doing his job. Any second now and Sabin would—

Sabin's whistle echoed.

Ding, ding. And there it was at last, the starting bell. Strider popped to his feet, the muzzles of both his guns outstretched. He aimed both at those gaps between the rocks and squeezed the triggers simultaneously. *Pop, pop.*

Screams erupted.

From the corner of his eye, he saw Reyes dart from

behind a tree trunk, sprint forward and climb the wall, tossing a knife along the way. There was another scream. Maddox sprinted forward as well, jumping over the wall with a single leap, gunfire ringing out. Only, Maddox hadn't carried a gun, Strider realized, stomach tightening. He was the target, using his body as a distraction.

Sabin quickly joined him and Kane attempted to do the same—until a bullet somehow ricocheted off a rock and embedded in his shoulder. Figured. Kane cursed loud and long as Strider rounded the wall, disabling as many guns as he could through the holes.

Then a gust of lemon-scented wind ruffled Strider's hair, and he stilled. Gwen, he thought. And sure enough, he spotted the blur of her hair as she darted up the wall and fell inside the circle. Sabin had clearly made good on his promise. Strider followed on her heels, remaining on the edge of the highest ledge, weapon trained, just in case.

He needn't have bothered. The Harpy squawked, claws raking, sharpened teeth chomping. Men screamed and collapsed. A few tried to run, to scramble over the rocks. They didn't get far. As fast as the tiny wings on her back allowed her to move, she easily caught them and snapped their necks.

And just like that, the enemy was conquered.

Yes. Yes! Defeat sang inside his head.

Too easy, he thought. He hadn't even worked up a sweat. Not that he was complaining. Much. The harder the victory was to achieve, the better the rush afterward. Occasionally, if the victory was sweet enough, his demon writhed in *pleasure* for days. Hot damn, that was better than sex. Better than anything, really. He'd only experienced such a thing twice, but he craved the next time like a drug.

Reyes and Maddox were bleeding profusely as they meandered through the masses, kicking away weapons. A few feet away, outside the enclosure, Strider heard the crunch of rocks and the snap of a twig. He turned, gun moving with him. He relaxed when he saw Kane settle against a tree trunk, trying to dig the bullet out of his shoulder. Disaster had had to mend himself from similar catastrophes a thousand times before, so he knew how to go about it.

Beside him was Amun, prone and writhing. The big guy must not ever have joined the fray. He'd clearly remained at the sidelines, the memories he'd stolen from that Hunter already overtaking him, demanding his attention.

"Gwen," Sabin called.

Once again, Strider's attention veered. A panting Gwen was pressed against the rocks. Blood coated her face and hands. All of the warriors had stepped away from her. All but Sabin. He was the only one capable of calming her down when her dark side overtook her.

As Sabin approached her, Strider joined the others in weaving through the fallen humans. Most were lifeless, silent. A few were moaning. He quickly aimed and fired, ending their misery. Except for one. That one, he crouched beside. There was something about the man... No, kid. Something about the kid that caused him to pause. And with the pause, reluctant compassion sparked to life.

That kid looked up at him through glazed eyes, realized who he was and scowled. "Bastard," he spat, blood spraying from his mouth. "Don't think this is the end. I'll rise from the grave if necessary. I'll end you."

Such hatred seemed wrong in someone so young. The boy could be no more than twenty years old and had dark hair and eyes, reminding him of Reyes when they'd lived in the heavens. There were cuts all over his face and holes in his left shoulder and stomach, both of which were gushing blood. They'd decided to kill these Hunters, decided not to take any prisoners, but Strider suddenly found himself regretting that choice.

Which made no sense. If the kid had been able, he would have gutted Strider without hesitation. Still. His strength in the face of defeat was humbling.

With a sigh, Strider removed his T-shirt, ripped the fabric into two pieces and used the first to bind the kid's shoulder.

"What the hell are you doing?" he ground out.

"Saving your life."

"When you just tried to end it? No. Hell, no. I don't want to be saved by a demon." He tried to scoot away, but was too weak and shaky to get more than a few inches.

"Too bad." Strider used the other strip to apply pressure to his stomach. "I never give Hunters what they want."

There was a tense pause. Then a weak, "This won't change anything."

"Good. I didn't want you to get the wrong idea."

Finally the kid gave up and just lay there as Strider bandaged him. Which was a good thing. The demon had begun to view their interaction as a challenge. "So what'd we do to you to earn your eternal hate?"

Eyelids that had been drifting closed snapped open. "As if you don't know," was the snarled reply.

Strider rolled his eyes. "Whatever, dude. Just so you know, we can't be everywhere at once, and we have enough trouble with our own lives. There's no way we could have done whatever it is you think we've done to those you love."

"My name isn't dude, asshole."

Nice of him to ignore everything else Strider had said. "Well, I thought it was better than calling you Holes."

"Go to hell."

"Been there, done that."

The kid ran his tongue over his teeth. "Fine. You want to know the name of the man who will one day destroy you? It's Dominic. My name is Dominic."

"Actually, I don't recall asking what your name is. I don't really care," Strider said, and it was true. "Now that I've saved your sorry ass, you can deliver a message for me. Tell Galen we know about the girl. The demon-possessed girl, if you need more clarification."

Already pale, Dominic became chalk-white. "I don't know...what you're talking...about." Blood loss had him gasping.

Yeah. Right.

Multiple shadows suddenly fell over the prone human, and Strider glanced up. Most of the others had closed in and were surrounding them. Not a single one complained about his disobedience. Compassion clouded their features the same way it must have clouded his.

He returned his attention to the boy. "And do yourself a favor," he said, finishing the patch job. "When you get back to wherever your hidey-hole is, take a good long look at your leader. I know those wings of his make it seem like he's the angel he claims to be. But guess what? He's just like us—demon-possessed. Only his demon happens to be Hope. Why do you think you feel so optimistic about the future every time you're in his presence? Why do you think you experience crushing disappointment every time you leave him? That's what he does, you know? The source of his strength. Building people up and tearing them down."

"No. No...wrong..." Dominic's eyelids drifted closed. This time, they didn't open. There were lines of strain and pain branching from his eyes and mouth now, and hollows were already forming in his cheeks. He needed a transfusion, but with no medical supplies here, such a thing was impossible.

"Text Lucien and tell him to try flashing here again, wherever here is." Strider's hand clenched. He didn't want this jerk to die. Not after all his hard work.

There was a shuffle of clothing as Gwen did as he'd asked. A few seconds later, she said, "Yes! He made it. He's at the temple and is going to follow our spiritual threads to reach us."

Lucien had been all over the world and could flash anywhere he desired. But he didn't know offhand exactly where someone he was tracking went. He had to follow the trails of energy they left behind in the spiritual plane.

Strider cupped the human's jaw and shook. "Open your eyes, Dominic."

A moment passed. Nothing. He shook again. Dominic moaned.

"Open. Your. Eyes." He made sure to inject enough

fury and menace into his tone to wake even the dead. Dominic had threatened to rise from the grave. No time like the present to prove he meant it.

The kid's eyelids finally cracked open. "What d'you want?" was the groggy reply. His breathing was more labored, coming in short bursts.

"Soon as he gets here, one of our men will be taking you to a hospital. You're going to live. And you're going to deliver that message I gave you. Oh, yeah. You want to know the name of the guy who just saved you? It's Strider. I'd also consider it a personal favor if you let Galen know I'm coming for him." And like Galen, Strider wouldn't show any mercy. Galen had made a mistake pairing Distrust with one of his soldiers, because now, *Strider* could kill *Galen*. And he could bind Hope with someone of *his* choosing.

Defeat laughed with glee. *Game on.*

Yes, Strider thought grimly. Game on.

CHAPTER FIFTEEN

AERON SOARED THROUGH the air, Olivia clutched in his arms. She had her own arms splayed, the wind whipping her hair in every direction. Every few seconds, she would sigh breathily and he would imagine her smiling. She had to miss flying.

"Having fun?" he couldn't help but ask.

She didn't reply.

She'd been silent since leaving Gilly's apartment. Clearly, she was irritated with him. He'd left her needy, after all, taking her to the edge of pleasure and then stopping before she could fall. But then, he was a *fool*. Why else would he have promised to show her the harsh realities of his life? Sooner rather than later? Something he couldn't do if he pleasured her every time she smiled at him. And sweetly begged him. And touched him.

Damned fool.

Her anger upset him, he would be lying if he said otherwise, but encouraging it was best. For both of them. When she surrendered, Legion would be able to return. Lysander would ensure Aeron and Legion were pardoned—or try to. Aeron hadn't missed the implication. Still. It would have been nice to have Olivia... No. *No.* Nothing else mattered. Not Olivia, and not building some kind of life with her.

The thought alone was paradoxical. If she stayed, he would have no life. Only a handful of days.

Suddenly he could hear... His brow furrowed in confusion.... Was Wrath...whimpering? He listened more intently. Dear gods, the demon *was*. Because they couldn't have Olivia?

They were both fools, then.

When they reached the fortress, he landed on the front steps and set her on her feet, the main door looming just ahead. No way he'd fly her through his bedroom again. Obviously, he couldn't have a bed and Olivia in the same vicinity without losing all common sense.

"Come on." He grabbed her hand and dragged her into the foyer. Once again, she was wearing her long white robe. A robe that bagged on her, hiding all those sinful curves. He'd flown to the fortress and retrieved the garment before flying back to her and bringing her here. A round trip that had been necessary for his own survival.

The woman was danger incarnate. When she'd stepped from that shower, damp and naked and clearly eager for him, he'd nearly died of pleasure, right then, right there. And the only thing he would have been sorry about had he died was that he wouldn't be able to see her like that again.

Her breasts were small but firm and her nipples that luscious plum. Her skin was like a fluffy cloud mixed with cream and sprinkled with ambrosia. And all that chocolate hair curling to her waist...*better for me to fist it,* he thought.

Which he'd almost done, but somehow hadn't. She'd moaned and writhed and begged him for more. Hell, *Wrath* had moaned and writhed and begged him for more. And he'd come so close to giving in to both of them. But then Olivia had gentled her kiss and he'd been disappointed and angry, and that volatile combination had thankfully snapped him into focus.

Yet, it shouldn't have been disappointment *or* anger that he'd felt. He should have been overjoyed, but he'd found himself wondering if her desire for him had waned. If she wanted someone else instead. Someone like Paris or William, both of whom she'd mentioned while showering, hands caressing her own body, lingering. With the thought, he'd once again yearned to have her completely out of control, because of *him,* sinking those nails into his back, scraping those teeth along his neck.

What was wrong with him?

"Did you hear that?" Olivia asked, tugging him from his dark and sensual musings. She slid her hand from his—*Mine,* Wrath growled, no longer crying but once again claiming—and stopped.

He'd told himself he'd protest these declarations from now on, but he couldn't force himself to do so. *Fool.* "Hear what?" He, too, stopped and listened. Aside from his demon's continued brooding, only silence greeted him. Frowning, Aeron faced her. As always when he looked at her, his heart rate quickened. "I hear nothing."

"But the voice…" She spun in a circle, gaze roving the foyer. "It's telling me to cup your balls with one hand and fist your cock with the other."

Was it possible she heard his demon and— Wait. *What?* "A voice is telling you to molest me?" Not Wrath, then. The demon had mentioned nothing that specific. Unfortunately.

"Yes."

"Is this an attempt to seduce me?" Tricky, delicious female, who wore scanty clothes, asked him naughty questions and emerged from the bathroom stark naked. "Is this supposed to—"

"No! I don't like this!" she interrupted. "I'm hearing the words, thinking them, but they don't belong to me. I know that doesn't make any sense, but I don't know how else to describe it."

Behind him, footsteps resounded. He turned. Torin was halfway down the stairs, taking them two at a time. Today he wore a black turtleneck, black gloves and pants that dragged the ground so that even if he sat down and his socks fell below his ankles, not an inch of his skin would show.

"Delicious," Aeron heard Olivia murmur. "I could eat you up."

"You have to stop saying things like that, Olivia." Aeron flicked her a glance—only to still, grind his teeth and curse under his breath. She wasn't peering at him as he'd expected; she was peering at Torin as if he was a piece of meat and she was starving.

Mine, Wrath warned.

Aeron popped his jaw in sudden irritation—with Torin. It wasn't that he cared who Olivia desired. It was just that she'd given up immortality for *him,* wanted *him* to provide her fun, wanted to welcome *him* inside her body; she shouldn't be so fickle.

"Uh, excuse me?" A confused Torin stopped at the bottom of the staircase.

Aeron studied his friend, trying to see him as Olivia must. Beyond that startling contrast of white hair and black eyebrows, that smooth, naturally tanned—and uninked—skin, and okay, okay, maybe those piercing green eyes, he wasn't *that* attractive. What's more, he was an inch shorter than Aeron and not as bulky.

"Ignore me," Olivia beseeched, horror drifting from her. "Please. I don't know what's come over me."

Torin, it seemed, was trying not to smile. "Glad you're not scared of me anymore."

Aeron wished he could say the same. "Let's get the meeting started." Surely that snapping, snarling tone wasn't his.

"Too late, I'm afraid." Torin leaned one shoulder against the banister, the picture of domesticated male. Except for the wicked gleam in his eyes. "Everyone's left."

"What!"

"You're not the only one with big news. Lucien flashed to Rome after Sabin and the others learned that Galen succeeded in binding Distrust to one of his soldiers. A female."

Aeron plowed a hand over his razored hair. Distrust, *Baden's* Distrust, was now inside a Hunter? He'd known Galen hoped to do such a thing, but still the knowledge stunned him. Unacceptable!

Punish, Wrath agreed.

No images flashed in his mind, but Aeron wasn't surprised. He was becoming used to his demon's more vocal presence. "Something will have to be done about that, but we'll have to tread carefully. Today I learned that Rhea, Cronus's wife, is aiding the Hunters."

Torin absorbed the words and paled. "You're kidding, right?"

"I wish."

Olivia clasped Aeron's hand, twining their fingers. Wrath's anger drained, leaving Aeron with a cuddly kitten. He favored the rage. "If there's anything I can do to help, please let me know," she said. "I won't even make you pay for it."

Her attempt to comfort him was…comforting. Damn it! Now he was like Wrath. Cuddly. And he didn't like it. But he liked her. More than he should have. He was used to bottling up his emotions, ignoring them so he could focus on what needed to be done, but she refused to accept anything but his complete capitulation.

Maybe that was why—realization hit him hard. Shit. It was. That's why he'd always preferred gentle women. Well, not preferred, but feared the other, stronger females. Gentle women didn't threaten to break the bottle that contained all those churning emotions. Stronger women could smash that bottle to pieces, forcing him to feel.

"What?" Torin asked, head tilting to the side.

"Nothing," he lied. No way he'd admit to such a weakness. "So look. Back to the Hunters. Rhea is hiding them from us while they're in town."

Torin's lips pulled back from his teeth. "First we learn Galen's leading the Hunters, and now a Titan is helping them, too. If there are more surprises, I don't want to know."

"Actually, Cronus—"

"Just visited me," Torin interjected, "but he conveniently didn't mention any of this. He just commanded us to get our asses in gear and find Scarlet, which is where the others are. Looking for her. He threatened us with the usual death and destruction if we failed to find her. Today."

The god king was certainly making the rounds, first visiting Aeron, then Torin. But why would finding Scarlet be so important to *him?* To ensure Rhea didn't get to her first?

Olivia's fingers squeezed his as she focused on Torin. "Looks like I can help, after all. Aeron wants me to show you where she's staying, and I agreed to do so."

Torin studied her closely. "Yeah, Cameo mentioned something about you knowing the girl."

When he'd said Cameo's name, his expression had softened. Interesting. Was it true, as some of the warriors suspected, that those two were involved? They couldn't touch one another, so, if they were lovers, they would've had to find other ways to please each other.

Aeron couldn't imagine being unable to touch and taste Olivia. He couldn't—focus, clearly.

"Tell him," he said to Olivia, forcing himself back on track.

She squared her shoulders and spouted off the location. That quick, that easy. If only.

"I'll text everyone," Torin said, relief dripping from the words. He didn't ask how Olivia knew, nor did he accuse her of trying to trick him. Even without that ring of truth in her voice, he would have trusted Aeron's judgment.

"No. Don't tell them where she is," Aeron said. He flicked a glance to the nearest window. The curtains were drawn, but there was a tiny sliver of open space between the two panels, allowing the barest hint of sunlight to seep inside. Darkness wouldn't fall for hours yet, which meant Scarlet was sleeping. "Tell them to come home. Olivia and I will take care of Nightmares. With Hunters in Buda and in possession of an artifact, I want as many warriors as possible here at all times."

"Done. Any way I can convince you to take a warrior or two with you, though? Backup's a great thing to have."

"Won't need any. She'll be sleeping until nightfall and no trouble. Right, Olivia?"

The angel nodded reluctantly. She clearly didn't like sharing information with anyone but him, but was doing so. For Aeron. Perhaps he could forgive her for her earlier fickleness.

Wrath went silent, for once not objecting to the thought of forgiveness—a concept that usually confused the demon.

"Oh, and I know you didn't want any more surprises tossed your way, but there's one more thing I've got to tell you about your buddy Cronus," Aeron said. "Turns out we have more in common than our mutual dislike of Galen."

Torin frowned. "I don't understand."

Only merciful way to do this was to say it quick. "He's possessed by the demon of Greed."

First, Torin's mouth fell open. Then his eyes widened. Then he stumbled back, hit the bottom step and nearly fell. "The god king is demon-possessed? How can you—"

"Lysander paid me a visit." Like him, Torin now knew angels couldn't lie. "Cronus was locked in Tartarus at the time we opened the box, so it makes sense."

"Wow. Just wow."

"Throw in an *oh, shit* and you've got my initial reaction."

"When did Lysander visit you?" Olivia asked. "What else did he say? Did he mention me? I know he mentioned me." Before Aeron could respond, she added, "And do you want to have sex before we leave?" She shook her head, as if she couldn't be sure she'd heard herself correctly. "Did I just ask you if you wanted to have sex with me?"

She had, and his body had reacted accordingly. He nodded because he didn't trust himself to speak.

The horror he'd heard in her voice a little while ago now flooded her features. "But I didn't say it. I mean, I did say it, and I want to do it, but that wasn't me. The voice…"

Torin's grin was all cat and cream. "So are you talking to Aeron or to me?"

"To me," Aeron barked, even as she said, "To you, of course."

"What?" Aeron and Wrath shouted in unison.

Mine!

Torin laughed, the bastard. "Wish I could, angel, but I really would kill you with my pleasure."

Her cheeks flushed, giving her skin a luminous glow.

Aeron's teeth did that grinding thing again. "You better tell that voice of yours to shut the hell up." Was someone speaking through her? Lysander certainly had the power to do so, but the warrior angel wouldn't say those kinds of things. Sabin, too, could do it, but he wasn't here.

Who did that leave? Cronus? Rhea? But why would it be either of them?

Olivia's shoulders straightened, her chin lifting in a way he now knew meant her stubborn streak had kicked in, and she glared up at him. "Maybe it wasn't the voice that time. Maybe it was me. You're not as fun as I thought you'd be. You don't even know how to give me a proper orgasm."

Torin barked out another laugh, and it was Aeron's turn to flush. "I could have given you one if I'd wanted."

"Yeah, well," she huffed. "Prove it."

Yes!

A growl sprang from deep in his throat and he stepped closer to her, leaned down and put them nose to nose. Give her an orgasm? There was nothing he wanted more. "If you aren't careful, you're going to—"

"Aeron, Aeron," a familiar voice called.

Aeron jerked upright as if he'd been caught doing something he shouldn't. Actually, he had. Legion was here. How could he have forgotten about her? About her safety? He should have been out there looking for her instead of responding to Olivia's taunts.

"I'm going to my room to summon Cronus again before the mud-wrestling starts," Torin said. "Maybe he'll show, maybe he won't. If he does, I'll ask him why he's not listed on the scrolls and if he can block *us* from *Hunters.* I'll let you know how it goes. See you guys later. Oh, and, Olivia. Good luck with that voice." With a wink in her direction, he turned on his heel and popped back up the stairs.

Touch what's mine and pay with—

Will you stop warning him away? Aeron snapped at his demon. *He can't hear you.* But don't stop staking that claim, he almost added. *Such* a fool.

A second later, Legion plowed around the far corner, red eyes wild. She halted when she spied Aeron, hissed when she saw Olivia, then tripped forward until she was standing in front of them. She was panting, sweating.

Instinctively, he moved in front of Olivia. "What's wrong?" he asked, guilt consuming him. If she'd gotten hurt because of him...

"Everything will...be...better sssoon..." The moment the last word left her mouth, her knees collapsed and she tumbled to the floor.

Aeron reached out, catching her before she hit and easing her down. She was so tiny, her weight barely registered.

"Aeron," she said on a sigh of relief—just before curling into herself with a pained grunt.

"Legion," he said, panic sprouting. "Tell me what's—"

Another grunt. Every muscle she possessed began knotting and relaxing, knotting and relaxing. Her body seemed to be...growing? Not possible. Or shouldn't have been. As he watched, her arms, legs and torso lengthened. Her scales even began to fall away like dew drops, leaving beautiful, golden skin in their wake.

Soon, though, the grunts became never-ending screams. And with her mouth open so wide, he could see that her teeth were shrinking, her forked tongue weaving together. Next, blond hair sprouted from her scalp and large breasts plumped from her chest.

"What the hell is happening?"

"She's becoming...human," Olivia whispered. Her words, so much softer than his, still managed to rival his in shock and horror.

Not knowing what else to do, Aeron popped to his feet and rushed around the corner. When he reached one of the living rooms, he grabbed a blanket slung over the couch. His mind churned with so many questions, he couldn't quite process what was happening. Legion. Human. Why? How?

At her side once more, he draped the blanket over her bare skin. She'd stopped growing, at least. Stopped spasming and screaming, too. Tears streaked her cheeks and her bottom lip trembled.

She gazed up at him with dark, liquid eyes, no hint of demon red. "Aeron," she said on a sigh. "I'm...so... happy to...see...you."

No longer did she sound like a child, all hint of her lisp gone. Though her words were hesitant, as if she didn't quite know how to use her tongue, she sounded like an adult, voice rich and husky.

Flabbergasted, he crouched beside her and smoothed the hair from her brow. "Tell me how this happened," he said as gently as he was able. He didn't want to spook her.

She reached up with a shaky arm and traced her fingertips over his lips, his jaw. "So beautiful, my Aeron is."

For the first time since he'd met Legion, he wanted to pull away from her embrace. He loved her, he truly did, but the adoration on her new face—adoration he'd seen a hundred times before, had once craved—was now...wrong. Because, without the glow of red in her eyes, he saw the sensual yearning banked there.

Dear gods.

She was a feast for the eyes, prettier than Olivia even. Skin like honey, eyes like cinnamon and lips as red as berries. Her nose was small and pert and her eyebrows perfectly arched. There wasn't a flaw to her. But...

His blood didn't heat, his fingers didn't tingle where he'd touched her and the thought of removing the blanket to peek at her curves was truly repugnant to him. He would rather gouge out his eyes. And while Wrath liked this girl as he had liked the old Legion, the demon was quiet, not staking a claim.

"There's only one way this could've happened," Olivia said with so much dread Aeron's stomach clenched. "She made a deal with Lucifer."

A deal with the devil? For what? She already possessed everything her heart could desire. "Is that true?" And if so, what did it mean for her? For him? What could Lucifer have demanded in return?

Wrath leapt into motion, prowling back and forth inside his head. There were no images flashing, at least, but the demon was suddenly restless, as if he didn't like what was going on.

Legion glared up at Olivia. "Of course it isn't…true. I would never do…such a despicable thing."

"You lie," Olivia replied. "I can hear the untruth in your voice."

He couldn't, but he *could* hear the truth in Olivia's. Still. He didn't know who to believe. Legion, whom he loved. Or Olivia, whom he hungered for but couldn't have.

Gingerly, Legion sat up, and the blanket fell to her waist. Aeron hastily looked away, but not before he'd caught a glimpse of her pearled nipples.

He wanted to scrub his corneas with sandpaper.

Would this day never end?

OLIVIA WATCHED AS LEGION held out one arm, looked it over, then held out the other and examined it, as well. She cupped her breasts, pinched her nipples and gasped in awe.

"I'm gorgeous," she said excitedly. Her words were emerging more fluidly now, smoother every time she spoke. She must be getting used to her new tongue. Her gaze lifted, smugness banked there as she met Olivia's eyes. "I'm a thousand times prettier than you are."

Maybe she was. Not that Olivia cared. Much. What did Aeron think about this? He was careful not to face Legion, careful not to touch her.

Kiss the back of his neck...lick it...and let Legion see you do it.

Olivia stopped breathing. There it was again. The voice. The temptation. Ever since Aeron had dragged her back to this fortress, it had been tormenting her, urging her to do all manner of things—all designed to lure Aeron into bed with her. Caress his penis, strip and dance for him, even flirt with his friend to drive him insane with jealousy.

None of which would have bothered her. Except the desires hadn't sprung from *her*. Yes, she wanted to caress his penis, and yes, she wanted to strip for him. As evidenced by the fact that she'd last approached him naked. And yes, she even liked the thought of his jealousy. But when the voice produced the desires, patches of darkness were left on her soul. She could feel them.

How was that happening? *What* was happening?

Aeron cleared his throat, tugging her from her thoughts. "Let's get you some clothes, Legion."

"I like being naked," she said with a pout.

"Too bad." Still keeping his gaze averted, he held out a hand. "Latch on and I'll pull you up."

"No." Watching Olivia, she drew herself up, threw her arms around Aeron's neck and pressed herself into the hard line of his body. "I want you to carry me."

He grimaced, but scooped her up. "All right. Olivia, come with us. Please." He didn't wait for her reply, but trudged up the steps.

No way she would have left him alone with the demon-turned-human, but she was gratified that he'd requested her company. Until, halfway to his room, she heard, *Pat his ass*…and actually found her fingers inches from his bottom before she even realized she'd reached out. She scowled and forced her arm to fall to her side, but it was too late. Another patch of darkness had already bloomed.

What would happen if that darkness consumed her?

Stop, she shouted inside her head. *Whoever, whatever you are, please stop.*

Legion rested her head on Aeron's shoulder, gaze returning to Olivia, and stroked the contours of his back. "So strong," she purred.

Olivia's eyes narrowed as rage infused every atom of her being. *He's mine to stroke. Mine to praise.*

Do something. You deserve Aeron, not Legion. So prove it to him. Get in front of him, drop to your knees, open his pants and suck his cock into your mouth.

She tripped over her own feet, rage quickly draining and leaving only despair. What would happen if the darkness consumed her? she had wondered. With this newest urging, the answer had slid into place. She would no longer be able to distinguish her own desires and emotions from those of the voice. What the voice had said, she wanted to do. Desperately.

Resist. She couldn't let that happen.

"I want to talk with you…privately," Legion continued, and that slight pause at the end had had nothing to do with her tongue and everything to do with sensual suggestion. "Send the ugly angel away."

"Stop that," he barked. Then more calmly, "You have to stop."

Finally the smugness drained from her and she turned a now-watery gaze to Aeron. "Don't you love me anymore?"

"Of course I do, but that doesn't mean... We can't... Damn this!" He snaked the corner, stalked down the hall and practically kicked his door from its hinges. He set Legion on her feet and backed out of the chamber. "Take anything of mine you want, just get dressed." He didn't wait for her reply, but shut the door with a firm snap and whirled on Olivia. "Tell me about her deal with Lucifer."

Drop to your knees...

"No!" One step, two, she backed away from him.

"Olivia," Aeron said, scowling. "Stop."

Kiss him, then...somewhere, anywhere...

Her attention fell to his lips, and she licked her own. A kiss, so innocent. So necessary. *Must...resist...*

"Stop that," he barked again.

She gulped. "Stop what?" Beyond the door, she could hear Legion stomping around, tossing things to the floor and muttering about "stupid angels."

"One, denying my command and two, trying to seduce me."

"Why would I try to seduce you? It's not like you're any good at the actual bedding." The moment the words escaped her, she plastered her hand over her mouth. Truly. How was this happening? she wondered again. That hadn't been her taunt, but the voice's.

Aeron bristled. "Not good? I gave you an orgasm the first time we...just the first time, damn it!"

Her eyes widened as realization struck. Another danger the voice presented: she liked the results. Aeron barely had a leash on his anger, and the thought of him out of control, determined to prove just how good he was at pleasing her, thrilled her.

Resist? Perhaps that wasn't such a good idea.

Really? Well, if that's the case, Aeron will fall for the voice, not you. Is that what you want? Finally. Rational thought. Thought that cracked through some of the darkness, allowing light to seep inside.

"What are you going to do about your little demon friend in there?" she asked him, returning to the only subject that mattered at the moment.

Aeron scrubbed a hand down his suddenly tired expression. He'd been doing that a lot lately. "I don't know what to do about her."

"To make a bargain of this magnitude, she would've had to promise something huge."

"Like what?"

Olivia shrugged. "Only she knows the answer to that. Well, and Lucifer, but I guarantee he won't tell us."

"How do you know she bargained with Lucifer rather than Hades? And does the bargainer matter?"

"Yes, the bargainer matters, but Hades is currently locked away and incapable of making such deals, so you don't have to worry about him." When the Titans escaped their immortal prison and overthrew the Greeks all those months ago, Hades had been included in their number. Lucifer, though, the Titans had left alone. Someone needed to be in charge of the underworld, she supposed. Even someone as vile as the devil, the creator of evil. Better him than the insane Hades, though.

Rub your body against his...

"Enough!" Any more of this, and she was going to bang her head into the wall until she passed out. No more darkness, no matter how much she liked the results. "I'm not going to do it, even though I want to, so you can just hush."

Aeron tossed up his arms, a man who'd said good-bye to the last of his patience. "Do what?"

"Never mind. Just, well, until you know more about Legion's end of the bargain, I wouldn't trust her. She could have shared secrets, promised to kill one of your friends."

He shook his head, suddenly confident. "She wouldn't do that. She loves me."

His faith in a conniving demon was irritating. Why couldn't he feel that way about Olivia, a former angel who never, ever lied? Why did he constantly try to push *her* away?

The bedroom door swung open, and Aeron stumbled backward. Legion caught him with a husky laugh. He quickly straightened and turned. She was wearing one of his T-shirts and a pair of his sweatpants and both bagged on her.

"Happy now?" she asked, twirling on her tiptoes. "This is…all I could find. But you know…what the funny thing is? I *still*…look good." In her exuberance, the hesitant pauses returned to her speech.

He backed away from her and into Olivia. Olivia flattened her palms on his shoulder blades to keep him from running, her heart picking up speed. Contact.

"Olivia and I have to go into town. You're going to stay here. And I mean it this time. Do *not* go anywhere. I need to talk to you when I return."

Her siren's smile quickly faded. "What! No. Hell, no. I'm going…with you."

"You're staying, and there'll be no arguing about it."

Expression petulant, she stomped her foot. "Why are you…taking the ugly angel then?"

I'm not ugly!

"I need her," was all Aeron said, but there was steel in his voice. Boiling steel.

Breath hissed between Legion's teeth as she leveled her gaze on Olivia, who was still peeking around Aeron's side. There was more hate in those eyes than Olivia had ever seen. "Touch him, and I'll…kill you. Under…stand?" The more intense her emotions, the more trouble she had speaking, it seemed.

"You will not harm her." Without pivoting an inch, Aeron wrapped a hard arm around Olivia's waist, his fingers digging into her lower back. "There'll be no more threats. Do *you* understand? I won't tolerate it."

Legion pressed her lips together, and a moment passed in silence. Then she smiled. A forced, too-sweet smile. "Any…thing you say, Aeron. I love you and… only want you happy."

A lie. Olivia heard it in the undercurrents of the demon's voice. Not about the demon's love for Aeron, but about her promise to leave Olivia alone. She would have to be on guard, for she'd seen demons at work and knew firsthand how insidious they were, how much destruction they could wreak.

"Try," she said, and whether the challenge came from her or that tempting voice, she didn't know. Didn't care just then. "Because I plan to do a lot more than simply touch him." Truth.

Aeron swung around, pinning her in place with his probing stare. His pupils were dilated, just as they'd been before he'd kissed her back at Gilly's, his chest moving up and down as if he couldn't quite catch his

breath. "Not. Another. Word. From. Either. Of. You,"
he gritted out.

Kiss him...

For once, she didn't resist. Darkness be damned, she
closed the distance between them, rose on her tiptoes
and planted her lips against his. Legion needed to know
Olivia was just as determined as she was to win this
man. To have him in every way imaginable.

Her tongue pushed inside his mouth, but only briefly.
Only long enough for a taste. He opened up, clearly
wanting more, which surprised her and heightened her
desire, but she forced herself to straighten and spin
away.

"Come, Aeron," she said. "We have things to do.
Together." Without a backward glance at either Aeron
or the now-cursing Legion, she strolled away as if she
didn't dread facing the rest of the day.

CHAPTER SIXTEEN

"I CAN'T SEE ANYTHING," Aeron whispered an hour later. "It's too dark." An unnatural darkness, at that. There wasn't a speck of light, and the flashlight he'd brought with him highlighted nothing, merely disappearing into the yawning thickness of gloom.

"The night Lysander appeared to me, he told me I would remain an angel in all the ways that mattered until my time expired," Olivia said. "I think I can—"

"Shh. Inside voice." He didn't want her to become a target. In fact, the thought enraged him, but he only had himself to blame. He shouldn't have brought her here, whether Nightmares was a threat or not. He just— he hadn't wanted to leave her within striking distance of Legion. Or touching distance of Torin. And he *had* promised to show Olivia the harsh realities of his life.

I'm such a fool. A fool drowning in a storm of his own making. Desire for Olivia—check, that hadn't lessened. Had only grown. A jealous, bloodthirsty pseudodaughter determined to end his angel—check. A vow to convince said angel to return home—check, even though he now hated himself for that vow. Send her away, never knowing how she fared? Torture!

"She's sleeping," Olivia said, and that, too, was stated at top volume.

"She can awaken," he gritted out. He'd never minded

the dark, but as he inched down the steps and felt his way along the walls of Scarlet's home, which just happened to be an underground crypt in the local cemetery, bumping into—furniture? coffins?—and having no idea what waited ahead, the possibility of leading Olivia into slaughter caused tendrils of fear to blend with his rage. How could he protect her like this?

"She won't awaken, I promise. *Anyway.* As my time has not yet expired, maybe I can..."

As Olivia's words trailed off, he stopped, pivoted. She knocked into him and *humphed.* Even though he'd felt her only briefly, he savored the contact. Soft, warm. Exhilarating. That's all his body needed to ready itself. Again.

Mine, Wrath said.

I know. You've told me. Over and freaking over again. And Aeron had let him, had stopped caring. Because... *No. Don't go there.*

A moment passed in silence, their breathing the only sound. The air was musty, thick with age, dust and death, but he would've been content to wait here forever. Here, she was safe. Here, they were together.

"Can what?" he finally prompted.

"This." Pinpricks of light flickered.

He blinked, rubbed his eyes. Those pinpricks were actually sparking off her skin, he realized, blending together and growing in intensity. Growing so much she was soon chasing away the shadows and his eyes were tearing.

"How—"

Slowly she grinned, her beautiful face illuminated, shining like the purest star, those dark lashes framing those sky-blue eyes. He could have kissed the breath right out of her. *Don't you dare.* But now that he knew her taste, now that he'd felt her rub against him, how was he supposed to resist?

Legion. Lysander. Freedom.

Oh, yeah. He could have cursed.

"Humans were sometimes trapped in darkness, and I had to show them the way out." Olivia shifted from one foot to the other, and motioned behind him with a tilt of her chin. "Scarlet is just around the corner. I can sense her."

"Thank you." Motions stiff, Aeron forced himself to turn away. His eyes immediately mourned the loss of her.

Wrath, too, howled in protest.

Calm. We're still with her. Aeron led his charge down the correct dirt path and soon found himself standing in a makeshift bedroom. Pikes sprung from several places in the floor, gleaming sharply and anchored firmly by concrete. Between them were trip wires, and at the far end of the room, guarded by the entire fun zone, was a coffin.

Why a coffin? Because she could close herself in for better protection? Smart woman, if so.

He palmed a blade and closed the distance, dodging those pikes. Olivia stayed close to his heels, every step measured.

"Careful," he muttered. "Stay behind me." He flipped open the lid, halfway expecting a fight.

Nope. As Olivia had promised, Scarlet slept peacefully, completely unaware of his intrusion. He studied her. Silky black hair framed her seemingly delicate face. She hadn't looked delicate before, when she'd cornered him in that alley. Her lashes were longer than he'd realized, like feathered fans reaching for her cheekbones. She had a small nose, and her lips were redder than before.

She wore a T-shirt and jeans, both black, and weapons were strapped all over her body. She didn't disarm, even to sleep. Interesting. Even he removed his blades before crawling into bed. He kept them nearby, of course, but not on him.

Relaxing, his gaze shifted. The walls were dirt, just like the floor, and there were blades peeking from several locations. Anyone who fell, either into the wall or onto the floor, would tumble straight to their death.

Nightmares could have placed traps at the doorway or even on the steps leading down here, but hadn't. Why? Perhaps she'd known the unerring gloom would frighten most people—most innocents—away. But the ones who persisted, the ones who kept going, would clearly have more sinister intentions. Perhaps those were the only people she wanted to hurt.

If that were the case, that would mean she killed discriminately. That would mean there was a line she wouldn't cross. Or perhaps she just liked the kills to be made nearby, so that the first thing she would see when she awoke was blood and death.

Either way, the woman was serious about protecting herself.

He almost hoped she would rouse and attack him. He *needed* a battle. His nerves were on edge and bloodshed would have calmed him. Too many things were happening, changing. Too many things were going wrong.

Baden's demon finding a new host, thanks to Galen. Discovering Cronus and Rhea were possessed. Everything with Olivia, of course, and her naughty clothes and searing kisses, with her irresistible suggestions (just then, he almost missed the voice) and her attempted seduction of another man, all of which were like matches on the kindling of his arousal. And jealousy. And anger.

Yes, he needed to kill someone today.

And if all of that wasn't enough to deal with, Legion looked at him the way he wanted Olivia to look at him. She'd made a pact with the creator of evil, and she'd blatantly lied to him about it. There at the end, just before leaving her behind, there'd been no more deluding himself about that. Sly determination had practically poured off her.

What was he going to do about her? How was he supposed to handle her? He still loved her like a daughter, still planned to keep her in his life. No way would he abandon her. There just…there had to be a solution.

Don't think about that now. You have a job to do. The job. Right. So. Back to Scarlet, the problem at hand. Did Galen know about her?

"She used to live in a church," Olivia said guiltily, before he could tell her they needed to leave. "But that didn't work out for her."

Why the guilt? Because she'd led him here? Probably. *Careful.* He couldn't let her guilt spark his own. "I believe I asked you to be quiet."

"I told you. She's not going to wake up."

"How do you know?" Silly question. Olivia knew everything, it sometimes seemed. Which meant Sabin was going to love her. Information was the man's best friend. Thank Olivia's One True Deity she would be gone before the warrior returned. Aeron would hate to have to stab his friend for interrogating his woman.

At the thought, Wrath chortled with glee.

Well, maybe he wouldn't *hate* stabbing the warrior. He owed Sabin, after all. *And she's not your woman!* "Never mind. It doesn't matter. We have to hurry before we run into other visitors."

"Like who?"

"Like Hunters."

"Oh."

Aeron might have craved a battle with Nightmares, but not with Galen's army. He didn't want Olivia involved in something like that. He'd show her the horrors of his life another way. From a safe distance.

Scarlet's crypt was a good distance from The Asylum, so that was a point in their favor.

"—so dark," an unfamiliar voice suddenly said, the words echoing from the concrete steps above and reaching into the small enclosure.

"My flashlight's not working."

"I can't see anything."

"Just keep inching forward, damn it."

Well, hell. This day could indeed get worse. Hunters were here, just as he'd feared. Had someone followed him? Used the Cloak of Invisibility?

Was someone watching him, threatening his woman, even now?

Aeron's hands curled into fists. He scanned the crypt anew, but saw nothing out of place. He glanced at Olivia, who was still glowing but frowning now. Next he glanced at Scarlet, who was still sleeping. After that, the doorway.

That dark, open space was the only way out of here. And to reach it, they'd have to run straight through the humans. The most likely *armed* humans.

Those humans couldn't see through the darkness, but

then, Aeron wouldn't be able to, either, without Olivia's light. But with her light, everyone would be able to see everyone else.

There was only one thing to do. Only one option that kept Olivia safe.

Aeron slapped a blade into her hand. "Keep it pressed to the girl's throat," he whispered. "If she moves even a little, don't hesitate to cut her."

Not giving her a chance to reply, he gripped Olivia by the waist and hefted her into the coffin beside Scarlet. The sleeping female remained exactly as she was, but Olivia gasped. Immediately he clamped a hand over her mouth and shook his head. She gulped in fear, but nodded that she understood what he wanted of her. Silence.

"Kill the light."

Again she nodded, and the glow of her skin washed out...dimmed...then disappeared completely. The shadows must have been waiting for just such an occurrence because they raced forward, enclosing every inch of space with that suffocating gloom.

"Shit! Watch where you're going."

"Sorry."

The voices were closer.

Big as Aeron was, he knew he wouldn't fit inside the coffin to act as Olivia's shield. Not without crushing her. Instead, he flattened his hand on her shoulder—or what he'd thought was her shoulder. He jerked that now-burning hand away because he'd actually cupped her beautiful breast. And her nipple had instantly pearled.

Mine. Protect.

Careful this time, he aimed higher. Shoulder. Good. Trembling. Not good. That meant she was as overcome—and distracted—by the mistake as he was. Or afraid. He preferred the thought of her overcome.

Clearly, *he* was the distracted one. Jolting back into motion, he pressed her to lie down and stay still. Thankfully, she didn't resist. Whether she did as he'd commanded and placed the tip of the blade at Scarlet's throat, he didn't know. Just to be safe, he angled his other hand over Nightmares's...face. Good. She was still motionless, her breath trekking onto his skin, warm, even.

He hadn't seen any traps around the coffin itself, so he inched his way to the front end, away from the corridor's entryway. Not once did he remove his touch from either woman. He wanted Olivia to know he was here, that he would guard her. Always. He would have closed the lid, but wanted access in case the girl did, in fact, awaken.

"Wait," one of the men said. "Stop."

"What?"

"Air. Do you feel the breeze?"

"We must be close to an opening."

Closer still.

There was a shuffling of feet. Multiple sets. Olivia's trembling increased, and he squeezed her in reassurance.

"It's gotta be a room." A pause. A crackle. "Yes. Yes! There's too much space for this to be another hallway."

"She can't be here. She couldn't have found her way inside."

"She's possessed by the fucking demon of Nightmares. Of course she could have found her way. Just... feel around. She'll be asleep. If you encounter warm skin, just start shooting."

How did they know so much? Had Cronus told his wife? Or again, had someone made use of the Cloak and listened to private conversations?

"Hell, no. No shooting. We'll just shoot each other."

"That's better than allowing a demon to go free."

There was a beat of shocked silence as the other Hunters absorbed the man's death wish.

"We either cut her, or I'm out of here," someone finally snapped. "I didn't sign up for a suicide mission."

"Then cut her, damn it, but make sure you incapacitate her so we can cart her out without fearing she'll be strong enough to attack. Every bad dream we've ever had is her fault. Every bad thing we've ever endured is her doing."

More shuffling. Aeron tensed, waiting. If any of them managed to make it to the coffin, he would have to—

A man screamed.

"What the hell—"

Another scream. A gurgle. Followed by another and another.

There would be no one making it to the coffin.

Nightmares's traps would see to that. Several of the Hunters discharged their guns, despite their fear of friendly fire, but the darkness hid the sparking of the powder. One of those bullets slammed into Aeron's shoulder, knocking him backward.

He caught himself as several more human screams rent the air. Though he didn't want Olivia trapped with the girl, unable to protect herself, he didn't want her shot, either. He slammed the coffin lid shut.

"What's happening?"

"Cut," someone managed to say between coughs.

Another scream, this one blending with the rising tide of pained moans and the wafting scent of fresh blood.

"Retreat," someone wheezed. "Re— Argh!"

There was even more shuffling, but the number of moving feet had severely decreased. And then, as more screams and moans abounded, the shuffling ended entirely. Over. Done. It was the battle he'd wanted, craved, yet he hadn't had to lift a single finger to win.

He waited until silence reigned before tossing back the lid and saying, "Light."

Immediately Olivia obeyed. Once again that nearly blinding light glimmered from her, grew, and conquered the darkness, and he saw that she was pale but unharmed. Scarlet still hadn't moved.

"Aeron, I was so—" Olivia sat up and twisted to face him. Her expression immediately became pinched. "You're hurt."

He gazed down at his wound. There was a hole in his shoulder; crimson seeped from it, riding the ridges of his stomach, each drop absorbing into the waist of his pants. Now that his concern for Olivia had faded, and his adrenaline had decreased, he realized it *hurt*. Fire spread, quickly, surely, as if his veins pumped gasoline rather than blood.

Didn't matter. "I'll be fine," he said. "Been injured worse, so it's nothing to worry about."

"I can't help it." Chewing on her bottom lip, she reached out and traced her fingertips over his jaw. "I'm worried."

The touch was meant to comfort him. But as always, the feel of her tormented him. He needed more. *Wrath* needed more, whimpering inside his head.

Now isn't the time. Bleeding bodies were piled upon bleeding bodies, blades protruding from each of them. Some had fallen face-first, and others had landed backward. Each had died. He would have to thank the girl for her decorating skills. They, rather than he, had saved Olivia's life.

He didn't know if any of the Hunters had managed to escape this room of terror, but he wasn't going to wait around to see if they returned with backup. After helping Olivia to her feet—*shit!* and causing his wound to split—he hefted Nightmares into his arms as he'd wanted to do before they were interrupted.

"Stay close," he said. "Only step where I step."

"I will."

He made his way to the open doorway, darting around bodies along the way, grimacing as the fire inside him intensified.

Hurt, Wrath cried.

His lips curved into a frown. *You, too?*

Bad.

We'll go home. Rest. There were no trails of blood on the stairs, not even a speck. Which meant no one had made it out. Excellent. Except...by the time he reached the top of the stairs, he was trembling. Weakening. His eyes were glazing over, creating a fog everywhere he looked.

Wrath moaned.

The fire finally died—only to be replaced by a frigid ice.

"Aeron?"

He slowed, his motions sluggish, his feet tripping over each other. "Reach into my back pocket. Grab my phone." At this rate, he wouldn't have the strength to fly both women to the fortress.

"What's wrong with you?" Olivia asked, doing as he'd requested. "Is it your injury? You told me not to worry!"

He ignored the question and the concern. He didn't want to lie to her—again—and tell her everything was going to be fine, but he didn't have an answer, either. Neither he nor Wrath had ever reacted this way to a simple gunshot.

"Do you know how to text?" They rounded a corner.

"No. I've seen humans do it, but I've never tried it myself."

"What about making a call?" Up ahead, he could finally see the sunlight pushing its way into the crypt. Sweat beaded every inch of him, yet that did nothing to melt the ice. His motions were slowing further, dragging.

"No," she said again. "I'm sorry."

Damn. If he released the girl, he wouldn't be able to pick her back up. That, he knew. Damn, damn, damn.

There were only two possibilities that explained this reaction, he realized. Either the Hunters had used some sort of special bullets or he hadn't truly recovered from their last attack, as he'd assumed. Neither boded well for him.

Outside—finally, blessedly—he searched for waiting Hunters. He didn't see any, but wasn't sure if that was because they weren't there or because his vision continued to fade. No one jumped out at them, at least.

Flying or not, he wasn't going to make it home.

He searched his surroundings once more, this time looking for a place to hide. There, a few yards ahead, was a large headstone, flowers of every color perched all around it, forming a hidden alcove.

"This way." He lumbered forward, weaker with every step.

Olivia wound her arm around his waist, acting as his crutch. "Here. Lean on me."

He didn't want to, was embarrassed that he needed to, was even *more* embarrassed that he actually liked having someone take care of him, but with her aid, he managed to make it. "Thank you."

He tried to ease Scarlet down, but his knees gave out and the two of them just sort of tumbled forward. She flopped unceremoniously to the ground, and he next to her. Not a peep did she make.

Nor did Wrath. The demon was silent now. Eerily so.

Aeron rolled to his side. Olivia, he saw, was busy rearranging the flowers to pin them in and shield them from prying eyes. "Good...girl," he told her.

The smile she flicked him was all bravery and iron will. It caused his heart to skip a damned beat. And either he was seeing things that weren't there or butterflies were actually floating around her head. Squirrels sat at her feet, as well, and birds picked at the grass around her. All of them were watching her, as though waiting for her attention.

Surely he was hallucinating. Which meant he was even worse off than he'd thought. Since he knew he wouldn't be able to read the numbers on his phone, he told Olivia what to dial.

"Ringing," she said, and pressed the device to his ear.

"Torin," he said after his friend answered. "Follow signal. Come get...us."

He didn't hear the warrior's reply. A darkness very similar to what he'd suffered inside that crypt closed around him, and this time, he could only welcome it.

CHAPTER SEVENTEEN

AFTER OLIVIA TORE a strip of cloth from the bottom of her robe and wrapped it around Aeron's shoulder, she withdrew one of the blades from the sheath anchored to his ankle. *I will protect him. No matter the actions necessary.* Just as he'd done for her. She crouched in front of him, waiting for his friends to arrive. Or Hunters. If anyone besides a Lord approached, she wouldn't hesitate to attack.

Never had she felt more like a warrior, more confident in herself, yet more afraid—for the man beside her. He'd taken bullets before; she'd seen him. He'd been stabbed, beaten and cut with knives and arrows. Yet he hadn't reacted like this. He hadn't gone pallid, hadn't moaned and trembled. Hadn't continued to bleed and weaken.

Minute after minute passed, and there was no change in him. Where in heaven's name were those Lords? They had better hurry, and not just for Aeron's sake. If they waited too long, dusk would arrive and Scarlet would awaken. And she would be very, very angry.

No one would survive.

At least that tempting voice had shut up the moment she'd left the fortress, and stopped urging her to do those vile—wonderful—things. Hardly a silver lining, though. Nothing was. The animals were even now crowding through the flowers and bushes, perhaps drawing the attention of passersby. Trying to get closer to her? Or Aeron? She didn't remember them ever approaching Aeron before, but couldn't figure out why the squirrels, rabbits, birds, cats and even a dog would seek *her*.

"Scat," she whispered, not wanting them hurt if a fight did, in fact, break out.

They didn't budge. No, they inched closer. To her. So she *was* the draw. Why?

"You have to leave now—"

A twig snapped, quieting her.

The dog growled and the cats hissed, but none ran away. They crouched, ready to leap into attack.

Her lips pressed together, every muscle in her body freezing. She even stopped breathing. Who was here? Lords? Or Hunters? The hand holding the blade trembled. *For Aeron,* she thought, readying like the animals. She was suddenly glad they'd stubbornly stayed with her.

Two men stepped past the foliage and at first, she didn't recognize them. She was too prepped, too determined to save this man she...loved? But just as she launched herself at one of them, the dog sprang forward, beating her to the target.

"Ow! Get off me, you mangy mutt," he gritted out.

She recognized the voice—William—but didn't lower her blade in time, her momentum too swift. Just before contact, a hard hand wrapped around her wrist, jerking her to the side before stilling her.

"Whoa, there, Liv," he said with a laugh. His voice was familiar, too. Paris. "I can call you Liv, right? Drop the blade for me, yes?"

Relief pounded through her, and she released the weapon.

"Now tell this mutt to let go!" William shouted.

"They're friends of mine," she told the dog. "I'm safe now."

The dog removed its teeth from William's ankle and each of the animals dashed away as if that was all they'd been waiting for. The assurance of her safety.

What little darlings. "Thank you," she called gratefully.

"Now that William's been properly welcomed," Paris said with another laugh, "we should get this show on the road." Concern lit his beautiful face when he spied Aeron. He bent down, slid his arms under the still-sleeping warrior and hefted him over his shoulder. "How long's he been like this?"

"Too long."

William limped to Scarlet and did the same, only he cradled her in his arms as if she were a precious treasure. "At least I get the pretty package."

"Yeah, good luck with her," Paris replied. "I'd say I got the better end of this deal. Apparently she's possessed by Nightmares."

William rolled his eyes. "And that's a bad thing?"

"If you don't like having your balls handed to you, then yeah, I'd say it's a bad thing."

"Come to Daddy," William said, holding Scarlet all the tighter.

Olivia listened to their banter, head zinging back and forth between them. "Enough. There were Hunters here, you know. This is a dangerous location. More than that, something's wrong with Aeron. I want him in bed."

"Sure, sure," William told her with a nod. "We've

known that from the beginning. But you're going to have to wait until he wakes up for that kind of sport. When you finish with him, though, I'd love a go at you myself. Show you what it's like to be with someone who knows what they're doing, and all that."

Her hands fisted. Did he take nothing seriously?

"We're parked over here." Paris jerked his head to the side.

Finally. "Let's go."

Together they broke through the bushes, and each man went on alert. In the span of a single second, it was as if they were different people. Hidden, they'd joked with each other and teased her about wanting to bed Aeron. Now, they were soldiers, hardened, capable of anything.

So many times, she'd watched the same change overcome Aeron. Until now, she hadn't truly appreciated it.

Aeron. Brave, injured Aeron. When her nine days ticked away and he was taken from her, where would she go? What would she do? She doubted these men would invite her to remain with them. And would she want them to? Aeron would no longer be there, the memory of him taunting her from every corner.

For the second time, Olivia found herself upset with the short amount of time she and Aeron had. Maybe there was a way to save him. Maybe there was a way for them to be together forever. Yes. Surely. Her Deity was the creator of love. Actually, her Deity *was* love. He would want two people who loved each other to be together. Right?

But she still wasn't sure beyond any doubt that she loved Aeron. Admired him, yes. Was aroused by him and craved his touch, oh, yes. But die in his place? she wondered again. Again, she wasn't sure. She'd given up everything to be with him—everything except her life.

Could she?

Plus, in dying for Aeron, she'd have to die for Legion, as well. Because she knew, *knew,* Aeron wouldn't be happy without the little—big now—tyrant. And if Aeron was going to live, she wanted him to be happy while doing so. Yet the thought of dying for such a lying, conniving brat didn't settle well.

More than that, Aeron would have to love *Olivia.* Right now, there was no question that he didn't.

Olivia sighed as she climbed into the SUV. Aeron was laid across the backseat, and she cradled his head in her lap. Paris took the wheel and William flopped into the passenger seat with Scarlet still in his arms. Her first time in a car, something she'd looked forward to, but now she didn't care. Her mind whirled.

Death wasn't something she'd ever considered for herself. Not really. She'd just always been and had known she would always be. Now she *could* die. Not to save someone, but just because, say, a car hit her. How did she feel about that? She didn't know. All she knew was that dying, without experiencing everything she wanted, was abhorrent. But afterward? Being without Aeron would be far more so.

She'd seen thousands, millions, of humans die. Not one of those deaths had ever affected her, for they had simply been part of the circle of life. Every beginning had an end. Perhaps that's why she hadn't mourned the thought of ultimately losing Aeron at first. It would be just another death in a long line of deaths she'd witnessed.

Now, his was personal. She knew him intimately,

had kissed and tasted him. Had experienced the ultimate pleasure with him. She had slept in his arms, curled into his side. He had protected her. He could have climbed inside that casket himself, but he hadn't. He'd placed her inside, ensuring *she* walked away unscathed rather than himself.

Therefore, he'd been willing to die *for her*. Why? Again, she had no illusions that he loved her.

She heaved another sigh and ran her palm along his scalp. As short as his hair was, the spikes tickled her skin. Later, she would summon Lysander. She would ask him about all of this—and also why he'd visited Aeron before. He wouldn't be able to lie to her. And if what he said was bad, destroying her hope for a future with this amazing man, she'd...what? She gulped.

"We shouldn't leave Gilly in that apartment," William said suddenly, drawing Olivia from her thoughts. "Not with your enemies buzzing around like flies."

"One, Aeron needs to get home. Two, she's better off there, disassociated from us." Paris fiddled with the rearview mirror, gaze darting in front of and behind him. "The Hunters have no idea—"

William slapped a hand on the console between them. "I beg to differ, Sex. They knew about Scarlet, and what contact have we had with her? Almost none. How much have we had with Gilly? Too much. And with Rhea on Team Dumbness, we can't leave Gilly out there on her own. Besides, Aeron is immortal. He'll keep. So again, we can't leave her out there on her own."

"Shit. You're right."

"I always am."

"We'll pick her up on the way to the fortress."

"She'll be at school," William said, and Paris cursed as he made an illegal turn, the tires squealing.

Olivia thought about complaining. She wanted Aeron safe and doctored as soon as possible, but the men were right. Gilly was human and needed protecting.

"Shit," Paris repeated. "She's at the American International School of Budapest, and it's located in the Nagykovácsi Campus. I think. Pretty good distance we've gotta go."

"Worth it."

There was an odd tenderness in William's voice when he spoke about the girl. She was too young for him, though. Too young for *any* of the men at the fortress. If Olivia had to warn the warrior away, he wouldn't like her methods. They'd involve a knife and a small plastic bag.

Embracing the warrior life you once so easily discarded?

"I doubt that she'll be happy to see us," Paris said.

"Speak for yourself. Anya says she has a crush on me." William sounded proud about that.

"She's just a child," Olivia reminded him. *And I don't care if I'm considered a warrior or not, I really will borrow one of Aeron's knives....*

William twisted in his seat to face her, hardly disturbing Scarlet at all. His lips were lifting in a naughty grin. "I know that, but when it comes to my appeal, you'll find that age doesn't matter. Gender, either. I'm irresistible."

"What are your intentions toward her?"

He rolled his eyes. "I have no intentions. I like to be admired, and she likes to admire me. That's the extent of it."

"Good." Olivia didn't hear a lie in his voice. Still. She wasn't taking any chances. Not with Gilly's well-being. "She's led a difficult life. Her mom's husband... did things to her." Perhaps she shouldn't be spilling Gilly's secrets, but she knew how the memories festered inside the girl. Finally bringing them into the light could be the first step to healing. "She told her mom, but the woman refused to believe her. Even accused her of trying to destroy her new, wonderful life."

"We know about that," Paris said gently. "Danika told us."

"Not me." William swung back to face the front, but not before she caught a glimpse of utter, undiluted fury on his face. "How do *you* know that?"

"I was once assigned to her care."

The rest of the drive was made in tense, oppressive silence. Finally they were winding through a neighborhood, a suburb, the houses utterly wonderful and inviting. Thick green trees surrounded the area, one side situated on a hill and rising majestically.

The car stopped in a parking lot, and Paris flicked William a glance. "I'll just be a minute. Watch the baggage."

Without warning, and moving so quickly there was nothing Paris could do, William dumped Scarlet in the demon's lap, no longer quite so careful. "*I'll* just be a minute. You scare Gilly, and I'm not having that. Not today."

"I don't scare women. I delight them. Besides, you aren't on the checkout list, and I am."

William rolled his eyes—a favorite action of his, apparently—and exited the vehicle. "Like that'll stop me. Have you seen my eyes? They're electric. Women take one look and I'm *immediately* placed on their check-out lists."

"Stop praising yourself and hurry," Olivia told him just as he slammed the door shut.

He saluted her with a grin.

She watched his progression into the school, fingers tracing over Aeron's warming brow. He wasn't getting any better, was even beginning to thrash a bit. His brow was beaded with sweat, and his teeth were digging into his bottom lip.

Not knowing what else to do, she began to sing. Sweet songs of peace and health. A few chords into the hymn, Aeron stilled, his pinched expression even relaxing somewhat.

"My gods," Paris whispered brokenly.

Her voice tapered off, and she looked up at him. "What? What's wrong?"

Aeron began thrashing again.

"Don't stop!" Paris said. "It's beautiful. My ears are already addicted and need more."

"Oh. Thank you." Olivia launched into another serenade. Outside, she could see all manner of animals emerging from the forest and approaching the vehicle. Once more, Aeron calmed and she could have wept with joy.

Would she die for him? Her finger traced one of the skeletal tattoos on his cheekbone. Maybe.

WILLIAM STOOD IN THE school's main office, waiting for Gilly. The receptionist had already called her. As he'd told the female that his name was Paris Lord, she'd summoned the girl without incident. List crisis averted.

She was short and curved, in her mid-thirties with a

sleek brown bob and brown eyes—eyes she was now in the process of stripping him with. A routine occurrence. One he usually enjoyed. Not so now. He just wanted to haul Gilly the hell out of here. He liked the little smart-ass, and wouldn't rest until she was safe.

He'd had no idea she'd led so terrible a life, and he was ashamed of himself. He knew women. He could figure them out in the span of a once-over. So why hadn't he realized Gilly was hurting?

Her fucking mother and would-be stepfather! Two people who were supposed to protect her. Well, William was with her now and William would ensure nothing like that ever happened again. He was tempted to cut her mother and stepdad's throats. Maybe give her their heads for Christmas or something.

"Are you Gilly's father?" the receptionist asked. She'd abandoned her post at her desk and now stood across from him at the counter.

Shit. He hadn't seen or heard her move. That level of distraction was dangerous. "Brother," he replied, a bit irritated that he looked old enough to have a seventeen-year-old daughter. Yeah, he was pushing two thou, but he didn't have a wrinkle on him, damn it!

"Oh. That's nice." She grinned and slid a piece of paper his way. "If you'd ever like to discuss her curriculum, here's my number. Call anytime."

"I'll definitely be in contact." He, too, grinned, though his was forced. He pocketed the paper, knowing he wouldn't use it. "Education is so important."

That earned him a giggle, and he tried not to cringe.

Women. They were both a blessing and a curse. Sex, he loved. Sex, he needed, craved. Sex with the wrong woman had gotten him locked up. Sex with the goddesses who visited him in prison had gotten him kicked out of the heavens. That hadn't stopped his libido, however. Actually, nothing stopped his libido. Even the curse hanging over his head.

One day, a woman of great beauty and power would tempt him. One day, that woman would trick him into loving her. One day, that woman would enslave him. And then, that woman would kill him.

It had already been prophesied.

Maybe—perhaps—okay, not really likely—he could have avoided females altogether and saved himself the trouble of such a death sentence. But even that wouldn't have saved him. That, too, was part of the prophesy. To avoid women and sex was simply to condemn himself to a much faster, much more painful death.

The only way to stop the unnamed woman and break the curse had been written in a book. A book that was nearly impossible to decode, so he had yet to find the answer. Also, the minor fucking goddess of Anarchy had possession of that book, returning it page by stingy page. He'd hate Anya for such a thing if he didn't love her so damned much.

They'd spent hundreds of years in Tartarus as cell neighbors. Her wit had been the only thing to keep him sane.

"William?" Gilly's husky voice suddenly rang out.

He turned on his heel and there she was, standing at the end of a long hallway. She was slender, dark haired, dark eyed, and more...knowledgeable than someone her age should ever be. That should have been clue number one, he thought.

Maybe he'd sensed it, but hadn't wanted to acknowledge it.

She wore jeans and a T-shirt, and sneakers that had a tracking device hidden in the soles, not that she knew it. Her hair was pulled back in a ponytail, not a speck of makeup on her face.

That didn't seem to bother the boy next to her. He was staring at her as if hypnotized. But having heard her say William's name, that boy had frowned. And when he followed the line of her gaze and spotted William, his frown deepened and he paled.

Boyfriend? Or potential boyfriend?

Someone would have to put a stop to that. She was too young, with too traumatic a past. She needed to be alone. Until she was *at least* forty.

"Hey, pet," William said with a finger wave.

Grinning, she rushed forward and threw herself into his arms. He hugged her tight before latching onto her wrists and gently pushing her back. He might enjoy her, might want the best for her, but he didn't want to encourage her crush anymore.

"What are you doing here?" she asked.

The boy she'd been with eased up behind her. He was tall for a teen, reaching William's ear, with brown hair and blue eyes.

"Who are you?" William demanded unceremoniously.

"C-Corbin, sir."

"What kind of a name is Corbin Sir? And if you ever hurt Gilly, I swear to the gods I will personally—"

Gilly slapped William's shoulder. "Stop. Cori's my friend. He just wanted to make sure I reached the office okay."

"Well, that's admirable," William said, never remov-

ing his narrowed gaze from the boy. "As long as protection was his only goal."

Corbin pulled at the collar of his shirt. "Are you
her...boyfriend or something?"

"Brother," William said as Gilly said, "Yes."

His gaze finally whipped back to her, and he arched
a brow. Yes? They needed to have a chat, then. Maybe
later, though. Hearing the word had caused something
to tighten in his chest. He'd figure out what that tightening meant first.

"So why are you here?" she asked again, her cheeks
reddening.

He didn't like that he'd embarrassed her, but there
was no help for it. "Aeron's been hurt. There are problems in the city, and we want you in the fortress with
the others until it's safe again."

"Aeron?" Corbin asked.

"Another brother," William informed him.

The boy's eyes widened. "How many do you have?"

"A lot," Gilly replied with a weary sigh. "So you'll
be there, Liam? At the fortress?"

Liam. Her nickname for him. Once he'd liked it. Now
he saw it as the endearment it was meant to be. Oh, yes.
They'd be having a chat. Damn his irresistible beauty.
"Yes, I'll be there. So let's go home, pet. Aeron's in the
car and he needs some medical attention stat."

Despite her fear of the Lords, she paled with worry,
grabbed his hand and led him from the building. "Bye,
Cori," she called over her shoulder.

"Bye," the boy returned, and there was a bit of an
edge to the sound.

William spied the Escalade but couldn't see Olivia
through the window tint, not to mention the god-awful

number of deer now surrounding the vehicle. However, he didn't have to see her to know that if they failed to get Aeron to the fortress safely, the angel, for all her goodness, would erupt into a seething cauldron of feminine fury. It was there in her eyes, a churning, unstoppable passion just waiting to boil over. Something she probably didn't realize she was capable of, but William realized it because, unlike his cluelessness with Gilly, he'd picked up on Olivia's dreams, fears and needs the moment he'd seen her.

Aeron was her everything. If the warrior died, even the gods wouldn't be able to stop her rampage.

CHAPTER EIGHTEEN

OLIVIA SAT AT THE edge of Aeron's bed, hip pressed to hip. Legion sat on his other side, hip pressed to hip. In their concern for him, they'd worked together to strip him. Olivia *hadn't* allowed herself to look at his penis, no matter how often the voice had told her to do so.

Oh, yes. The voice of temptation had returned.

Weak as Aeron was, any peeking on her part would have been wrong. He was so weak, in fact, that he hadn't stirred once. He'd even stopped moaning, though she wasn't singing, and she didn't think that was a good sign.

His wound was still seeping, and even though the piece of her robe wrapped around his shoulder was self-cleaning, it couldn't keep up with the flow and was soaked through. His tattooed skin was clammy, no longer hot with sweat. To warm him up, they'd placed blankets all around him, but it hadn't affected his plummeting temperature.

As a last resort, they'd sat beside him, hoping their body heat would be the magic cure.

"What did you do to him?" Legion demanded, hands rough as they petted him.

"Nothing," Olivia replied, though she couldn't keep the guilt out of her tone. She should have done more for him. "He was shot by Hunters."

"Because you didn't protect him."

Slap her.

Ignoring the voice no longer proved difficult, her concern for Aeron overshadowing everything else. "What could I have done?" The question brought a fresh wave of torment.

"You could have taken the bullet for him. I would have."

Yes, Legion probably would have. *I'm a failure as a girlfriend.* Not that she was his girlfriend. But she wanted to be, therefore she should have acted like one. "Even if he survives this—" which he would, she would accept no less "—he's going to die in a few days because of you." Oh, Deity. Sorrow joined the torment.

"Liar!" Though the word was snarled, Legion leaned down and gently kissed Aeron's brow. "Do you hear this, darling? Your angel is a liar. You will never die. I won't let you."

Shove her away and claim your man.

Again she easily ignored the voice and the darkness that came with it. "In nine days, an angel assassin will come for him. That assassin will take his head. Because of you. Because you wouldn't stay in hell where you belonged." Rage now.

Legion straightened, twisted toward her, teeth bared in a glower. Once more, her eyes were glowing that demon red. "Another word and I'll stab you while you're sleeping."

"While I'm sleeping next to Aeron?" The taunt was all her own, and she couldn't regret that she'd said it.

"You bitch!"

"Uh-oh. Catfight," an amused voice said from the doorway.

William.

If only it had been William to fascinate her, she thought then. He would have seduced her that very first day, and because his attention span lasted only a few days, she easily could have given him up at the end of her two-week trial.

Then again, she probably would have taken his head if ordered, so she wouldn't have sacrificed her future for a little time with him in the first place. Where Aeron was selfless, William was selfish, a trait that would have been irritating in anyone else. William wore it well, that was for sure.

He had one shoulder pressed into the door's frame, arms crossed over his chest. "Sorry we tried to stab you when we got home," he said to Legion. He and Paris had been completely taken aback when they'd spied the strange female flying down the steps and shouting Aeron's name.

They'd tackled her to the ground. Only Olivia's explanation about who she was—and how she'd gotten that way—had stayed their hands from delivering a deathblow.

Should have stayed quiet, she thought. Not that it would have done any good. Torin, who had eyes and ears all over the fortress, it seemed, had quickly confirmed her story.

"You can't blame us, though," William continued smoothly. "The change is mind-blowing. Besides, I figured we'd reached our limit on pretty females long ago and couldn't possibly be lucky enough to score another."

Ugh. Flirting. Did William never stop? The only time she hadn't heard him flirt was on the drive back to the fortress. Gilly had tried to gain his attention, but he'd been strangely silent.

"Well, it's not like you would provide a real fight for me," the demon girl grumbled, probably charmed despite herself. Weren't they all?

"You wound my honor." He clutched his chest. "We'll have to fight again later and see who actually comes out on top. I prefer my battles naked. You?"

"You said you were going to talk to the others," Olivia interjected, moving them along. "Does anyone have any idea what could be wrong with Aeron?"

"That's actually why I'm here," William said, accepting the change of topic without protest. "Torin thinks he's been poisoned."

Poison. That made sense. And considering the people in high places the Hunters knew, she would bet that poison was heaven-sent. Human poison, like human alcohol, wouldn't have affected him this severely. "Does Torin have a remedy?" she asked hopefully.

William gave a grave shake of his head. "He's got the women searching through old scrolls Reyes has, so I'd give them another few hours before you start panicking."

Hours? Did Aeron have that long? She gulped, tears burning her eyes. Perhaps it was time to change the subject again. If she broke down, she'd be no help to anyone.

"How's Scarlet?" she asked shakily.

"Locked up and still sleeping. Cute little thing," he added as an afterthought. "I might have a go at her."

"Well, I think she's ugly," Legion huffed. "Just like the angel."

"Fallen." Olivia didn't spare her a glance, instead

remaining focused on William. "That *cute little thing* can kill everyone here. Tell the Lords and the women to stay awake if at all possible. The moment they go to sleep, Scarlet can invade their dreams even when she's asleep herself. They'll think what's happening in those dreams is real, and their bodies will react accordingly, making any injury they sustain in the dream a reality."

Wait. Aeron…asleep…nightmares… Had Scarlet already attacked Aeron? Olivia had to stifle a cry at the thought. She had to wake him. Soon.

William pursed his lips. "You couldn't have told us that little gem before we brought her here?"

"Would it have mattered?" Saved Aeron? *I'm an even worse girlfriend than I'd realized.*

"No," he said with a sigh. "Probably not."

The truth, or was he trying to absolve her of culpability?

"Oh, and speaking of nightmares," he added, "there are animals all around the fortress, just like there were around the car at Gilly's school and in the cemetery. Want to explain that?"

"I wish I could," Olivia replied, suddenly grateful to him and eager to help him any way she could. "Ever since I left that crypt, they've been seeking me out and I don't know why." Last thing she'd done was summon her inner light and—

And there was the answer. Her inner light. Of course. They'd sensed that light, and now sought the source. She explained to William.

"Cool trick, but it's really freaking everyone out. And by everyone I mean everyone. Lucien flashed the rest of the men here. You know, the ones who were in Rome. And here's a little tidbit of gossip." Grinning, he rubbed his hands together. "Flashing makes Reyes ill and while vomiting, he had to fight off birds and rodents."

"I'm sorry."

"Sure you are." Legion shot her a scowl. "You're a troublemaker. Nothing goes right when you're around."

"Oh, shut up!" Olivia snapped. "We should be thinking of ways to help Aeron. Or, at the very least, finding him a doctor."

"He doesn't need a doctor. He just needs me. And I'm going to be there for him." Legion began peeling off the dress she'd found while Olivia and Aeron had been fighting for their lives. A barely there dress clearly meant to rival Olivia's slut-it-up outfit.

Olivia gaped at her. "You plan to be there for him by ravishing him while he sleeps?"

"That's right." Naked, completely unabashed, Legion pinched the covers around Aeron and pulled them back, clearly meaning to do as she'd claimed.

"Well, that's gonna have to wait. Legion, honey, I need you to come with me," William said with a crook of his finger.

Frowning, she paused, and her huge breasts jiggled. "Why?"

"Why?" he asked, as if he hadn't thought that far ahead.

"Yes, why?"

"Oh, well, I need to introduce you to the warriors who've been out of town. That way, they won't try to attack you when they come to check on Aeron. And they will. Check on him and attack you, I mean."

He was making it up as he went along, Olivia suspected, trying to give her some alone time with Aeron. She could have hugged him.

"But I can't leave him," Legion whined.

"We'll only be a moment." He smiled a beautifully practiced smile. "Promise."

"Fine," Legion grumbled, jerking the dress over her head and smoothing the white material down her dangerously curved hips. She hissed at Olivia. "If you touch him, I'll eat your eyes in front of you and you'll have to watch, unable to stop me!"

Olivia didn't point out the flaw in her plan as the two left the bedroom and shut the door behind them, William winking over his shoulder. Not knowing how long this reprieve would last, she didn't waste any time stretching out beside Aeron herself.

Kiss him...

When things settled down, she was going to figure out who was invading her head and why.

She wouldn't kiss him, but she *would* pray.

As she caressed her hand down Aeron's chest, she closed her eyes. "Dear Heavenly Deity. I come to You now, as a humble servant who loves You. This man, he isn't evil, despite the evil inside him. He's kind. He's considerate. He's capable of great affection and boundless loyalty. Those are the very things You value most. He's to die, I know. But not now. Not like this. You, who can work all things, even the worst of things, to our good, can heal him, making him ever stronger. You, who long ago conquered death, can save him."

Please hear me. Please help me.

"Why are you doing this to yourself, Olivia? He's going to die eventually, anyway."

Lysander. That was even faster than she'd hoped. *Thank you, thank you, a thousand times thank you!*

The voice—Temptation, she was going to call him—screeched in frustration. *Not him. Anyone but him. I can't stand that bastard.*

"Then leave," she snapped, a suspicion blooming. Temptation clearly hated her mentor, an angel, and the only beings to hate angels were demons.

That meant Temptation was a demon.

I will. So for now, later, baby.

When this demon returned, and he would, she had no doubt, she would have to be better guarded.

"Olivia?" Lysander said.

She opened her eyes a crack. Sure enough, her mentor stood off to the side. Tall, imposing, pulsing with power. His golden wings arched over his shoulders, and his robe swayed at his ankles.

What had he first asked? Oh, yes. Why are you doing this to yourself? "Aeron doesn't deserve to die like this."

"Many do not deserve the deaths that come for them."

She curled into Aeron's side, acting as *his* shield, as a proper girlfriend should do. "You were given a second chance with your Harpy. I deserve a second chance with Aeron."

"And when his time is up, will you request a third?"

To answer as he wished was to lie. "Why are you here, Lysander?"

A muscle ticked in his jaw. "I'm here to tell you that your prayer was heard. I'm here to tell you that Aeron will be healed, but that you must make a sacrifice in return, as is our way."

Sacrifice. Yes, that was usually the way of things.

Since the beginning of time, self-sacrifice, undiluted proof of love, had always held the power to sway her Deity—and change the world. "I accept. Therefore, you may do what you were sent to do and leave."

He remained unmoving. "Do you not care to know what you will be losing?"

"No."

"Are you sure? Well, no matter. I will tell you, anyway. You will lose your Voice of Truth. No longer will others believe everything you say. No longer will you never face doubt. No longer will you recognize a lie the moment it's spoken. And if you decide to return to the heavens and be the angel you were meant to be, you still won't have your Voice of Truth. It will be gone from you forever."

Automatically, her hand sought her throat. Lose her truth? She would rather lose her hands as Gideon had. How would she deal with Aeron doubting her, when she would know in her soul that what she spoke was true?

Her gaze flicked to him. So still, so pale. So gaunt.

"Think carefully," Lysander said. "Every hour, every minute, the path you are on develops more dangerous curves. And do you know what I see at the end of that road, no matter the direction you take? Do you know what awaits you there? Death, Olivia. Your death. And for what? A few more days with him. A few more days with a man who made a deal with me."

"Wh-what deal?"

"I vowed that if he can convince you to return to the heavens, I will try and convince the Council to spare his life as well as his demon companion's."

Her mouth floundered open and closed. In shock, yes, that Lysander was now willing to fight the Council when he'd always denied her pleas to do so, but mostly in hurt. This explained so much. Lysander's secret visit with Aeron. Why Aeron hadn't given her that last orgasm. Why he'd wanted her to see him fight, showing her the harshness of his life.

She meant nothing to him. Not really. How could she, if he were so eager to use her as a bargaining chip? And yet, he was still a man she admired. He was willing to do anything to save someone he loved. To save Legion.

If only that loved one could have been her.

"If I return with you, you can guarantee he will live?" she croaked.

"I can try." Which didn't sound like a guarantee to her. "What's important here is that he agreed," Lysander added before she could reply. "He's willing to part with you to save himself."

The hurt expanded, consuming her, choking her.

"Does that change your mind about this healing?" Lysander asked quietly. Hopefully. "This sacrifice?"

"No," she answered without hesitation. Aeron had placed Legion's well-being above hers, yes, but she'd expected that. What she hadn't expected was to lose him before their time was up. Despite everything, she couldn't lose him. "I still wish to make this bargain."

Sadness filled Lysander's eyes. "Then so it shall be done."

As the last word left him, her vocal cords seized. For a moment, she couldn't speak at all. Couldn't even gurgle or gasp or breathe. She clawed at her throat, her mind fogging as ice and fire melded in her blood.

"It will pass," Lysander said, suddenly in front of her and stroking her temple. It was what he'd done anytime she'd failed to bring her human charges joy. Offered comfort. He had always wanted the best for her, and clearly did now, as well. He was not a bad man, and she would do well to remember that.

As he'd promised, oxygen finally began to seep past her throat and into her lungs. The fire dulled, the ice melted. The fog dissipated. Grateful, she sucked in breath after breath.

"Would Aeron have done the same for you?" Lysander asked. "No. Do not answer. Just think about all I have said."

She nodded. She would be able to do nothing else.

"Be prepared, sweet Olivia. Aeron could very well be injured like this again. I fear Rhea has given the Hunters water from the five rivers of the Realm of Hades."

Olivia flinched. Such water used as a weapon meant certain death. A sip, a touch, and goodbye forever. Even the soul withered. The only way to combat the vile poison was to drink from the River of Life. A river even she didn't know how to find.

"They've been making their own bullets and each of those bullets contains a single drop of that water." He withdrew a small vial from his robe. "Aeron needs only a drop of this to heal. The rest I would hide. Just in case. Use it carefully, however, for when it's gone, you'll receive no more."

River of Life? Hand trembling, she claimed the vial.

"But don't think, even for a moment, that this will save him after his head is taken. And it will be taken, Olivia. An assassin will come."

Her gaze fell. Lysander knew her well; she *had* been thinking along those lines. No matter. She shook her head, tossing away her disappointment and renewing her determination. She would simply find another way.

"I thought you meant to petition the Council for him."

"And so I shall. *We* know the results such a petition will wield. He does not. They were lenient with you, but then, you are one of us. He is a demon. There will be no leniency."

Would telling him do any good?

"How you worry me, Olivia." Lysander sighed. "I will leave you to your task."

CHAPTER NINETEEN

GIDEON, KEEPER OF LIES, tossed and turned atop his bed. His boxers were glued to his sweat-soaked skin, his bandaged hands—or lack thereof—throbbing painfully. Blood had beaded on those bandages and as much as he'd healed, that hadn't happened in weeks. Regression?

He was asleep but still aware, which was weird as shit, and trapped in the thickest darkness he'd ever come across. Again weird, if not technically true. Not for his demon, at any rate. The darkness inside Pandora's box had been just like this, suffocating and maddening. Something Lies hadn't stopped screaming about since entering the strange realm—screams that blended with the ones layering the darkness. Thousands and thousands of discordant shrieks, each one more tortured than the last.

Clawing his way out proved impossible.

"Gideon. Gideon, man, wake up. You're not supposed to sleep."

He heard Paris's voice, wanted to obey, but again, he couldn't. The darkness was too cloying, wrapping around him, holding tightly, nearly drowning him. And then he *did* drown, losing that thread of consciousness altogether. *Can't breathe...*

The gloom parted, and he sucked in a greedy breath—only to scramble backward. Oh, hell, no. *Spider!*

Don't calm, his demon told him.

You don't calm! Panting, trying not to screech like a pussy, he flattened himself against the wall. The monstrous spider followed, those eight hundred legs stabbing into the ground, those beady eyes practically peering into his soul.

Enemy, Lies said. Meaning, friend.

Hardly. *Shit, shit, shit.* Every brain cell he possessed—all of which were trapped in that shit-haze of panic—suddenly let him know, in high-def detail, that he would be this creature's dinner. He'd rather be set on fire. He'd rather be hanged. Hell, he'd rather be gutted.

"I'll be so tasty," he said desperately. Truth was, he'd taste like shit, but then, even in his dreams, he couldn't say what he meant. At least, he didn't think so. He'd never tried it. And wouldn't. The consequences could be just as devastating as when he did so in real life. Pain, pain and more pain.

Memories of his last tangle with truth were fresh in his mind. A few weeks ago, he'd told a Hunter what he really felt—*hate*—and what he really wanted to do—*hurt, maim, kill.* All because he, who could spot a lie from a few thousand miles away, had been tricked into believing Sabin, keeper of Doubt, was dead, slain by Hunter hands. Stupid of him. But as the pain racked him, he'd thought *what's a little more* and had volunteered himself for torture to save his friends from having to endure it.

That's when he lost his hands to a hacksaw. They were now stubs with a few fingers. Even in his dreams. Therefore, he couldn't defend himself properly against Mr. Hungry—who was still eyeing him as if he were a slab of beef as he tripped from one corner of the dream room to another.

Those corners closed in on him, the space shrinking. Hell. No. "Come closer!" *Stay away!* "You want to do this." *You don't want to do this*.

Don't calm, Lies repeated.

There was no time to analyze his demon's odd behavior. One of those hairy legs swiped out. The tip was sharp, bladelike, and sliced his thigh. Maybe that tip had been dipped in poison, because the sting that next exploded through him sent him to his knees, causing his muscles to lock onto his bones, nearly breaking them in half.

"Do that again," he rasped. *Shut up, just shut up!* He rarely despised his demon. Most days, he even liked the bastard. Was glad to be a stronger, harder soldier because of the little fiend. But not now. He wanted to curse that damned spider to everlasting hell.

Why he was so afraid of spiders, he didn't know. The fear had simply always been there.

Another swipe of that leg. Another cut, this one on his back as he tried to spin away from impact. The sting spread quickly, his muscles twisting. The bones in his arm *did* break this time.

"Again," he repeated, the word like an arrow as it left his clenched teeth. "Again."

Don't calm!

The spider stilled, its disgusting head tilting to the side. Watching him, studying him. Damn it! He couldn't scramble away, was now locked in place.

"Stay!" *Go!* The thickness of his breath, beating against the too-close walls, echoed.

"Why do you say the opposite of what your expression tells me you mean?"

The voice came out of nowhere. Or maybe the spider was talking. Except he would have thought a spider that ugly would be male, and this voice had been pure femininity. Familiar somehow. Soft, yet strong. *Relax,* that voice said.

Lies sighed with contentment.

"Stay!" Gideon shouted to the beast. He wouldn't be tricked into passivity like his demon.

Slowly, too slowly, the spider faded, shimmering out of view. *Another trick. You have to—*

A woman stepped from the ensuing murkiness. She was tall and lean, with shoulder-length black hair that possessed not a single curl or hint of wave. There was something as familiar about her face as there'd been about her voice.

Who was she?

She had eyes like black velvet, a regal nose and lips so red they were like thousands of tiny, freshly polished rubies that had been pressed together and cut into a heart. Her cheekbones were sharp, her chin stubborn, but by the gods, she was lovely. A warrior queen.

His heart continued its frantic beat, even as Lies uttered another of those sighs. The panic left him, leaving behind a white-hot fascination. A trick? Who cared! His mind had surely used his deepest fantasies to create her.

The sweat dried on his body, and the ice left his blood as a consuming fire washed through him, blistering everything it touched. So badly he wanted to reach out, to touch her, to caress her face and run his fingers through her hair. To know if she was as soft and silky as he thought she would be.

"Why do you say the opposite of what you mean?" she asked again.

"Don't know," he said, meaning that he did, in fact, know the answer. He could have lied in more detail, allowing her to decipher the truth, but a single thought had stopped him. What if she was Bait, a female sent to help destroy him?

Were Hunters now so powerful they could invade dreams?

Possible. Torin had visited him earlier and told him that Galen had an artifact, that the traitor had successfully bonded the demon of Distrust with a dark-haired female and— A dark-haired female?

He stiffened. Like the one he was staring at?

"Come to the dungeon," she said. "Alone."

"Who aren't you?" he demanded.

"Who aren't *you?*" she shot back.

Silence slithered between them, and anger filled those black eyes. Anger and still that churning curiosity.

"Come to the dungeon, or I'll bring back the spider." With that, she disappeared.

Gideon's eyelids flew open, his conscious mind propelled from that dream-state as if riding a rocket.

"Thank the gods," a frantic Paris said. "Finally."

Gideon was panting. Unlike in his dream, his sweat was not dried. It poured off him, drenching him. Just like in his dream, however, his arm, thigh and back were throbbing, bleeding from where they'd been cut.

"What happened?" he demanded shakily. "Small, hairless mosquito…"

"Bad dream, as I feared."

Fading sunlight trickled in through the only window in his room, but his overhead light was on, illuminating his friend. Paris's hair was multihued, and each of those hues gleamed brightly. His skin was pale, yet it held the shimmer of a pearl.

Now, Gideon might have acted like a pussy, but Paris *looked* like one, he thought with the first threads of humor returning.

"You fell asleep before we could tell you not to and must've met our new guest."

The girl. "Who isn't our guest?"

"Scarlet's her name, and she's a Lord of the Underworld. Or Lordess, I guess."

They'd actually found one of the missing links and brought her here? "What's she not a keeper of?" He would have scrubbed a hand down his face to clear away the remnants of sleep, but couldn't.

Paris sensed his need and wiped his eyes with the edge of his sleeve. "Nightmares, apparently. Pretty thing, if you like 'em rough, but evidently she's as crazy as the Hunters."

Nightmares. For some reason, the word alone was nearly enough to give his own demon an orgasm. And Gideon, well, he was suddenly wondering why the girl had seemed so familiar to him.

Stay, stay, stay, Lies demanded inside his mind.

"Olivia helped us capture her, and she's locked in the dungeon," Paris continued.

"She's hurt, right?" he demanded, throwing his weakened legs over the side of the bed.

"What are you doing, man?"

Gideon managed to stand, swaying but thankfully not falling, his gaze sweeping over his body. He still wore those boxers, was dirty from the sweat and probably smelled.

It wasn't vanity that propelled him unsteadily toward the bathroom, he told himself, but a sense of politeness. No reason to torture the girl—Scarlet, Paris claimed—when she had yet to do anything wrong. Well, kind of. His newest wounds *hurt,* dripping blood all over his clean floor. Her fault?

Aeron, housecleaner extraordinaire, would be pissed, a prospect that had his lips twitching. If nothing else, that'd be fun to watch. Aeron with a mop. Classic.

All the Lords had assigned chores. A great thing for his friends, sure, but Gideon kind of excelled at freeloading. A title he'd once worn with pride. Then Paris had guilted him into helping with the shopping. They'd taken turns, each going to the grocery once a week, Paris at the beginning of the week and Gideon at the end.

He wondered if someone else had taken over the chore since his injury and if so, what he'd have to do instead once he recovered fully. Probably help Aeron with maid-service.

His lips stopped twitching.

"So what'd she do to you?" Paris asked, sidling up to him and acting as his crutch the rest of the way to the bathroom. Once there, Paris even started the water. Scalding hot, just as Gideon liked it. "You mentioned a small, hairless mosquito and I gotta tell you, I have no idea what that means."

With a little more help, Gideon managed to strip. He stepped under the spray. He'd never been modest and he knew Paris, who'd been with thousands and thousands of women, and even the occasional man over the years, wouldn't care.

For a long while, he simply stood immobile, stubs

braced on the wall in front of him, broken arm throbbing as the water poured over him, burning his face and body. Then his good wrist was captured, his bandage upturned and a bar of soap placed atop it.

"No thanks," he muttered. How was he going to manage this?

"It lives," Paris muttered back. "You never answered my question. What'd she do to you with those mosquitoes?"

"Nothing," he said, meaning something.

"I know that. Start talking."

As he scrubbed himself with the soap as best he could, considering he was handless and reduced to using only his right arm, he explained in Gideon-speak. His meaning was clear—*Awake, I got to party with my favorite thing ever*—even without having to resort to the truth.

"You know what this means, don't you?" Paris asked grimly.

"Yeah." No. What the hell? His brain must be addled. All he could think was that Scarlet knew how to conjure insects, but then, a three-year-old could have figured that out by now.

"She knew what scared you most. Only logical conclusion is that the woman can sense our deepest fears and present them to us while we're sleeping. Hence, nightmares."

Great. Exactly what his life had been missing. "I'm not going to pay her a visit."

That earned a *No, thanks* from Lies.

"Now hold everything."

"You're totally going to be able to talk me out of this, so I wouldn't shut up if I were you." Took him a bit, but he managed to switch off the water. "Don't get me a towel."

A growling Paris tossed a fluffy white bath mat at him. Gideon missed, his bandaged nubs simply not fast enough. He bent down and after several attempts, managed to lift the material. His arm throbbed. Stupid broken bones! He tried to dry himself, he really did, but he didn't do too good a job.

Finally Paris snatched the cotton and patted him dry. "You're worse than a baby, you know that?"

"Don't grab me some clothes."

Shaking his head, Paris disappeared into the room. A dresser drawer slid open, slammed shut, then another, and then he was striding back into the bathroom, holding out a pair of shorts and a T-shirt.

Gideon had already stepped from the stall. He could have dressed himself, but that would have required the rest of his energy. "I'm not going to let you do it."

Another shake of that head. "You're going to go see her, at least take some weapons." Paris tugged the shirt over his head and helped him pull his arms through. He only cringed once. "Like me."

"Sure." Gods, this was embarrassing. Being this helpless. His friend was so matter-of-fact about it, though, that some of the sting eased.

Paris rolled his eyes as he held open the shorts for Gideon to step into. "Just because she's locked up doesn't mean she's harmless." His gaze dropped pointedly to the still-bleeding wound in Gideon's thigh.

Gideon shrugged. "Could you have picked anything more masculine for me?" he asked with disgust as he eyed himself. If he hoped to impress Scarlet—which he didn't, he assured himself—he would fail. A plain white shirt too small for him and gray running shorts. Fabulous.

Paris crossed his arms over his chest. "So you're thinking about going without me?"

"No." *Alone,* she'd said. If he brought a friend, she might zip her pretty lips, and that he wouldn't tolerate. He wanted answers, damn it. Namely: how the hell did he know her? He wouldn't be averse to listening to her apologize for slicing him, either.

"Gideon," Paris warned.

"She's not locked up, right?" He lumbered into the bedroom, throwing over his shoulder, "I'll be in danger the entire time."

"Frustrating ass. Fine, but be careful," Paris called.

"Won't."

After two winding hallways and a flight of stairs, he had to prop himself against a wall to remain standing. Along the way, he'd run into several of his friends, and each had tried to help him back to his room. He'd shooed them away as politely as possible. They were worried about him, and he loved them for it. Not that he could ever tell them that. "I hate you" was the best he could do. But he wasn't backing down for this.

He forced himself back into motion. As he crossed the threshold into the dungeon, the air changed completely. It was dirty now, laden with blood, sweat and even urine. Hunters had been tortured here, over and over again. How disgusted the girl must be. Perhaps huddled in a corner, shaking. Crying.

What would he do if that were the case? Probably run screaming, he mused. Only thing worse than spiders were feminine tears.

Grappling with dread, he turned the final corner. At

last she came into view, and he stilled. Awareness consumed him. First thing he noticed: she wasn't crying. Or scared. Second: she was far lovelier in person than she'd been in his dream.

She gripped the bars, waiting, expression blank. "You came." She didn't sound surprised, just resigned.

"No, I didn't." As if in a trance, he closed the distance between them, the scent of night flowers suddenly filling his nose. He breathed deeply. So did Lies.

Her gaze raked him, taking his measure, cataloging his every flaw. "Maybe you shouldn't have."

Again he was struck by how familiar she was, both her voice and her face, but he still couldn't figure out where he'd met her. "Don't tell me why."

Her dark eyes narrowed. "Tell me I'm pretty."

Conceited, was she? Well, she wouldn't get what she wanted from him. "You're ugly."

Part of him expected her to gasp in horror. She didn't. In that same resigned voice, she said, "Tell me I'm smart."

"You're stupid."

Slowly her lips curled into a smile. "Well, well, well. Lies. It really is you. We're together again at last."

CHAPTER TWENTY

A DROP OF WATER hit Aeron's lips, cool and tingling, before sliding over his tongue, down his throat and into his stomach, absorbing there, then entering his bloodstream and traveling to each of his organs. Moment of contact, his heart began a perfect beat, his lungs filled with more oxygen than they'd ever had and his skin reached the perfect temperature, neither too hot nor too cold.

Suddenly he could hear the birds chirping outside his window, the wind dancing past the line of trees that surrounded the fortress. Could even hear his friends in the rooms above and below his, discussing what was to be done about Scarlet, about the Hunters, and lamenting his illness.

And his nose... He breathed deeply, catching the scent of bark, dewy leaves, sweat, the lemon soap Sabin used, Paris's aftershave and his personal favorite...wild sky. Olivia.

Olivia was here with him.

Maybe that was why Wrath was purring so contentedly.

Aeron pried his eyelids apart, and immediately regretted the action. So much light. Light from the bulbs in the ceiling, light from the bathroom. His walls, which he'd once thought were pale silver and crumbling stone, gleamed as if those stones had somehow trapped a rainbow.

"You're alive," Olivia said with palpable relief.

There was something different about her voice, he thought as his gaze sought her out. It was still beautiful, more so now that he could hear the subtle nuances—a low rasp, banked sensuality—but still different. She was perched at the edge of his bed, sky-blue eyes peering down at him. Her dark hair was in tangles around her, framing the delicacy of her features. The white robe he'd forced her to don however long ago still draped her, free of wrinkles and dirt.

Her skin was… His breath caught. Majestic. That was the only word to describe it. *Majestic.* No, not the only word. *Flawless* worked, too. He could have stared at her for hours, days. Forever. She was pure, white cream.

He wanted to touch her. Had to feel how soft she was. How warm she was. Had to know she was healthy and whole and she'd escaped without harm.

Escaped. The word tormented him. He remembered they'd been inside that crypt, and he'd been shot. He'd carried Nightmares into the cemetery, fallen to his knees, waiting for his friends, but he didn't recall anything after that. He fisted the sheets. Answers first, then he could allow himself a single touch.

Single?

Concentrate. "What happened?" Odd. Olivia's voice wasn't the only one to have changed. His had never sounded so smooth or strong.

She offered him a shaky smile. "We thought we'd lost you. You were shot, and the bullet was laced with immortal poison, slowly killing you."

Yes, that made sense. A bullet had never affected

him like that, but this one had weakened him unbearably. "How'd I get here?"

"Paris and William came and got us."

"No trouble?"

"With Hunters?" She shook her head, that cloud of hair dancing around her shoulders. "None. We even picked up Gilly on the way back here, but we never encountered them."

It was only a matter of time, though. As close as they were, and with the success of their demon-possession, they would attack soon enough. "How's Paris?"

"He's fine, strong and taking care of himself now."

Or he'd tricked everyone into thinking so. Paris was good at hiding his actions—or lack of action—behind humor and smiles. Most likely he was drinking ambrosia and neglecting his body's needs.

"I'm not going to say that!" Olivia suddenly snapped.

Aeron frowned. "Say what?"

"Sorry." Her shoulders slumped. "The voice returned, telling me to do all kinds of things to your body. I've named him Temptation, and I'm pretty sure he's a demon."

A demon? None that he knew, which could mean that someone else listed on the scrolls was hiding in town. But why torment Olivia? And with sexual thoughts, of all things?

Whatever the reason, he wouldn't stand for it.

Punish, Wrath said.

Aeron was glad the demon had recovered, as well. And yes. He wanted to punish the ones who had hurt them. He just had to—

"Oh, no," Olivia said with a shake of her lovely head. "I can see the thoughts spinning behind your eyes. We'll worry about the demon later. He's irritating, that's all. Right now, I'm more concerned about *you*."

Sweet, darling Olivia. His protector, something he'd never thought he'd need. Something he'd never expected to want. But he did want, desperately. Need, certainly. Yet he had to convince her to return to the heavens. In—how long?

He glanced at the window, the split curtains framing a waning moon. "How long did I sleep?"

"Most of the day and night. You're still naked, if you hadn't noticed." A blush stained her cheeks. "Not that that's important right now."

Most of the day and night. Which meant morning would arrive all too soon. Which meant he had eight days to convince Olivia to return home. Eight days to save himself and Legion.

Eight days to resist her.

He wouldn't last. A single touch wasn't going to be enough, he admitted that now. He would want more. He would have more.

More, Wrath echoed.

Yes, more. He wasn't going to stop himself. Not this time. Selfish of him, yes, but selfish he would be. He could have died out there. Died without warning. Without knowing what it was like to sink inside her, feeling her clench around his cock, clawing his back, gasping his name.

When he knew, he would stop wondering, stop craving. He could continue on as before. And she would have had her fun. She could go home satisfied.

Selfish? Ha! He was a *giver*.

"How did I heal?" he asked. Better question: would he lose steam midway? He didn't want her leaving this bed until she reached her peak twice. At least. He owed her. Her crack about his lack of prowess still stung.

Olivia's gaze shifted away from him. "An antidote."

Why couldn't she meet his eyes? "An angel antidote?"

"Yes." She motioned to a glowing blue vial on his nightstand. "Water from the River of Life. One drop, and death is chased away."

No wonder his senses were heightened.

"Once we run out," she continued, "we'll be given no more. Which is a shame. Lysander told me the Hunters have many, many more of those poisoned bullets."

"How long will the effects last?" He would've expected Wrath to fume at being fed a heavenly substance. Instead, the demon purred a little louder, as if given a great gift.

In a snap, Aeron thought he understood. Legion represented hell, and Olivia heaven. The latter he'd already figured out, but the former... He realized now that Wrath missed his home. *Both* his homes. High Lords had once been angels, Olivia had said, before falling from the sky. Home number one. And landing in hell. Home number two, though Wrath hadn't considered it as such until he compared it to Pandora's box.

Heaven and hell, he thought again, unsure how he'd missed the connection before. Olivia and Legion. Two halves of a whole, just as he and Wrath were.

Speaking of... "Where's Legion?" he asked, gazing around the room in search of her.

"William's distracting her, but I'm not sure how long that will last." Olivia traced a finger along his breastbone. "Your heartbeat is improving. Strong."

His flesh heated where they connected. *More.*

His ears twitched as he listened to a conversation a few rooms over. Sabin and his crew had returned from the Temple of the Unspoken Ones. A lot of them were injured, but recovering. As soon as they were better, they were going to raid The Asylum and destroy the Hunters residing there.

No one was coming to check on him, then, and there was nothing for Aeron to do at the moment. Except Olivia.

"As you pointed out, I'm still naked," he found himself saying. "Are you ready to have fun?"

First her jaw dropped. Then she closed it with a snap. Then it dropped again. Unwilling to wait for her to acclimate to his intentions—no more waiting period— Aeron reached up and cupped the base of her neck, drawing her down until she was practically on top of him. Her breath hitched, and the softness of her breasts pressed into his chest.

Yes, he would have this woman. Those breasts, too. The sweet spot hopefully moistening for him even now, definitely.

"Wh-what are you doing?" The breathy question warmed him body and soul, because there was longing in every word.

"Having you." Finally.

He lifted his head and meshed their lips together. She didn't resist, not even for a moment. No, she opened for him, meeting his tongue with her own. He could taste the freshness of the water she'd given him, as well as the cinnamon of her breath.

Trembling hands flattened on him, and his heart increased in speed, racing to meet them. Her skin was hot rather than warm, and burned him just right. Silky curls tickled him.

He anchored his free hand under her bottom and tugged her the rest of the way atop him. Their bodies fit together, and her legs opened automatically, cradling him perfectly. He moaned. Yes...yes...

Yes! Wrath agreed.

"No," she rasped, and wrenched away. She even scrambled from the bed and stood to trembling legs, nearly teetering over.

Both he and the demon wanted to roar. Instead, Aeron settled his weight on his elbows and watched her. *Calm.* "You want me. I know you do." Gods, he could smell her arousal just then, heady feminine musk.

"Yes, but I won't let you rouse my passions and then leave me before I can finish." She fisted her robe, inadvertently raising the fabric and showing a hint of those beautiful calves. Calves he *would* lick.

"Olivia, I—"

"No," she said again, spinning away. Twice she tripped over her own feet as she made her way to his dresser. There, she propped her elbows on the surface and held her head in her upraised hands. "I can't bear it."

Was she...crying?

Aeron swallowed the sudden lump in his throat and stood. Not that. Anything but that. He was as naked as she'd promised, his erection waving proudly. "I want you. I'm not going to deny either of us again. This I swear to you, Olivia."

"Oh, shut up!"

He blinked. Was he making no progress, then? Had his actions ruined everything? "Make me," was all he could think to say. With a kiss. *Please.*

"Not you," she murmured. "The voice. Temptation. He wants me to raise my robe and show you that I'm not wearing anything underneath."

She wasn't? Aeron licked his lips and approached. Nothing, not even one of the Hunters' bombs, could have kept him away after learning that. "I'll find out for myself."

Olivia gasped when he placed his now-trembling hands on her hips. Her head lifted and she twisted to peer up at him. Her eyes were huge, watery, and his heart lurched in his chest.

"What—what are you doing?"

"Finding out, like I told you." First he played with her breasts, cupping, thrumming the nipples, until *she* trembled. Then he dropped to his knees, his hands never leaving her delectable body, but following him down. "You wanted to have fun, so I'm giving you fun."

"D-don't do this if you're going to stop midway. I've been through too much the past few days and I—"

"I won't." The scent of her arousal was stronger, a sultry night he wanted to lose himself in. "Nothing could stop me now, angel. *Nothing.*"

Slowly, so slowly, he lifted the hem of the robe. Not once did she protest, not even when goose bumps broke out over her legs. Her smooth, firm legs, a mix of honey and vanilla. When he revealed her bottom and saw that she *wasn't* wearing any panties, his cock jerked in re-action. *Beautiful.* Even his wings ached from inside their slits.

Mine.

Actually, mine. He bunched the material around her waist, holding it prisoner against the dresser and leaving her lower body bare. He cupped her, spreading his fingers over those delectable cheeks. Again she gasped. Between each of his fingers, he placed a kiss.

"More?" he asked.

"Yes," she and Wrath breathed in unison.

He kissed the underside and encountered the softest skin her Deity—his Deity now, too, for he realized he would always worship the one responsible for creating her—had probably ever created.

"Aeron," she said on another of those wispy catches.

"Spread your legs for me." He clutched her thighs and prodded her into action, even nudging her feet apart with his knees. His blood was like fire, his need sharpening to a razor point. "Now bend over. As far as you can."

There was only a slight pause before she complied. For a moment, only a moment, all he could do was stare. So pretty. So sweet. So pink. So wet. For him and him alone. Even the thought of sharing with his (once again purring) demon was abhorrent. But he would. He would take this woman any way he could get her.

"Going to taste you now." He dipped his head and sampled her fully, distantly hearing a slap of flesh upon wood.

"Aeron!"

His gaze flicked up. She'd settled her hands on the mirror in front of her and flattened her temple against the dresser. Her eyelids were squeezed shut and her breaths shallow, her teeth chewing at her lips.

"Don't...stop," she begged him.

He didn't. He ran his tongue over her femininity again, lingering against her clitoris, flicking it, sucking on it. *This* was ambrosia. Her. Soft and pouty...his. Accepting what he did, *liking* it.

Though he wanted to consume her, he didn't allow himself to rush. He'd gone that route with her before. This time, he would savor. This time, he would learn everything about this beautiful body.

"I'm going to... Aeron..."

"Good girl." He moved his tongue faster, harder against her. Her hips arched forward and back and when he found her opening, he thrust deep inside. She screamed, shuddering with her release.

He didn't know how much time—minutes, hours, days—passed before she calmed enough that he was able to bend down and kiss—and lick—the calves he'd so admired before rising and paying proper homage to her lower back. There were two indentations, and as he swirled his tongue around them, his hands slid up... up...and cupped her breasts the way he knew she liked. Both of her nipples were still gloriously hard, like little pearls, and he rolled them between his fingers.

More.

"I'm ready," Olivia said between pants. "Come inside me."

"Not yet." She was wet, yes, but he wanted her dripping. He wanted her beyond ready. She was a virgin, and he would make this as easy as possible for her.

His first time had been with a minor Greek goddess. One of the three Furies. Megaera, the "jealous one," as she'd often been called. Her brand of loving had been violent and painful, and yet another reason he'd always avoided females who preferred a strong hand from their lovers. With Olivia, though, it wasn't that he preferred gentle women over wild women, or wild women over gentle women. It was that he preferred *Olivia*.

As he stood, he traced his tongue up the ridges of

her spine—there were scars where her wings should have been, and he kissed them, too, laving them with his attentions—all while yanking her robe up and over her head. Silky hair cascaded down her shoulders and back, even obscuring her breasts from the mirror's view. He had to see those breasts, he thought, brushing that hair aside.

Through the glass, those frosted nipples came into view. He tweaked them, and she dropped her head upon his shoulder, eyes closing to half-mast. The thick length of his erection pressed between her bottom, desperate for contact, and he hissed between his teeth.

There would be no more savoring if he kept this up.

Down, down his hand went, until it reached the apex of her thighs. His fingers tunneled through the fine tuft of dark curls and into that hot, wet mound. One, two, he pushed them inside her.

They both groaned. Aeron placed a kiss at the curve of her neck, watching himself all the while. What a sight they were. His dark tattooed body behind her. Her softer, cloud-tinted one writhing in front of him. By far the most erotic sight he'd ever beheld.

No. Wait. Her arms reached back, one hand gripping his head to angle him down for a kiss, the other clasping his ass. *This* was the most erotic sight he'd ever beheld.

"I'm ready, I swear."

Almost…almost… He worked a third finger inside her, stretching her, spreading that glistening moisture. And when he encountered the proof of her virginity, he paused, reveled in the sense of possessiveness flooding him—*mine, all mine*—and then gently broke through.

Mine. A cry from Wrath.

Mine. An insistence.

She tensed, even stilled against his mouth. "Aeron."

He'd rather hurt her with his fingers than his cock. "Sorry. Pain. Feel good. Swear." He sounded like a Neanderthal, but he just couldn't form proper sentences. Olivia was his. Utterly his. His mind was stuck on that fact, and that alone.

When she relaxed, he reclaimed her mouth, playing with her tongue, feeding her kiss after needed kiss, and soon she began writhing against him again, lost to the pleasure. Soon she was dripping, as he'd craved.

Now she was ready.

Though he hated to release her, even for a moment, he did so to grip his cock. The throbbing length practically leapt into his touch, hungry for more, so much more, yet he feared spilling at first contact. *Diversion.* He bit down on his tongue until he tasted blood, and the boiling need was tempered. *Achieved.* Tenderly, he pushed Olivia back on the dresser with his free hand, chest to wood, then poised the tip of his erection at her opening.

"Still ready?"

"Now, Aeron. Do it now!"

Inch by inch, he drove it inside her, allowing her to grow accustomed to his size before giving her more. All the while she gasped and moaned and beseeched him. Wrath, too. Finally, he was in to the hilt, his eyes fogging over with the force of his need to pound and pound and never stop.

"Aeron," she groaned, and he knew it was another plea.

He pulled out, almost all the way, before sinking back in. A curse rushed from him—she had arched her hips to meet him, and rational thought fled, something inside him breaking. A tether of some sort. A tether on his restraint.

Just like that, he lost himself. Lost control, lost who he was, lost everything but the need to fill this woman with all that he was. In and out he pounded inside her, just as he'd wanted. Determined, driven, possessed by far more than a demon.

He was gripping her hips, probably bruising her, surely crushing her bones, but he couldn't stop himself. He was wild, feral, existing for only this moment. This woman. Just then, she was his everything. She was as much a part of him as Wrath. He couldn't live without her. *Wouldn't* live without her.

"Aeron." She was no longer panting; she was shouting. "Don't stop, don't stop, don't you dare stop. More. More!"

In his mind, only one word echoed. *Mine. Mine, mine, mine.* He'd heard it a thousand times before, but then he was *shouting,* "Mine, mine, mine," and the sound was filling his ears, sweeping through him, heating him another degree, branding him, destroying who he'd been, what he'd been, then building him back up, into something new and fine and right, into the man he'd always been meant to be. Her man. And that's when *mine* faded and another word took its place, stronger, far more necessary. *Yours.* He wanted to belong to her, to be hers. To be everything she'd ever dreamed, to fulfill every wish she'd ever made.

"Aeron," she gasped.

Yours.

He should have seen this coming, should have known what she was beginning to mean to him, but his resistance had blinded him. Now, reduced to his basest self, he was raw, vulnerable, operating on a visceral level.

She was his, and he was hers.

He kicked her legs farther apart, and she fell down a little, deeper into his thrusts. The gap from the dresser allowed him to reach around and stroke her where she needed. With a scream, she erupted, and as those lush inner walls gripped him, Aeron hurtled over the edge himself, hot seed jetting inside her.

"Aeron," she cried.

Yours.

He collapsed on her, panting, and realized there was a flaw to his "only once" plan. Once would never be enough. Not for him, and not for his demon.

They needed more; they couldn't possibly be satisfied until they'd taken her in every way imaginable. And they could. He could. Without fear. He'd lost control, but Wrath hadn't attacked her. He'd lost control, but he hadn't hurt her.

She'd been irresistible before, but now... He needed to be with her or his life would not be complete. He needed to make love to her every night and wake up to her every morning—to make love to her again. He needed to pamper her and give her the things she craved. Like fun. Like joy. Like passion.

Like him.

"Olivia," he said, the syllables broken but still a promise from him, a promise for all the "more" she desired. Forever?

What are you doing? What are you thinking? You can't do this. His sweat-slicked chest pressed into her back, and he forced himself to rise.

Wrath whimpered.

"Aeron," she said. Then, "Aeron!"

No, that last shout hadn't belonged to Olivia. He twisted, as did his angel, and they stiffened at the same time. William and a pretty blonde—Legion, he reminded himself, surprised all over again by the change in her—stood in the open doorway.

Aeron forced his wings out of hiding and wrapped them around Olivia, shielding her from view. Meanwhile, William held the humanoid demon back, but strong as he was, she was dragging him forward, her murderous gaze locked on the angel.

CHAPTER TWENTY-ONE

OLIVIA COULDN'T BELIEVE what had just happened with Aeron—and what was happening now with Legion. Naked. Sex. Pleasure. Happiness. Hope.

All dashed.

Trembling, she bent down to retrieve her robe and wrenched the material over her head. Thankfully, Aeron's wings kept her concealed the entire time. How she would have loved to bask in the afterglow. To discover if Aeron had been as affected as she was.

Sex was...so much more than she ever could have imagined—and she'd imagined a lot, since the first orgasm he'd given her. The pleasure, the satisfaction, the power of knowing you were driving someone out of their mind. The closeness, the sharing, the giving, the taking. Every minute was a miracle.

She'd been alive for centuries. Why hadn't she been doing this all that time? Although, she suspected the act would not be the same with any other man. Only Aeron. Her Aeron. The man who made her ache...dream.

Legion's high-pitched screeches drew her back to the present. "Bitch! Whore! I'll kill you!"

Temptation laughed inside Olivia's head. He'd been silent during the act, having gotten what he'd wanted. Why had he returned?

William still had a grip on Legion, but that grip could

fail at any moment. Olivia kind of hoped it did. Someone needed to put Legion in her place, and she would be more than happy to do so. She wanted her afterglow, damn it!

"Dress," Olivia told Aeron, hating that another woman—especially *this* one—was seeing him like this. All those tattoos should be hers, and hers alone, to feast upon. Visually or otherwise. She wished she could have licked them.

Next time.

Would there be a next time?

His expression was hard, unreadable, as he tugged on his pants and fastened them at the waist. Because his wings were still expanded, he couldn't don a shirt. At least dressing spurred him into action. He kicked forward, wrapped an arm around Legion's waist and hefted her into his side like a sack of potatoes.

The demon's flailing never ceased. "Let me go! Let me at her!"

"You can go," Aeron told William. "I'll handle things from here."

There were cuts on William's face and arms, and all of them were bleeding. The warrior nodded, his lips twitching in amusement. "Good luck, my friend. Oh, and just so you know, a meeting's been called. Entertainment room, ten minutes." With that, he strolled into the hallway, shutting the door behind him and whistling under his breath.

Aeron carted his bounty to the bed and tossed her onto the mattress. She bounced up and down and tried to scramble off, gaze still locked and loaded on Olivia.

"Stay," he barked.

Legion froze, glaring up at him—until an obvious

sense of self-preservation took hold and she smoothed out her features. The self-preservation was quickly followed by determination, though, and she settled on the edge of the bed, elbows behind her, breasts thrust forward, legs on the floor but spread and ready to wrap around him.

"Care to join me?" she asked huskily.

Oh, no, she didn't, Olivia fumed as Temptation yelled his own denial. *Enough!* She stalked forward, bypassing Aeron without a word, and stopped in front of Legion. Before either of them knew what she was about, she punched Legion in the mouth.

Legion's head whipped to the side, her bottom lip split and already bleeding. Olivia's knuckles throbbed, but she welcomed the sting. *Try to kiss him now.*

Hard, hot hands settled on her shoulders and spun her around. Aeron wasn't looking at her but over her shoulder at Legion. "Stay."

The command was met with a growl, but Legion obeyed.

Aeron's gaze finally shifted to Olivia. Surprise began to swirl in those lovely violet irises, chasing away his fury. "I never thought I'd have to tell you to behave."

She raised her chin. "I will not tolerate being called such vile names."

"You won't have to." Once more his gaze moved to Legion. "Understand?"

The support surprised *her.* Was he…could he be choosing her over Legion? For a moment, Olivia couldn't breathe. Could barely stand. There wasn't time to bask in the wondrous sensation, however. Aeron moved around her as if she were already forgotten and crouched in front of Legion.

"There's no need for you to hurt my—the angel. I love you," he said. "You know that." His tone was soft, caring now. "Tell me you know that."

"Yes. I know it." All the anger drained from Legion, as well, and she reached out, cupping his jaw, trying to pull him down for a kiss. "I love you, too."

Aeron removed her hands with a gentle yet forceful jerk. "I don't love you in that way. I love you like a daughter. Tell me you know *that*."

First, anger reclaimed the demon's features. Then shock. Then fear. All in the span of a single second. Her chin trembled, and tears of abject misery filled her eyes. "But I'm pretty."

"You were pretty before, but that doesn't change how I feel."

Legion shook her head in denial. "No. You have to be with me. You have to—"

"That's not going to happen, baby."

Several droplets spilled, tumbling down her cheeks. "Is this…is this because of the angel?"

"Olivia has nothing to do with what I feel for you."

Olivia suddenly wished she were someplace, anyplace else. She shouldn't be here. Shouldn't be witnessing this private moment. Yes, that's what she'd do. Go anyplace else. Her knees knocked as she walked to the door.

Stop! Where are you going? Temptation. When would the demon leave her for good?

"You're lying!" Legion spat. "You love her."

Her hand froze on the knob.

Silence. The answer…she had to know.

Then, "Legion," Aeron said on a sigh.

Disappointment choked Olivia, but still she couldn't force herself to exit. Not yet. Maybe he would—

"You can't love her," the demon shouted. "You have to love me."

"I told you. I do love you."

Stomach clenching... Say them. Say the words.

"No! You have to love me like a wife. You have to pleasure me with your body. Otherwise..."

"Otherwise?" he demanded harshly.

Olivia tensed. Oh, Deity. The bargain. She'd forgotten about Legion's bargain with Lucifer. Dread, so much dread. She turned and pressed her back into the wood, shaking. Waiting. This, more than a declaration, she had to hear.

"Tell him," she commanded. "He deserves to know."

"Tell me," Aeron parroted.

Legion gulped. "If I fail to seduce you in eight days, Lucifer will...he'll...he'll possess my new body," she whispered. "If I fail, he'll...he'll use me to kill you and your friends."

No. *No!*

Aeron flicked Olivia a quick, unsure glance, not comprehending Legion's confession. "Physically, he can't leave hell. He can't—"

"He can. If he possesses her, he can do anything," Olivia croaked, hand closing over her throat. Her horror didn't last long. Blood chilled in her veins, numbing the emotion. She'd been so close to paradise, only to be thrust into hell. "He can breed her with anyone of his choosing, assume control of the Hunters, influence humans and turn them against you. He can even see into the angelic realm and slaughter my kind."

Aeron's spine became as rigid as a steel pipe. "Why would he want to do any of that?"

"Why else? Power. Freedom. Spite. He despises angels. They were supposed to follow him, yet they chose to remain with the One True Deity instead. But most of all, he despises the True Deity. His destruction is what Lucifer craves most. With his demon High Lords freely roaming the land, he'll have a better chance of that."

Enough of this foolishness. Shut her up, Temptation commanded.

Olivia ignored him, only to blink in bewilderment a moment later. Him. She'd already known the voice belonged to a male, but she now realized this male wanted her to win Aeron—and more specifically, for Legion to fail. This male wanted to prevent Legion from convincing Aeron to bed her.

Not a demon, after all.

Lucifer, she realized. Lucifer was her Temptation. He didn't have to leave hell to cast his voice elsewhere, or to whisper to one particular person. He merely had to link with a soul open to corruption.

Bye-bye blessed numbness. Her horror returned, as did her dread, both mixed with shame. How could she not have known? How had she missed the truth? *Stupid angel.*

"Why would you make such a bargain?" Aeron demanded.

The tears continued to flow down Legion's cheeks. "I wanted to be pretty. To be what you needed. I thought I would win you, make you forget the angel. I thought I would make you happy."

Aeron scrubbed a hand down his face, his nails scraping, leaving angry red welts. "I can't believe this.

Do you have any idea what you've done? Do you have any idea of the things you've put into motion?"

Legion nodded, chin trembling. "I'm sorry. So sorry."

A pause, then a sorrowful, "So am I."

With those words, Olivia knew. She *knew*. He'd already made up his mind. Aeron would sleep with Legion. He would enter her body the same way he'd entered Olivia's. To save the little demon from possession. To save his friends from Lucifer. To keep the Hunters from victory.

Tears filled her own eyes, but she blinked them back. With this act, Aeron would prove that what he'd done with Olivia meant nothing. With this act, she would leave. He had to know she would leave.

Had that knowledge made the decision easier for him? she wondered with a bitter laugh. No way she could stay here, knowing he'd bedded another woman. No matter the reason.

Olivia had her own choice to make, then, it seemed. She would leave, there was no question of that. Not now. But would she return to the heavens, possibly saving Aeron's life, or simply travel to a new location here on earth?

Here, most likely, for how could she possibly return home now? She was changed, human in all the ways that mattered. She would be miserable up there, bringing joy to no one, least of all herself. She would be useless. And if ever she changed her mind about having returned, she wouldn't be allowed to fall again. No, she would be put to death or permanently cast into hell. There could be no other choice for an angel who lost her way twice.

But how could she stay here and live with herself,

knowing she could have saved Aeron and hadn't? Even though saving him meant that he would be with another woman?

Was she truly that selfless?

No, she wasn't. She should have killed him when she'd had the chance and saved each of them this pain. Another bitter laugh filled her head, but this one escaped.

Aeron rose, the action stiff, uncoordinated. "We have a little time. We don't have to take care of this right this moment."

So he didn't plan to sleep with Legion right away. That was a small comfort, at least.

"Thank you," Legion said, grateful, pleased and shamed all at once. "I promise I won't—"

He turned, cutting her off, and Olivia's gaze ate him up. His masculine beauty, his power. No, she wasn't that selfless, but she was that in love, she realized.

Love. The word echoed in her mind. She loved him. Fully, utterly, wholly, completely. He was the reason her heart beat, the source of her joy. She *would* die for him. He was strong and brave, fierce and caring. Giving, selfless himself. What wasn't to love?

She would stay here with him until he bedded Legion. She would soak up every moment she had with him. And then…then she would return to the heavens. She would ensure Lysander kept his end of the bargain and petitioned the Council for Aeron's life.

Still. That didn't guarantee their cooperation.

Well, she would just have to find another way.

What a difference a few days made, she thought sadly. She'd come here resigned to Aeron's approaching death, happy with the time they would have and determined to experience joy as humans did. Yet she'd spent time with her warrior, and everything had changed. She could no longer accept the thought of him dying. Of his courage and strength being extinguished.

"Don't worry, Aeron," she said, squaring her shoulders. "Soon I'll leave, and you and Legion will be safe." A promise welded to her soul.

Legion gaped at her.

Lucifer screeched an unholy sound inside her head.

Aeron's lips pulled tight in a scowl, his teeth bared, his eyes red, glowing. Demon eyes. "I said we have time. We don't have to take care of this now. Therefore, you will stay. Now, enough about that. I have a meeting to attend. I'm going to leave the two of you in here and you *will* play nice. Understand? You won't like what happens if you harm each other, I promise you that." He didn't wait for their replies but stormed from the room.

Unlike William, he didn't gently shut the door behind him. He slammed it, rattling the pictures on the walls.

After everything she'd just agonized over, realized and decided, a little compassion—and a goodbye kiss— wouldn't have been amiss.

Olivia stared over at Legion. Legion stared back.

"Well," Olivia said, at a loss. She still ached from Aeron's possession. Still felt the wetness he'd left behind. Yet very soon this female would be with Aeron the way she had just been with him.

"I won't stay here with you," Legion lashed out.

"That makes two of us. I'm leaving."

Grinning, Legion jolted upright. "You're returning to the sky already?"

"Not yet. I'll be listening to what's said at the meeting."

Her grin faded, but she glanced at the door. "Your ears are probably so feeble you'll need someone there to interpret the murmurings."

She offered no reply, wanting to hate the woman but unable to do so. Hate required energy, and just then she had none to spare. Besides, this demon would have been like her stepdaughter if things had progressed the way she'd wanted. More than that, Legion had done what was necessary to win her man. Just as Olivia had.

Only, Legion had won.

IT WAS GOOD to be home, Strider thought, gazing around the entertainment room. All the men and women were accounted for. All three thousand of them, it seemed. Except for Gideon, who—according to the gossiping hens and William, the gossiping cock, as he happily called himself—was in the dungeon making nice with the newest prisoner.

The warriors, with their big, hard bodies, seemed to consume every inch of space, saturating the air with testosterone. The women perched on the couches and chairs, forcing the men to stand against the walls. Those who weren't otherwise occupied, that is.

Lucien and Sabin were playing a game of pool and talking amongst themselves, probably trying to sort things out before they spoke to the group. William was sitting in front of the TV, playing a video game. Aeron and Paris were in the far corner and passing a flask back and forth. Both looked miserable. Especially Aeron. His expression was carved from granite—livid granite—and his tattoos were stark against his now-pale skin. And his eyes…hell. They were demon red.

Still healing from that poisoned bullet? Or something more personal?

Strider had only been home a day, but he'd already heard about the man's angel problems from three different sources. Cameo, Kaia and Legion—an unbelievably improved Legion. All three had been a font of conflicting information. Cameo liked Olivia, talked about how knowledgeable and helpful she was. Kaia talked about how delightfully naughty the real Olivia was. And Legion thought she was a bitch who would murder Aeron in his sleep.

Kaia thought Aeron would marry the girl. Cameo thought Aeron would kick the girl out and never see her again. And Legion thought she was a bitch and a murderer. (That was pretty much all Legion had said. Oh, wait. She'd asked Strider to kill that "bitch and murderer.") When he'd refused, she'd threatened to pay someone to "do him prison-style."

"I'm waiting," Strider called. "Me no likes to wait."

Finally, Lucien and Sabin ended their game, nodded to each other as if they'd reached an understanding and approached the front of the room. Conversations tapered to quiet.

Both men anchored their arms behind their backs, their legs braced apart. They were ready for action. Good thing. Everyone else in the room was tense and ready to receive that action.

"We called this meeting so that each group could bring the other up to speed on what's been happening in Rome and Buda," Sabin began. "I'll go first. The Unspoken Ones want us to bring them Cronus's head, but that little deed will free them, and if they're freed…" He shuddered. "No telling what evil they'll unleash."

"However," Lucien said, picking up where Sabin had stopped. "They've hedged their bets and asked the Hunters to bring them Cronus's head, as well. Whoever succeeds in doing so, us or the Hunters, will be given the fourth and final artifact."

The Paring Rod. No one knew what it did. Not really. Even if it was useless, Strider would've massacred an army to possess it. If there was the slightest chance it was powerful, and there was, it couldn't end up in his enemies' hands.

"But Cronus is a god," Maddox said. And they'd all been up against the gods before. That's why they were here, rather than in the heavens. That's why they were demon-possessed. "We can't contain him." Despite the grim topic, the man had never looked happier.

Why? *Later.* The gods had always been more powerful than they were, able to strike them down with only a wave of their capricious hands.

"But he's also possessed," Cameo said. "His demon will have a weakness. All of ours do."

Oh, the agony of her voice. Strider was too busy cringing to process her words.

"His demon is Greed." This was said by Aeron, and the agony of his voice was a thousand times worse than Cameo's.

Holy hell, Strider needed to gouge out his ears and— Wait, wait, wait. Backtracking. Cronus was possessed by Greed. Lucien had told him this already, but Cameo had made a very good point. All the demons had a weakness. That weakness made the warriors vulnerable. His was losing and the coma that followed. Anyone could attack him then, and he wouldn't be able to protect himself.

What was Cronus's weakness?

That kind of intel would be critical in a fight…not that he planned to fight the god king, but a guy had to be prepared.

From the corner of his eye, he saw Amun sign with his hands.

"What of Danika's painting?" Strider translated. "The one where she predicted that Galen would take Cronus's head?" For himself, he added, "I know we're hoping we can change the course she saw, but maybe the way to change it isn't to kill Cronus ourselves. Maybe we should increase our efforts to kill Galen."

"But Galen has the Cloak," Reyes said, striding to the couch, lifting Danika, sitting down and pulling her into his lap. "He might be harder to destroy than even a god."

"Galen has the Cloak," Aeron repeated, "so why hasn't he acted against us? His troops have been here a while. So again, why haven't they attacked us?"

Maddox shrugged. "Maybe they were waiting for their little Distrust experiment to succeed. And now that it has…"

"We have to strike first," Aeron said, "and catch them unawares. Hopefully we can cut their numbers significantly, buy ourselves time to figure out what to do about Distrust and maybe even force Galen out of hiding."

Good rationale, but was his bloodlust returning? Besides that glint of red in his eyes, his hands were clenched and his posture rigid.

"Will they be unaware, though?" Reyes asked. "What if they're waiting for us to attack?"

The soldiers on the island had waited. That might be the new Hunter M.O. Plus, a lot of warriors were still recovering from that battle. They weren't at their strongest, and their strongest would be needed for a victory of this magnitude. "And let's not forget they've got Rhea on their side. No telling how she'll aid them."

"Not true," Torin said, speaking up for the first time. He'd placed a speaker and monitor in the room so that he could attend the meeting without actually having to enter the too-crowded room. "I've spoken to Cronus. He's distracting his *beloved* wife as long as he can today. That's why I asked Lucien and Sabin to call this meeting now. Anything we do today, we do without godly interference. From the queen *or* the king."

No one to hinder, but no one to help, either.

A murmur drifted through the crowd. And then a single word began to echo from everyone's lips. "Yes."

"We can't sleep, anyway," Maddox grumbled. "Not with Nightmares in residence. When are we going to get rid of her, by the way?"

No one had an answer to that. The other, however, was quickly decided. Tonight, they would attack.

CHAPTER TWENTY-TWO

GIDEON COULD HEAR the warriors shuffling around above him. Their footsteps were harried, and he thought he even detected the click of guns being locked and loaded, the whistle of metal being sheathed.

He didn't care. Didn't budge. Nearly a full day had passed since he'd first entered the dungeon. After Scarlet had made her announcement—*Lies, we're together at last*—she'd hissed a curse at him, said, "And now that I know it's you, you can go," then turned her back on him, lain down on her cot and ignored him, humming under her breath as if she hadn't a care. She'd fallen asleep at sunrise, nothing he did or screamed able to rouse her, and had only woken up a few minutes ago as the sun set again.

She'd sat up with a gasp, her gaze frantic. When she'd spotted him, the wildness had left her, replaced by anger and resentment—neither of which he understood—and she'd flopped back against the mattress.

"I can't stay here all day, you know," he said. Torin, who watched him from the many cameras set up down here, must have felt sorry for him because Disease had long ago brought him a chair. A chair he had pushed as close to Scarlet's cell as possible. His long legs were outstretched, his ankles propped on the bars.

"Go away."

Hearing her voice after all that silence was like finding a pool of acid with Hunters already inside it: a whole lot of awesome. He even shivered. Thank the gods he'd never be able to admit that aloud, though. Em-bar-rass-ing.

"What, you're ignoring me now?" she grumbled.

It would serve her right, as much as she'd ignored him. "Yep. Ignoring you." Every cell in his body was attuned to every move she made, so even though he would've liked to give her what she deserved, he couldn't.

Shameful. Men were supposed to be in charge, and women were supposed to be grateful for their attention. Men were supposed to give orders and women were supposed to obey them.

Okay, fine. He'd never wished for that before but he abso-fucking-lutely wished for it now. Didn't help that Lies was freaking putty in her hands, quiet now, but humming softly in appreciation, just happy to be near her.

Another bout of silence ensued, and he knew she was punishing him. For what, though, he didn't know. He hadn't been the one to lock her up. Sure, he hadn't set her free, either, but give him props for his intelligence, for gods' sake. She would have run away.

Scarlet—he really liked that name. It fit her. Fit the curve of her wicked lips, the ease with which she flayed him and the darkness of her personality—scrubbed a hand down her face. "Just go, okay. I'm done with you."

Finally. More talking. He'd stay here forever, he thought, just to be near her. Which didn't make any damn sense! "My name isn't Gideon." There. Simple. Easy. And hopefully she would begin to reveal personal information about herself in exchange. Like how she knew him. Like how he knew her but didn't remember her.

"Duh," was all she said.

She knew? How? He doubted she'd tell him, so he didn't bother asking. "I know a lot about you. Such as, you can't enter other people's dreams."

"No shit."

Not so simple. Not so easy. "I'd really hate it if you left my friends alone."

"Well, then. Consider it done. I'll mess with them all night long, just to keep you happy."

He stared up at the ceiling for a moment, praying for divine patience. "Please do." Damn it. He rarely minded that he could only speak in lies, but right now it was irritating the hell out of him.

"Or would you like it better if I only concentrated on you?"

"No." Yes. While he wanted his friends to be able to rest peacefully, that wasn't the real reason he wanted this woman to stay out of their dreams. He wanted her to himself. All of her. Even her ability. Just until he figured this out.

Even still, that didn't make any sense. He wasn't a possessive man. More than that, he had no reason to be possessive of this woman.

"Sorry," she said, sounding anything but. "I can't promise that."

"They won't consider drugging you."

"What kind of drugs? Can I request Vicodin?"

So she enjoyed human drugs. He couldn't blame her. He'd indulged a time or twenty. Not that they affected him much, but a little was better than nothing. "How'd you know I loved spiders so much?"

"Ugh, you're talkative. If I tell you something, will you shut up? I'll take your silence for a yes. How did I know you loved spiders? Because I enter a person's mind and just sense things. That's how. Now shut it for good."

Truth. His demon recognized truth as if it were a lone Hunter in a lineup with Lords. His demon usually hated it, was usually disgusted by it, even as Gideon always savored it. Today, the demon remained quiet and happy. No matter what poured from the girl's beautiful mouth.

"That how you didn't know my name?"

"I see bargaining isn't a skill you possess." She slapped the wall, and dust plumed around her. "So, what? You're going to irritate me until I tell you everything I know?"

He didn't want to admit that he just wanted to be with her, so he held up his bandaged hands and waved them. "There's so much more I could be doing right now. Like fighting with my friends."

"Injuries wouldn't stop a real warrior."

Ouch. "Yeah, 'cause a real warrior likes to get in everyone's way and actually aid the enemy."

"A real warrior succeeds despite his handicap." She snorted. "I said *handicap* and you don't have hands."

Yeah. Funny. "If I didn't have all my fingers, I totally *wouldn't* be flipping you off."

"The action of a man with more bark than bite. Figures you fall into that sad, sad category."

What's your problem? he wanted to demand, but the words would emerge as something like: *Why don't you have a problem with me?* and he didn't want to hear her

GENA SHOWALTER   363

say, *Stupid question. I do have a problem with you.* He'd
say: *Well, I don't want to know what it is,* and she'd say:
Good, because I didn't plan to tell you.

He'd had similar exchanges in the past. He was already frustrated, confused, curious, eager, and each
emotion was pushing him closer and closer to the edge.
An edge that always urged him to say things he didn't
mean and do things he couldn't reverse.

"How'd you lose the hands, anyway?" This was
asked grudgingly, as if she didn't like that she wanted
to know.

Her curiosity pleased him, and he lost some of his
frustration. "The hands, well, they didn't disappear
through torture."

"You break?"

"Of course." There was pride in his tone. He hadn't
broken. Hadn't spilled a single secret.

"Just as I suspected."

His jaw clenched. Somehow she knew he was Lies.
Had known all along. She also knew he couldn't tell the
truth, yet she continually pretended to take his words at
face value. Just to piss him off? Because she was angry
with him? An anger he still didn't understand.

"Hunters do it?" she asked.

"No."

"How's that going, by the way? The war with them?"

So she knew about that, as well, when he'd never
heard of her involvement. How? Actually, she knew a
lot that she shouldn't. "We're losing." Winning, but just
barely. Two artifacts against one. The liberation of all
those halfling children the Hunters had created through
hideous means. The discovery of their Buda hideout.
Not that he could explain that to Scarlet. "Since you

don't seem to know me, I'm wondering if you didn't come here for *me*."

"Whatever," she sputtered. "Look, I told your friend I just wanted you guys to leave me alone. I knew you were searching for me. I wanted you to stop. That's all."

No. That wasn't true. Couldn't be. Only, he couldn't prove it. Lies still wasn't helping. "How do you not know me? How do I feel like I don't know you when I've met you before?"

Her gaze flicked to him, narrowed and once more filled with that anger. "You don't remember me?" Okay. *Anger* wasn't a strong enough word. Outrage had layered every word. "You don't remember specifics?"

"I do no—" *Lie, lie.* He shouldn't have had to remind himself, damn it. "Yes. I do." But he couldn't have met her. He would *not* have forgotten a woman like her. Beautiful, wild, a predator. Blunt, hard yet somehow vulnerable.

Yeah, he'd been with a lot of women over the years. Mostly one-night stands. Women didn't come back for more when the man they were with constantly told them how ugly and stupid they were. Or when the man didn't speak at all. And no, he didn't remember all their faces, but as he'd already reasoned out, this was not a woman he would have forgotten.

"We were lovers," he said to get them started, "so that's in." Out.

"Ha!" Her gaze returned to him and lingered, perusing him up and down. "I'm not sure I approve of the packaging, so *no,* we weren't lovers."

"I'm not sure I know what you mean," he said, because he did know. She didn't like the looks of him.

His hands fisted. "For your information, I'm as ugly as they come."

There was something smug in her eyes as she said, "Yeah. I know. That's what I just said."

He ran his tongue over his teeth. *I'm sexy, damn it!* Yeah, his appearance was a little unorthodox. Blue hair, a few piercings. Tattoos—although nothing on the scale of Aeron's. Boy was covered. Gideon, at least, had himself and the ink under control. He'd chosen designs that meant something to him.

A pair of black eyes he saw every time he closed his eyes. A pair of bloodred...lips... He sat up with a jolt, staring over at Scarlet. Who had black eyes. Who had bloodred lips.

"What?" she snarled. "I know I'm gorgeous, unlike you, but come on. Show some manners, for gods' sake."

For as long as he could remember, he'd had images in his mind. Black eyes, red lips, even a phrase he thought of only during the darkest time of night: *TO PART IS TO DIE*. Bright red flowers curved beneath them.

In his mind, he'd seen those words and flowers wrapping around a woman's waist. His heart accelerated every time he thought of them, so he'd had the words— and yes, the flowers—tattooed around his waist, as well. Girly of him, and something many people had teased him about, but he didn't care.

"I don't want to see your lower back," he told her starkly.

She stilled completely, not even daring to breathe. "Not just no, but hell, no."

"I'm not willing to beg." He had to see. Had to know. "I *haven't* seen you before. I don't know that you have a tattoo of flowers there." She did, he knew she did.

"You're wrong. I don't."

Lie, surely. "Don't prove it, then."

"I don't have to."

Argh! Frustrating woman. He pushed to his feet. He'd been sitting so long, his muscles ached in protest and his knees shook.

"What? You don't get your way so you're leaving? Fine. Go sulk like a child."

First she'd wanted him to leave and now she threw a tantrum because she thought he was doing so. Women.

Bandaged as his wrists were, it was hard to grip the hem of his shirt, but after several agonizing minutes, he managed to do so. He raised the material and turned, offering Scarlet his back. At first, she gave no reaction. Then he heard a sharp intake of breath, a rustle of clothes, the patter of footsteps.

Warm fingers met his flesh, and he had to bite his bottom lip to contain his pleasured moan. Her skin was callused—from using weapons?—and abraded deliciously as she traced every word, every petal.

She could have had a blade hidden, could have stabbed him while he was distracted, but he couldn't make that matter. She was touching him. It was more arousing, more…everything than being inside another woman.

"To part is to die," she whispered brokenly. "Do you know what it means?"

"Yes. Don't tell me." *Please, gods, please.*

"I—I—" Her hand fell away. One step, two, she increased the distance between them.

Gideon whipped around. For a moment, he forgot about the bars and reached for her. His wounds hit the metal, and he cringed. Scarlet blanked her expression as she danced out of reach.

"Don't tell me," he commanded.

"I told you to go away, Gideon."

Gideon. For the first time, she'd used his name. It affected him deeply. Slithered through him, burning each of his organs—especially his speeding heart. Because...because...while this was the first time she'd said his name during their conversation, it wasn't the first time he'd ever heard her say it.

Just then he knew, *knew,* that he had heard her say his name before. Somewhere, sometime. She'd shouted his name in passion; she'd whispered his name in entreaty. She'd growled his name in anger; she'd cried his name in pain.

He *had* been with her.

"Devil," he said, wishing he could say her name instead.

She must have heard the riotous emotions in his voice because for once, she didn't have a sarcastic comment.

"Just go, Gideon, as I asked you to do in the beginning. Please."

Please. He doubted that was a word she said often. But then, she sounded close to tears and she didn't strike him as a woman who would relish crying in front of a man. Ever, over anything.

Except, she had before. He knew it. She'd cried and he'd held her. When? Where?

The only possible time would have been while he'd lived in the heavens. Since she was possessed by one of Pandora's demons, she had once been a prisoner of Tartarus. He hadn't locked her away, but could he have seen her there when he'd deposited other prisoners? Could he have spoken to her?

How could they have had a relationship, though, and he not recall it?

Could someone have erased his memory? Gods were capable of such things. Gods were capable of all kinds of cruel things. But that raised the question of *why* someone would have wanted to erase his memory. What could such a deed have gained? Prevented?

"Do you not have a man?" His voice was so raw, so hoarse, anyone hearing him would have thought he had yet to recover from a severe throat infection. A husband, though, would have wanted Gideon out of the picture.

"No," she whispered, so sad her tone brought tears to *his* eyes. So sad her tone rivaled Cameo's, Misery herself. "I do not."

"No father?"

"My father is dead." She lay back on the cot, peering up at the ceiling. "Has been for a long, long time."

Truth? *Damn it, demon! Help me.* "No mother?"

"My mother hates me."

He would just have to take her words as gospel. "Is there anyone who would want to see you...happy?" *Please understand that I mean miserable.*

Rather than reply, she rolled to her side, facing away from him. "If I tell you what you want to know, will you leave me alone? I'm not pretending to bargain with you this time, Gideon. If I do this, and you don't leave..."

He didn't want to leave. Now, more than ever, he wanted to stay. But he had to know the answer. Perhaps it would help him piece this mystery together. "No. Tell me and I'll stay."

A pause. Then, "I lied to you earlier, when I pretended not to recognize you. I did, from the very beginning I did. To part is to die," she croaked. "They were words you once told your...wife."

CHAPTER TWENTY-THREE

AERON STOOD ON THE balcony next to his room, clutching the railing, peering into the indigo-tinted sky. Most difficult choice he'd ever had to make, deciding between Legion's life and Olivia's. If he'd picked Olivia, as he'd so desperately wanted—*still* wanted—Legion would have suffered eternally. His friends would have been in danger. From Lucifer, no less. By picking Legion, he'd saved her *and* his friends, and Olivia could return home, unscathed. As he'd once tried to force her to do. As he now yearned to wail against. As Wrath *was* wailing against.

Keep her. Please. We need her.

Block it out. Don't listen. A demand for himself.

Had Legion appeared just then, he might have shaken her. The position she'd placed him in...the things he would have to do...to her, to Olivia... His nails elongated and bit into his palm, and the metal whined, arcing out of place. The worst, though? The things he *wouldn't* be able to do to Olivia. Not anymore.

No more making love. And that's what it had been. Making love. He hadn't wanted it to be, had tried to resist, but in the end, even his body had known. Being with Olivia was right. Perfect.

But now, he *couldn't* keep her. Even if sending her home were not a life-and-death situation, no woman would stay with him knowing he would soon sleep with someone else. And he would. Bile rose in his throat. He wouldn't allow Legion to be possessed. He wouldn't allow the destructive Lucifer into this realm.

Eventually, Olivia will thank me for this. At least, that's what he told himself in a bid for solace. If she stayed here, she would be human. She would wither and die and he would have to watch, helpless to save her. It was a prospect that had always baffled him. A prospect that had always horrified him, yet just then, he would have given anything to spend more time with her.

Can't lose her.

We must. He would have liked to hold her, there at the end of their loving, as his mind became wrapped in thoughts of being together forever. Now he had to live the rest of his life without her, knowing she was out there, that he would forever be unable to see, hear or smell her.

No!

How was he going to bed Legion when Olivia was the only female his body responded to? He laughed bitterly. He'd gone from having no girlfriends, cockily assured he didn't need or want one, to basically having two. One he didn't desire. The other was ready to leave him.

Soon I'll return, Olivia had said.

Instantly he'd panicked. *Can't lose her now,* he'd thought. So he'd told her they had time and that she was to stay here. All he'd done was prolong the inevitable, making the split more painful when it finally happened. But he hadn't fucking cared!

"Aeron," a soft voice beseeched from behind him.

Heaven. Wrath sighed.

Stay strong. Resist. He didn't allow himself to face her, but called, "Out here."

Soft footsteps resounded, then Olivia was beside him, gazing into the approaching night, her wild scent enveloping him. Smelling her without touching her was torture. Torture he deserved.

"Where's Legion?" he asked, expecting the girl to burst through the door at any moment.

"Sleeping."

Without Aeron's presence? "That doesn't sound like her."

Olivia shrugged a delicate shoulder. "If you must know, I drugged her. And I'm not sorry!"

His lips twitched. Gods, he lov—admired this woman. The smile, small as it'd been, fell away.

One of Wrath's visions suddenly opened up in his head; it was of Olivia and Legion sneaking through the fortress halls, careful to tiptoe, even while pushing each other out of the way. Legion held a bottle of wine. Olivia held two glasses.

Clearly, they'd gone to the kitchen. And for alcohol, of all things. But where else had they gone and why?

They reached his bedroom and Olivia said, "A toast to your success."

"That's right," Legion said smugly. "*My* success. I told you Aeron was mine and would never be yours."

Again, Aeron wanted to shake her.

"And you were right." The color drained from Olivia's cheeks as she poured the drinks. With her back to Legion, she ripped a tiny piece of her robe from the sleeve. She then dropped that little speck of material into one of the glasses.

"Sleep," she whispered as the material dissolved,

then rotated to Legion with a forced smile. "I know when I'm beaten."

The demon claimed the glass greedily and even before she swallowed the last drop of her wine, she began wavering on her feet. Her eyes leveled on Olivia. "Something's...wrong..."

"Of course it is. Did you really think I wouldn't doctor your wine?"

"Bitch," Legion slurred, as her knees buckled. She hit the floor snoring.

Olivia's robe could clearly do more than Aeron had realized, and at that moment, he should have been filled with a desire to drug *Olivia*. But to his utter amazement, Wrath was...charmed by her actions. "Heaven" had merely played with "Hell," and the demon wanted only to hold the winner of that game.

"Are you angry with me?" Olivia asked, drawing him from his odd thoughts.

"Grateful." He was too raw to deal with Legion right now. Too raw to think about the girl he considered a daughter. *Change the subject. Now.* "There's something different about your voice. I noticed it earlier, but now, it's even more obvious." She'd told him about Legion, but he'd felt no compulsion to believe her.

"Yes," was all she said. "Something's different."

"What?" he asked, though he thought he knew the answer. She must be losing more of her angel-abilities the more time she spent here.

How would her fellow angels react to that when she returned home? He didn't like the thought of them shunning so precious a female.

She gave another shrug, but this time her skin brushed his. He closed his eyes for a moment, savoring the softness. And when a cool breeze swept over the balcony, lifting her hair and tossing the strands against his bare chest, he thought his tenuous hold on sanity completely severed.

Mine. Yours. Ours. Forever. Cries from the demon, from him.

Never. A stark reminder.

When he opened his eyes, he returned his focus to the sky. "You used to live up there," he said, his voice hoarse.

"Yes."

"What was it like?"

"We live in clouds, which are far more than you imagine." Her affection was obvious. "They have rooms, and whatever we command, they produce. We're hidden from the rest of the world, but we can still see what's happening around us. Like angels flying past, or warriors corralling demons. We can see storms but not be touched by them. We can see the stars, blazing so close, but not be burned by them."

Palpable excitement from the demon. *Yes, yes.*

"And you gave it all up." For him. For fun. He was humbled. Guilty. Ashamed. For the most part, he'd given her only pain and worry. But he was also…glad.

"Yes," she said again, as simply as that. Then, shifting uncomfortably, she changed the subject. "Why do you have two butterfly tattoos? I've always wondered."

"The one on my back is the mark of my demon, and the one on my ribs is of my own making. I wanted to always see, to always know the narrow ledge I walk."

"I don't think you ever needed visual aid. You never seem to forget." Sadness had replaced the affection.

"Enough reminiscing. I know you're heading into battle tonight."

A sobering reminder. "Correct." He didn't ask how she knew about the coming fight. He could guess. She and Legion had spied on him. That's why they'd left his room.

"I want to go with you," she said. "If I return home now, I'll be able to join you and the Hunters won't know I'm there. I'll be able to protect you, like a shield. I'll be able to—"

"No!" He cleared his throat and offered more gently, "No."

The railing whined again, bending, and he pulled his fingers free, one by one. Again, he thought, *Can't lose her now.* Again Wrath whimpered. "That's not necessary."

They still had time, damn it.

"I have to leave anyway, so why not now? Why not do so while I can help you?"

Any other time, he would have admired such determination. Now he turned to her, snarling, "Why would you want to help me? Why aren't you screaming at me? Ranting about what I'm going to do?" That would have been easier to deal with.

Instead, she gazed up at him through calm eyes. "There's no need for me to resort to such emotions. I'm an angel."

"Fallen," he corrected darkly, then blinked. This was the first time he'd ever acknowledged the distinction, and oh, the irony sliced deep.

There was a pause, a regretful sigh. Then, "Not for much longer I'm not."

Mine.

He crowded her, closing the rest of the distance between them, fisting her robe and anchoring the handfuls of fabric against the railing so that she couldn't escape. Did she not care that they would be parted? Did she not care that they would never again be together? That they would never again make love? That he would soon do something vile, unforgivable?

"Let me go, Aeron." Still so calm.

Never, he thought.

Never, Wrath agreed.

We can't think like that. "Will your people treat you differently when you...go back?" Even saying it was difficult, but he needed the reminder. "You won't be the same person you once were."

"They'll welcome me home." She shook her head and more of those silky tendrils danced over him. "With the exception of our Council, they're very tolerant. Very patient."

"Lysander doesn't strike me as either one of those things."

She smiled wryly. "Well, he isn't a typical angel."

That smile...he needed more. Had to have more. As many as possible, until... "There are seven days left." The words croaked from him. *Stupid.* Still, he pressed their chests together, felt her nipples bead, and just like that he hardened, ready. "Promise me you'll stay six."

The calm finally left her, a storm brewing. "Wh-why?"

"Just promise me. Please."

Please, Wrath echoed, as pitiful as Aeron. Who would have thought they'd be reduced to this?

"I can't," she said. "I'm sorry." She looked away from him, over his shoulder.

But not before he saw the tears swimming in her

eyes. Tears that undid him...emasculated him. He reached up and cupped the back of her neck, forcing her to face him, to see his desire—and a determination that surely rivaled hers.

"So that's a maybe?"

A shaky laugh escaped her. "No. That's a no."

I did that. I made her laugh. "What *can* you promise me?" At this point, he'd take anything.

"A...a day," she offered shakily.

A day. A day wasn't enough. Eternity might not be enough. His grip on her tightened. "You'll stay until I return from town. Even if that's a little longer than twenty-four hours. Please."

"Why is that so important to you?" she demanded, letting loose the first hint of that churning tempest.

Because I need you. Because I want you. Because I hate the thought of being away from you. Because, if it were only you and me, and my decisions didn't affect anyone else, I would willingly die just to have another minute in your arms.

"You'll stay?" he insisted, ignoring her question. "If I think there's a chance you'll leave, I won't be able to concentrate." He'd never manipulated before. He stated facts, for better or worse, unconcerned by the results. Now... "I'll be an easy target, perhaps injured again. So tell me. Tell me you'll stay."

She licked her lips, and her shoulders sagged. "I— All right."

Not good enough. "Say it."

"Yes," she whispered. "I'll stay until you return from town."

Without that layer of truth in her voice, he didn't know whether she lied to him or not. But he chose to believe her, because he couldn't stand the thought of her absence.

"Now that we've got that settled, will you let me go?" Even as she spoke, she placed her hands on his chest, not pushing him away but tracing his tattoos.

Mmm. Wrath sighed.

She might not want to want him just then, but want him she clearly did. "Why do you desire me?" he demanded, another fierce reminder of the obstacles between them. "Why did you pick me? Beautiful as you are, smart as you are, sweet as you are, you could have anyone. Someone not covered with pictures of their sins."

"Because." A mutinous answer, though she didn't back away.

"Why?" He shook her now, desperate for the truth for reasons he didn't care to contemplate. "Please, Olivia. Tell me."

Perhaps it was the *please* that swayed her. Perhaps the savageness of his actions. Either way, she shouted, "Because you aren't what you believe you are. You aren't what everyone else believes. You might have delivered countless deaths but you love more fiercely than anyone I've ever known. You give of yourself with no thoughts to your own happiness." She laughed, and it was as bitter-sounding as his own had been. "Funny, isn't it? The very qualities that brought me to you are the things that are sending me away."

Stay.

He quashed the plea before it escaped. Loved more fiercely? By gods, he would. Now, this moment, before time betrayed him.

Without any warning, he meshed their mouths together, unable to stop himself, thrusting his tongue inside. She opened without protest, eagerly accepting his brutality. Good thing. He had no control, and was glad for it. He had only a beginning—Olivia—and the hated end—her loss. And that loss…gods. Losing her would slay him.

No, he thought then. Her kiss would. His demise rested in this meeting of souls, he realized, and again, he was glad. He tasted and claimed and conquered without reservation. He gave and he took.

If this were the end, he would die like a warrior.

"I will make you mine, woman." He jerked her robe around her waist. Her legs, bared. Her core, his. Still she wasn't wearing any panties, and the knowledge nearly floored him. One day, he wanted her on a bed. Wanted to remove her clothing slowly, take her lingeringly. Savoring every second, every breathy sigh.

Now, he just wanted her.

Urgency rode him as he reached for the button on his pants, tried to open—it caught, so he ripped them apart. His cock sprang free. "I hope you're ready for me, Olivia."

READY FOR HIM? Olivia thought she would be ready for this man every minute of every day for the rest of her life. He was peering down at her as if she were necessary for his survival. As if he lived only because she did.

And this would be the last time she ever experienced such a gaze.

Sadness threatened to overwhelm her, but the force of her desire beat it back. Later. Later she could wallow in her misery. But for now, she was in Aeron's arms.

Her body was on fire for him. She was wet and shaky and aching all over.

This was what she'd given up her wings for, after all. This was what she'd given up eternity for. And here it was, hers for the taking. No matter what happened next, she would always have this.

"Olivia," he said, her name a guttural beseeching.

"Ready. Promise."

He cupped her bottom, lifted her, and as she wound her legs around his waist, he drove inside her, all the way to the hilt. She cried out, unable to strangle the sound. As big as he was, he stretched her, but as sore as she should have been, considering they'd done this not long ago, her pleasure was unparalleled.

"Need you." In and out he thrust.

"Yes!" Her nails dug into his back, scouring. There was no holding back, not for her. She needed this. Needed this memory to keep her warm at night. "Just like that."

Harder and harder he pounded inside her. It was heaven and it was hell. So good, so close to ending. *Last forever,* she prayed, but she knew it wasn't a prayer that would be heeded.

The railing rocked with them, whining, then finally giving out entirely. Over they tumbled, falling...falling...Aeron never slowed his thrusting. She loved it, reveled in it, the wind whipping around them. Freedom and love and pleasure, all wrapped together. Without fear or regret. Aeron would keep her safe.

And he did. Just before they hit, he twisted and his wings expanded, gliding them to a slow stop. He settled her gently on the ground, those thrusts continuing still, never ceasing. She kept her legs locked around him, accepting him, arching up into him, desperate and eager and lost.

The sun fell steadily, pretty and pink, and anyone looking down would be able to see them. She didn't care. Her need was too great.

"Olivia," he panted.

"Aeron."

Their gazes met, his violet irises wild. His expression was taut, feral, his lips thinned and bleeding from where she must have bitten him. There was something so hauntingly beautiful about him like this. Something so savagely tender.

"You are mine," he gritted out.

More than anything, she wanted to be. "Yours." Until he gave himself to Legion. Then, as the girl had said, Aeron would be hers. *Stop. Enough.* She had now, this moment.

As though sensing her thoughts and wanting to drive them away, he lowered his head and kissed her again, this one even more wonderfully vicious than the last, his tongue stabbing at hers, his teeth grinding against hers. So much passion…

She scratched and bit and shouted, hurtling over the edge of sanity, once again falling, this time spiraling apart, screaming, clutching at her lover, every muscle in her body spasming deliciously. *There. Oh, yes, there.* He hit her just right, and her orgasm soared higher. She couldn't see, her eyelids squeezed firmly, but she felt him shudder over her. Heard him roar her name.

When he collapsed on top of her, his weight crushed her, but she loved it too much to offer a rebuke. If only they could stay like this forever, lost in the here and now.

"Olivia," he croaked.

Slowly she blinked open her eyes. Aeron was watching her, his features somehow stripped bare. Open, needy. "Don't say it," she said. If he planned to tell her that this had changed nothing, she knew that and didn't need him to sink the knife deeper into her chest. If he planned to ask her to stay, even though he had to be with Legion, even only once, she would be tempted to do so. Even though the Council would send someone to kill him. Even though images of him with the demon would haunt her forever.

No matter which way this played out, they were doomed.

"I have to." His voice was throaty. "I want you to know—"

"Uh, Aeron," someone called. "Hate to interrupt, but it's time to go."

Caught again, she thought with a sigh. Would they never be allowed to enjoy the afterglow humans so praised? Except, this time she was glad of the reprieve. She scooted out from under Aeron and stood, smoothing her robe to her ankles.

"Go," she said without looking down at him. "As promised, I'll be here waiting." *And then we'll say good-bye.*

CHAPTER TWENTY-FOUR

3:00 A.M. MOONLIGHT WAS no longer quite so bright, and the streets were deserted. Shops were closed, and partying humans had finally left The Asylum. The lights were out, not a single movement inside.

About a hundred yards away, Aeron was crouched beside Strider in a shadowed corner. The warrior held a remote control and a tiny four-wheeler with an even tinier camera attached to its roof. Apparently that camera could cut through the dark, filming faces and bodies as clearly as if they were bathed in sunlight.

Torin always found the coolest toys. The proof rested in Strider's wide grin as he launched the vehicle forward.

The rest of the men were scattered around the building. A building they'd once helped restore—a building they were about to destroy. Some were high on rooftops, gun barrels pointed down. Others were on the street like Aeron, hidden in different locations.

Aeron lifted the portable monitor that would allow him and Strider to see through the camera's lens. And sure enough, the buildings and roads he'd traversed since their creation were visible. Amazing.

"We're good," he told Defeat.

"We're ready for you, Willie," Strider said into his earpiece.

Aeron wore a headset, as well, and heard William's reply. "Gods, I can't believe I let Anya talk me into this. I'm going in."

A few seconds later, William abandoned his post and rounded a corner. His clothes were disheveled, and he clutched a bottle of whiskey. He bore no resemblance to himself, his dark hair now bleached, his piercing blue eyes hidden by dark contacts. And his face...somehow, he'd roughened his skin and changed the shape of his features.

Every step he made looked as if it threatened to topple him over, but he managed to belt out a love song while moving forward.

Mocking bastard. Not that he knew Aeron planned to betray Olivia.

Sweet Olivia.

Mine, his demon stated.

Ours. No. He nearly smashed the device he held. *No one's.* Not Wrath's, and certainly not his. Except...

How was he supposed to go on without her? She was light, and she was happiness. She was love, and she was bliss. She was...everything.

"You with me, Wrath?" Strider muttered.

The question came just in time, drawing him to the present. He watched as William tripped, as planned, and crashed into the front door of the club. *Distraction.* Glass shattered as he fell. He lay there a moment, sputtering drunkenly. The remote-controlled truck raced over the shards of glass, slipping inside the building unnoticed.

Didn't take long for a flood of armed men to come barreling toward the immortal.

"What are you doing?"

"God, he reeks!"

"Get him out of here and clean this up. Now!"

Two of the guards latched onto William roughly, hauling him to his feet. "Hey, gents," he slurred in an appalling British accent. "This where the party's at? Oh, lookie. A gun. How bloody manly. But I should probably warn the angels on the hill. Can't encourage crime, you know."

"Boss?" one of the men holding William said. "We can't just let him roam. He's seen too much."

"First, I'm not your boss," William said, then he frowned and clutched his stomach. "Second, I think I'm gonna be sick."

The man in charge—Dean Stefano, Galen's right-hand man, Aeron realized, even as Wrath prowled through his head, ready to hurt, to kill—flicked his attention to William before turning back to the shattered remains of the door. "Make it look like he was mugged. And do it away from the building. I don't want anyone sniffing around here."

A cold, utterly uncaring death sentence for a man they assumed was human. Humans, the very beings they allegedly strove to "protect." But then, Stefano was a cold, uncaring man. He blamed the Lords, particularly Sabin, for his wife's suicide, and wouldn't rest until all of them were dead.

Punish...

In the past, Aeron would have secretly loved the demon's command and hated himself for it. No matter how much the victim deserved what he dealt. But no longer would he castigate himself. Losing Olivia was reason to rage. Destroying someone evil? A reason to rejoice. And he would.

He'd have *fun*.

Soon.

The two guards jerked a now-protesting William outside. "What's going on? Just let me go and we'll—"

"Shut up, asshole, or I'll cut out your tongue."

That's when William began sobbing like a child. If Aeron hadn't known better, he would've thought the warrior was truly scared. But he did know better. This was all part of the role William had volunteered to play. And by "volunteered" he of course meant "caved to Anya's threats to burn his book if he didn't cooperate." They'd hoped it wouldn't come to this, to what was about to happen, but deep down they'd all known it would.

William couldn't free himself and run; that might raise their suspicions, put them on guard. He had to take whatever was dished, and let the men walk away afterward.

The guards rounded a corner and hurried down a back alley, out of sight. Even though Aeron could no longer see them, he could hear what was happening through his earpiece.

When they reached their destination, their footsteps tapered to quiet.

"I didn't mean any bloody harm," William cried.

"Sorry, pal, but you're a liability now." Next there was a slide of metal against leather, followed by the rip of flesh and muscle. A grunt. Another rip, another grunt.

William had just been stabbed. Twice.

Aeron flinched in sympathy. To take whatever was dished, just to leave an enemy unsuspecting, required guts—guts William was probably spilling all over the pavement. He'd survive, though, and he'd be able to repay the favor. They all would.

He heard clothing rustle, then a thump. William must have dropped to the ground and slumped over as if dead. The footsteps started up again, and then the two guards—smiling now over a job well done—were once more rounding the corner. They headed back inside.

Strider kept the hidden car trained on Stefano and the workers even now boarding up the hole. Finally, they finished up.

"Fuckers," William grumbled in his ear. "Those two are mine. They went for my sweet, innocent little kidneys."

There was nothing sweet or innocent about William. Not even his kidneys.

"Just a few minutes more," Aeron promised.

"I want two guards at this door until morning," Stefano barked. "The rest of you go back to what you were doing. And for fuck's sake, someone contact Galen. Better we tell him what happened than he hear it from someone else."

The two who'd stabbed William nodded and claimed their posts.

So Galen wasn't there. Disappointing.

As Aeron watched, the rest of the Hunters filed out of the lobby, through the club and down a hallway. Strider stared at the monitor as he maneuvered the car silently behind them. In that hallway were several doorways. One, the camera showed, led to a room where a few Hunters were relaxing in front of a TV. In the second room, a few were peering at screens and clicking at computer consoles, much like Torin did. In the third, bed after bed stretched. Several Hunters were clearly sleeping in them.

Stefano entered the fourth, an empty room. There were no people and no furnishings. There was only a rug. A rug that had been flung aside to reveal a dark, yawning void. A void into which Stefano descended.

An underground tunnel.

Digging their way to the fortress?

Planning to sneak inside, never having to deal with the traps on the hill?

"We have the location of their hideaway," Strider said smugly.

Go time. For Aeron at least.

"You know which way you have to go?" Strider asked.

"Yes." As he'd watched the monitor, he'd memorized his path.

Strider patted his shoulder. "May the gods be with you, my friend."

"And you." Aeron pushed to his feet. He hadn't worn a shirt because he'd known he would be flying. With a single mental command, he popped his wings free from their slits. Grateful for the freedom, they stretched to full length.

"Good luck, my man," Paris said.

"Be careful," a few others echoed.

"If anything happens to me," he said to no one in particular, "make sure Olivia returns home safely."

Aeron didn't wait for their replies, but shot into the air.

Punish...

He soared high...higher...moving so quickly he would be no more than a blur to any camera in the area. Even one that could cut through shadows. Finally, he leveled out and hovered.

Punish...

Below him was the club. He searched the darkness, but there were no Hunters on the roof, and he couldn't see the Lords he knew were scattered nearby.

Tonight, victory would be his.

Punish...

My pleasure. "Descending now." Down, down he fell, wind whipping over his skin, wings tucked into his sides, increasing his momentum. When he reached the building, he flattened out and burst through the wooden slats that had just been erected. They brutalized his wings, cutting and breaking them, but they also knocked down the guards.

Aeron didn't pause, but flew through the lobby, the dance arena, and then the hallway. Hunters had heard the newest crash and were springing into action, but they were doing so behind him, too slow to catch him. Only when he reached the room with the rug did he finally stop.

Wrath laughed, images flashing through Aeron's mind. The sins of his targets. Beatings, stabbings, kidnappings. So much violence, so much hatred. These men deserved what they got.

"Demon!"

"Stop him!"

He hid his wings—or tried to. Once again they were too mangled to fit into their slots. No matter. He strode toward the repositioned rug just as Hunters reached the doorway. A bullet cut through his back, but he didn't slow. He simply spun as he walked, withdrawing a gun from his underarm sheath and firing, sending several men ducking for cover.

A reprieve. He threw back the thick, colorful mat.

"Bastard!" Another bullet whizzed behind him and slammed into his side.

He returned fire.

Amid the new gunshots, he heard his friends pounding into the building. Soon there were grunts and screams. Shattering glass. No time to rejoice. Yet another bullet hit him, this one in his thigh, dropping him to his knees.

"Some help," he gritted into his earpiece. He continued to fire, sending the Hunters back into hiding. He couldn't hold them off much longer. The gun's clip was—empty. Shit. He tossed the now-useless piece to the floor.

Punish. More. More!

"Almost there," Strider panted as the shooting started up again.

Aeron withdrew a second gun just as his friend arrived. Within moments, bodies were falling forward, motionless, then Strider was peeking inside. Blood splattered his face, but his eyes were gleaming brightly and a smile kicked up the corners of his lips.

"Get everyone out," Aeron told him. "It's about to blow."

Strider nodded and was off, shouting warnings to their fellow warriors.

Aeron jerked at the latch on the tunnel door; it held. Though his arm was throbbing, trembling, he squeezed his weapon's trigger over and over until the metal splintered apart.

"Now!" Strider's shout echoed through their ear-pieces.

Aeron didn't allow himself to wallow in the pain he felt—pain that would soon intensify. He didn't allow himself to acknowledge the drugging lethargy even then working through his bloodstream. Courtesy of the Hunters' poison, he was sure. He simply grabbed a grenade from the pouch at his waist and pulled the pin with his teeth.

He tossed open the door—multiple guns fired at him simultaneously, hitting, hitting, peppering his body with holes—and, pushing himself into the air with what strength remained in his legs, he dropped the grenade.

Wrath uttered another of those joyful laughs. *Punish! Boom!*

The ensuing blast of air sent him crashing through the roof. When he stilled, he grabbed another grenade, pulled the pin, and dropped it through the void he'd created.

Boom!

Wood and glass shards soared in every direction, cutting him further, knocking him off course. Still he persevered. His wings were now so broken they barely flapped, but he managed to work himself higher. At a safe distance, he stopped. Hovering, though, proved impossible.

As he fell, he swept his gaze around the surrounding area. Plumes of black smoke shielded the building. But through them, he could see crackling gold flames licking their way toward the sky.

None of the humans could have survived this kind of carnage. He, however, was unwilling to leave any-

thing to chance. He withdrew the third grenade and as
he closed in on the building, he dropped it.

Boom!

Once again, he was shot upward. The new flames
made contact, singeing his skin. He twisted midair, letting his back take the brunt of the damage before twisting again, changing direction and finally falling and
hitting the ground where he'd first waited with Strider.

His friend was already there. "I could kiss you,"
was the first thing the warrior said. "Even though you
look like shit."

Aeron would have laughed, but he'd inhaled smoke
and his throat was raw and swollen. He was barely
breathing. His eyes teared from the burn, and he didn't
have the strength to swipe the drops away.

"I'm sure you want a report," Strider added, helping
him to his feet. "William managed to cut the throats
of the guys who cut his guts. Paris took a bullet to the
stomach, and Reyes got hammered in the kneecap. They
aren't faring so well, so Maddox and Amun are helping them home. Exactly where you need to be. Lucien's
gonna remain behind to escort the dead souls to hell,
and Sabin's gonna stay with him just in case he has to
leave his body behind. Or there are survivors. If the
tunnel is deep enough, those who ran could have been
protected from the blast. And you know how Stefano
likes to run."

Dizziness swept through him, mild at first, then rag-
ing, flooding, and if it weren't for Strider's arm snaking his waist, he would have fallen. Worse, darkness
was descending.

"They used poisoned bullets, definitely," Strider
said, mirroring his earlier thoughts. "Like the one that

almost killed you. How'd you survive? What did you do? We should have asked before, but with everything else going on…"

Aeron's thoughts fragmented, but he knew there was something he needed to tell his friend. Something vital. Something about life and death. Yes. That was it. Life! "Men…shot…die…need…water," he managed.

"I don't understand."

Shit, shit, shit. If he passed out before he explained what was needed, his friends would suffer. They might die before he awakened or Olivia explained. "River. Drink."

"You're thirsty?"

"Water. Men. Must. Drink. Water. Life."

"Aeron, I don't understand," Strider said, his frustration clear. "The men who were shot need water? How will water save them?"

"Water life. Only need…little. Olivia. Olivia…know." And then the darkness dragged him under completely.

CHAPTER TWENTY-FIVE

OLIVIA PACED THE CONFINES of Aeron's bedroom. Legion was still sleeping, but she'd been moaning the past hour so Olivia knew she would awaken at any moment. And wouldn't that just be a treat?

—*can't give up*, Temptation—Lucifer—was saying. He'd been jabbering for hours. *You must win Aeron.*

Allowing a prince of darkness to win, as well. Never. That was something she'd fought against her entire life. Victory was all that truly mattered, even at the expense of her own happiness. And that's exactly what the price was. Her happiness.

He needs you.

"Quiet."

He'll be miserable without you.

"And he'll deserve every bit of that misery." Holy Deity, who was she becoming? That kind of attitude wouldn't serve her well in the heavens. Yes, angels were tolerant and patient, as she'd told Aeron, but that didn't mean they had to like who she'd become.

If you leave, you'll never be allowed to taste him again.

A whimper escaped her. She wanted to hit the wall. "You are a thief, a liar and a destroyer. You will leave me alone. Or by my Deity, I will request Lysander be sent into the depths of hell to silence you. We both know that request will be granted. You are not to consort with the angels."

You're no longer an angel.

"I will be."

Lucifer screamed in frustration, but didn't say another word.

"Your voice is *so* annoying," Legion mumbled as she sat up. She rubbed the sleep from her eyes. She must have forgotten how she'd fallen asleep, because she didn't leap up and attack. Either that, or she didn't care about retribution now that she knew Olivia would be leaving. "Where's Aeron?"

Anger draining as concern swept through her, Olivia stopped at the vanity and plopped into the chair, facing the bed. "He's raiding a Hunter camp." Was he all right? She'd left his balcony doors open so that he could fly straight into this room. Though *forever* had passed, he hadn't yet appeared.

Legion yawned. "Oh. Well. He'll be home soon, then. My man kills quickly."

Her man. Yes. He was now. Once again, Olivia wanted to punch the wall. A hole would leave some reminder of her. A reminder they could patch up when she was gone, but whatever.

That wasn't important now.

A cool breeze had been dancing in through the open door, but for the past few minutes, she'd felt something sinister in the air. A sign of Lucifer's presence, perhaps, or something else? The dark hints of smoke stung her throat, burned her eyes.

Perhaps the battle had already erupted.

Was it over? Was Aeron hurt?

Licking her lips, she wrapped trembling fingers

around the vial she'd slipped into her robe's pocket. The River of Life. She lifted the cold glass and studied the swirling blue liquid. Only a drop had been used, and there was plenty more. Would he need another drop this night? More than a drop?

If so, how long would the contents last?

"What's that?" Legion asked with a yawn.

No longer did Olivia have to tell the truth, so she could have lied to Legion and kept the healing water a secret. But she wasn't going to be around much longer, and she wanted the Lords to have access to the contents.

She explained what it was while reluctantly approaching the girl. When she held out her hand, the precious vial resting in her palm, she said, "Here. I want you to have it."

"Hell, no." With a grimace, the demon batted her hand away.

The vial slapped against the mattress, and Olivia anchored her fists on her waist. "Legion!"

"Your River of Life *ruins* our water system. We can't even bathe after a single drop of that crap has contaminated just one of our five streams."

"How sad for you. Just make sure the Lords use it sparingly. The longer it lasts, the more times you can bring Aeron back from the brink of death."

"It can save Aeron?" Legion's distaste had yet to dissipate, but she pinched the vial between her fingers, then smashed it between her cleavage. "I'll use it sparingly. Promise."

Olivia believed her. If anyone would see to Aeron's health and make sure the warrior came first, it was Legion.

Should have been me.

She moved to the terrace but remained just inside, resting her head on the door frame. The moon was still high, still golden, but the stars were hidden behind that smoky film. She couldn't see the city lights any longer, just trees and hill. Her worry increased.

You need a distraction. "Why do you love Aeron?" she asked before she could stop herself.

A pause, then, "He plays with me. He makes sure I'm happy. He protects me." Legion probably didn't realize it, but she sounded defensive.

Hinges squeaked as the bedroom door suddenly swung open, and Olivia turned, heart suddenly slamming against her ribs. "Aeron?" No one replied because no one was there. And with the door now thrown wide, she could see that the hallway was empty, too. The breeze must have been stronger than she'd thought. *When* would he return?

The others, the women, were camped out in the attic with Gwen, Sabin's wife, acting as their protector. Just in case someone dug through the floor, Torin had explained. Something Olivia didn't understand, though he'd mentioned a text message. Anyway, she liked Gwen, had from the first moment she'd seen her, scared to be here, hating what she was. Now Gwen was confident. Happy. *Like I want to be.*

She'd been grateful for the woman's offer to join her and the others, but Olivia hadn't wanted to leave Legion sleeping helplessly. And when Gwen had offered to carry the demon to the upper level, she should have caved, but again, she'd said no. This was her last night inside the fortress. She hadn't wanted to spend it with a group of women she knew but who didn't really know her. They would have questioned her about Aeron, and she just couldn't deal with that right now.

Besides, Torin watched every inch of this place. He would sound an alarm if anyone besides a Lord even approached it.

With a sigh, she strode to the door and closed it, then ambled back to the terrace entryway. Her gaze flicked to Legion along the way. The demon was still lounging on the bed, but now she was studying her nails as if she couldn't believe how pretty they were.

Where had they left off? "If you love someone," Olivia said, "you want them to be happy. Right?"

"Uh, yeah. Hence the reason I'm going to sleep with Aeron. It'll make us both happy."

Had Olivia ever been this clueless? "No. It'll make *you* happy. He thinks of you as a daughter. By forcing him to do this, you're going to destroy him. You're going to keep him wallowing in guilt, just like his tattoos do, a constant reminder of what he is, what he's done and what he can never have."

Those nails ripped into linen. "And you think you can make him happy?"

"I know I can," she said softly. Or knew she would have. The way he'd made love to her that last time…that hadn't just been about pleasure. That had been about a meeting of souls. A promise of what could never be. "He needs me."

There was a very masculine laugh behind her. "Well, well. A demon Lord in love with an angel. I can't believe my luck."

Olivia's eyes widened as she spun. She didn't recognize the voice—not Lucifer, then—nor did she see anyone in the room. Great. Another invisible tormentor. Who was it this time? Was this her payback for all the times she'd spied on Aeron unseen?

"Who said that?" Legion demanded.

"You heard him?" What did that—

Strong hands suddenly settled atop Olivia's shoulders, propelling her outside and forcing her to face the sky. Before she had time to resist, those hands shoved her over the railing she'd repaired in Aeron's absence, and she was falling down, down, down.

For the first time in her life, falling terrified her. "The water," she screamed to Legion. "Don't forget the—"

She would have said more, but something hard clamped over her mouth. Something else, just as hard, snaked around her waist, jerking her back into a solid wall. She leveled out, began to lift higher, higher still.

A man, she realized. A man was holding her. Not Aeron and not Lysander. Menace poured from this one. Using all the strength she possessed, she struggled for her freedom, scratching at the skin she couldn't see but could now feel, kicking at the legs resting atop hers.

"I wouldn't do that if I were you," he said. The voice from the room.

"Who are you? What do you want with me?"

They broke through a layer of clouds, hiding them from view. "I'm hurt, truly. I thought my reputation preceded me."

Galen, she realized. Aeron's greatest enemy. He had found the Cloak of Invisibility; Aeron had said as much to Torin. That's how he'd entered the fortress undetected. That's how he'd snuck into Aeron's bedroom.

That's how he would ruin what was left of her life.

Torin didn't have cameras in the bedrooms, but there

were cameras outside them and those would have captured her jumping and flying. Anyone watching the feed would believe she'd simply been heading back to the heavens. Unless Legion told him what had really happened, Aeron would assume Olivia had lied to him. He would think she'd left him without saying goodbye.

Blood froze in her veins. She *had* to convince Galen to take her back. "I'm not sure what you hope to accomplish, but I assure you, you won't get your wish. Aeron doesn't care about me." Not the way she dreamed, hoped. "He's letting me go."

"I highly doubt that, but you weren't the reason I was in the fortress. You were simply a last resort."

"And what did you hope to accomplish?"

His arms tightened around her. "Do you really think I'll spill all my secrets?"

"Are you going to hurt me? Tell me that, at least."

"And spoil the surprise?" He chuckled. "No. I'd rather show you." His wings snapped closed, and they began to fall....

AERON CAME AWAKE with a jolt. One moment he'd been lost to the burning pain working its way through him, flaming his organs to ashes, and the next a cool rain had swept through him. A cool rain he'd instantly recognized. The River of Life. Olivia was here, and she had healed him once again.

Except, when he focused, he saw that it was Legion who loomed over him, and he fought a wave of disappointment.

"It worked." She smiled, all pearly whites and happiness. "It really worked."

Though he badly wanted to ask about his fallen

angel, he couldn't. Not without causing all kinds of problems. "The others?" His voice was rougher than usual, and not because of damage from the smoke inhalation. The water had healed him. But thoughts of Olivia always filled him with need.

"Who cares? You know," Legion added, tracing a finger down the line of his breastbone. Her lashes dipped to half-mast, though he could still see her eyes. They weren't glazed with desire. No, it was determination that swirled in their depths. "Now that you're healed, we have some unfinished business to attend to."

He grabbed her wrist and held her hand at bay. "The others, Legion? How are they?"

With a sigh, she waved away his concern. "They're still sick. Okay? All right? But they'll get better on their own. I'm sure of it."

Not with those bullets spurting poison into their systems. "You're telling me they haven't been given the River of Life?" Perhaps that's where Olivia was now, seeing to his friends' well-being. How like her. Caring, helpful.

"No, they weren't." There was a growing rigidity to Legion's features. "Now, about that unfinished business…"

Damn her. She was going to make him ask. "Does Olivia have the vial?"

Finally giving up her attempts at seduction, Legion looked away from him. At least she hadn't erupted into a rage because he'd mentioned that—beautiful, perfect—name. "No," she said. "Because we ran out. Sorry."

Hardly. Last time he'd used it, there'd been enough to save an entire army. Aeron sat up and scrubbed a hand down his face. So. If Olivia didn't have the water, that meant Legion did, since it had just been given to him and she was the only one here.

But why would Legion— The answer slid into place, and he scowled. Of course. She was saving the rest for *him*.

"Why don't I change into something more comfortable," she suggested.

Not done with the seduction, after all. He shuddered. "Give me the water, Legion, and stop trying to sleep with me. I know we have to, just not now."

Wrath stirred inside his head, stretching and yawning.

"No, I—"

"Legion. I'm giving up my life to save yours. The least you can do is give me the water."

Frowning, she crossed her arms over her ample chest. "You make it sound like I'm...I don't know, *ruining* you."

He cocked a brow, his silence answer enough, and her anger increased. Any life without Olivia would indeed be a ruined one. *Legion's your bratty kid.* "Baby girl" no longer seemed appropriate. *You can't hate her.* Fine. "Give me the water or I'll finally give you the spanking you deserve."

Now Wrath purred.

The demon *liked* the idea of punishing her? He never had before.

"Fine," she grumbled, and tugged the vial from between her breasts. "They only get one drop each. No more."

Because no more than a drop would be needed, he said, "I promise," and grabbed the glowing blue vial, the glass so cold it seemed refrigerated. He pushed to a stand and gazed down at himself. He was still blood-soaked and soot-covered from head to foot. His jeans were ripped and he wasn't wearing a shirt. Good enough.

"Stay here." With every step toward the door, his blood flowed faster and his strength intensified.

"If you're going to look for the angel," Legion called tightly, "you should know that she left."

The purring faded.

Aeron stopped and turned. "Left? As in went to another room?"

"Nope. She left the fortress."

No. No. She wouldn't have done that. She'd promised to stay until he returned and they'd spoken.

Wrath remained deadly quiet.

"You don't believe me, I see." Legion sighed and flopped back against the mattress. "She jumped from the balcony and flew away. She didn't even tell me to tell you goodbye. Which is rude, if you ask me, but I doubt you will," she added with a grumble.

No!

His own protest echoed the demon's. He pounded out of the room and down the hall. Legion must have followed him, because she was suddenly beside him, her hand resting in his, trying to drag him to a halt.

His steps never slowed. "Olivia!" he called.

Heaven!

"I told you. She left. She's gone forever."

He jerked free from her hold and his hand curled into fists. Olivia wasn't a liar. Despite the fact that her voice no longer possessed that ring of truth, she wouldn't have lied to him. It wasn't in her nature. He knew that. He knew *her*. Something must have happened. What, he didn't know, but he *would* find out.

"Olivia!"

Wrath whimpered.

We'll find her. He stopped the first warrior he found—Strider—and tossed the vial of water into his hands, tossing instructions, too, but not slowing in his quest to find his angel.

"Aeron," Legion said, a desperate quality to the word. "Please. You were going to lose her anyway. And you better give me back that bottle the moment you're done, Strider, or I will ensure you never have children!"

Aeron stormed back into his room and weighed himself down with weapons. "Doesn't matter if I'm losing her or not." Olivia, the one woman he realized he would always chase after, pride and circumstances be damned, was out there. "She's mine. Ours," he added before Wrath could protest. "And we won't rest until she's returned."

CHAPTER TWENTY-SIX

SLAP. HER LIP SPLIT.

Punch. Air abandoned her lungs.

Crack. A hard fist slammed into her lower arm, shattering bone.

Olivia remained mute through it all, enduring, but she couldn't help the tears that swam in her eyes. The torture had begun an hour ago. An eternity. Her wrists were tied to the arms of a small, wooden chair; she was bruised, bleeding and broken.

Her hair was soaked from the many times the man called Dean Stefano had held her head underwater, preventing her from breathing, forcing her to suck in mouthful after mouthful of liquid. Now those ice-cold droplets covered her, keeping her awake, ensuring she felt every bit of pain.

Not as bad as hell, she told herself. *You'll survive. You have to survive.*

"Galen left me in charge of your care," Stefano said, his face streaked with soot and patches of his skin blistered, "specifically asking that I interrogate you. And I will. I promise you. Your friends did this to me, you see. They burned me and what had become my home. I barely escaped, and owe them one. Or two."

She looked away from his wild eyes. She was in a warehouse of some sort. A warehouse with a concrete floor and metal walls. The room she now occupied was small. There was a table piled high with knives she fully expected the bastard to begin using any moment now. There was a basin of water deep enough to drown her in, which she'd already gotten up close and personal with more times than she could count, and the chair she sat upon.

"Ready to talk now, angel?" How calm he suddenly sounded. Not at all like the cruel man he was.

If only she'd tell him what he wanted to know, she would be saving the Lords the agony of losing a war, she thought, then bit her tongue. No. *No!* Galen must be nearby. His demon, Hope, must be playing with her, for that thought had not belonged to her.

Stay strong.

"All you have to do is tell me where the Lords have hidden the Cage and this stops." Stefano offered her a kind smile. "Surely you want that."

Did she want it to stop? Yes. Who wouldn't? But once she told him what he wanted to know, he would kill her. *Don't forget that fact.* She pressed her lips into a mulish line.

He plucked a feather that had fallen to the floor when Galen dumped her here and caressed the tip along her jaw. "The Cage. Where is it? Tell me. Please. I don't want to hurt you anymore."

You know what you have to do, a voice suddenly growled through her head. Not Lucifer, not Galen. The third that day. This time, she fought back a sob of relief. Lysander. He was here. She couldn't see him, couldn't sense him, but she knew he was there.

She wasn't alone in this any longer.

"Angel," Stefano snapped. Directly in front of her, he

curled his hand into a fist, preparing to hit her already-shattered arm. The feather had floated to the floor and now mocked her with its softness. "Talk."

"I don't...I don't know where it is," she rasped. A lie. She'd never thought she would be grateful for the ability to tell them, but she was now. Of course, that meant the human could choose not to believe her.

Olivia. Say the words, and I'll take you home.

Oh, she knew she could leave. Knew she could return to the heavens as planned and escape this. All of it. The pain, the humiliation. But she'd made a promise to Aeron, and it was a promise she intended to keep. She had to tell him goodbye. She *would* tell him goodbye.

"You do know," Stefano said. "You traipsed that fortress for weeks without anyone knowing you were there. You had to have seen it."

Olivia, please. Return with me. I can't stand to see you like this. I can't stand this sense of helplessness, of knowing I can save you but being unable to act.

"I can't," she told him.

Stefano punched her arm, just as she'd known he would, and a small cry finally found its way free. Stars winked over her vision, and dizziness rushed through her head, slamming from one temple to the other.

Olivia!

"I can't," she said again, gasping for breath.

Slap. "You can," the human replied, thinking she had spoken to him. "You're not giving me enough credit for what I can and *will* do to you, and that hurts my feelings."

The sting inside her already-cut mouth spread.

Olivia, Lysander snarled again. *This is madness.*

Nothing is worth this. Come home. Please. I can't help you any more until you do.

"Your wife...would not have...wanted this." This time she was speaking to Stefano and ignoring Lysander. She was glad he was here, yes, but she wouldn't cave in this matter.

Through her spying, Olivia knew that Darla, the wife in question, had committed suicide. Because of Sabin, keeper of Doubt, *and* Stefano—the two men who had loved her. She'd been locked in a tug-of-war between them, death her only escape.

Stefano's eyes narrowed, shielding the darkness of his irises. "She was tricked. The demons tricked her into liking them." He leaned down, flattening his palms on her bound arms—on her broken bone—and pressed. "If she'd been in her right mind, she would've wanted me to do *more*."

Another cry escaped her. The pain was so sharp, it traveled through her entire body before collecting in her stomach and burning.

Olivia!

"Aeron will hate me more than ever, as well, when I send him one of your fingers," Stefano said, as calm as when he'd caressed her with that feather. "Then he'll come for you. He'll end up dying for you. Is that a price you're willing to pay? Tell me where the Cage is, and I'll spare his life."

There it was again. That hope for a better future. If she told Stefano what he wanted to know, she would go free, return to Aeron, and they could be together forever. They could make love again, and even start a family.

Did Galen know what his man was doing in a bid

for the answers he sought? Did he care? Did he realize what his nearness was doing to her?

Olivia, damn you. You don't have to tell him and you don't have to endure. Just come home.

In and out she breathed. Fighting herself, her desires. Fighting that silly hope. Fighting the pain. She opened her mouth. What she planned to say, she might never know. Stefano hit her and she couldn't form a single word...was fading...sinking...blessedly lost...

"IT'S GOING TO take a while and could yield no results."

Aeron studied his friend, barely able to stop himself from latching onto those massive shoulders and shaking. Lucien's mismatched eyes, one brown, one blue, were regarding him with grim resolve. "I don't care how long it takes. Just do it."

He wanted to shake himself for not thinking of this sooner.

Everyone here thought that Olivia had returned to the heavens, as Legion had claimed. Hell, they'd all watched the video Torin's camera had recorded. The one of her jumping from the balcony in his bedroom.

The scene played through his mind constantly. She'd been standing inside his room, staring out at the night. She'd stiffened, turned. Then she'd turned again, walking outside, her mouth moving as if she were talking to someone—Legion said she'd been mumbling about her excitement to rejoin her friends—but it had been *terror* that had bled from her expression. *Then* she'd leapt. Fallen, fallen, begun to soar. Without her wings.

How could she have flown without her wings? Why had she been afraid?

The others assumed that terror stemmed from the

unknown, of wondering how the angels would receive her. Aeron knew better. Olivia wouldn't fear that. She'd told him the angels were forgiving—*patient,* had been her word—and that they would welcome her with open arms.

The only rational conclusion was that Legion was lying. Again. Which meant Olivia had been taken, as he'd first assumed. And there was only one way that could've happened. Galen. Galen had used the Cloak of Invisibility.

Save her. Punish him.

That the demon wished to save first and punish second proved the depths of his affection.

Aeron had scoured the entire city of Buda. He had raided buildings, terrorized citizens and killed. Oh, had he killed, and happily, too, no trace of guilt, having discovered many Hunters still lingering nearby. He might never be able to remove the blood from his hands. But there'd been no sign of Olivia. No hint of her scent. No rumors, no sightings. He. Was. Desperate. And only growing more so.

"Come. There's no better time to begin." He led Lucien down the hallway to his bedroom, where he threw open the door.

Legion, who was once again lounging on the bed, sat up. The sheet fell to her waist, revealing bare breasts. "Finally. Are you ready to do this or what?"

He ignored her—as he had since tossing that vial at Strider—so angry with her he no longer knew how to treat her, and stepped aside, allowing Lucien deeper inside the room.

Legion released a frustrated sigh. "Company? Now?"

Wrath hissed at her.

Aeron sensed that the demon liked her still, as he did, despite his rage, because there were no urges to hurt her. But no longer was Wrath calmed by her. She'd destroyed their piece of "heaven," and neither of them could forget.

Lucien was careful not to glance toward the bed. He stopped in the center of the room and spun slowly. He was here to lock on to Olivia's spirit trail—a trail he could then follow to wherever she was being held. Aeron's hands fisted.

"Gods," Lucien said, the awe in his tone clear. "She has the purest spirit I've ever beheld."

Aeron couldn't see it, but he could feel it, and nodded. "I know."

"Who?" Legion asked with a pout.

Again, he ignored her. Six days left until he had to be with her, but just then he wasn't sure he could do it, even to save his friends.

"I'll follow it as far as it goes," Lucien told him, "and if I—"

"When you," Aeron corrected, a low growl forming in his throat. *She is* fine. *She has to be fine.*

The warrior nodded. "*When* I find her, I'll come back for you." With that, Lucien disappeared into the spirit realm to follow that trail.

Gods, he felt helpless. He wanted—needed—to be out there, actively looking for her himself. But his first attempt had wielded no results, and deep down he knew his second wouldn't, either. Galen could have taken her anywhere, and Lucien would reach her much faster. If Aeron left the fortress now, Lucien would then have to hunt *him* down, once the warrior discovered her location.

"Aeron!" Legion jumped to her feet, scowling over at him as she clutched the sheet around her. "This is about the angel, I take it. Well, she's gone. Let her stay gone. We're better off. Why can't you see that?"

"We aren't better off without her," he shouted, no longer able to temper his ferocity. He faced her, pinning her with the fierceness of his stare. Why couldn't *she* see how much he needed Olivia? "She's better than any of us."

Disbelief glimmered in her eyes like tears. "I didn't believe her, but she was right. You...you love her."

Aeron didn't allow himself the luxury of answering. If he admitted, even to himself, that he loved Olivia, he wouldn't be able to let her go when the time came. He would keep her, no matter the consequences. "Tell me what happened when she left. Tell me the truth, damn you!"

She opened her mouth. To lie. He knew it; Wrath sensed it. "Don't." With anyone else, the demon would have plagued him with an urge to lie in return. Legion's sins had never bothered Wrath before, hadn't even registered, but as pissed as they were with her, things were changing. "The truth, godsdamn it. Only the truth. After everything I've done for you, do I deserve anything less?"

"Y-you're right. I—I'm sorry. I just thought...I thought it'd be easier for you if you thought she was... willing to leave you."

No. Fuck, no. A raw cry from him, from Wrath. "So Galen..."

"Has her. Yes. I'm sorry, Aeron. So sorry."

Having his suspicions confirmed...well, he might as well have cut the heart from his chest and torched it.

His beautiful Olivia was indeed with his enemy, probably hurting unbearably, for mercy was not something Galen's army practiced.

He tilted back his head and roared.

"Aeron. Tell me what I can do to—"

"Quiet!" As he glared over at her, he bit the inside of his cheek until he tasted blood. "You've hurt a woman who gave up her life to save us. *Us*. Not just me, but you. She's the reason you're still here."

"I'm sorry," Legion repeated raggedly, pulling from his gaze and peering down at the floor. "I really am."

"Doesn't matter." That didn't bring Olivia back.

Punish.

Wrath's demand, tossed out so determinedly, threw him. Even though the demon had been edging in that direction already.

She betrayed us.

Careful. *Wouldn't you rather save Olivia?* Aeron asked.

Anger morphed into sorrow. *Heaven.*

He'd take that as a yes. Pushing Legion from his mind, Aeron stalked to the closet and began to prepare for Lucien's return, strapping on as many knives and guns as his body could hold.

Just in case, he also grabbed what remained of the River of Life. Half the bottle. Strider hadn't heeded his instructions all that well, but a little was better than none. Hopefully, Olivia wouldn't need any. But if Galen *had* hurt her, there wasn't a hole the bastard would be able to hide in or a piece of fabric he'd be able to shield himself with. In the end, Aeron would find him.

Vengeance.

Yes. Vengeance would be his.

WHAT HAVE I DONE? Legion thought, horrified, as Aeron stalked out of the chamber he'd decorated to amuse her. He was suffering. And she was the cause. He was right. He'd only ever treated her with kindness, and she'd reduced him to *this*. His eyes were bleak, his voice ripe with despair.

Her stomach churned with sickness. She would have done anything, *anything,* to make this better for him. Maybe…maybe even step aside so that he could be with Olivia again. *No. Don't think like that.* Because she'd made that wretched bargain with Lucifer, her course was set—and so was Aeron's.

There had to be something else she could do, though. Something that would make him happy again. Something like…

The answer hit her, and she closed her eyes. *No, no, no,* she thought. Then, *Only way.*

For Aeron.

With shaky hands, she tugged on her clothes. A pair of pants and a T-shirt she'd borrowed from Danika. She could get the angel back. Not for Aeron to be with, but so that he could finally tell her goodbye. Legion couldn't follow spirit trails like Lucien, but she could sense her brethren. That's how she'd found Aeron the day they'd first met. She'd sensed his demon nearby. She could sense Galen, as well.

I should never have let him leave with the angel. Despite the Cloak hiding him, she'd known the moment he stepped into this room. She'd said nothing, too busy hoping he'd destroy her competition. *I'm a bad, bad girl.*

Find him. Yes. Okay. That's what she'd do. She'd present Aeron with both Olivia and Galen. And then Aeron would love her again.

"Leave me alone, child."

"I'm not a child." Gilly placed her hands on her hips, the picture of feminine pique. Too-young feminine pique. "You need someone to care for your wounds."

"My wounds," William told her with a frown, "are healing just fine." Since the moment he'd returned to the fortress, riddled with slices, she'd been fussing over him.

Yeah, he liked it. What man wouldn't enjoy being cared for? But the fact that he had to keep reminding himself that Gilly was too young for him was freaking him out. He shouldn't have to remind himself that he preferred older, more sophisticated women.

He shouldn't have to remind himself that he even preferred married women. Gods, did he love married women. The brokenhearted, too. They were easy pickings. Actually, anyone with low self-esteem was an aphrodisiac to him. He seriously jonesed, watching them bloom under his flattery. But adorable little Gilly?

No. No, no, no. Off-limits. Always. No matter her age. With all the women he'd been with—and yes, there'd been thousands—he knew you didn't play with the toys in your own home. That left too big a mess. You played with other people's toys in *their* homes.

"Why are you being this way?" She tucked a dark strand of hair behind her ears. A delicate ear. An ear made for nuzzling.

Idiot! "Get out," he said more harshly than he'd intended.

She flinched, and then a blanket of hurt fell over her lovely features. "And go where? The other girls are with their boyfriends, and I don't like hanging out with the single men."

Uh, hello. "I'm single."

"Yeah, but you're not like them," she said, gazing down at her shoes.

That was true. He was way more handsome and intelligent. Probably a little more deadly, too. "Gilly," he said on a sigh. "I think it's time we had a chat. I've sensed that you have some…feelings for me. I don't blame you. Hell, I commend you for your intelligence and keen appreciation of beauty. But we're friends, you and I, and that's all we can ever be."

"Why?" Those big eyes with their too-long lashes flicked up, pinning him in place, giving him ideas he shouldn't be having. Like teaching her that pleasure didn't have to be ugly.

You're worse than an idiot. He made sure to moderate his tone. "Because you're too young to be with a man and understand what that means."

She laughed bitterly. "I've known for years *what that means.*"

There it was again, a verbal confirmation that things had been done to her. Things that should never have been done. "Whoever was with you was wrong," he said tightly. "Very, very wrong."

A blush bloomed in her cheeks, and he wasn't sure if the color was born of shame, embarrassment or relief that someone recognized the ill-treatment she'd received. She didn't know that he knew about the stepfather, and he wasn't going to tell her; she only knew that William blamed the one who had hurt her, not Gilly herself.

Which was true. Her stepfather should be shot. And gutted. And then hung. And then set on fire. And William would see to it. In fact, that would be his next mission. Her mother wouldn't fare very well, either.

"It wouldn't be wrong with you," she whispered.

Gods, she was killing him. "Why do you want to hang around me, anyway?" He wouldn't tell her what he planned. She might try and stop him. "What makes me different from the others?"

She licked her lips, the pink tip of her tongue hiding away before he'd gotten a good enough look at it. "Well, you don't smoke."

That's what she found appealing? "Neither do the other men here. But unlike them, I've been meaning to take up the habit." And would do so, immediately. "And I won't be using a filter!"

She crossed her arms over her chest and drummed her nails. "It's more than that. You're beautiful, as you've already told me."

"As always, there's no denying that."

"Modest, too," she added dryly.

He was what he was. He knew his appeal, and wasn't ashamed to admit it. "Looks aren't everything, though. Especially since I'm as shallow as a rain puddle. I use women, Gilly. I sleep with them and then I'm done with them, even if they want more from me." He hated to taint her illusions about him, but it had to be done. One of them had to be smart about this.

She shifted from one foot to the other, once again looking away from him. "I knew all of that. I've heard talk about you."

"From who?" Whoever gossiped about him needed to be—

"Anya."

THE DARKEST PASSION

Spanked. Hard. "Whatever she told you, just remember that she's a liar."

"She said you can make a woman forget her troubles. So much so that the woman is happier when you leave her than she was when you found her, no matter the broken heart you leave behind."

Oh. "Well, for once she spoke true." His touch *was* magical. "But listen. In a few years, the *right* man is going to come along and make you happier." Sure, that man would have to meet William's standards and gain his approval, but they would jump that hurdle when they came to it. "As for me, I'm not that man. I'm not right for anyone long-term."

Again, hurt fell over her face. "But—"

"No. We aren't going to happen, Gilly. Not now, not ever."

She gulped, visibly gathering her composure. "Fine," she finally said. "I'll leave you alone. As you prefer." True to her word, she stalked from his bedroom, slamming the door behind her.

Unfortunately, she left the sweet scent of vanilla in her wake, taunting his bastard of a nose.

William pushed to his feet. His sides hurt, the wounds still in the process of scabbing over, but he had to get out of here before he followed her. The more distance between himself and Gilly the better. Besides, he had cigarettes to buy.

Maybe he'd help Aeron find his angel—who cared if she was findable or not—and then, when he was at full capacity, he would track and kill Gilly's family.

A good plan, if he did say so himself, but why did he suddenly feel so…incomplete?

A WIFE, GIDEON THOUGHT, dazed. He'd had a wife. A wife he didn't remember. How was that possible?

After Scarlet's announcement, he'd just sort of stumbled from the dungeon. He hadn't known what to say to her. Hadn't known whether he could believe her, Lies absolutely no fucking help. All he'd known was that he hadn't wanted to leave her, but he'd promised to do so, so he had.

Except, he'd stayed nearby, in the stairwell. Waiting, thinking, floundering, hoping she would call for him. She hadn't. Now, hours later, she was sleeping and he was headed...somewhere. He gazed up, meaning to keep track of his surroundings, when he bumped into an equally distracted Strider.

"Watch where you're going, my man," his friend said with a grin. "And shouldn't you be in your room?"

He had his shoulder propped against the wall for support, was panting and sweating. He hadn't eaten in forever, and was weakening by the second. "Probably not. No help needed."

Concern chased away Strider's smile. "Let me."

A strong arm clasped his waist and Gideon shifted his weight. "No thanks, enemy."

"You're welcome." Along the way, Strider told him about the bombing of The Asylum, and their victory. That explained the happy glow in the warrior's eyes. But there was something else in his eyes. Something out of place. Something...dark, upsetting.

"That's not great, but what about what's not troubling you?"

Strider looked over his shoulder, then scanned the hallway, ensuring they were alone. They were. Even so, he remained silent until he got Gideon inside his room and situated atop his mattress.

He sat on the chair Ashlyn—and then sweet Olivia—had once occupied, propped his elbows on his knees and leaned forward, head dropping into his upraised hands. "So get this. We met the Unspoken Ones. They're bad, dude. Bad. They know where the fourth artifact is, and they're willing to give it to whoever brings them Cronus's head. Even the Hunters."

"So we won't—"

"No, we *won't*. You remember the painting Danika made of Galen?"

Shit. Yeah, he remembered. In it, *Galen* had taken Cronus's head.

"If that comes true," Strider continued, "the Unspoken Ones, who are extremely powerful, will be freed from Cronus's rule, and they'll be able to do whatever they want. Like, I don't know, eat every human on the planet. I noticed they prefer an organ-rich diet."

Shit didn't cover it. "That's awesome."

"I summoned Cronus, hoping to talk to him about this, to see if there was any way we could destroy the Unspoken Ones before Galen got creative with his blade, but he's ignoring me. Torin summoned him, too. Nothing. And get this. I just ran into Danika. She'd just finished her newest painting."

Dread curled through Gideon. Usually, Strider relished an upcoming challenge. Now he just looked sickened. "I don't want to know."

"You might change your mind when you hear this. It was of Cronus and his wife, Rhea. Oh, yeah. Did anyone tell you Rhea is helping the Hunters? Anyway, they were with Lysander, Cronus fuming and Rhea cheering. You know Lysander, right? He's the angel shacking up with Bianka."

"No." Yes.

"No biggie, right?" Strider said. "So what if Cronus is pissed at Lysander and Rhea is pleased with him. The angel doesn't really concern us. Well, your demon will really dig this. That's a lie. The angel concerns us *big-time*."

"Please, don't go on, then. Don't hurry with the details. I mean, I love that you're dragging this out." Which he was probably doing because he didn't want to drop the bad news at all and was having to work up the courage. Still. Gideon couldn't take much more.

Strider looked up, expression grim. "Aeron was there, in the painting. Lysander had just taken his head."

CHAPTER TWENTY-SEVEN

IT WAS THE PAIN that woke her.

Olivia slowly cracked open her eyes. *Beep, beep.* At first, the room was hazy, as if someone had smeared it with oil. But then, bit by bit, clarity descended. Not full clarity—her eyes were swollen—but enough to see that she was still in the warehouse, though in another room. This one had hospital gurneys. She was hooked to an IV, and electrodes covered her chest, monitoring her heartbeat. Her broken arm wasn't in a cast, she noted, but was cuffed to the bedrail.

"Lysander?" Even speaking those few syllables caused her throat nothing but agony. Tears flooded her ravaged eyes.

There was no reply.

She tried again. "Lysander."

Again, nothing.

He was gone, then. He wouldn't have ignored her, that wasn't his style. He would have yelled at her some more and right now, that yelling would have been welcome. She was alone and scared.

No, not alone, she realized as her gaze scanned the rest of the room. Beside her was a man on a gurney of his own. A man she didn't recognize. He was young, perhaps early twenties, and there were bruises under his eyes. His cheeks were hollowed out and his skin a little jaundiced.

He was watching her.

When he realized he'd been found out, he blushed and said, "Uh, hi. Glad to see you're awake. My name's Dominic."

"Olivia," she replied automatically. Ow. That had hurt even worse.

"You sound terrible." Remorse and guilt poured from him. "We're supposed to be the good guys, you know. Stefano told me you're Wrath's girlfriend, but I don't care. You shouldn't have been hurt like that. No human should be hurt like that."

She didn't have to ask who "we" was. The Hunters. Her gaze shifted over the boy's body, checking for injuries. He was shirtless and there were bandages around his shoulder and middle. The one around his middle was dotted with dried blood. He wore a pair of loose scrub pants. "Hurt…you, too?"

He didn't seem to hear her, too lost in his own thoughts. "They told me our leader is a demon, too." As the last word left him, he began coughing. Coughing so forcefully, he spit up blood. When he finally calmed, he added, "I should have believed them. After what was done to you, I *have* to believe them."

Them. The Lords? She couldn't sense a lie in his tone, but then, she couldn't sense the truth, either. Either way, she knew deep in her bones that he wasn't going to live much longer. She hated that he would die like this, in here. As she probably would.

No. No. She shouldn't think like that. She was a joy-bringer at heart, yes, but that didn't mean she was helpless. She'd withstood the fires of hell. She'd endured having her wings ripped from her body. She could escape this. She *would* escape this.

Dominic sat up, wavered a bit and rubbed at his temples. When he steadied, he kicked his legs over the side of the gurney and stood.

"Careful," she managed to croak.

Again, he didn't seem to hear her. "They found me on the streets. I was a thief and a whore, and they told me it wasn't my fault." There was shame in his voice, shame far greater than his remorse had been. "They told me it was *their* fault. The Lords. That the demon of Defeat was feeding off me and my circumstances. I believed them because it was easier than blaming myself."

"Lied," she said. He was making a last confession, and that nearly made her sob. Death shouldn't bother her. It never had before. But now she knew the finality of it. This kid, for that's what he was, should have had a chance to live a long and happy life. Instead, he'd known only sorrow and regret.

One wobbly step, two, he worked his way around his gurney, approaching hers. "I know they lied. Now. The Lords, they sent me back. Set me free. They didn't want to, but they did it. *Defeat* did it, and there was compassion in his eyes. I saw it. Evil doesn't feel compassion, does it?"

"No."

"I studied him, you know? More than the others. I wanted to kill him myself, but he saved me. And Stefano, what he did to you…" Dominic shook his head, scowled. "There's no compassion in the act of beating a defenseless woman. Galen was pissed when he found out, but the *angel* didn't punish Stefano for his actions."

Galen, upset at her mistreatment? Surprising.

When Dominic finally reached her, he offered her a small smile that managed to be sad and happy at the same time. "Those bastards never thought I'd help you." He pulled one of the ties from his pants and there at the end hung a thin strip of metal. "They were wrong. Over the years, I learned to always be prepared for anything."

Her eyes widened in surprise as he worked at the cuff holding her captive. They teared again, as well. The pain was unbearable, nearly sending her back into that welcome black void. Thankfully, the metal clicked before she fell, freeing her, easing the agony somewhat.

"Thank you."

He nodded. "We've got ten minutes. Maybe. Someone's always coming in here to check on you." As he spoke, he helped her sit up. "Plus, I was supposed to call Galen when you woke up. Of course, I won't do that." With barely a pause, he added, "At the door, we're going to turn left. We'll walk past all the other doorways, and hopefully my body will block yours. There are men here, only a few, but even though they're the medical staff, they won't hesitate to gun you down if they realize who you are and that you're free."

Uncertain, Olivia placed her weight on her left foot, then her right. They held. A sigh of relief parted her lips—and made her cringe. Her lips were cut and the action, small as it had been, split the abrasions apart.

"I can't leave without the Cloak," she said. "Where is—"

"Impossible. Galen keeps it with him at all times. The only way to get it is to confront him, and you won't survive if you do that."

Dominic was right. She didn't have the strength to defeat Galen. But she couldn't leave that Cloak in his possession. Someone else could be taken by him. And would be. Galen wouldn't hesitate, and he might not be so...lenient with the next person.

"Come on," Dominic said, and with his arm around her waist, he led her toward the only door.

"Where's Galen now?"

"Oh, no. I know what you're thinking, but I already told you. We can't do it. There's just no way."

"I have to try," she said, letting her determination seep from her.

He stilled, closed his eyes. She could feel his heart banging against his ribs, erratic, too hard. "He's here. Waiting. Impatient." He laughed bitterly. "I tried to wake you sooner, but you were pretty out of it."

If she left, Galen would leave this warehouse and never return to it, knowing she could bring the Lords here. She'd no longer know where to find him, and that was an edge she wouldn't give up.

"I want you to go on without me," she said. She spouted off directions to the fortress. "The Lords will spot you once you reach the hill. Ask for Aeron and tell him—"

"No." Dominic shook his head. "How many times do I have to tell you? You can't beat Galen. He'll kill you before he parts with that Cloak. I'm dying, anyway, and don't care if I do so here or somewhere else. But you... No," he said again. "I won't let you. I won't die knowing I did nothing to help you."

She opened her mouth to protest, to tell him anything needed to convince him to do as she wanted, but the sound of pounding footsteps and a distant shout stopped her.

Dominic stiffened. "He's coming back to check on

you," he whispered, horrified. "Shit. Shit." He dragged her to the door and pressed her against the wall next to it, where they would be hidden when that door opened.

"I can't leave without the Cloak. I just can't."

Again Dominic closed his eyes, as if he were weighing his options. Only took a second, a second that seemed to drag into eternity, but when he opened them, there was more resolve banked in his expression than she'd ever seen in anyone before.

"The Cloak will be in his pocket. As it folds, it shrinks. It's gray, soft. Grab it and run. Don't look back. Just run. Okay?"

Like his, her heart was pounding against her ribs. Sweat was beading over her skin, her limbs were shaking and her mouth drying. "What about you?" He claimed he was ready to die, but she wasn't ready to watch him do so. He was a nice kid who'd seen too many bad things in his short life. He deserved a happily ever after.

"I'll handle Galen. Okay?" He pulled the other tie from his scrubs and there was a blade attached. His knuckles whitened as he clutched the hilt. "Just reach into his pockets, grab whatever you can and run."

Pockets. Galen wore a robe just like Olivia's, so she knew that there were three pockets. Two on the right and one on the left. It would be impossible to frisk all three at the same time. Still, she said, "Okay," and prayed she chose correctly.

The door swung open, and Galen strode inside. He stopped in the center of the room, head swinging left and right to survey the empty gurneys. She didn't think about her next actions, just propelled into him and slid her hands along his sides, into two of his pockets.

He cursed and tried to push her away. Perhaps Lysander was helping her, after all, because Galen did not succeed.

Her broken arm throbbed, the fingers swollen and slow to react to mental commands, but she grabbed everything she touched, turned and ran. Just ran. Just as Dominic had wanted. Fingers snagged in her hair and jerked, but she kept moving.

She passed the door, halfway expecting hard hands to settle on her shoulders or tangle in her hair again, but that never happened. Instead, she heard a shout, a roar of pain, and knew Dominic had just stabbed Galen.

A stabbing wouldn't keep the immortal down for long.

Through the open doorways of the other rooms, several men raced into the hallway. As their confused, panicked gazes hit her, she increased her speed and peered down at her bounty. There, in the center of her palm, was a square of gray material.

Relief. Excitement. Yes, she experienced both. They gave her strength. Olivia dropped everything else, it wasn't important right now, and shook the material out. Because of her inattention, she plowed into a solid wall of man.

The action jarred her, hurt her, but not enough to stop her from continuing to shake out the material as she fell. Just as the man bent down to grab her, she wrapped the Cloak around her shoulders.

One minute she could see her limbs, the next she couldn't. *Don't even breathe.* Be quiet.

All of the men spun, frowning, looking for her. They fired at where she'd been, but she'd already moved. She pressed against the wall, and they finally darted past her, shouting for help.

Galen stomped out of the room, blood spurting from his gut. He was scowling and dragging an unconscious— *please, let him be alive*—Dominic behind him.

"Where'd she go?" he demanded.

"I don't know."

"She just disappeared."

Galen ran his tongue over his teeth. He dropped Dominic, who didn't even utter a gasp. "She couldn't have gotten far. She's injured. Spread out and move toward the demons' lair. That's where she's headed. If you feel anything you can't see, shoot. If you hear a woman panting but can't see her, shoot. Do you understand? I'm done playing nice. She has something that belongs to me. Do not set foot on the hill, though. The Lords will see you, and I'm not ready for that yet."

A chorus of yeses rang out, and the men were off.

Galen stood there for a long while, popping his jaw, breathing deeply. Olivia didn't dare risk an exhalation; she simply held the oxygen in her nose and waited. Finally, he stormed off, following behind the men.

She tiptoed forward and placed her fingers at Dominic's neck. No pulse. Her chin trembled, and tears once again filled her eyes. He'd been ready to die, had wanted it even, but it still broke her heart. He'd never known joy. He should have known joy.

Pray for his soul. Later. You can't help anyone if you die, as well. Olivia stood, her tears pouring down her cheeks like rain. She could barely see in front of her, but she stumbled forward, taking the same path as Galen.

The hallway led to an empty area, but that empty

area led to a closed doorway. The exit? Most likely. The seam between the double doors revealed a stream of sunlight.

Gulping, she held out her uninjured hand and pushed the panels open. Warm air instantly enveloped her. And sure enough, the sun was shining brightly over a parking lot. Too brightly for her now-sensitive vision. Still, she blinked against those rays as she trudged onward.

Until a smiling Galen stepped into her path.

His wings were spread wide, and she was moving too quickly to stop. She knocked into him and careened backward, falling into the metal wall of the warehouse. With a shocked, pained gasp, she slid to the rock-laden ground.

"I thought you'd stay behind to check on the boy," he said, grin widening. "Your friends caused his death, yet still you thought to return to them. So disappointing. So predictable."

Bastard!

He lunged for the wall, and Olivia rolled out of the way, clutching as many rocks as she could hold. She scrambled to her feet, careful not to make another sound, and Galen ended up slamming into the building.

He straightened. "Doesn't matter. I can see your footprints. It's just a matter of following you now."

Thanks for the warning. She zigzagged left, right, gaze continually moving, searching for a path to safety. Only dirt and gravel greeted her. Which meant anywhere she stepped, he would continue to see her prints. And he did. He followed her.

"Escape me, and I'll go after Aeron next. I'll cut off his head while you watch, helpless."

He was taunting her, trying to trick her into retreating.

Slowly, inch by agonizing inch, Olivia moved backward. Still Galen followed. She threw a glance over her shoulder. A hundred yards away was a busy area, with a high-traffic road and many other buildings. Hunters had probably chosen the location as a way of hiding in plain sight, but what they hadn't counted on was that it would be easier for their *prisoners* to hide, as well. All she had to do was make it there, and then she would be safe. He would never be able to pick her out.

Problem: he was fast, faster than her, and uninjured. If she ran, he could catch her. *Worth the risk.*

Drawing on a reservoir of strength she hadn't known she possessed, she spun around and sprinted forward. There was a crunch of gravel, and she knew that Galen was still hot on her trail. Her entire body screamed in protest each time she threw one leg in front of the other, but she only increased her speed.

Almost there… Galen gripped the Cloak and jerked. Yelping, fisting the material with her free hand to keep it around her, she rounded a corner and slammed into a group of pedestrians. Two fell backward as her shoulder and arm were revealed. Panting, Olivia refit the material around her, then plastered herself against the nearest wall.

She tossed her handful of rocks into a pole. *Pop, pop, pop.* She watched, hopeful, as Galen soared past her toward the pole, giving chase to where he thought she'd gone.

So close. So close to disaster. But she'd done it. She'd really done it.

Hot breath slammed in and out of her nose, burning her throat and lungs. Sweat was pouring obscenely now, and she probably smelled. Her limbs were once more shaking. Unfortunately, she couldn't go to the fortress. Galen's men would be surrounding the place by the time she reached it. She couldn't call Aeron for a pickup because she didn't know his number.

She had to do something, go somewhere; she couldn't stay here. Using the wall to prop herself up, she careened forward, winding around several corners, letting herself become lost in the different crowds and locations. Finally, she spied a shadowed, empty alley and sat. Mistake. The moment her body stilled, she knew she wouldn't be able to force it into action again. Her muscles clamped down on her bones, and every spark of energy drained.

"Lysander," she whispered. Waited.

Once again, she received no reply.

Alone. A terrible thought. This wasn't the best location to hide. Someone could stumble over her invisible legs. More than that, Hunters would probably be searching all the alleys when she failed to reach the fortress. But…

She'd rest her eyes, she thought. Just for a bit. Catch her breath, too. Then she'd pick herself up and start moving again. Except, she must have fallen asleep, because when she finally opened her eyes, still unable to move, she saw that the sun had set and the moon was glowing prettily.

Her pain was magnified, her resolve finally shaken. She couldn't do this. She couldn't go on. Death would be welcome. She wouldn't fight. She would—

"Olivia," a male voice said, startling her. "Come on, sweetheart. I know you're here. Your spirit trail ends here, but I can't see you." A second later, a body materialized.

Lucien. She recognized him, though they'd never been properly introduced, and knew he carried the demon of Death. How appropriate. He could escort her—

"I'm not going to hurt you. I want to help you. Aeron's looking for you."

Aeron. Death could suck it. With a shaky hand that felt as if boulders anchored it in place, she reached up and tugged the Cloak from her shoulders. "H-here. I'm here."

Lucien's eyes widened when she suddenly appeared. "Oh, sweetheart. I'm so sorry. Everything will be—" He shook his head. "No time to explain what's going on. There's a soul at the warehouse where you were tortured, and I need to escort him into the hereafter."

"His name's Dominic," she said in that savaged voice of hers. "He saved me. Be gentle with him, please."

"I will." Lucien disappeared.

She folded the Cloak as best she could, expecting— Lucien reappeared with Aeron.

All other thoughts faded. Aeron. Unexpected. Welcome. "I thought you were...the soul..."

"That's what I'm doing next. See you back at the fortress," Lucien said, and once again disappeared.

"Oh, baby," Aeron said gently as he crouched beside her. Despite the gentleness, she could hear his worry and his fury. But he was here, he was safe after the earlier battle. "What did they do to you?"

Like Lucien, she didn't have time for explanations. "They're out here, looking for me. Waiting by the fortress."

He immediately stiffened, his gaze sweeping the area. "No one's near us. You're safe. And I'll call Torin and warn him about what's going on. Anyone in the area will be taken care of before we get there." With a tender expression, he withdrew a vial from his pocket and held it to her lips. "Drink, baby, drink."

She shook her head. There was no need to waste a drop on her. She'd be going home soon and—

Determined, he parted her lips himself and tipped the glass. The cool liquid slid down her throat, more than a sip, and settled wonderfully in her stomach. Within seconds, that liquid was deluging the rest of her, giving her strength, peace. The pain left her entirely, leaving a cool hum of pleasure in its place.

Stubborn man. "You shouldn't have given me so much." Even her throat was healed, the words leaving her smoothly.

"I would give you all of it."

What a sweet thing to say. Sweet and wrong. She didn't want to hear things like that. Not now. It would make leaving him that much harder. "How did you find me?"

His eyes narrowed. "I knew you wouldn't leave without saying goodbye, so I had Lucien hunt down your spirit trail. Which means he saw where you'd been, what paths you'd taken. I will never forgive myself for how long it took us to locate you. And I will murder that fucking bastard Galen if it's the last thing—"

"Aeron," she interjected. She wouldn't have him endangering himself for her. "Just hold me."

His arms settled under her knees and at her back, and he lifted her, cradling her against his chest. "When we get home, you're going to tell me everything that was done to you. You might as well tell me what the demons did to you that first night, as well." With every word, his voice hardened. "And then I'm going to find Galen *and* the demons and return the favor. No one hurts my woman and lives."

CHAPTER TWENTY-EIGHT

AERON LAID OLIVIA on his bed as gently as possible. The swelling was gone, her cuts and bones healed, but he wasn't taking any chances. Legion was absent, and he was glad for that. He didn't know where she was; all he knew was that he couldn't deal with her right now. His darling Olivia...when he'd found her...

His hands fisted. Wrath screamed for vengeance, and Aeron wanted to give it to him. Now. No waiting. He wanted Lucien to flash him to wherever Olivia had been held and just start killing. Actually, the "want" was more of a need, like breathing and eating. But the cowards had already run away, the warehouse empty. That much Lucien had told him before carting him into that alley. Not that that mattered to his demon.

Clearly Olivia had been beaten, tormented. Lucien had told him her energy had been bright red with pain and fear. Aeron didn't care what he had to do to find Galen. He was going to do it and finally kill the bastard.

Slow and painful, Wrath said.

Slow and painful, he agreed. First, though, he would battle past those dark urges and have his promised chat with Olivia. Her comfort, *her* needs, came before everything. And also, he couldn't punish Galen properly until he knew exactly what the asshole had done to his woman.

He was going to punish him properly.

Relax. For Olivia. Aeron crouched beside the bed and Olivia rolled to her side, maintaining eye contact. "I would've understood if you'd gone...home during Galen's interrogation," he said. In fact, he would have preferred it if she had. He would rather have lost her forevermore than know that she'd suffered.

"I didn't want to leave. Yet. I had to make sure you got this." She lifted a small piece of folded gray material. "It's the Cloak of Invisibility."

For a moment, he could only blink in astonishment. Then he shook his head and laughed. His first in forever, it seemed. This tiny woman, this fallen angel, had done what an army of immortals had not been able to do. She'd stolen the third artifact from under the Hunters' noses—and she'd trounced Galen in the process. Pride swelled his chest.

Reward.

First the demon had wanted to chastise Legion, now Wrath wanted to give Olivia a prize. *We're on the same page, demon.* "Thank you. Not that those two little words express the depths of my gratitude, but thank you all the same."

"You're welcome. So, what do you think of it? The artifact, I mean."

"Looks so small." He studied it from every angle. So innocuous, too. "How does it—"

"Cover an entire body? It expands as you unfold it."

He didn't want to leave her, even for a second, but he had to ensure the Cloak's protection. "I'll be back in a minute," he said, and she nodded.

He kissed her forehead, then stood reluctantly, practically sprinting from the room. The first warrior he ran into was—Strider. Again. Aeron shoved the material into his hands and said, "Cloak of Invisibility. Give it to Torin for safekeeping. Thanks." There. Done. Not his problem anymore. And then he was off, heading back to his room.

Strider caught up to him just before he reached the door, grabbing his arm and jerking him to a stop. "How did you get this?"

"Later."

"Fine. Deets about the Cloak are on hold. We've got more important things to discuss, anyway."

"Later." He only had five days left with Olivia—*if* he could convince her to stay for the rest of that time. If not... Hell, no. He would. He was a warrior. He would act like one. Victory, at any cost.

Heaven. Any cost.

Two against one. He liked his odds. Then, when their time was up, *then* he'd finally have his vengeance.

"This can't wait," Strider insisted.

"Too bad." His fingers curled around the knob.

His friend gave another jerk.

Aeron swung around, scowling. "Let go of me, man. I'm busy."

"For news like I've got, you need to make time for me. 'Cause, here we go. You're about to lose your head. Literally. I wanted to break it to you gently, but you were too much of an ass."

He froze. "What do you mean, lose my head? How do you know?"

"Danika painted a new picture. In it, your head was detached from your body."

He was going to die? So far, Danika's paintings had never been proven wrong. The Lords hoped they could change some of their outcomes, sure, but had never really learned whether they could or not. Which meant it was more than likely that he was going to die.

He waited for rage to fill him. It didn't. He waited for sadness to overwhelm him. It didn't. He waited for the urge to drop to his knees and cry and beg for more time to claim him. Again, it didn't.

He'd lived for thousands of years. And now, having met Olivia, he'd led a full and glorious life. Because he'd loved. His friends, definitely. His surrogate daughter, Legion, despite her recent actions. But mostly Olivia. He loved her. He could deny the emotion no longer. She was his. She was Wrath's. Their reason for being. The source of their happiness. Their obsession.

Their heaven.

He would have chased her all over the world, just for a few more minutes of her time. Minutes. Perhaps all they had left now, he mused, rather than the days he'd thought to fight for. She was his everything, and he wasn't going to waste any more of their remaining time away from her.

Finally, he understood the humans. They didn't beg for more time because they wanted to spend what they had left enjoying each other. Not wishing for what could have been.

Wrath must have understood, as well. The demon wasn't crying, wasn't urging him to change his course. Without the angel, they had nothing. And as long as they completed their mission—Galen's destruction—they could die happy.

"Aeron," Strider prompted.

He forced himself back to the present. "Who takes my head?" He would still have to be with Legion. That couldn't change. He wouldn't allow his friends to deal with a mess of his creation without him, but he would take care of that once Olivia was gone and avenged. And then, then he could die in peace. It would be better that way, anyway. He didn't want to live without his Olivia.

Now he wouldn't have to.

"Lysander. I think. Cronus and Rhea are there. I've talked to the others and we decided—"

"Later," he said. What the others speculated didn't matter right now. If they didn't have facts, they didn't have anything he needed. "Tell me later. I appreciate the warning, but like I said, I'm busy now." He pushed his way back into his bedroom and shut the door, his gaze remaining on Strider until the wood blocked them.

Any other time, the confusion and concern on Strider's face would have made him laugh.

There was a knock. "Aeron. Come on, man."

"Go away or I swear to the gods I'll cut out your tongue and nail it to my wall."

That earned a growl. "Shut your mouth, Wrath. I'm trying to ignore the challenge in your tone, but it's not working. Now listen. We can't lose you. We can't go through something like that again. We just can't." As he spoke, Strider pounded at the wood. "You remember how it was after Baden."

Not going there. Aeron opened the door, punched his friend in the face and shut it again.

Only a heartbeat later, Strider opened the door himself, punched Aeron twice, smiled sweetly, although a bit sadly, and replaced the block between them. "I won. As for the other thing, you've got thirty minutes, and then every single one of us will be inside that room to talk to you. Understand?"

"Yes." Unfortunately.

Footsteps echoed.

Behind him, Aeron heard Olivia sit up. "What's he talking about? Losing you? And why were you punching each other?"

At the sound of her voice, Wrath uttered a sigh of contentment.

Slowly Aeron turned and faced her. Having her worry wasn't something he would allow, so he offered her a grin, one he hoped conveyed everything he felt for her. Perhaps it did. Her eyes widened, and she nervously licked her lips.

"Ignore him. I think he's suffering from brain damage." Which wasn't necessarily a lie. Aeron had always considered the warrior a bit deranged. "Besides, we have unfinished business. I've never had you in a bed, and I *really* want you in a bed."

Yes!

At first, she gave no reaction. Then, before panic could bloom inside him at the thought of a rejection—*no!*—she reached up to the collar of her robe and pulled. The material parted, revealing those beautiful breasts with their pink, pearled nipples, that smooth stomach and those long, perfect legs.

"I would like that."

Yes, yes.

A tremor traveled the length of him, his shaft filling, hardening. He stalked toward her, stripping along the way. A process that included kicking off his boots and stumbling over himself because he refused to stop, even for a second. Skin to skin. That's what he needed. When he reached her, he was as naked as she was.

He crawled up her luscious body, settling some of his weight atop her.

Perfect. Heat, so much heat. They both hissed in a breath. She closed her eyes and arched against him, even as her hands clutched at his back. Her neck was exposed, her pulse hammering wildly. Her lips were parted, and her hair in tangles around her shoulders.

Passion had never looked more exquisite.

He should have spent every minute of their half hour pleasuring her senseless. Licking her, tasting her, sucking her. He should have started at her toes and worked his way to her mouth. He should have lingered over her thighs and her breasts. But he didn't. He couldn't. He had to be inside her, couldn't go another minute without being joined, totally and completely, with her.

"Lock your ankles on my back," he commanded.

She didn't hesitate. Obeyed instantly.

The moment she was opened up to him, he was shoving inside. Deep, so deep. As deep as he could go. A moan left her, because it wasn't the easiest of fits. His second thrust was a little smoother, though, and his third a rapturous glide.

"Aeron," she gasped out.

Mine.

Ours. Learn to share, Wrath. I've had to. He braced his hands at her temples and rose, just a little, drinking her in while he moved in and out, in and out. He couldn't have stilled had Galen burst into the room and placed a gun to his head. This woman delighted him, frustrated him, enraptured him, angered him... belonged to him. As he belonged to her. He wanted to brand her, so that she'd never forget him. He wanted to erase himself from her memory, so that she'd never remember him.

He didn't want her to suffer when they parted. He wanted her to find someone else—just as much as he wanted to kill that someone else. But mostly, he wanted her to be happy. To smile. To have her fun.

Fun. Yes. That's what he'd give her this day. Fun.

"Did I ever tell you why it's bad to be a penis?" he asked, slowing his thrusts.

Her eyes blinked open. Passion still glowed in those sky-blue depths, but mixed with it was sudden confusion. "Wh-what?"

Paris had told him a lot of jokes over the years, but he only recalled this one. He'd never been able to scrub the thing from his mind. "Why it's bad to be a penis." He twisted his hips on the inward glide, hitting her in a new spot.

A cry of delight parted her lips. "No. No, but it doesn't matter right now, I want you to—"

"It's bad to be a penis because there's a hole in your head."

Her lips twitched as she clutched at him. "I never thought of it like that."

"Well, it gets worse. Your owner is always strangling you."

The twitching became a half smile. Her knees tightened at his hips, and she bit her bottom lip. "What else?"

"You shrink in cold water."

There was a strangled chuckle.

"And you're forced to hang around with two nuts."

The chuckle became a full-fledged laugh. Gods, he loved the sound of her laughter. It was pure and magical, washing over him like a caress, dessert for his ears.

He felt like a king, that he had been the one to cause that reaction in her.

"Well, your penis can hang out with me anytime he wants."

Now *he* chuckled. He wished. Oh, how he wished. "Baby, sweet baby," he said. "My baby."

Ours. Learn to share.

He twisted his hips again, and she again closed her eyes and cried out. She reached for the headboard, meshing her breasts into his chest, and met him thrust for thrust. Common sense slipped away, the need for completion taking over. Yes, yes, so good.

Her body squeezed at him, wet and warm and silky smooth. Faster and faster he pumped inside her, unable to slow, unable to savor. He had to hear her cries of abandon. Had to spurt his seed inside her. Had to brand her, just as he'd wanted.

Soon she was thrashing beneath him. Soon she was calling his name over and over. She was all he could see, all he could hear, all he could smell, and he wanted that to last forever. But the more he pounded into her, the closer he came to the end. His muscles tensed, his blood heated to boiling, burning him up, ruining him for anything else. Anyone else. This was it. All he existed for. All his demon craved.

"I love you," he roared, pushed over the edge.

Just like that, she climaxed as well, spasming around his shaft, hands back on him, nails digging deep. She even leaned up and bit the cord of his neck. Perhaps she drew blood. He didn't know, didn't care. Only knew that his body continued to rock into her, spurting and clenching and burning some more, his demon humming, purring, as lost as he was.

And when Olivia finally settled, when he finally caught his breath, he collapsed atop her before rolling to the side. Immediately she burrowed against him, several minutes passing in silence. Never had an orgasm been so intense, so consuming.

He'd wanted to brand her, but he was the one who'd been branded. She was all over him, inside him, his everything. His every breath. With her, he was calm, the demon was calm, and life was everything he'd ever dreamed.

"That was...that was..." She sighed with contentment. One of her fingertips traced a heart on his chest.

"Amazing," he said. "*You* are amazing."

"Thank you. You are, too. But...but...did you mean what you said?"

Tread carefully. If he told her the truth, she might decide to stay, even though he had to be with Legion, even though his end was near, forcing her to witness both his betrayal and his death. Forcing her to live without him if—when—Danika's vision proved true.

"Yes," he said, then cursed under his breath. Still, regret wouldn't come. She deserved to know. She was more to him than sex. She was more to him than, well, anything. "I love you."

"Oh, Aeron. I love—"

"Do not say another word, Olivia," a male growled from the center of the room.

At the interruption, Wrath snarled in fury.

Aeron stiffened, already reaching for the blades resting on his nightstand. He didn't relax when he spotted Lysander, gold wings outstretched, white robe glowing in the moonlight. The man's eyes were narrowed with fury.

Who takes my head? he'd asked Strider.

Lysander. I think.

"Lysander," Olivia gasped out, holding the bedsheet to her chest. "What are you doing here?"

"Silence," he commanded.

"Don't talk to her like that." Aeron stood, jerked on a pair of pants, and said, "Tell us what you want and leave." *Don't be here for the reason I think you're here. I'm not ready yet.*

Lysander met his stare and uttered the words Aeron dreaded hearing. "I want your head. And I won't leave until I've taken it."

CHAPTER TWENTY-NINE

FINALLY, LEGION FOUND GALEN. He was in a dingy pub in London. She'd been flashing all over the place, from Buda to Belgium to the Netherlands, and now London. The coward had flown himself here and was nursing a glass of whiskey in a shadowed corner. She could smell the ambrosia he'd already consumed; she recognized the sweet scent because Paris always smelled like that, and she knew Galen would be drunk very soon. She had only to wait.

She was too impatient to wait.

Her gaze raked over her own body. She still wore that T-shirt and jeans. They were plain but clean. And though they weren't revealing, her breasts were so large they stretched the material. Several men had noticed her already and whistled as she strolled by. Outwardly, she'd paid them no heed. Inwardly, she'd thrilled at being viewed as something other than ugly, disgusting or at best, something to be tolerated.

She stopped at Galen's table, and he looked up through the dark shield of his lashes. "Go away."

Steady. Instinct demanded she attack first and ask questions later. *Resist.* Galen delighted in tricking the Lords, in sending Bait to distract them before acting. Today, she would be *their* Bait.

"You're beautiful," she said, and he was. With his

pale hair and pale blue eyes, with his flawless features and sensual mouth, he was every woman's fantasy. But he'd helped destroy her Aeron's life, and for that he would pay. "I want you." Dead, but she didn't add that part.

He arched a brow. "Of course you do. You can't help yourself. None of you can." He almost sounded...upset by that. "Here's a little news flash for you. No matter what I make you feel, hopeful for a future, a wedding, babies, you're not going to get it from me." There at the end, he'd been sneering. He drained the rest of his drink. "Now go away like I told you. I came here for peace and quiet."

He was the second man to turn her away since her transformation. She couldn't help herself; she slapped him. His head whipped to the side, and a trickle of blood formed at the corner of his mouth. *Guess I'm stronger than I thought,* she mused smugly. Good.

When he faced her this next time, his expression was lit with interest. "Why did you do that?"

"Perhaps you didn't hear me when I said I wanted you."

"And you thought slapping me would win me over?"

"You're still here, aren't you?"

He studied her before moving his gaze across the bar. "So where do you want me?"

"Bathroom." No witnesses. Not for what she had planned. "And by the way. I don't want to wed you and I don't want your babies. We're gonna have sex, and you're gonna like it."

"Forceful little thing, aren't you?"

"You have no idea. So we doing this or not?"

Those lush lips twitched. "Let me get this straight.

We're going to the bathroom, and I'm going to fuck you, and you don't even care to know my name?"

"I'd actually prefer it if you'd keep your stupid mouth closed." Oops. Her hatred was slipping out.

"Well, well. You might just be my soul mate." He was on his feet a second later, his chair skidding over the sticky floor. He didn't say another word as he kicked into motion, arm snaking around her waist and pulling her along with him.

There was a woman in the bathroom, washing her hands, and Galen pushed her out without preamble.

"Hey," the girl cried in irritation. She softened as her gaze raked him. "Hey." Sultry now.

"Stay out or die," he told her flatly. And then he slammed the door closed and whipped around to face Legion.

She trembled, she just couldn't help herself. There was so much heat in his eyes she was momentarily shocked stupid. It was what she'd wanted from Aeron. What she might never get.

One step, two, he approached her. She backed away. *Attack now. Kill him.* But she didn't.

"Scared?" he asked silkily. "You should be."

She raised her chin, looked behind her—and saw the counter and the mirror. Her reflection stunned her. The fall of golden hair, just begging for a man's hands. The wide, dark eyes so filled with longing.

Longing? She wanted him? *Him?* How could she want Hope? He was her enemy. He was Aeron's enemy.

Strong hands banded around her waist and hefted her up. She gasped as she returned her focus to him. He was already working the button of her jeans. That button gave easily and then he was jerking them off her legs.

He chuckled. "No panties. You *are* eager for me."

His amusement irritated her—even as it spiced her desire up another notch. That wasn't because of him, she told herself. She refused to believe so. She'd wanted to have sex; that was one of the reasons she'd bargained for this body. She'd expected it to be with Aeron, though.

Yet he might never want her that way. Not really.

"Who said I was eager for you? You're beautiful, yeah, but you're just a substitute for someone else." Truth. A truth she liked. She could use him. Have the sex she wanted and *then* kill him.

Galen's eyes narrowed to tiny slits. "Is that right?"

"There you go, talking again. I thought I told you how much I hated that."

"You're the one who better watch her mouth." With a growl, he ripped off her shirt. She wasn't wearing a bra, either. He didn't ask for permission, but leaned forward and sucked a nipple into his mouth. A mouth that was hot as fire and had her moaning. In pleasure.

This was...wonderful.

Yes. Yes, she'd have the sex she wanted. It would distract him so that she could more easily go in for the kill. That was all the rationale she needed to spread her legs and jerk him into her. His pants-clad erection hit her sweet spot, and she cried out.

Wonderful was not the word to describe *that*. *Perfection* was. How much better would it have been with Aeron, then? Aeron. She didn't want to think about him right now. She only wanted to feel.

"More," she found herself commanding. She arched into him, rubbing herself against him. Her skin was sensitized and only growing more so. There was an ache inside her, a heat like the one she'd seen in his eyes. Both were building.

"Don't even want foreplay?" Galen worked at his pants, freeing his erection. It was big. So deliciously big. Demons often had sex while in hell—with each other, the damned souls—so she knew big was preferred and small ridiculed.

"What's foreplay?" Truly. She had no clue.

He chuckled again. "I like you, female. I really do." He tried to kiss her, but she turned her head. He followed the movement, and she turned her head again.

"No kissing," she rasped. She wanted to, oh, did she want to, but kissing would kill him before she was finished with him. She looked like a human, yes, but her teeth were pure poison. She could taste it.

She settled her ankles on his lower back, digging in, forcing him to move against her. Mind…fogging… body…burning…

"Kiss me," he commanded.

"No."

"Kiss."

"No!"

"Why not? Not like it's anything special."

"Cease…talking!" she growled.

His snarl was like a caress. "Fine. You want a quick fuck, that's all you'll get." He gripped the base of his erection and aimed it between her legs, then he was thrusting forward, all the way inside her.

She cried out in pain, but the pain disappeared as quickly as it had sprouted, leaving only a feeling of utter possession. "More." He stretched her, filled her up, and it was heady. No wonder all manner of beings did this so often.

"Virgin?" he gasped out, clearly shocked. Wonder of wonders, it appeared as if his expression was softening.

"None of your business. Finish."

He bared his teeth at her, but in and out he pumped. The stretching and the fullness only increased, pushing her toward...something. Soon she was thrashing against him, desperate for that something, willing to kill everyone in this building if she didn't get it.

"Hurry."

"Gods, you feel good."

She clawed at him, hurtling over...finally over... drifting, spinning, floating, seeing stars winking over her eyes. Every muscle in her body clamped down, let go, clamped down again. It was powerful, it was moving, but all too soon it faded. Leaving her strangely shattered.

Her eyelids flickered open. She was panting. Galen was still inside her, still moving in and out. Absolute pleasure consumed every inch of his features. He must be getting close to his end, as she had done.

And she couldn't allow that, she thought. He didn't deserve to feel like that. Even though he'd made her feel better than she ever had before. Even though sex was her new favorite game and she planned to have it as often as possible.

"Galen," she said, and his shocked gaze met hers. A tremor moved through her, reigniting the fire in her blood. How odd. But there was no time to enjoy another round. "See you in hell."

With that, she sank her teeth into his neck, clamping down as he roared. A roar born of pain rather than completion. He shoved at her, trying to rip her away, but she held tight, pumping her poison deep into his vein. Only when the last drop left her did she lift her head and smile at him. He'd gone pale, almost green.

"What did you…do to me?" His knees gave out and he sank to the floor.

Silent, she hopped to her feet and dressed. Her knees trembled the entire time. Part of her wanted to stay, to ease him, but she couldn't forget who and what he was—not again. This had to be done. For Aeron. She owed him this much, at the very least.

"I planned to take you to my man and have him kill you, but this is better. Have a nice life," she said, and then blew Galen a kiss. "Not that it'll last much longer."

AERON STARED OVER at Lysander. The threat of decapitation had been issued, the angel's determination unwavering. "Olivia," he said. He hadn't moved from beside the bed. He and Wrath were both oddly calm. "Return home. Now. Please."

"No. No." She threw her arms around his waist, pressing her cheek into his back. The wet warmth of her tears scalded him. "Don't do this. Please, don't do this."

"You have caused her nothing but pain, demon," Lysander gritted out. "You did not see her tortured at your enemy's hand. I did. You didn't beg her to return home to save herself the pain. I did. And why did she deny me? Because she'd made a promise to you. Because she wanted to say goodbye. Again, *to you*. I will not give you time to wheedle another promise from her. I will not give you another opportunity to make a mockery of my pact with you. This ends now. Today." One moment his hands were empty, the next he clutched that sword of fire. A sword he twirled, sparks of flame crackling from it.

Not yet, Wrath cried. *Not yet. We must kill Galen first.*

"Lysander, no!" Olivia cried. Realizing she'd get nowhere with Aeron, she attempted to move in front of him. "Not the sword. Anything but the sword. I'm begging you."

Reeling from the force of his guilt, Aeron pushed her back onto the bed and spread his wings to full length. He wanted this battle out of the room and away from Olivia. And there would be a battle. He wouldn't simply lie down and die. Not yet, as his demon had reminded him. He had too much to do.

"You want me," he told the warrior angel, "then come and get me." With that, he launched himself out the window, breaking the glass with the force of his momentum before soaring high into the sky.

Along the way, he dropped his daggers, watching them thump harmlessly on the ground. Olivia loved Lysander. No matter what, even to save himself, Aeron wouldn't kill the warrior. That would hurt Olivia, and Aeron vowed then and there never to do so again.

No matter the consequences.

Lysander was quick to follow. He knew because Olivia screamed, "No, Lysander. Don't do this! Come back."

He hated her worry, her despair. Later, if he still lived, he would soothe her. Give her anything she desired. He would also find a way to save Legion from Lucifer's possession without having to touch her. He had to. He couldn't give himself to any woman but Olivia. He had no illusions about that now.

She'd stayed for him. She'd endured a Hunter's brutality for him. He would not penalize her for that.

Reward.

Always. Aeron twisted midair, and sure enough, a scowling Lysander was only a few feet away. He no longer held the sword, his hands empty but balled. The moment their gazes met, both of them stilled, hovering, not quite within striking distance.

"It doesn't have to be this way," Aeron said.

"It can be no other way. You claim to love her," the angel snarled, "and yet you would keep her here while you bed another. You would ruin her spirit."

"I had planned to let her go first!" But would he ever have been able to do so? He'd wanted to kill something every time he'd considered it. And when she'd wanted to go, he'd convinced her to stay a little longer. Despite the danger.

No, he never would have been able to let her go. He never would have been able to sleep with Legion.

He would have reached this decision eventually. Lysander had merely sped it along.

"I will only ever be with her," he said with a proud tilt of his chin.

"And that's worth continuing to allow her to put herself at risk? Do you know what the Hunters did to her?"

He shook his head, stomach clenched painfully. "No. But I saw her, saw the end results, and I will be haunted by that image for all eternity."

"That's not enough! Listen. And know. Stefano hit her with a closed fist, as well as an open palm. He broke her bones. Tried to drown her. She, who has not a single thread of malice inside her. And the demons, the ones she battled to reach you? They touched her in places only a lover should. But she endured it all. *For you.*"

Hearing that, Aeron spread his arms, face lifted to

the highest part of the sky and roared. Roared with
fury so potent he had never known its like. He'd known
Olivia had been hurt; as he'd said, he'd seen the evi-
dence. He'd raged even then. But now, having the details tossed at him, sharper than any blade...that rage
intensified. Grew. She was so delicate, so fragile. She
could have died, alone and human. Wrecked by pain.

Punish.

"Stefano will pay. By my hand." Target, switched.
End result, the same. Another vow. He'd already decided to kill anyone involved, but this...Stefano would
be brought to the brink of death over and over again,
only to be revived so they could start again. "The demons, too."

PUNISH!

"I have stood back and watched all of this, helpless
to stop it from happening." Some of Lysander's own
rage seemed to cool. "I tried bargaining with you. I
tried helping your cause, even distracting the gods who
pulled your strings. But no longer. You will feel pain by
my hand. You will suffer as my Olivia has suffered."

Pinpricks of red dotted Aeron's vision. "She is not
your Olivia. She is mine."

Ours. Ours to protect, ours to reward.

"For how much longer?" the angel snapped.

"Forever."

"Don't you understand?" Lysander shouted. "You
can't give her forever. You decided not to bed the demon
Legion, only Olivia, so Lucifer will be coming for you.
There's no way around that. Your friends will die, one
by one. Their demons will not be able to defeat their
master. And that's what Lucifer is to them. Master.
The women will be next. Think that your woman, your

human woman, will be overlooked? Only your death can fix the problems you have wrought."

Wings flapped, a war cry sounded, and then Lysander was there, all distance between them conquered. They collided, rolling through the air. Fists hammered at him, even as his own hammered at the angel in defense. There were grunts and groans, explosions of breath. Their legs tangled, kicked.

So engrossed did they become, they forgot to flap their wings and began to fall toward a rocky cliff in a clashing heap. Just before contact, Aeron realized what was happening and latched onto the angel's hair, pushing his wings with all his might. The two of them darted back into the sky.

Lysander ripped free and nailed Aeron in the mouth. Pain exploded through his teeth and gums, blood trickling down his throat. As the angel came at him again, Aeron kicked him in the stomach, sending him propelling backward. They'd reached the fortress, and the angel slammed into a wall. Stones crumbled and dust plumed around him.

Through that dust, he shot forward, knocking into Aeron and sending him hurtling back toward the ground. This time, he didn't catch himself and hit full force. Oxygen abandoned him, nothing more than a sweet dream. A few bones even snapped apart.

He quickly stood—cringed as his ankle gave—and pushed back into the air. One of his wings was broken. *Not again,* he thought, ignoring the pain screaming through him. Where was Lysander? His gaze circled the area, but he— A hard weight punted him in the back, spinning him through the air.

He knew Lysander would be waiting, ready to punch

him the moment he stilled. And so when that inevitable moment of stillness came, *he* slashed first, managing to make contact with Lysander's side. Perhaps smashing a kidney.

That would have felled anyone else. The angel merely grunted. But he didn't attack again. He remained in place, golden wings gliding smoothly up and down. "You want to save both Olivia and Legion, as well as your friends?"

Aeron, too, remained in place, panting, sweating. "Yes." More than anything.

"Well, the only way to do that is to die."

Of course Lysander would say so. "Legion's bargain—"

"Is voided if you die before the allotted time. That was part of their terms."

Voided. Voided with his death. She would be free. His friends could live without the threat she now presented. But... "Olivia?" he asked through the sudden knot in his throat.

"Will be able to go home, without the guilt of knowing you hurt someone you loved because of her. Without the burden of wondering if you will one day resent her. Without the shame of leaving you behind, if she decided you *would* one day resent her. Without being captured once more by your enemy. Without fearing she'll be forced to kill you."

She would do anything for Aeron. He knew that now. She would endure any hardship, any mental or physical pain. And that's what his life would bring her. Pain. No matter what he did, how he lived, he would bring her pain. Key word: *lived*.

He couldn't do that to her. Couldn't give her that

choice. She shouldn't have to endure anything, whether she was willing or not.

Without him, she could live without guilt and shame. Without pain. And that was what got him. The thought of her living as she was meant to: happy, free, safe.

We are to die now? Wrath asked, knowing, as he always did, the direction of Aeron's thoughts.

I am.

And me?

You will continue on. Crazed, but Aeron didn't remind the demon of that.

To punish. A statement, not a question.

Yes. To punish. He prayed the demon remembered this after their parting. *They hurt her.*

So they will die.

So simple. *Thank you for everything.* Now, for the rest. "You'll protect her?" he asked Lysander. "Always?"

"Always."

"And my demon?" If the angel meant to—

"Your demon will be contained. Galen now has Distrust, therefore to balance the scales, I will capture Wrath and give him to Cronus. I have already spoken to the god king, and he has chosen a body. A body that belongs to someone he'll be able to monitor himself, ensuring she doesn't aid your enemy or hurt your friends."

Panic bloomed. "She?" Not Olivia, not Legion. Surely.

"No, not Olivia or Legion," Lysander assured him, clearly sensing his thoughts. "Have no worries on that score. Legion will return home. And as I told you, I will see to Olivia's care myself, now and always."

"Wrath has a mission to complete. Will you ensure that Cronus—"

"I sense the nature of the mission, and I *will* ensure it's completed. In a manner you would find highly satisfactory."

Very well, then. Though he hated that he would have no part in the upcoming massacre, and that's what it would be. "I have one last request, before I allow you to end my life."

A nod. "Ask."

"Olivia craves fun. She *needs* to have fun."

Before the last word had left Aeron's mouth, Lysander had begun shaking his head. "Such a need stemmed from her association with you. Once you are gone—"

"Vow it or the fight continues!" On this, too, he would not bend.

Lysander scowled at him. "I will do my best."

"That isn't good enough," he gritted out. "You live with Bianka, a Harpy. I know the little witch is fun incarnate."

"Yes," Lysander said, and there was pride in his tone. Pride Aeron probably exhibited himself when he spoke of Olivia. "Very well. I will make certain they spend time together."

All the details were taken care of, then.

Death, he thought next. Here it was, staring him in the eye. It had finally caught up with him, and he was willing. There was no resistance on his part. Again, he waited for emotions to consume him but again, they remained absent.

He would have liked to say goodbye to Olivia, to remind her that he loved her. But she would try and talk him out of this. He knew it, just as he knew he would crumble. This had to happen now.

Aeron drew in a deep breath, held it…held it… Then, as he slowly released it, he splayed his arms. "Do it. Take my head."

Lysander merely looked at him, head tilting to the side curiously, as if he hadn't expected Aeron to comply. "You are sure?"

"Yes."

The angel stretched out his arm and the fiery sword once more appeared.

"No!" Olivia screamed from below them. "No! Aeron! Lysander! Please, no!"

Aeron didn't want her to see this, but it was too late to ask Lysander to whisk them to another location. That sword of fire was already arcing toward him.

Goodbye, Aeron, Wrath said softly.

He felt the first sizzle of contact, and then he knew nothing more.

OLIVIA SCREAMED AND SCREAMED and screamed. Aeron. Dead. Gone forever. His beautiful warrior's body had gone limp, had fallen from the sky. A fall that had seemed to last forever, slow and agonizing, taunting her and making her hope that maybe, maybe, he would land softly, and he would be okay. She had only to reach him…

"Please," she sobbed, racing out of his bedroom and heading outside. But deep down, she knew. Reaching him wouldn't make a difference. Aeron. Dead. Gone forever.

LEGION HAD JUST flashed back to the fortress to tell Aeron what she'd done when she felt her bond to him break. And she knew. *Knew.* Only one thing would break a bond like theirs.

Death.

She was alive, so that meant— No. No! Never. She shook her head violently. "Aeron! Aeron!" Without their bond, she couldn't remain here. She would—

"No," she screamed, even as she was tugged from the fortress and back into hell.

As the flames enveloped her, she heard Lucifer's scream echo her own. "No!"

CHAPTER THIRTY

OLIVIA CRIED UNTIL she had no more tears left, Aeron's body clutched in her arms. She barely noticed as the sun fell and rose again. Barely noticed as Aeron's friends descended. Upon seeing what had become of the warrior, Strider had dropped to his knees and howled. Torin had wept. Lucien had waited to escort his soul, but was never summoned, and no one knew why. Maddox had raged for answers, and most of the others had stood staring in shock and disbelief, pallid, shaking. Even Gideon had stumbled his way outside, and oh, his tears had destroyed her. But the reaction that had slayed her most, the one that had torn her up and left her raw, was Sabin's.

"Not him," the warrior had uttered brokenly. "Not this man. Take me instead."

A sentiment she, too, wallowed in.

Like her, they refused to leave the hill. Cameo tried to convince her to rise, to let Aeron go, so that others could hold him and say their goodbyes. She refused. Even slapped those strong arms away from her. Finally, they left her alone, but she knew they waited nearby, watching, wanting their turn.

This couldn't be the end, she thought, dazed. It simply couldn't be. No immortal could recover from decapitation. She knew that. But this just couldn't be the end.

Aeron couldn't die alone.

The words drifted through her mind once, then a second and third time. Aeron couldn't die alone.

Aeron couldn't die alone.

On every level, this death was wrong. Needless, senseless.

Aeron couldn't die alone—and he wouldn't.

Hope suddenly bloomed from the darkness of her soul, and though it required every ounce of strength she possessed, Olivia at last released the warrior—*no, hold him, never let go*—and picked herself up off the ground. Oh, no. He wouldn't die alone, she vowed.

"Olivia," one of his waiting friends said, closing in on her, projecting so much sorrow, so much regret, so much pain.

Ignore. Closing her eyes, she splayed her arms and lifted her head to the gleaming sun. *Act.* "I'm ready to return home. To claim my rightful place in the sky. To be the angel I was created to be."

Instantly she was caught up in the sky, wings sprouting from her back in one glorious wave. She curled them around herself and looked them over, shocked to see no threads of gold. No longer a warrior, then. Funny. No longer a warrior, yet never in her life had she been more intent on fighting for something.

Aeron wouldn't die alone.

Lysander was beside her a second later, his expression so tortured he looked as if he were in physical pain. "I'm sorry, Olivia, but it had to be done. It was the only way."

There was true remorse in his voice, and she nodded to acknowledge it. "You did what you had to do, just as I will." She didn't give him time to question her. No, she marched toward the tribunal chamber, ready to face the Council.

AERON SLOWLY OPENED his eyes. The first thought to hit him: how was he able to do so? Frowning, he reached up, and wonder of wonders, he had eyes, a nose and a mouth. His head was attached to his body, but strangely enough, there were no scabs on his neck—or tattoos on his arms, he realized with shock when he spotted smooth, tanned skin.

Frown intensifying, he sat up. He experienced no dizziness, no pain, just a cool breeze that wrapped around him as if hugging him in welcome. His gaze moved over his body. Intact. Unharmed. He was lying on a marble dais, and he was wearing a white robe, much like Olivia's. His legs were also devoid of tattoos.

How was that possible? How was any of it possible? Lysander hadn't missed. He'd felt the burn.

So what had happened? And where was he? He studied his surroundings. There was a mistlike quality to the air, as if he were trapped inside a dream. There were no houses, no streets, only alabaster column after alabaster column with dewy ivy that climbed the sides.

Heaven? Had he somehow been made into an angel? He reached around and felt his back. No. No wings. Disappointment rocked him. As an angel, he would have been able to search for Olivia, to be with her.

Olivia. Sweet, sweet Olivia. His chest ached and his hands itched to touch her. He would miss her every day of his…life? Death? Utterly and without waning. Where was she now? What was she doing?

"Aeron."

The deep voice hit him, and he shook in recognition and shock.

Though thousands of years had passed since he'd heard that raspy timbre, he knew who it belonged to instantly. Baden. Once his best friend, but centuries deceased. Aeron pushed to his feet and turned, unsure of what he'd find. How…?

Baden stood only a few feet away.

Aeron battled through the shock. His friend looked the same as when he'd been alive. Tall, muscled, bright red hair that shagged around his face. Brown eyes, sun-darkened skin. Like Aeron, he wore a white robe.

"How are you…how are we…?" Still the questions wouldn't form, so great was his astonishment.

"You've changed. A lot." Baden grinned, revealing straight white teeth, and rather than answer, he raked Aeron with his gaze. "But gods, I've missed you."

And then they were running toward each other, wrapping their arms around each other. Aeron held tight. He'd never thought to see this man again. Yet here he was, holding his best friend close.

"I've missed you, too," he managed to choke past the hard lump in his throat.

A long while passed before they pulled back. Aeron still couldn't believe this was happening. That he was here, with Baden. Touching him, seeing him.

Last time they'd been together, before Baden's beheading, Aeron had wanted to set the man on fire. Or rather, Wrath had wanted him to do so. Baden had torched an entire village, certain they plotted his murder, and Aeron's demon had yearned to repay him in kind, fire for fire, even though guilt had ravaged Baden, perhaps even leading to his "trust" in Hadiee, the Bait who'd led him to his slaughter.

Now Aeron felt…nothing but kinship. No menace of any kind. No urge to grab a match. There were no images inside his head, either. No screams in his ears. Actually, he didn't sense Wrath at all.

That made no sense. He still had his head, so Wrath had to be inside him. *Right?*

"Where are we?" he asked. "And *how* are we here?"

"Welcome to the afterlife, my friend. Created by Zeus after our possession, just in case our demons killed us. He didn't want our tainted souls able to reach him. And yeah, I know it would have been nice to know we had a place to stay, but the old bastard never breathed a word." Baden pivoted and waved his hand over their surroundings. "I call it Bad's Land. Get it? *Bad*en."

"Yes, I get it."

"Still no sense of humor, I see. We'll have to work on that. Anyway, I know it's not much to look at and the place is boring as shit, but it's better than the alternative."

The alternative? "So I really am dead?"

"Afraid so."

His shoulders slumped, a paltry motion for the sense of crushing loss suddenly plaguing him. No chance to search for Olivia, then.

And no Wrath, he realized with a sharp inhalation. His demon had been taken from him, released when he died. He was alone. Truly alone, for the first time in centuries.

He was…saddened. Yes, saddened. There at the end, they'd reached an accord.

"Are you and I the only ones here?"

"No. There are a few others, but they keep their distance from me. I don't know why. I'm as sweet as a sugar cookie. Not that I've gotten to enjoy one lately,"

Baden grumbled. "Pandora, though…" He shuddered. "She also resides here and she does *not* keep her distance. Unfortunately."

Again Aeron battled back his shock. Pandora. The woman who'd been given charge of *dimOuniak,* the box holding all the escaped demon High Lords captive. The woman who had taunted him and his friends with her elevated status, reminding them over and over again that the gods had overlooked them.

Once he'd despised her. Now…so many years had passed since he'd even thought of her, he couldn't dredge up the hate. Was he overjoyed to know she was here and nearby, however? Hell, no.

"Why haven't you killed her?" he asked. "Again."

"He's not strong enough," a female said from behind them.

In unison, they spun. Pandora rested against one of the columns, arms crossed over her chest.

Seeing her, even though he'd been warned of her presence, was like being punched in the face with brass knuckles. Aeron looked her over. Like him and Baden, she was tall and muscled, though on a much smaller scale. Her brown hair hit her chin and trapped her face. A face too harsh to be pretty. Her eyes were gold. Too gold. Too bright. Otherworldly. And filled with disdain.

The same look she'd always given him in the heavens.

Ah. There was his old sense of loathing, rising inside him, filling him. Even in death he was to have an enemy, it seemed.

"Must be my birthday," she said with a cruel smile. "One by one the men who sent me here have decided to join me."

"You're mistaken. The gift is mine. Now your eternal torment can be ensured."

She stepped toward him—to attack?—but stopped herself and offered another smile. "So. How's Maddox? Dying, I hope."

Maddox had been the one to kill her. The warrior had been lost to his demon, Violence, and had stabbed her, over and over again. "You'll be disappointed to know he's well. He's even expecting a child."

Breath hitched in her throat. "Is he now? How wonderful." She exhaled, and with the release, a dam seemed to break inside her. "That bastard! He doesn't deserve to be happy! He killed me, allowed my box to be stolen, and now no one knows where it is. It's our ticket out of here, but *nooo*. Even I can't find it. He ruined everything and now his dreams are coming true? You think I didn't know that he always wanted a family? I knew! But he was supposed to die! He was the one who—"

"Oh, get over yourself already." Baden tossed Aeron a see-what-I've-had-to-endure look. "Gods. You're just as much of a bitch now as you were then."

Silence. Panting. Her eyes narrowed on the redhead. "Feeling invincible now that you have a friend to protect you?"

"Hardly. I'm invincible either way."

They continued to bicker, but Aeron tuned them out, his attention locked on part of Pandora's impassioned speech. Finding the box, *dimOuniak,* would free them from this realm? Truth or lie, he didn't know. What he did know? If he could escape, he could search for Olivia, as he'd wanted.

Would she be able to see him?
Yes or no, he didn't care. He would be able to see her.
That box is mine.

CHAPTER THIRTY-ONE

OLIVIA STOOD IN FRONT of the Heavenly High Council, life and death in their hands for the second time. For days she'd pleaded her case, refusing to give up or leave, but they'd continued to reject her, too satisfied with the outcome. Aeron was dead, as they'd wanted, and Legion returned to hell. Her home. Something Lysander hadn't fully explained to Aeron.

She splayed her arms, her wings, and turned, letting them see her. All of her. Aeron's blood had been cleaned from her robe, but not her hands. She hadn't let her hands even graze the material. She wanted those in charge to see what they had wrought.

Her gaze locked with every member, perched as they were atop their thrones. They were beautiful, each of them. Strong and proud and pure. They felt justified. They felt exonerated. They did not flinch under her probing stare.

Do not waver. You are confident, aggressive. "By punishing him," she called, "you have punished me. Eternally. I fell, yes, but you allowed me to return. I am once again like you. An angel. That means my soul is as pure as yours. Therefore I ask you—what have I done to earn such a punishment?"

At last, a murmur arose.

Hope bloomed once again.

"What do you mean?" one of the males asked her. "Allowing you to return here was not meant to be a punishment, but a privilege."

"I love Aeron. I cannot be happy without him."

"You can," one of the females said. "You just need time to—"

"No! No time. I deserve to be as joyful as I have made thousands of others, and I have told you what that will entail."

This time, there were no murmurs. Only silence. Heavy silence. Defeating silence. Still she didn't bow her head or apologize for her impudence. She wouldn't back down. Not about this. If they would not give Aeron back to her, she would die with him.

He would not die alone.

Confident. "If you leave things as they are, a good man slain, you will be no better than the ones you protect the humans against." They would be like the demons. She left that unsaid, but her meaning was clear.

"Good men are slain all the time, Olivia. That is the price of free will." Another of the females, her tone softer now, bearing a hint of compassion.

Aggressive. "We punished Aeron for his choices. Why can't we reward him, as well? For that is what truly sets us apart. Our compassion, our kindness. Our love. Love he himself has demonstrated to a humbling extent. He gave up his life for mine. Does that sacrifice not outweigh his crime? Has he not proven beyond a shadow of a doubt that he's worthy of redemption?"

Murmurs again. And then, finally, a sigh.

"Perhaps something can be arranged…."

THE DAYS PASSED in quick succession, one fading into another. Aeron spent all of his time with Baden. They talked, laughed, cried and caught up, all the while dissecting possible locations for Pandora's box. His determination to find that box was stronger than ever. Not to stop the Hunters—though that would be a wonderful bonus—but for Olivia.

He found that he didn't need to sleep, and he didn't need to eat. He merely existed in the endless white, his resolve unwavering.

So far, they'd developed a few good theories. The box was hidden in plain sight. Perhaps stored in a realm like this one, no one able to flash inside. Perhaps buried at the bottom of the sea. Who had taken it, though, and why, they still hadn't figured out.

"I want to go back so badly," Baden said as they walked through the mist. They did their best thinking this way. "Every so often, at random times, we're given glimpses of life down there, but they're never enough."

"What have you seen?"

"A few of Sabin's battles with Hunters before he moved to Budapest. Your fortress. The explosion that brought you all back together. Each of the women who've helped you. Lucien is a lucky bastard. His woman is my favorite."

"You'd probably offer him condolences if you actually met Anya."

Baden laughed. "A troublemaker, is she? But then, aren't they all." As his amusement faded, he slapped Aeron on the back. "I think I miss a woman's softness most of all."

Thinking of Hadiee? "Why did you do it?" Finally Aeron asked what he'd wondered for centuries. "Why did you allow the Hunters to take your head?"

His friend shrugged. "I was tired, so tired of con-

stantly looking over my shoulder, suspicious about anything and everything. I'd even begun to doubt *you*."

"Me?"

"All of you, really." Baden sighed. "I hated it. I hated
that I expected each of you to turn on me when I knew
in my heart that it would never happen."

"You're right. We never would have hurt you."
They'd loved this man too fiercely. Despite his demon,
Baden had been the one each man relied on. The one
each man sought for guidance and support.

"And then the woman came," his friend continued.
"I suspected she was Bait, but what made it worse was
that I *hoped* she was. So I did it. I escorted her home, let
her seduce me, even though I knew the Hunters would
show up. I was…relieved when they finally approached.
I didn't even fight them."

Like *he* had ultimately refused to fight Lysander.
"Are you happy with the way things ended?"

"To be honest, I don't know. Pandora is all I have for
amusement and as you saw, she isn't very amusing."

There was no denying that. "Speaking of Pandora,
she seems to have disappeared. I've caught no glimpse
of her since I first arrived."

"That's the way she works. She gives you a few days
of peace, lulling you with a false sense of security, and
then strikes. But enough of her. Why did *you* do it?"
Baden asked, flicking him a glance. "Why did you
allow yourself to be killed? And yes, I know you allowed yourself to die. You're too good a soldier to have
been taken any other way."

Aeron sighed, the weary sound a mimic of Baden's.
"All these years I've feared death, but there at the end,

you're right. I, too, welcomed it. Not because I was tired but because I wanted to save my woman."

"Ah, a woman. The downfall of us all. Tell me about her. I have yet to be given a glimpse." Baden rubbed his hands together, ripe with anticipation. "I want to know what kind of creature captivated so leery a man."

"Yes, Aeron, I want to hear this, too."

Aeron stilled. "Did you hear that?" He spun, gaze searching wildly for the woman he craved more than life. He found no sign of her.

"I heard," Baden said, frowning now. "A female voice, right?"

He wasn't insane, then. "Olivia?" he shouted. He would have sworn his heart began pounding in his chest. "Olivia!"

Several yards away, the air began to shimmer, dappled glitter in a canvas of pearl, and a shape took form. Dark curls. Bright blue eyes. Flawless skin. Heart-shaped lips. Circles of rose painted her cheeks, and glorious white wings were stretched behind her.

Wings. Angel. She'd gone home.

"Can you see me?" Desperate, he kicked into motion. "Can you see the dead?"

"Oh, yes. I can see you."

When he reached her, his arms banded around her and lifted her up. He held on to her as he'd never held on to another, spinning her. Here, she was here. With him. Never would he let her go.

Her head fell back and she laughed with carefree abandon. That laughter...how it soothed his soul.

"Olivia." Desperate to taste her, he meshed their lips together. She opened willingly, eagerly, and he fed her kiss after kiss, savoring everything about her. The warmth of her body, the sweetness of her curves. His. And his alone.

"Aeron. There's so much I have to tell you."

Trembling, he set her down and cupped her face, never losing contact. "Sweetheart, what are you doing here? *How* are you here? And I see you're an angel once again." *My angel.*

"Yes. A joy-bringer, no longer a warrior."

"You were always my joy-bringer, but how... I don't understand."

She beamed up at him and traced her fingers all over his face, as if she, too, couldn't bear to let go. "My Deity is the creator of life, and He has offered you a new one. Just as the Heavenly High Council offered me my old job back—even though they say I'm now better suited for the warrior class. From now on, I will be your personal joy-bringer. They realized you couldn't be happy without me, and I would have no joy without you."

He still couldn't wrap his head around the details. "Why would they care? They were the ones who wanted me dead in the first place."

"You sacrificed everything. For me. My Deity acknowledged your sacrifice and sought to reward you. He will return you to your body, heal that body, and you may return to the fortress. We can be together."

"Together." He wanted to fall to his knees in thanks. He wanted to shout and to dance. He could only marvel. Olivia was his.

Her gaze became questioning, unsure. "Are you happy about this?"

"I'm happier than I've ever been, sweetheart. You are all I want, all I need."

Another smile bloomed. "I feel the same." That smile

dimmed somewhat. "Wrath...your demon cannot be returned to you, I'm afraid. I tried. But he's been given to another already."

"Who?"

"A woman named Sienna Blackstone. Once a mortal, killed by gunshot. But Cronus saved her soul and has kept her with him."

Paris's Sienna. Of all the outcomes... What did that mean for poor Paris? He could have his female back, after all, it seemed, but she would be crazed by Wrath for many years to come. She would exist only to exact vengeance upon those who sinned.

Aeron would do everything he could to ease her transition. And hopefully, the demon would recognize him. They still had a job to do, after all. Stefano's punishment. The demons who hurt her, too.

"Will I be mortal?" he asked. Not that he cared. He would be with Olivia. What did an aging body matter?

"No. You'll be immortal, just as before. In fact, your body will be restored to what it was at its creation. You will be without your tattoos, without your butterflies. Without your wings." Again she appeared unsure. "Is that okay?"

"Okay? That is magnificent." Laughing now, he spun her a second time. Could life get any better? Maybe not. She didn't look as happy as she should have. "What's wrong?" he asked as he stilled.

"Legion. She's back in hell, bound once more to its flames because her bond to you was destroyed."

Ice crystallized in his veins—right along with realization. That's what Lysander had meant by the words "she will return home." He should have known, suspected at the very least.

"Lucifer is so angry with her, he's left her in her human body and the demons are tormenting her ceaselessly. Galen's looking for her, and I think…I think he'll even venture into hell for her. He wants to kill her because apparently she tried to kill him."

Aeron's eyes widened. Legion had tried to kill Galen? So much had happened since his passing. "I can't leave her there," he said. Despite everything that had happened, he still loved the little demon.

"I know. Which is why I've spoken to the Council about my new duties. As your joy-bringer, I explained that you need the demon in your life or that life will not be complete. They have agreed that if you decide to go get her, they will let her stay with you, because what she is enduring now is a hell that will last her a thousand lifetimes. Upon her rescue, though, she will be assigned a guardian angel to ensure she harms no humans."

"Yes, yes, I accept for her." Legion hated angels, but she could deal. She'd have to get used to his Olivia, anyway. "Yes," he said again. He didn't even have to think about it. "You, Olivia, are even more amazing than I realized. You did this, and I can never thank you enough." He rained little kisses all over her face. "You have given me everything."

"Just as you have given me everything."

"I will spend the rest of my days ensuring you have your fun."

"All I need is your love."

Aeron dove in for another deep, penetrating kiss, and soon they were lost in it, their hands all over each other, eager, ready for more, determined—

"Uh, guys." Baden's voice pushed through the illusion of privacy and both of them turned toward him. He waved at Olivia. "Hi. I hate to break this up, because wow, but what about me? I want in on this action. I want to go back to my body."

"I'm sorry," she said. "You have made no sacrifice. I'm afraid you have to remain here."

Regret and sorrow instantly tainted Aeron's new-found peace. He'd only just found Baden, and now he was supposed to abandon him?

Baden's shoulders sagged. "Is there anything—"

"No," Olivia interjected softly. "I'm sorry. You are already dead. There's no sacrifice you can make."

"I'll find a way to get you out," Aeron vowed. "Pandora mentioned the box. I'll never stop searching for it, I swear on my life."

His friend nodded, but there was sadness in his voice as he said, "I will miss you."

"And I you." Tears now burned his eyes.

Baden smiled, though even that was sad. "Tell Torin he owes me a sword. Tell Sabin I haven't forgotten how he cheated at chess. And tell Gideon I want a rematch. He'll know what you mean." He rattled off a message for every warrior, and damn if they didn't break Aeron's heart. By the end, his tears were flowing freely. "Until we meet again, Aeron."

"We will. Meet again."

"I will never lose hope." Without another word, Baden walked backward, step by agonizing step. So badly Aeron wanted to shout for him to stop, but just as he opened his mouth to do so, unable to take the grief, the warrior disappeared in the mist.

"I'm sorry," Olivia said, petting his chest.

Aeron jerked her back into his arms, grip tightening.

"This is not the end. I swear it." He buried his face in the hollow of her neck. He could never repay her for all that she'd done for him. "I love you. So much."

"I love you, too."

"I'm going to make you happy. Of all the things I've sworn, that is the most important to me."

She pushed to her tiptoes and kissed him. "You already have made me happy. Now let's go home. There are lots of people eager to see you."

"First, and I can't believe I'm saying this, but fly us to my bedroom. We need a proper reuniting. *Then* we'll meet with the others."

That earned him another laugh. "That's right. I have wings now and you do not. Guess that means I'm in charge of our more…illicit activities, too. So you can consider it done. Seeing to your happiness is my job, after all."

"For which I will be eternally grateful."

They kissed again before heading home.

* * * * *

LORDS OF THE UNDERWORLD

Glossary of Characters and Terms

Aeron—Keeper of Wrath

All-Seeing Eye—Godly artifact with the power to see into heaven and hell

Amun—Keeper of Secrets

Anya—(Minor) Goddess of Anarchy

Ashlyn Darrow—Human female with supernatural ability

Baden—Keeper of Distrust (deceased)

Bait—Human females, Hunters' accomplices

Bianka Skyhawk—Harpy; sister of Gwen

Cage of Compulsion—Godly artifact with the power to enslave anyone trapped inside

Cameo—Keeper of Misery

Cloak of Invisibility—Godly artifact with the power to shield its wearer from prying eyes

Cronus—King of the Titans

Danika Ford—Human female, target of the Titans

Darla Stefano—wife of Dean Stefano; Sabin's lover (deceased)

Dean Stefano—Hunter; Right-hand man of Galen

dimOuniak—Pandora's box

Dominic—A young Hunter

Elite Seven—The most prestigious faction of angels

Galen—Keeper of Hope

Gideon—Keeper of Lies

Gilly—Human female, friend of Danika

Greeks—Former rulers of Olympus, now imprisoned in Tartarus

Gwen Skyhawk—Half-Harpy, half-angel

Heavenly High Council—Angelic governing body

Hera—Queen of the Greeks

Hunters—Mortal enemies of the Lords of the Underworld

Joy-bringers—Angels tasked with watching over mortals

Kaia Skyhawk—Harpy; sister of Gwen

Kane—Keeper of Disaster

Legion—Demon minion, friend of Aeron

Lords of the Underworld—Exiled warriors to the Greek gods who now house demons inside them

Lucien—Keeper of Death; Leader of the Budapest warriors

Lucifer—Prince of darkness; ruler of hell

Lysander—Elite warrior angel and consort of Bianka Skyhawk

Maddox—Keeper of Violence

Olivia—Fallen warrior angel

One True Deity—Ruler of the angels and head of the Heavenly High Council

Pandora—Immortal warrior, once guardian of *dimOuniak* (deceased)

Paring Rod—Godly artifact, power unknown

Paris—Keeper of Promiscuity

Reyes—Keeper of Pain

Rhea—Queen of the Titans; estranged wife of Cronus

Sabin—Keeper of Doubt; Leader of the Greece warriors

Scarlet—Keeper of Nightmares

Sienna Blackstone—Female Hunter

Strider—Keeper of Defeat

Taliyah Skyhawk—Harpy; sister of Gwen

Tartarus—Greek, god of Confinement; also the immortal prison on Mount Olympus

Titans—Current rulers of Olympus

Torin—Keeper of Disease

Unspoken Ones—Reviled gods; prisoners of Cronus

Warrior Angels—Heavenly demon assassins

William—Immortal warrior, friend of Anya

Zeus—King of the Greeks

*If you liked THE DARKEST PASSION, you'll love
Gena Showalter's next captivating tale in the*
LORDS OF THE UNDERWORLD *series*
THE DARKEST TOUCH
*in which Torin, keeper of the demon of Disease,
must fight his every urge to touch
the woman who drives his desires...
since giving in could mean her eternal demise...*

FOR THE ETERNITY it took Keeley to submerge under the cover of the water, Torin had to fight his most basic warrior instincts. Touch. Take. *Own.* Then never let her go.

She would be his, only his.

He laughed bitterly. It was a fantasy destined to remain forever unfulfilled. The demon of Disease lived inside his body, bringing excruciating pain, illness and death to anyone foolish enough to touch him skin-to-skin.

But still…this woman was so gorgeous his insides were ripped to shreds every time he looked at her. She was open and honest, a rarity. She was also fearless, the first potential lover to mention the giant demon in the room—*did your girlfriends leave you because you couldn't meet their needs*—as casually as if they were discussing the weather.

Everyone else had always tiptoed around the issue as if the truth would somehow break him, never realizing he was *already* broken. But this girl…she didn't seem to understand he would never be enough for her. That she would soon need more than he could give her.

Hell, why didn't *he* understand? His hands still itched for her. Those breasts…that tuft of cobalt between her legs…he could play with her…sink his fingers in nice and deep. He wouldn't be too aggressive for her, not again. He wouldn't squeeze her too tightly, or thrust too forcefully. He wouldn't let himself. She would like what he did.

Or not.

Disappointment was his specialty. As he'd just proven.

Keeley leaned over the spring's edge and dug through his backpack. The tips of her exquisite breasts peeked up over the line of water, her nipples like ripe little blueberries.

Look away.

She withdrew a bar of soap and held it up like the prize it was, grinning seductively. But then, everything about her was seductive, stealing bits and pieces of his sanity.

"I'm about to become the queen of clean, what what," she sang. Then, voice dipping huskily, gaze sweeping over him, she added, "But I could certainly be convinced to get dirty all over again."

Had a man ever died from too much desire, or would Torin be the first?

What did she want from him?

How had Hades pleased her?

Stupid question. One Torin despised. The guy was at the top of his must-kill list. Enemy one.

Need distance. Now! "I'll hunt us some dinner and return."

Keeley jolted, gasping out, "But—"

"You gonna complain about missing me, princess?" He put just the right amount of sneer into his tone, guaranteed to irritate her. "How sweet."

Her eyes narrowed to tiny slits. "If I'm a princess, then you're Prince Charming. So you go ahead and take all the time you need, Charming. Right now I'm pretty sure I'll have more fun on my own, anyway."

Direct hit.

He turned to go.

"Torin," she called, her tone no longer giving anything away.

"What?" he snapped.

"It's due to rain soon. Trust me, we want to be long gone from the realm when that happens."

"Why?"

"Do you like drowning?"

"Does anyone?"

"That's why."

What did a little rainfall have to do with drowning? "I'll be back when I'm back." He took off as if his feet were on fire. The rest of him certainly was.

Why was she doing this to him? Acting as if all was forgiven? As if she cared about his well-being…and would die if she didn't get him in her bed? Or on the ground. Or in the tub.

Punishment? Maybe. But he didn't think so. The way she'd looked at him before stepping into that bath… as if she could already feel him thrusting inside her…

He had to readjust his pants before his erection burst free.

Was she truly attracted to him? He wasn't irresistible like his friend Paris, the keeper of Promiscuity, or determined like Strider, the keeper of Defeat, but okay, yeah, he rocked warrior fierce. Since his possession, many women had tried to get a little some-some of his goods and services.

Can't even toe the line of dangerous with Keeley. Gloved touches here...there. Can't live with the consequences if I mess up.

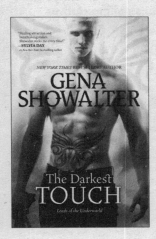

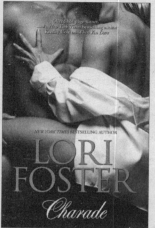